The Bone Ship's Wake

RJ Barker

orbitbooks.net

ORBIT

First published in Great Britain in 2021 by Orbit

Copyright © 2021 by RJ Barker

Inside images © 2019 by Tom Parker

Excerpt from *The Black Coast* by Mike Brooks
Copyright © 2021 by Mike Brooks

A CIP catalogue record for this book is available from the British Library.

ISBN 978-0-356-51186-3

Typeset in Apollo MT by Palimpsest Book Production Limited, Falkirk,
Stirlingshire
Printed and bound by Clays Ltd, Elcograf S.p.A.

MIX
Paper from
responsible sources
FSC® C104740

Papers used by Orbit are from well-managed
forests and other responsible sources.

Orbit
An imprint of
Little, Brown Book Group
Carmelite House
50 Victoria Embankment
London EC4Y 0DZ

An Hachette UK Company
www.hachette.co.uk

www.orbitbooks.net

The Bone Ship's Wake

A darkne   inst the d   A shape detaching from the night. A ship on the   n glowing corpselights dancing above it. No honesty in its approach. A black ship, coming in fast on the winds of a gullaime, and before she could open her mouth the call was going up from Tafin, and the deckchild on the tower opposite. Panic in their voices.

"Black ship rising!"

". . . ship rising!"

And she was already halfway down the tower, sliding down the rungs. In the town and on the docks alarm bells were ringing and she knew every woman and man would be pulling on clothes, reaching for weapons.

Feeling fear.

By RJ Barker

The Wounded Kingdom
Age of Assassins
Blood of Assassins
King of Assassins

The Tide Child
The Bone Ships
Call of the Bone Ships
The Bone Ship's Wake

For my Dad, who introduced me to the romance and beauty of sailing ships

Contents

PART II: THE SHIPWIFE

PART III: THE WAKE OF SHIPS

Berringholme Sound

Namwen's Pass

Keyshanhulme Sound

GAUNT ISLANDS

Sparehaven

The Song of Lucky Meas

The tide it ran for miles
Left ship and crew a-dry
Don't sacrifice the babe
The sea put out the cry.
But the hagpriests didn't listen
Said "The babe must surely die."

Thirteenbern called out
"Give the child to the ships!"
And the sea came to her rescue
As word left the Bern's lips.

PART I
THE BLACK PIRATE

1

The Terrible Here and the Terrible Now

Waves as monuments. Vast and cold, brutal, and ugly. Waves washing over all sound and sight and sense. Waves leaving you breathless. Waves leaving you gasping. Unstoppable, agonising waves.

"And how do you raise the sea dragons, Meas Gilbryn?"

As the waves withdraw, the tempest eases, the agony flows away and leaves behind a thousand other little pains. Her wrists and ankles, where the ropes hold her on the chair, the skin rubbed raw by straining against twisted cords. The gnaw of hunger in her belly, the rasp in her throat from screaming, the ache in her feet from toes broken and never reset correctly. The sharp catch of the clothes on her back against the scars left by the whipping cord.

The throb of a tooth in the back of her mouth going bad, one they are yet to notice. She takes a little comfort in that. That one little pain is *hers*, one little pain they could exploit but have not. Not yet. One day they will, no doubt about that. They are as fastidious in her pain as they are in their care of her. But today it is a small victory that she will claim over her tormentor.

"I do not know how to raise a sea dragon."

A sigh. Meas opens her eyes to see the hagpriest sat before her on a stool. She is beautiful, this girl. Her brown eyes clear, dark skin unblemished and shining in the light coming through the barred window. Her white robe remains – miraculously, given her profession – free of blood or stain as she places the glowing iron back in the brazier. Meas smells her own flesh burning. It makes her mouth water with hunger, even as the pain from the burns sears across her nerves.

They burn her on the back of the calf. It is as if they do not want their cruel work to be immediately apparent.

"This could all stop, Meas, you only have to tell the truth."

She has been telling them the truth for weeks, but they do not believe her. So she starts in the same place. The same place they always start.

"My title is shipwife. And if my mother wants my secrets, then tell her to come and ask for them."

Laughter at that. Always laughter.

"You are not important enough to bring powerful people down here," says her torturer. She stands, walks to the back of the small, clean white room and opens a cupboard. "You should know I am the very least of my order, the most inconsequential of novices. I am all you are deemed worth, I am afraid." She takes a moment, staring at the shelves, choosing from the instruments stored there. Eventually settling on a roll of variskcloth which shifts in her arms and clinks with the sound of tools hidden within. Meas's heart starts to beat faster as the hagpriest returns to sit opposite her.

"I know I am important," says Meas, sweat starts on her brow, "and I know my mother comes down, for I hear you talking outside the room to her. I hear you, no matter how low you keep your voices." She was so sure.

The hagpriest smiles and places the roll of variskcloth on a small table by the brazier.

"I am sorry to disappoint you, Shipwife Meas, but that is simply another of my order. I am told your mother has never so much as mentioned coming down here." She stares at Meas. "Or mentioned you."

Something small but important breaks within her at that. She has been so sure. But in the hagpriest's words is the ring of truth.

"Now, Shipwife Meas, let us look to your hands." The hagpriest's hands are gentle when they touch her, soft, so unlike Meas's own, hardened by years at sea. But they are also strong as she forces Meas to uncurl her fingers from the fists she has balled them into. "The nails have grown back remarkably well," says the hagpriest. "Sometimes, after they have been ripped from the nail bed, they grow back malformed, or not at all. But you are strong." She lets go of Meas's hand and turns to her table, unrolls the variskcloth to reveal the tools within. Sets of pliers of various sizes with strange jaws and beaks, although Meas is far more familiar with them than she had ever wished to be. The hagpriest picks over them, first taking one out and inspecting it, then another. "It is sad for you, that you hold such an important secret. And sad for me also, I suppose. I must be careful with you, oh so careful, and we must take our time. Were your secrets less important, our relationship would be far more agreeable." She clacks a pair of pliers together in front of Meas's face.

Open. Shut.

Open. Shut.

"By which I mean short, for you, Shipwife. Oh, agonising, indeed, far more agonising than anything I have yet put you through. But you would thank me when I brought out the knife that would send you to the Hag, if that is your fate." She puts the pliers back. Takes out another, smaller pair.

Open. Shut.

Open. Shut.

She turns to Meas. "They often do thank me, you know. Women and men have so many secrets, and they become a burden. I allow them release from their burdens. And I allow the pain to end." She forces Meas's hand open again and places the pliers around the end of the nail on Meas's longest finger. A gradually rising pressure in the nail bed. "They cry, Meas. They thank me and they cry with joy when I end them." More pressure; not pain, not yet. Just the promise of it. "Now, tell me, how do you raise the arakeesians, Meas Gilbryn?"

Meas stares into the eyes of her torturer, finds no pity there. Worse, she is sure what the torturer believes she feels for Meas is compassion. That she thinks she is a woman doing an important job, no matter how unpleasant it may be. And she really, genuinely, pities Meas. That she thinks it a shame that Meas's end could not be quick, if agonising. The pressure and the pain in her nail builds and builds. And she knows, as she has known so many times before, that she can bear it no longer.

"I cannot raise keyshans." Words like shame, burning her throat as if poisonous. Bringing tears and choking sobs with them. "It is my deckkeeper, Joron Twiner. The gullaime name him Caller and he sings the keyshans up from their sleep."

The hagpriest staring into her eyes.

"The same lies, Meas, they do not become more truthful just because you repeat them. But I admire your strength. We will find your deckkeeper, do not worry, and I will speak with him." Meas steels herself, ready for the rip and the agony. Instead the pressure falls away. "I think, sweet Meas," says the hagpriest, and she strokes her cheek, "that we are done for today. You are tired, and you need to rest. Think about today, and what may come in our future. Think about secrets and what you can share to end your pain." She rolls up her tools, walks over to the cupboard and replaces the roll. "I will have the seaguard come, take you back to your rooms. I have had a bath drawn for you." She turns, walks back to Meas and then she changes, from gentle to hard. Grabs Meas's face, pushes her head back so she looks up at the hagpriest through tears of shame. "You are a handsome woman, you know? You are very fine looking." She leans in close. "I am hoping," she whispers, "that if I ask nicely enough, they will let me take one of your eyes."

The hagpriest lets go, walks away, leaving Meas alone with two opposite thoughts warring in her mind:

Joron, where are you? You said you would come, and *Joron, stay away. Whatever you do, you must not let them take you.*

2

The Terrible Now and the Terrible Here

Skearith's Blind Eye had closed and Deckkeeper Deere walked through night as thick and black as congealed blood. The gentle hiss of the sea on the shore like the drawing of breath, in and out and out and in. The crunch of shingle under her boots as she walked toward the lookout tower. Up the ladder on the stone pier, along the walkway of stout varisk, cured and black with age. The wind touched her face, cooling for now, not long until it became the biting cold of the sleeping season when ice would coat everything in Windhearth and the boneships would come in, heavy with ice as white as their hulls, seeking new supplies before they resumed their patrols of the northern waters. Not as numerous now those boneships, not calling as often. The sea was more dangerous than it ever had been; keyshans roamed, keyshans and much worse out there on the water.

Touching the hilt of the straightsword on her hip for reassurance.

"Bern keep me safe," said under her breath before starting the climb up the ladder to the tower – the rungs cold enough to numb her hands.

"D'keeper."

"Seen anything, Tafin?" The man shook his head, his body crouched, encased in thick robes against the night chill.

"S'quiet."

Wind against her face.

"The breeze seems to be picking up," she said. "I feel it when I turn to the sea." Saw the screwing up of the deckchild's face, knew it for disagreement. One of those many hundreds of little ways the old hands told you that you had said something wrong or foolish. "What is it, Tafin?" She waited for the man's gentle instruction. She liked him, he never made her feel stupid.

"Winds is always off the land at this time, see. You . . ." His voice fell away.

A darkness against the darkness. A shape detaching from the night. A ship on the water, but no glowing corpselights dancing above it. No honesty in its approach. A black ship, coming in fast on the winds of a gullaime, and before she could open her mouth the call was going up from Tafin, and the deckchild on the tower opposite. Panic in their voices.

"Black ship rising!"

". . . ship rising!"

And she was already halfway down the tower, sliding down the rungs. In the town and on the docks alarm bells were ringing and she knew every woman and man would be pulling on clothes, reaching for weapons.

Feeling fear.

Her feet hit the stone pier and she stumbled as she heard the warmoan, the sound of wind over the taut cords of the gallowbows, loud in her ear. The familiar sound of loosing, the high elastic twang of the cord, the thud of the bow arms coming forward, the hiss of the wingbolt. A moment later the sound of varisk and gion smashing and the screams of deck-childer, as the towers were hit by heavy stone. Too dark to see the far tower but she heard the groan and crack of the varisk structure as it toppled, the huge splash as it hit the water. Knew it lost. Then she was throwing herself to the floor as she heard the tower behind her coming down. Rolling over, as if the massive, crushing weight coming toward her should be met head-on. As if she needed to face her death bravely, but at the last moment she brought her hands up – a natural reaction, though what use she thought her slender arms would be to ward off the jointweight of that broken mass of gion and varisk spars, she did not know.

At the last she screamed.

Felt shame.

Felt shock.

Horror as Tafin landed by her, his head broken, body pierced by spars. Smelling like a butcher's row.

But she lived.

Had the Hag smiled on her today? Not so much as a cut on her and the lookout tower had fallen neatly around her. She rolled over. Stared into the harbour as the black ship cruised past. The crew throwing lamps over the side. At first, she thought of it as light for the archers in the rigging but it was not. No arrow or crossbow bolt pierced her flesh, she was either not seen or not cared about. No, these lights were not to find her, they were so people like her could see this ship. Could see the cruel keyshan beak that crowned the front of him. Could see the spikes and burrs. See the skulls that topped the bonerails along the side, and under the brightest lamps could see the name. The most feared name in the Hundred Isles, and the most wanted.

Tide Child.

As the ship passed she saw its crew, saw the deckchilder arrayed for war, crying out for blood and plunder, saw *Tide Child*'s seaguard, stood like statues in clothes as black as the ship. Saw the gullaime, dressed brightly in thick robes and surrounded by six of its own in ghostly white. Saw the command crew on the rump. The burned woman, the massive forms of Hag-cursed Muffaz and Barlay Oarturner. Between them all, he stood. Stock-still and swathed in rags, even his face covered, all hidden apart from his eyes. Did he turn as the ship passed? Did he see her on the ground? Did he watch her as he glided into the harbour? A shiver of fear went through her, for no woman or man was more of a danger to the Hundred Isles fleet than that one.

The Black Pirate had come to Windhearth.

And where the Black Pirate went, death and fire followed.

She heard his voice, loud, but fragile, like the croaking of a skeer.

"Bring him to landward. All bows at the ready. Put fire to my bolts, my girls and boys, and fire 'em well."

With that order she knew her one hope – that *Maiden's Loss*, the two-ribber moored at the harbour might save them – was gone. Oh, *Tide Child* might be a pirate right enough, but they flew him well, manoeuvred him sharp and fleet as any ship. He came about, pulling side-on to *Maiden's Loss*. Her ears hurt as the gullaime brought their power to bear to slow the ship.

Fire streaking through the night as *Tide Child* loosed its great bows and its underdeck bows in one devastating volley into the smaller ship. All was fire then. No more need for lamps. Boats let down from *Tide Child,* and more black ships coming through the harbour mouth. A grappling hook chinked against the stone of the pier as a smaller black ship came to a stop and then Deere was up, running for the town as fast as she could. She was hurt, not bleeding but bruised. Forced to run at a limp. Aware that behind her more grappling hooks would be coming. The ship would be pulled up next to the pier. Pirates would swarm ashore.

How quickly the world changed. A few minutes ago it was as cold and crisp and dull as every other night. Now it was a nightmare, firelight turning her world into a crackling, screaming landscape of jumping shadows.

The sound of feet. People running. Hers or theirs? She threw herself between two buildings as a group of deckchilder ran past. Hers? Or theirs? She did not know. She ran for the main square, where any defences would be found. Had Shipwife Halda been on *Maiden's Loss*? She hoped not, for Shipwife

Halda was the only officer on the island with any experience of war; if defence was left to Shipwife Griffa, who had never commanded anything more fleet than a loading crane, they were lost already.

Running. Running. Running.

Into the square, fighting everywhere. If there had been order it was lost. Bodies on the ground, peppered with crossbow bolts. Almost getting tangled up in her own sword as she drew it. Striking out at the vague shapes around her. Aware she did not know who they were. Hers or theirs? Breathing hard, frightened. She did not know. Too frightened to care.

Strike. Cut. Blood. Scream. Shout.

She wanted to live. It was all she cared about. In among the heaving bodies. The running bodies. The panicked women and men. She wanted to live.

Found herself in a space. Fire from the burning ship painting the buildings orange, changing their shape, making everything alien. Strange, screaming, fierce faces looming out of the night. She slashed at a figure. Felt resistance as her blade was met. Staggered back. Face to face with a small woman, pinch-faced, mean eyes.

"Come to Cwell, lass," said the woman.

The fear was liquid within her. This was the Black Pirate's shadow. Deere lunged. The shadow parried, twisted her blade, pulled it from her hand; then, with a hard push, sent her sprawling back onto the dirt.

"Don't kill me!" Those frail arms of hers coming up once more.

"Officer is it?" said the shadow.

"Deckkeeper," and she cursed herself for stuttering with fear over her rank.

"Well, he'll want to speak to you then." And the shadow swung the weighted end of her curnow and all was darkness.

Waking. Tasting blood in her mouth. The warmth of Skearith's Eye on her face. The sound of skeers on the air. The sound of women and men on the ground. Crying and begging and laughing. The burn of ropes around her wrists and ankles. She opened her eyes. Lying on her side above the beach. Black ships filling the harbour. Lines of women, men and children kneeling on the beach. All tied.

She tried to move. Groaned.

"Another one awake." A voice from behind her.

"Bring her along then, quicker it's over with quicker we can leave. I heard Brekir saying fleet boneships were near." A sudden spike of hope in her chest. She rolled over. Saw the gallows. Four bodies hanging from it. A fifth, Shipwife Griffa she was sure, stood atop a barrel with a rope around her neck. The Black Pirate before her. He took a step back, raised his bone spur foot and kicked the barrel away. Shipwife Griffa fell, her drop abruptly stopped by the rope and she swung like a pendulum as the noose tightened, her legs kicking as she gasped for air. Then Deere was picked up, the rope between her ankles cut and her legs almost gave way beneath her. But the deckchilder did not care. They dragged her along the dock, past the jeering crews of the black ships. At the end she managed to find her feet, to stand as they threw a rope over the cross bar of the makeshift gallows. Placed the noose around her neck. Placed a barrel and lifted her onto it. Pulled on the rope until she had to balance on tip-toe to breathe.

Only then did the Black Pirate approach.

He was well named. Not only was what skin she could see dark, but his clothes also. Black boots, black trews, black tunic and coat. Black scarf swathed around his face so only his eyes showed. Eyes full of darkness.

"What is your name and rank?" he said. The voice, when speaking, surprisingly musical.

"Vara Deere. I am deckkeeper of the *Maiden's Loss*."

"Well, Vara Deere," he said. "I am afraid your ship is gone and your rank is meaningless to me."

"You hide your face," she said, finding the imminence of death made her braver than she had ever thought she could be. "Is it because you are ashamed of what you are? Ashamed that you betray the Hundred Isles? Kill its good people and loyal crews?"

He stared, brown eyes appraising her.

"I cover my face for my own reasons, and it is not shame," he said, and it surprised her, as she had not expected an answer. "And as for betrayal, that is all the Hundred Isles have ever shown me, do you wonder that I pay it back?"

"You were an officer," she said, and when he replied there was venom there.

"I was a condemned man, Vara Deere, never anything else. I was sent to die and in death found purpose." He stepped closer. He smelled wrong, overly sweet, like he had bathed in some sickly unguent. "Now, I have answered your question. Will you answer mine?" He did not wait for a reply, only hissed words at her. "Where is she?"

"Who?"

"Shipwife Meas Gilbryn, Lucky Meas, the witch of Keelhulme Sounding. I know Thirteenbern Gilbryn has her, where is she?"

"I . . ." She wondered if he was mad, that he expected some lowly deckkeeper from a poorly kept-up two-ribber at the rump end of the Hundred Isles to know such things. "I do not know."

He stepped back and she braced herself. But he was not finished.

"Will you serve me, Vara Deere? I have all the officers I need," he said. "But I always need deckchilder."

She stared at him, and found, in those deep brown eyes, something that she did not understand. Almost as if he were imploring her to say yes. To join him in the pillaging and destruction of the Hundred Isles that the Black Pirate had indulged in for the last year, that had set every boneship they had searching for him to end his reign of terror.

She stood a little straighter on the barrel.

"They will find you, and you will hang, then," she said. "So to join you is only to postpone my death a little." She put her shoulders back. Made her voice as loud as she could. "You and your deckchilder are murderous animals. And I am fleet. I will not join you." He stared at her. Nodded.

"Well," he said. "I expect you are right enough about death, Deckkeeper Deere. And I admire your loyalty. I will toast gladly with you at the Hag's bonefire." Then he kicked away the barrel and the rope bit and all she was became concentrated on one thing, a desperate need for air.

Then darkness.

All was darkness.

3

The Black Pirate

He had thought to meet in the largest bothy in Windhearth, an old building, held together as much by vines as by clever stonework. But in the end he had decided it better to meet in the familiar confines of *Tide Child*'s great cabin. Above he heard the thud of feet on the deck as his officers – Farys his deckholder, Barlay his oarturner, Jennil, called his second – shouted orders and the ship went about its business. By him stood Aelerin his courser and behind him stood Cwell, his shadow. Few looked upon her without some worry, for she was a woman who radiated violence, and enjoyed and gloried in it.

But she was not alone in that. Shipwife Coult of the *Sharp Sither* raided with great joy, as did Turrimore of the *Bloodskeer* and Adrantchi of *Beakwyrm's Glee*, and Twiner made no attempt to hold them back. Other, less severe shipwives also joined him: Brekir of the *Snarltooth* stood at his side, always loyal, and Chiver of the *Last Light* and Tussan of *Skearith's Beak*. Six black ships in the harbour, and that in itself worried Joron Twiner. That would be the first thing he addressed.

"Welcome, shipwives. Windhearth is ours."

"Those who would join us are being taken to the ships," said Coult. "Those who will not are being dealt with."

"He means they will be taken to the Gaunt Islands, Deckkeeper Twiner," said Brekir.

"If we have room," said Coult, but not loudly, not to the room. He let the words out to be heard, to test them.

"I am sure we can find room," said Joron. "But first, charts. Six ships in one place is too many so I would tell you what to be about. Aelerin, if you would." The courser stepped forward, their robes bright white among the black of Twiner's shipwives. They spread a chart over the table.

"We are here," they said, soft voice filling the room. "Windhearth. The majority of the Hundred Isles fleet has drawn back to be nearer Shipshulme Island so they can protect Bernshulme from incursions now we have weakened their fleet so. Though there are still many patrols, and a couple of big ships out looking for us."

"So it is important we are not trapped here. Coult," said Joron, "I would like you to take *Bloodskeer* and *Beakwyrm's Glee* and head here." He pointed at an island. "It is another store island and should be no more well defended than this place." He looked up, Coult nodded. "Go now. The less time we are here the less likely we are to be trapped."

"And if I see Hundred Isle ships, Deckkeeper Twiner?"

"If they are small and you can catch them, destroy them. But take their officers and question them first. Be wary of being led into a trap."

"And I would be nothing else."

"Of course," said Joron. Then turned from him. "Brekir, take *Snarltooth*, Shipwife Tussan and *Skearith's Beak* and head for here," he tapped the map, "Taffinbur. We are told there is some sort of message post. I would have it destroyed, and if you can take the messages and someone who understands the codes then all the better."

"Ey, I shall do that."

"Good. I will take *Tide Child* and, accompanied by Shipwife Chiver with the *Last Light*, head back to the Gaunt Islands to speak to Tenbern Aileen and see what she plans for us.

We have wreaked enough havoc and weakened the Hundred Isles in a thousand ways. She must be ready to assault Bernshulme now." Nods and smiles met his words. "Then be about it, I will not have us caught here." He touched Brekir on the arm.

"I would speak with you alone a moment," he said. She nodded and smiled, it had become a habit of his that he indulged when he could, to talk with her after a meeting. They waited as the other shipwives left the cabin. Then Brekir took a step nearer; he smelled her perfume, a mixture of salt long soaked into clothes and the earthy smell of the gossle that she burned in her cabin, to chase away the pains of long years on the sea and the many wounds and aches it had brought her.

"Meas may not be in Bernshulme, Joron," said Brekir.

"She must be," he said.

"It has been a year, Joron. And no one has heard a thing about her." She touched his arm, gentle, comradely. "Maybe it is time you stopped calling yourself deckkeeper and took on the two-tail . . ."

"No," he said and knew the word came out harsher than Brekir deserved. "When all avenues are exhausted, when every island has been searched and nothing found. Then, maybe then, I will call myself shipwife, but she is Lucky Meas, Brekir." Was he begging her, was that the tone in his voice, the catch in his throat? "She is the one the prophecy of the Tide Child speaks of. She will bring the people together in peace. She cannot be dead. Cannot. And if I were to take on the two-tail, what message does that send to the crew, to all the crews? That I have given up hope." Brekir nodded. Took her hand from his arm.

"It is a lonely thing, command, Joron Twiner."

"Ey, well, I do not dispute that." Behind Brekir sat the great cabin's desk, as comfortable in its place there as he was not. And behind the desk sat Meas's chair and from the upright of the chair hung her two-tailed hat, the symbol of a shipwife's command.

"Well," said Brekir, stepping back, "do not forget, Joron Twiner, you have friends among those you command."

"Ey," he laughed. "And rivals."

"There is always that."

"And worse."

"That is partly why I would ask you again to put on the two-tail, Joron."

"Wearing a shipwife's hat will not make me any more legitimate in the eyes of Chiver and Sarring, Brekir."

"No," she said, "they are fleet through and through and will never truly accept one of the Berncast in command over them, you are right. But just wearing that hat will make you harder to undermine."

"Among the officers, maybe," he said. "But among the deckchilder?" He stared into Brekir's eyes. "No. I made a vow. They will never respect me if I go back on it. They will see me as unlucky and to lose the deckchilder is to lose our fleet, Brekir. Let Chiver and Sarring complain, as long as I have the deckchilder by me they can do nothing." She nodded.

"How hard it is, to command a boneship, to juggle all these duties and loyalties so the thing will fly," said Brekir. "I think few are aware of it. Even fewer how hard it is to command a fleet of them." Now it was Joron's turn to nod. "Just so you know, they mean to call you out at the next meeting of shipwives."

A settling within him, cold still water. He had always known this would come.

"A duel?"

"No, they cannot duel you; to fight a one-legged shipwife, and a man at that, would be beneath them. They will say we fight for nothing." Joron turned and took the seat behind the desk which sat so comfortably in its position, motioned Brekir to take the one opposite him and she did. Folding her tall, long-limbed frame up in thought, her skin even darker than his, her face gifted by nature a constant look of sorrow.

"Maybe they are right, Brekir. Meas had a plan no doubt, for ending war. I have no such thing. Sometimes I wonder if it is that which drives me to find her, not loyalty." He took a bottle of anhir from the drawers of the desk and poured two cups, passed one over to Brekir.

"Do not doubt yourself," she said. "You have served us well this long. They will argue for carving out a berndom of our own, that we have enough ships to do it." Joron turned away, so as not to expose the ruined skin beneath the wrapped scarf he used as a mask as he sipped the anhir, let the liquid add to the constant burn in his damaged throat. Pulled down the soft black material and turned back.

"Well, maybe that is one way to stop the war. I can think of few things that would bind together the Hundred and Gaunt Islands quicker than someone stealing their land for a new Berndom."

Brekir leaned forward.

"Just to play Hag's lawyer on this, Joron," she said. "We could hold our own, we have a mighty weapon, in you."

That cold ocean within him became ice. His words emerged as cold and sharp as the frozen islands that would slice a boneship open from beak to rump.

"We do not talk of that."

"I think we must, Joron, you can raise keysh—"

He cut her off, his voice quiet but stern and brooking no further argument. "And the moment I act, raise a sea dragon, Meas is dead, you know that. They have her because of what they believe she can do. If they know she cannot do it, then they have no reason to keep her alive."

"The keyshans are rising anyway, Joron. Small ones are being seen all the time, fifteen at the last count."

"If I break another island and one person escapes to tell of it, Brekir, she is dead. I will not do it." Brekir nodded, sipped her drink.

"I knew you would say that, and you are right of course, but it may come to it, Joron, one day, that you have to choose. Our fleet or her." He took a drink and Brekir leaned forward. "Some friendly advice," she said.

"Always welcome from you, Brekir."

"Chiver is the more forceful of the two personalities. You should have Cwell pay them a visit in the night. Then all of your problems are over and you can either advance their deckkeeeper, who will owe you, or put your own woman in. Sarring will not speak out without Chiver to back them up, most likely Sarring will slink back to the Hundred Isles with news of us and hope for a pardon."

"I am no murderer, Brekir."

She did not reply, only stared over his shoulder and out of the great windows in the rump of the ship. Joron turned to do the same, saw the bodies hanging from the gallows, the bodies strewn across the docks.

"They are the enemy," he said, "and would do the same to us."

"True," she said.

"Do you disapprove?" As he spoke he watched the first of his black ships begin to glide out of the harbour, Coult's *Sharp Sither*. Behind it the others were readying themselves. Smoke was rising from the small port.

"I understand," she replied.

"That is not approval." He turned back to her. "We cannot leave our enemies behind us." Brekir stood.

"I should return to *Snarltooth*. As you say, there are patrols searching for us, and it would not do to be trapped here."

"Yes." She turned to leave, paused in the doorway.

"The deckchilder, they love the destruction we leave in our wake, Joron. But, and I know I did not serve as closely with Meas as you did, I cannot help wondering whether she would approve of the bloody swath we cut across the sea."

"She was hard, Brekir," he said, and his own voice was full of that same hardness.

"She let you live," said Brekir, and then turned and vanished into the darkness of the underdeck, leaving him with unwelcome thoughts.

He wanted to pursue Brekir, to scream and shout, tell her

she was wrong. Where was her loyalty, to question him so? He found himself standing. The familiar ache on the stump of his leg as he moved his weight onto it. He stopped. Remembered Meas, so long ago, telling him how the deckkeeper's place was to question their shipwife. Make them consider their actions. And though shipwife of her own ship, the *Snarltooth*, he knew Brekir played that role to him in this fleet. He sat again. Turned his chair so he looked out the great windows at the small town. At the hanging bodies. At the corpses. At the fire as it took hold.

This was his. He had done this and he would not run from it. Brekir was right, there were those of his deckchilder who revelled in the destruction, who inevitably took things too far. He did not believe he did. A year, and he had heard nothing of Meas. He believed she must be in Bernshulme somewhere. To get his shipwife back, he needed the Gaunt Islands fleet to assault Bernshulme. Before they would do that, the Hundred Isles fleet must be weakened. And that was what he would do, what he did. If he met their ships on the sea he destroyed them. When he could not destroy their ships he destroyed their supplies. When he could not destroy their supplies he killed their officers. And when he could not kill officers he stripped them of their deckchilder.

Whatever it took

Whatever was needed.

This was war.

No quarter and no mercy shown. In return he expected the same. He only gave in kind what his enemies would give to him. And if this was not what his father had promised, if this was not the glorious stories of being fleet, of proud boneships and honourable shipwives, well, that was because life was not stories. Life was painful, and it was hard and it was cruel and full of loss. And if this was not the peace Meas had wanted, had fought for, well, that was because there was no peace without war. He watched the bodies on the gallows sway in the breeze. Heard that young deckkeeper's voice.

You and your deckchilder are murderous animals. And I am fleet.

"Maybe we are all animals, ey?" he said to himself. Then he reached for the bottle of anhir and poured another drink. Lifted the scarf then the cup, felt the familiar burn of the strong alcohol in the back of his throat.

The alcoholic burn he had left behind under her, becoming more familiar every day.

"I will find you, Meas," he said quietly and he spoke only to the bones of *Tide Child*. "I must find you, for I fear that every day without you I drift further from the course you set me upon."

4

Once More to Sea

He stood on the rump of *Tide Child*, a familiar place, a familiar feeling under his one foot as the ship moved across the surface of the water. And yet, all was different to how it had once been – as, he supposed, was the nature of life. He commanded this ship now, and by him stood his people: his deckholder, Farys, and by her was his second and leader of his seaguard, Jennil. Gavith, once a cabin boy who cowered whenever Meas turned her eye on him, was now bowsell of the maindeck. Some figures remained from Meas's command, stood as if immovable: Barlay at the steering oar, Solemn Muffaz, the deckmother; two solid pins that anchored him here, let him know this was still the same ship he had boarded many years ago, following Lucky Meas as she entered the years of her disgrace. And sometimes Muffaz would glance to Farys, look upon her like the proud father she had never had. Sometimes Farys would glance to Gavith, look upon him in a way Joron knew he should watch but had not yet found the right time to speak of it, or the way to speak of it. He would ask Solemn Muffaz to speak to her, the two were close.

Mevans was still steward, refusing any form of advancement but somehow managing to be involved in every facet of running the ship. Fogle remained his seakeep though not for much longer, he feared. Last few times he had spoken to the woman he had smelled drink on her breath and he could not have a drunken seakeep.

Rich, for him to say such a thing.

Aelerin the courser and the Gullaime were absent from the deck, and maybe it was their absence that filled him with melancholy. *Tide Child*'s clothing of war was long removed, Windhearth a month behind them. The bows tied down, the sand swept away, the chains unstrung from the rigging and the skulls taken from the bonerail. In the centre of the deck the new gullaime worked, a ring of white-robed windtalkers that sang gently as they brought the wind to move the ship. Joron was careful with them, never worked them too hard or forced them into pain, but there was little kinship between him and these gullaime. They had been chosen by Madorra, who guarded Joron's friend, the first gullaime he had ever met, jealously. And though he had made the windshorn promise never to speak of the prophecy – the foretelling that *Tide Child*'s gullaime was the Windseer, meant to free all gullaime from the bondage of women and men – he did not believe that promise had been kept. He knew in the way these new gullaime were around him, too quiet, not suspicious of him but reverent. Because to them he was the Caller and to be that was to be bound within the mythology of the Windseer; whether he was a servant to it, or doomed by it he did not know and none would tell.

But the gullaime obeyed him, in most things.

"Farys," he said.

"Ey, D'keeper?"

"I am going below, you know our course."

"Ey, D'keeper," she said and he left her on the rump, sure in the knowledge that she would mind the ship and steer it as careful as any who lived.

And down, out of the cold which bit his cheeks and nose, even through the scarf wrapped around his face, and into the damper cold of the underdeck where the glowing eyes of wanelights showed the way and he passed through to the Gullaime's cabin. At the door stood Madorra, clad in white, one fierce eye looking out at him.

"Madorra," he said, always aware of the rasp in his throat that had destroyed his singing voice. "I would speak to the Gullaime."

"Busy," said Madorra, then hissed. "Too busy for you. Busy."

"I command this ship, Madorra, no one is too busy for me." He made to walk past the windshorn – one of those gullaime who could not control the wind, and had acted as both guard and captor to its own people back in the Hundred Isles – but it did not move. "Gullaime," shouted Joron, "I would speak with you." Madorra hissed at him again but the Gullaime's voice could be heard above it.

"Come, Joron Twiner, Come." Joron waited, staring at the windshorn, he noticed its white robe had acquired a garland of shells, sewn in around the collar. It did not escape him that they were guffin shells, the creatures within the pearlescent white curls famously poisonous to humans, a delicacy to the gullaime.

"Well?" said Joron to Madorra. The windshorn blinked its one good eye and moved aside. "Thank you," said Joron and he opened the door, moved within, from the cold and damp to the warm room, heavy with the scent of gullaime, hot sand and salt. They had twelve gullaime aboard now – five currently on deck, his gullaime, Madorra and five others in here. He did not know the names of the ten new gullaime, and they would not talk to him or meet his eye.

They sang constantly and though they followed the gullaime everywhere, were always with it, they seemed to obey only Madorra and not the Gullaime, which sat within their circle and looked mournfully up at Joron.

"Away go," it said to them, sadly. Once it had been a whirlwind of anger and fury but now it only seemed tired. When the gullaime around it did not move, but continued singing their low and mournful song, a little of the Gullaime's fire returned. "Away go!" it snapped at the one nearest to it and, as one, they withdrew to the door, though they did not leave the room.

"You were asked to leave," said Joron to the group of gullaime, and they cooed and clicked but made no move on his say-so.

"Will not leave," said the Gullaime. "Will not." It settled down into its nest, its robe, once torn, filthy and ragged, now the finest thing on the ship. Sewn with cloth of many colours, jingling with shells and trinkets and feathers and bright things given to it by others of its kind and by the crew. Joron could not help feeling the robe was as much prison to the Gullaime as command was to him, that the windtalker was trapped within it, unable to share, unable to escape.

"Find ship woman?" it said.

"No, she was not there, and none knew of her." He shook his head. "If you would have these gullaime removed from your cabin, I can have that done." The Gullaime shook its head.

"No, no no. Madorra not leave. Madorra fight, Madorra kill. Not do, not do." It sounded on the edge of panic. Joron nodded.

"You would not have cared about it killing us once," said Joron. The Gullaime yarked quietly, a sad laugh to those who understood its ways.

"Not care much now. Care for Joron Twiner." Its masked head turned to him. "Joron Twiner sick," it said quietly. "No make Joron Twiner's life hard."

"My life is already hard and I do not think it will get much easier, Gullaime." It nodded sadly.

"Not want," it said.

"No," said Joron. "Well, I only wanted to look in on you. I must see the hagshand now, and Aelerin. If there is ought you want, then call on me."

"Call," it said, and Joron pushed through the little gaggle of white-clad windtalkers and out of the door, only to be hissed at by Madorra as he passed. He ignored it – the windshorn were seen as outside the command of the ship, so for Madorra to act in such an insolent way was no more a threat to his command than if a kively pecked him or a longthresh bit him. Still, it rankled at Joron as he made his way deeper into the bowels of the ship to where Garriya, the hagshand, waited for him in the hagbower where the sick and the wounded were brought. It was empty today, their raid had seen no casualties. It was often the way. To turn up with overwhelming force was part of it, but more than that was his reputation, the Black Pirate who left none alive, the only proof of his passing in the swinging corpses and burning towns.

An exaggeration, of course, and he understood it was necessary – that in the long run his reputation saved the lives of his people, and it was what he hoped would lead them to Meas. He liked it no more for that though.

In the hagbower, Garriya sat on a stool, no hammocks for her, and laid out by her were the tools of her trade. *Could take her for a torturer as much as a healer*, he thought. The old woman was a mass of contradictions, fastidious about washing her hands, but never washed any other part of herself. Played dumb half the time but fooled no one any longer. A powerful intelligence worked behind those bright eyes.

"Caller," she said. "How goes it?"

"I hear more and more reports of keyshans rising throughout the seas, and yet I have not sung them out."

She chuckled, passed a hand over her tools as if wondering which would cause the most pain.

"You think you are all there is in the world?"

"No, but we called a beast, we . . ."

"Did not raise the first one, Caller," she said, then rolled up her tools and stood. Making her way to the shelves and jamming the roll behind a rope before taking out a cloth and a bottle.

"Well, no . . ."

"You can speed a thing on a little," she said, "but you cannot stop a thing once started."

"What do you mean?"

"Take your scarf off, sit on the stool. Let us see how we do today."

He did as she bade, it felt strange, the air against his skin rather than the warmth of his breath, caught by material. She came before him, ugly, old, skin ingrained with dirt.

"Anyone on that isle know where she is?" He shook his head. "Of course not, why would they send anyone that important way out here." He was about to answer but she lifted his head by putting her hand under his chin and pushing up, effectively stopping him talking. "The sores are no worse," she said. "Any dizziness?" Shook his head. "Nausea? Find time missing?" Shook his head. "Made any decisions you regret?"

"Many." She smiled as she soaked her cloth in liquid from the bottle.

"Made any that made no sense to you later?"

"Not recently."

"Good. Now, this will hurt." She dabbed on the liquid and he hissed; it felt as if his skin caught fire, but if this was what was needed to keep the keyshan's rot at bay then this was what they would do.

"How is Coxward?" he said, in one of the short respites.

"I could keep him here no longer," she replied. "Now he is restrained in the brig." Another dab. Fire running over his skin. "It'll be a long time before you are in his condition though. He's had the rot for many years."

"I could have done with him, none know a ship the way he does," he said. "Can you make him well?" She shook her head.

"Once the rot has reached the mind, only the Mother can fix it, and I am not her." Dab. Pain. "It would be kinder to let him go, Caller," she said, her voice low. Pain. "There is naught left in this world for him."

"He has been with us from the start." His voice caught. "I do not want to lose—"

"Sometimes it is not about you," she said. Dab. Pain. "You

know, Caller, life is loss, and much has been taken from you: Dinyl, your leg, your song and your shipwife. And if you think you can dilute your pain in blood you are wrong. Blood will only feed it."

"It is not vengeance, Garriya." He moved her hand away, caught a whiff of the liquid she had in the bottle and it made his eyes water. "She is in Bernshulme, I am sure of it. And I need Gaunt Island ships to assault the capital, but they will not give them to me while the Hundred Isles navy is strong." He picked up the scarf and tied it once more around his face. "So I weaken them."

"And yourself."

"We lost no one."

"Yet."

"We lost no one, old woman." He stood. She stared.

"Go visit your bonemaster in the brig."

He turned from her, fully intending to go back up the stairs and through the underdeck and the hatch until he was on the slate and in the light of Skearith's Eye far above. But guilt nagged at him. Coxward had served him well until the rot had taken his mind, and Joron owed him a visit at least. So he turned, heading further down and further into darkness, the only lights the small glow of the wanelights positioned along the tight corridors. He heard Coxward before he saw him. Heard the raving and crashing as he threw himself around the small room that housed him. The brig had been made as comfortable as possible, as the man had done no wrong, not really. He had caused a few bruises, but that was the disease, not the man.

". . . fire is coming!" he roared. "It'll all end in fire and teeth. You hear me? I am the teeth! I am the fire! I am the place beneath. I am the Hag's own vengeance. You come upon me! You come upon me! I will kill you. I will . . ." He quietened as Joron stepped into his line of sight. He had been a large man, once. Now he was not, his flesh hung from his bones, skin mottled with sores and dried blood.

"Shipwife!" he said. Hand coming to his chest in salute.

"I am not . . ."

"They have locked me in here, Shipwife," said Coxward, and he pushed himself up against the barred door. "It is mutiny, Shipwife. Mutiny. I know about the crew, listen to me." Joron stepped nearer; the sores of keyshan's rot filled the air with the smell of rotting flesh. *This awaits me*, thought Joron. *This awaits me.* "Listen, Shipwife, they think me mad, but I know the truth." He sounded less manic than he had the last time Joron had seen him. He stepped nearer.

"Truth?"

"Ey, many aboard are new, they resent you, Meas, resent you. Know you fell from grace right off the beak of your ship, eh? Well, they are planning and things." Was he almost lucid? Did he, despite thinking Joron was Meas, actually talk of something real? Joron stepped forward a little more. "And worse, Shipwife, you think they are women and men yet they are not, they are borebones, borebones in human flesh. They wear women and men as we wear coats." His voice was rising with every word, with every syllable and Joron had no doubt the man was tormented, that he believed every word he said. "It is all true, Shipwife. It is all true, I feel them beneath my flesh! They think me mad! I see the fire and the death!" Spittle flying from his mouth and Joron stepped even nearer.

"Coxward," he said softly, "I am not Meas. She is gone."

Like cloud passing to reveal the light of Skearith's Eye. The sudden return of lucidity.

"Joron?"

"Ey, it is me, Coxward."

Coxward put his hands on the bars, brought his face right up to them. Tears in his eyes.

"Served well, didn't I?"

"Ey, Coxward, you have. None better."

"I cannot abide this, Joron."

Joron put an arm in through the bars and around the man. Pulled him close.

"You have served this ship and me, Coxward. You served Meas and you have served as well as any woman or man ever could."

"You believe me then," he said, a froth of white in the corners of his mouth, "about the borebones? About the fire?" The cloud returning, the light going out.

"Ey," said Joron quietly. "I will sort it, do not worry yourself." The torment receded a little, as if Coxward had only needed to hear those words, and when Joron saw peace enter the bonemaster's eye he gave him a smile.

Then Joron drove his bone knife deep into the man's heart. Watched the light in his eyes go out, and hoped what he saw at the last was gratitude, that he had freed him from the madness. "Rest easy, old friend," said Joron, letting the body down. "You rest easy."

He stared at the still body of the bonemaster and inwardly, he cursed Garriya.

"*We have lost no one.*"

"*Yet.*"

Then he heard the call from above, the one he feared most, and the one that sent a thrill of excitement running through him.

"Ship rising!"

5

And I Saw a Fair Ship

Amazing how quickly you became used to something. He stood in the swaying tops of the spine, the slate of the deck far below him. Leg and bone spur braced against ropes as he lifted the nearglass to his eye. Not so long since he had thought he would never ascend the spines of a boneship again. Not so long since he thought the loss of his leg made it impossible. First he had ascended a little, then a little more and then a little and a little more, for how could he command a boneship if he would not do what he expected of his crew? And though each step had been tentative, each time he used his false leg, his spur, to move along a rope or spar he had been sure it would slip. But, just as with walking, and running and fencing, he had slowly become used to it, slowly worked out how to translate the pressure on his stump into a semblance of feeling, and now he climbed the spines of the ship as well as he ever had, better even.

He stared through his nearglass – *her nearglass* – at the horizon. Passing his eye along the grey sea while the topboy, Havir, gave instruction.

"Saw it just five off the shadow to the rump, D'keeper, only a hint see, but sure it was the flags waving off the tops of a boneship."

"And not one of ours?"

"No, I'm sure o'that. Not flying the black were they, though?"

Joron nodded, continued to stare through the nearglass though he did not doubt Havir; the man was an old salt, a skilled deckchild with years of service under his belt. Joron spoke to make conversation while he waited for the moment when the sea rose below *Tide Child* and gave him that little more distance to his vision. Havir had said the ship flew just below the horizon.

Did it follow him? And if so how long for? Or was that paranoia, for paranoia was a symptom of the rot. He'd seen it creep up on Coxward, heard him talk of how Hewes, the bone-wright below him, was plotting against him. The eventual violence that had risen before he'd been forced to move Hewes over to another ship, bring aboard a woman called Colwulf, and then things had been fine, for a while. Until the paranoia had started again.

But that was over now, for Coxward at least.

He took the nearglass from his eye, wiped sweat from his forehead, raised the glass once more. How long could he be up here? How long to wait? How long to stare into that circle, perfect hemispheres of sea and sky punctuated by the gliding dots of skeers as they danced above the waves?

There! A single line, unnaturally straight, jutting over the horizon.

"I found his tops, Havir."

"And I knew you would."

"Seems he's no longer shy, three spines rising, rigged like us, so a four-ribber no doubt, full corpse lights." He moved the focus ring. "There's a second ship."

"Ey?" He could feel Havir close to his side.

"Two-ribber."

"Evenly matched, ey, D'keeper?"

"Ey, evenly matched indeed." He leaned over so he could shout down to the decks. "Barlay, steer us two points toward the shadow!" He felt the ship come about, the kiss of the wind move from the side of his face to the back of his head, blowing the tangled locks of his hair around as he made his way down the rigging, not fast, maybe, but steady and even until he jumped from the spine to the deck, landing sure-footed and running, at an unseemly rate for the commander of a ship, up to the rump where Farys waited, hands behind her back, overseeing the deck.

"Two ships, Farys, four-ribber and a two-ribber."

"You mean to give chase, D'keeper?" She smiled at him, the burned skin of her face pulling her eyes into slits.

"Well," he said, "they call us murderers and marauders, let us not disappoint them, ey?" He grinned a murderous, piratical grin and raised his voice. "Full wings, give me all speed. Sound the bell, beat the drums! Clear my decks for action! Signal Chiver on the *Last Light* to do the same!" And all became seeming chaos around him, the ship stripped for war, deck-childer running hither and thither as he watched, a smile hidden beneath his mask for he saw the patterns within the seeming chaos. Saw that every woman and man knew their job and their place and he was pleased, for this was the ship he wanted to bring his shipwife back to, an orderly, well-run ship of war. He turned his head to the horizon, lifted the nearglass to study his quarry. Two ships side-on to *Tide Child*, white as new sand. The wind blew the tail of his hat around his arm, tangling with it and the long locks of his hair. He pushed it away. Went back to staring at the ships and the smile that had so recently been on his face fell away.

"Seakeep," he shouted, "call Aelerin for me." He watched the two ships while he waited for the courser to announce themselves in that soft voice he was so familiar with.

"You wanted me, D'keeper?"

"Ey, Aelerin," he said. The courser's robe was as pure and white as the hulls of the boneships ahead. "Two ships out there," he pointed. "They have made a show of themselves and now they run, inviting us into a merry chase."

"That explains all the noise," said the courser, a hint of humour there.

"Indeed, but they run toward the wind."

"That will work their gullaime hard."

"It will, and they must know we have gullaime of our own, so they should save their windtalkers, there is a brisk enough wind to run with."

"It is what a sensible shipwife would do."

"Ey, so, I ask you this, why may they not?"

"I would think they seek to lead us away from something? Or toward something?" Joron nodded, collapsed the nearglass and placed it in his jacket.

"Have you studied the charts around here?" He knew the question needless, for Aelerin studied charts obsessively. "Is there anything that they may want to tempt us toward or away from?"

Aelerin stood, hands clasped before themselves, absolutely still as was their way when deep in thought.

"There is little the way they head, just the near northern isles, low and cold. A poor place for a trap."

"And where they come from?"

"Open water until Skearith's Spine is all."

"Curious," said Joron and he squinted into the distance; he could make out the ships without the nearglass now.

"There is one thing," said the courser.

"Ey?"

"There were reports of keyshans, small ones. Not that way, but given how fast they swim it would not be impossible for one to have made it that far. Maybe they hunt one?"

"You would think they would have learned their lesson about that by now?"

"You would think. But maybe Sleighthulme is back in production of its poisons? Could they have perfected hiyl?" Joron thought a little on that, on what he had seen in Sleighthulme before the shipwife gave herself up. Vast cauldrons mixing human and gullaime flesh in search of the recipe for hiyl, a poison powerful enough to hunt keyshans with, for all other attempts simply ended up with women and men on their way to the Hag. He raised his voice.

"I think we shall return to our original course," said Joron, "see what our friends out there make of that."

"Ey, D'keeper," said Farys and she called out the orders to Solemn Muffaz who called them back to Barlay and *Tide Child* heeled over, his wings creaking and complaining, spines echoing those complaints as he came back to his original course. If Joron heard the sighs and words of disappointment from his crew, that they were robbed of a fight, then he gave no sign. Instead he raised the nearglass and watched the ships so far away, waiting for the moment when they realised he no longer gave chase, letting time tick past and pretending to be unaware of the women and men scurrying around him, loosing some ropes, tightening others, making work in hope of over-hearing his plans.

"What do you think, Farys?" he said after staring for long enough to be sure, then he passed her the nearglass. She raised it, found her quarry. Studied them.

"They want to be chased, D'keeper, are slacking some wing, letting it billow so they slow. Wait, the two-ribber has lost a top spar." She passed the nearglass back and Joron returned to gazing through it. Saw that the smaller ship was indeed wounded, its highest crosspiece having fallen, bringing the white wing with it.

"Well, now he trails a wing like an injured kivelly."

"A mess of rigging and gion is a lost topspar."

"It is," said Joron slowly, "if it is real, but if I were to fake damage then that would also be what I would choose to do. Rigged right it is a simple enough thing to pretend."

"Ey," said Farys. "They must be fair desperate for us to follow."

"Which begs the question what is so interesting on our previous course, ey?" He dropped the nearglass from his eye, folded it and placed it safe in his jacket. Raised his voice. "Listen well my women and men, my girls and my boys." All heads turned to Joron, all work momentarily pausing, then well practised hands continued in their tasks, even while gazes were focused elsewhere. "I'd not have you think I stole a righteous fight from you, but those ships want us following, and I reckon that means there's something over the horizon they don't want us finding. So we'll do finding not following, ey?"

A rousing shout of "Ey!" in return.

"And we'll keep *Tide Child* rigged for war, as if I am any sort of commander at all then I reckon I know what will happen soon. Those two ships will see we do not fall for their ruse, and they'll be chasing us." Looks and smiles were exchanged on the deck of *Tide Child*, and in the rigging of *Tide Child* and in the gloom of the underdecks where Joron's voice reached and even in the deepest hold, where word was passed down from deckchilder to deckchilder. And each and every one of them knew he was right, for Joron Twiner had proved himself a fighting shipwife, even though he'd take the skin off the back of anyone who called him ought but deckkeeper; they knew what he was and where he took them, and they would follow him. For among the deckchilder of Meas's fleet a rumour had grown up, one that had passed from idle gossip into an undeniable truth in the mind of every woman and man who flew those ships. Was Joron Twiner not Lucky Meas's son? For what else made sense? And was not Lucky Meas a figure of legend, the Tide Child? The peacebringer? Unkillable, unbeatable, just biding her time afore she came back and led them all in glory? None doubted these were facts as true as the sea and the Hag and the Mother and the Maiden.

"So," said Joron, who knew what was said of him and how very wrong it was, though he did nothing to stop the rumours persisting, "you mark my words, girls and boys, women and men, we'll get our fight. Those ships will come after us soon enough, and maybe more will be waiting over the horizon." He ran over to the bonerail, raised himself onto it. One hand on a rope as with the other he lofted his straightsword.

"Sharpen your curnows, ready your blades and your gaffs and gallowbows, for I see a bloody day ahead." At that a riot of shouts, a joyous cacophony from his crew and Joron felt it too. Until he saw Garriya, the old woman's head just above the hatch which led to the underdecks, and then came a dark cloud over him.

"*We have lost no one.*"

"*Yet.*"

A shudder ran through his body.

"Now," he shouted, "back to work the lot of you, I'll have no slate-layers on my ship! Rig for speed, tighten the wings and put out the flyers!"

They went to work, excited and gossipy and ready for the coming battle as *Tide Child* scudded over waves which glinted and winked in the light of Skearith's Eye, every scrap of variskcloth raised to catch the wind. Once more Joron brought up the nearglass and trained it on the ships now vanishing behind them. Smiled to himself in vindication as he saw the two-ribber hoisting its fallen spar back into position. "Clever," he said quietly, "many would have fallen for it." Then he turned, putting away the nearglass and staring down the deck of *Tide Child* toward the future. "Best speed we can make in this wind," he shouted. "Barlay, keep our last course for that was what worried them. Topboy!" he shouted. "You keep me appraised on those ships, I want to know the urgency with which they chase!"

"Already turning, Deckkeeper, wings a-full of wind!"

Then it became a race, though not a true race, for Joron knew it was unlikely *Tide Child* would be caught, they had the wind still, and if those ships flogged their gullaime hard for extra speed then Joron had gullaime of his own, and they needed no flogging to work for him. Were glad to, for they named him Caller, and saw in his words the nearing of the Windseer's time and if they were right, that brought nothing good. But Joron knew prophecy was a fickle thing, for Meas had been named in one, and where was she?

Where was she indeed.

On flew *Tide Child*, cutting through air and water, making such speed that it caught the breath from the lungs of those who rode him. And if there was a greater joy in the world than a ship under full wing then Joron did not know it. That he flew toward danger did not matter in this moment. This was what every deckchild lived for, just them and the sea and the wind and the way it carried them. A shout went up, that made so much sense but also filled Joron with fear. For what else was worth so much in the Hundred Isles that two ships would risk sacrifice to keep him away from it?

"Keyshan rising!"

6

The Cause

What fear and amazement. What wonder and terror those words brought to every woman and man in the crew. "Keyshan rising!" For many among them had seen the keyshans, knew the majesty and the danger that came with them, knew the creatures could smash a ship like *Tide Child* to nothing and barely even notice. Those of the crew who had not seen a keyshan had heard talk of them, heard it so often that to every woman and man among them it was as if they had seen the keyshan themselves. Like they had felt the heat coming from it, the splash of the water as it breached the surface, heard the terrible cacophonous song that beat against the ear like a hammer.

And each and every one of them knew that they were somehow linked to the keyshans by their special gullaime, and some believed by their shipwife, who had raised one from the dead rock of an island and given herself up to the enemy so that they may escape.

Or so they thought.

And Joron let them.

And if some remembered otherwise, well, they never spoke of it to their deckkeeper.

As the crew wondered and worried and talked among themselves Joron stared at the world through the convex circle of the nearglass. First over the beak of the ship, toward the horizon where the topboy said the mighty form of a keyshan awaited him, then over the rump of the ship. Behind him and to seaward, the black form of the two-ribber, *Last Light*, black as *Tide Child*, but smaller. Only two spines and wings triangle-rigged, not square like the bigger ship's, and corpselights glowed above it marking that it had come over from the Hundred Isles fleet and was not a true black ship. He was built for speed and quick hit-and-run attacks with his twenty smaller gallowbows. Then Joron tracked back toward the two white boneships, towers of billowing white varisk cloth growing larger every moment.

"They punish their gullaime to catch us," he said.

"Should I bring up ours?" said Farys.

"No," he said, turning back to the beak, "let them tire their gullaime, we will keep ours fresh. Make sure Chiver on the *Last Light* knows that too."

"Ey, D'keeper," she said and ran to shout out instructions for the signals to be given. *Tide Child* flew on, his beak smashing through waves, sending spray up in twin arcs as he barrelled forward. In the convex world Joron looked through he saw the first sign of the keyshan, a huge flipper, almost as long as the ship that followed them. He waited for the thrill to run through him, the shock and awe at the creature. Yet it did not come.

Where was the heat?

The joy?

The song in his heart?

Where was the terror?

The majesty?

The sheer and overwhelming presence?.

Somewhere, deep inside, he felt a darkness. Knew a truth.

"Dead," he said quietly.

"D'keeper?"

He focused the nearglass on the beast, saw its belly, as big as an island, thick with white feathers and as he scanned along it, the creature's body bending in the imperfections of the glass, he saw it was spattered with blood. And that blood surrounded the creature, a slick of black, and within the black a million jewels. He struggled to understand it. Was this some property of keyshan blood? Did jewels run through its body?

On closer inspection he saw a line of wounds across the beast's body.

What weapon could do this? What vast engine had been created to make this series of punctures across the body of something as mighty and indomitable as a keyshan, empress of all the seas?

No woman or man of the Hundred Isles had caused this.

And no woman or man of the Gaunt Islands either. He looked harder, saw how the regular the wounds were, how they were shaped, long and narrow like a beak.

Bite marks.

A fight?

It must be. Over what he did not, could not, know. Territory? Mates? Some terrible sub-aqueous grudge? How could a man understand a keyshan? None could, not really. Not even himself, who had, in some unfathomable way, a connection with them. But he was also not surprised by the violence. How could he be? He had seen them smash ships, seen them open their mouths to reveal a cave of huge teeth. He had, unthinkingly, presumed them simply for hunting. Never thought of them fighting.

"It's dead?"

He turned to find Farys, staring across the water. She looked stricken.

"Ey, so it seems," he replied. "No wonder they wish us away, there's enough bone there to keep the Hundred Isles fighting for another generation, and with the damage we've done to their fleet it's bone they need."

"So what do we do?" she said.

"We fight, Farys; what choice do we have?"

"Ship rising!" shouted from the tops.

"Tell of the ship, Topboy," shouted Joron, and he hoped it would be one of theirs — Brekir, maybe, having turned back for some reason.

"Boneship, D'keeper, coming from t'ward the Eaststorm, four-ribber, I reckon."

"A pair of four-ribbers and a two-ribber against us," said Joron. Beneath the mask he grinned at Farys, and Farys, knowing him well enough to read the movements of his eye and the cloth across his face, grinned back.

"Seems unfair on 'em, if you ask me," she said.

"Jennil," shouted Joron, "get your seaguard fully armed, I went half of them up the spines with crossbows. The rest belowdeck, ready for boarding. Solemn Muffaz! Clear my ship for action! And I want . . ."

Before he could finish speaking the Gullaime exploded from belowdeck in a blur of bright colour, flapping robes and noise.

"Stop ship! Stop ship!" screeched at the top of its considerable voice. Behind it came Madorra, also screeching.

"Listen! Listen!"

"What do you mean, Gullaime?" roared Joron in his best storm voice. "The creature is dead, there is no danger."

"Dead! Dead!" shouted the Gullaime, speeding down the ship toward the beak so it could look over the sea at the rapidly growing corpse. "Much danger! Much danger!"

"From what?" said Joron as the Gullaime turned and ran back up the deck.

"Poison! Poison!"

"Hiylbolts," said Joron, "they have managed to make them at last?"

The Gullaime screamed at him, opened its beak wide showing the cave of spines within and screeched for all it was worth, before spinning round on the spot twice in frustration.

"Poison! Poison! Sea sither poison!"

"They are not poisonous, quiet yourself. I have read the

books, Gullaime, and granted, death is never pleasant, especially the death of a creature so great."

"No!" it screeched, shaking its entire body. "Stupid human. Stupid."

"Gullaime, I—"

"Stupid! Keyshan dead. Keyshan dead. Dead keyshan bad. Poison!"

"Gullaime," he stepping toward it. "Speak more slowly. Please, I do not understand."

"The fire in the heart. Heart break, fire unleashed."

"There is no fire, Gullaime," said Farys.

The Gullaime turned slowly, first its head, then its neck, then its body. The mask that covered its eyes focused on Farys.

"Stupid human. Not see fire. Poison fire." All around the Gullaime the women and men of *Tide Child* were smiling and grinning to one another at this display of strangeness and insubordination – they had come to expect such things from their gullaime. It was a creature of odd passions, given to taking against the strangest things. Then Solemn Muffaz stepped forward.

"My mother used to say 'sooner break a keyshan's heart', if she were making a promise she would never break," he said.

"I have heard such a thing," said Joron, "may even have said it myself but . . ."

"Among the bonewrights," said Colwulf, stepping forward, speaking quietly, still unsure of her position on the ship, "'tis well known the flensers never allowed a heart to stay near a town."

"Ey," said Cwell from behind him, "those born near a heart-ground seldom come out right or live long."

And as each spoke, the Gullaime's masked head flicked from them back to Joron.

"Listen!" it squawked. "Stupid ship man!"

Joron was about to explain to it that it was wrong, simple superstition. That they could not simply believe it and allow the bones to fall into the arms of the Hundred Isles. That to do so was to supply material for more boneships. To undo their work in weakening the Hundred Isles to bring Meas back. To make the fight for peace when she returned harder.

Something black caught his eye. Something black and strange and boneless moving across the huge corpse. He lifted the nearglass once more. A shudder ran through him. A tunir, the black-spined, three-legged killing machine he knew to fear like few other beasts. Yet it moved like no tunir he had seen, it crawled across the body, plainly struggling. Then it staggered, tripped over its own rubbery legs and fell, rolling down the sheer side of the keyshan as slack as seaweed tipped from a bucket until it splashed into the water. As he watched he realised this scene was wrong. Where were the skeers? There were no skeers flying above the corpse. Anything that died on the ocean attracted the carrion birds and yet here, the biggest creature alive in the entire archipelago had died and there were no skeers.

Tide Child flying full speed toward the corpse with all his wings out, his commander wondering why there were no skeers around the corpse.

Was he being foolish?

Something hazy above the carcass. Like heat on a summer's day. But the air was cold.

He let the nearglass dip.

The water full of jewels.

No.

Fish.

Dead fish.

And in among the fish there were the skeers, or their corpses. Attracted by the bounty. Killed by something invisible.

"Hard to landward!" he shouted and ran to the rear rail of the ship. "Hard to landward!" he shouted at the smaller ship behind them and then *Tide Child* tilted, the sea rushing up to meet them, the edge of the circle of dead birds and fish that marked the radius of the poison so much closer than it had been before. "Hold on! Hold on!" he shouted. The ship came around, tilting further and further, the turn feeling impossibly tight for such a large ship. The circle of death drawing closer. Behind them the smaller ship turned in a tighter circle and he could hear the Gullaime screaming out a raucous squawk, "Poison! Poison!" The deck now heeled over so steeply Joron had to pull himself along one of the ropes, finding the gullaime.

"How far does it reach, this poison?"

"Not far?" The ship shook and creaked. "Long way? Not know! Not know!" The circle of deathly water grew nearer.

"How long does it stay?"

"Long and long, many lives." The ship creaked and shook, the circle of deathly water still nearer.

"How quickly does it kill?"

"Weeks, hours, year. All different." He stared into the colourful feathered mask of the Gullaime and heard a cheer as the ship began to right itself, skirting the edge of the poisonous water, the giant hill of the keyshan's corpse moving to seaward of them. At the furthest edge of the turn, where *Tide Child* almost touched the deathly circle around the corpse, Joron finally felt the heat he associated with the vast beasts, yet this was different. Where before it had been warming, like lifting his face to Skearith's Eye, this was a scorching heat, a flaying heat, like the wind after a hagspit strike, a devouring heat that set the sores on his face burning. The poison from the beast was not some ichor that leaked from it despoiling only the water, it was something on the air, some unknown element within that radiated out from it, killing all that came too close whether over or under the water. Silently, he thanked the Gullaime for warning him, if not for it they would have flown straight into the poison and all aboard would have died. He felt as sure about that as the slate beneath his feet.

"Barlay!" he shouted. "Bring us alongside the *Last Light*. Seakeep! Bring in the wings, slow us down." He stared over the side at the Hundred Isles boneships, still a good way off. His mind so used to measuring time and distance and wind he did not notice the effort of the calculations even as he did them, did not consciously consider any one of these things as they had become a part of him, like breathing, like pain, like disease and like loss. Four turns of the glass away at least, even with gullaime to assist them. "Heave to! Solemn Muffaz! Bring him to a stop!"

"All stop!" shouted the giant who stood before the main-spine, "let out the seastay!" Over the side went the concertina of rope and varisk cloth that would hold the ship still and *Tide Child* came to rest beside the *Last Light*. Joron went to the rail.

"Ho the *Last Light*!"

"Ho the *Tide Child*!" came the reply and Shipwife Chiver, a tall man who wore his long hair in a thick braid that fell down his back and the sculpted trews and leather straps of the Kept, he was as pale as Joron was dark. His face thick with scars earned fighting in Joron's fleet. "It seems we have found a mighty prize out here!"

"Ey, but this cup is poisoned, Shipwife," Joron shouted back. "Look in the water around it, it brings only death."

"So what is your plan then, Deckkeeper?" and when he said the rank, it took Joron back to the days it had been first given, when no one had respected him or thought him worthy.

"Well, there is a great jointweight of bone there in the water, Shipwife," he said. "I plan to give those ships out there what seems a very generous gift."

"If you are wrong about this poison, it is a costly mistake." Chiver did not hide his scorn.

"Feel free to take your ship nearer, if you, wish, Chiver," said Joron. All action stopped aboard *Last Light*. The crew looked to their shipwife, who stared at the circle of black water, full of dead creatures. Chiver also looked, for a moment. Then turned back to Joron.

"They will think it odd if the Black Pirate simply runs away, D'keeper," He shouted over the water.

"Ey, they will. So we must bloody ourselves a little." He saw a smile appear on Chiver's scarred face. "But not you, I am afraid, Shipwife. Given long enough to think about it they may make the link between the old heartgrounds where all is death, and the poison around this keyshan. They must not think. I want them to take it in tow, and if they get it back to Bernshulme then it could destroy their entire fleet."

"So what is your plan?"

"I want you to run, as if you are going for reinforcements. There will be no new scars for you today."

"I will not pretend I am less than disappointed, D'keeper," he shouted back, "but if we simply run they will know something is wrong – that is not the reputation the Black Pirate has cultivated. Would be stranger to run than stay and fight."

"Ey," Joron shouted back, "*Tide Child* will engage, but then break off. They will think we got a little full of ourselves then thought better of it. But your escape will have them worried that more of our ships are coming. I am sorry to deny you a fight, Chiver."

He grinned, and waved a finger in the air.

"Well, the Hag knows the black ships, and she will scar me another day, no doubt. Fly well."

"And you, Shipwife Chiver." He turned away, calling out to his crew, and the ropes were pulled and the wings hoisted. He watched, always a beautiful sight to see the serrated and hooked hull of a boneship go from still to moving, the way the wings billowed then snapped tight as the wind caught them. The sound of women and men heaving on ropes and the slow, almost imperceptible first movements as he caught the wind and the ship gathered impetus. Then building up of speed until the movement seemed unstoppable, and the speed seemed limitless and Joron knew he could watch happily until the *Last Light* vanished over the horizon and the wake of white water faded into one with the sea, as everything must eventually. Maybe in another life he would have done just that, and spent his days on a beach somewhere, watching the boneships come and go.

But this was not that life, and he turned from *Last Light*

and back to his own ship, saw his crew arrayed and waiting on his word, like longthresh sniffing blood, eager and ready. "Hoist the mainwing! Untruss the gallowbows! Get yourselves ready for there will be blood, and there will be suffering and there will be death!" He walked among them. "But let that be at our hand, and let the Hag hear my voice, and know we do not act in vain, for we do this for the black ships, for the Hag, and for Lucky Meas!" And the cry was returned,

"For Lucky Meas!"

And the wings went up, and *Tide Child* began to move, and in the distance two boneships, white as fear, grew larger and larger.

7

Blood on the Water

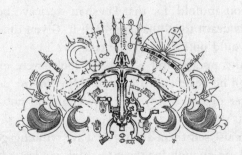

Tide Child gripped the wind. Cut through water. His music the rhythmic crash and hiss of the beak smashing through waves. The beat guiding the song of the crew as they pulled on the ropes, tightened wings, altered rigging. Two white ships growing larger.

Corpselights glowed above them. Too far to make out the colours yet.

He knew that across the water, the shipwives of those ships would mirror him. Stood on their rumps between their officers. Staring down the deck, between the gallowbow crews crouched around their weapons. Shot and bolt stacked. Gullaime gathered before the mainspine. Deck strewn with sand to soak up the blood. Ropes and nets through the rigging to catch falling spars and wings. Weapon racks brought up.

Ships of war.

Not long now.

Far behind them a third enemy ship now approached and *Last Light* made his escape, though Joron had already put Chiver's vessel out of his mind. He had a plan, and that approaching third ship was part of it though he did not intend to fight it, and it would play no part in his current calculations for the coming battle unless something went terribly wrong.

"My crew! My proud women and men, my black pirates!" To this a cheer. "The time for blooding comes, but we will play a fancy trick. What pain they take out of us, they will suffer a thousandfold, for that keyshan we leave behind is a poison, it is death to all that approach it. Given time, a clever shipwife would notice, as we noticed, ey?"

"Ey!" And nudges and winks and looks were exchanged, for although he never called himself shipwife, the deckkeeper was a clever one all right, and how could he not be, being Lucky Meas's son?

"So we must sell them a ruse; first we will engage. Not for long, just long enough for them to think we leave because of that third ship. And they will think that we leave to get help. So they will hurry to lash up that keyshan and tow it away. They have no loyal gullaime to warn them of the danger! So, I tell you this, the Hag may take from us today, she'll want paid in blood, and we'll see little from it, for I do not want those ships destroyed or crippled. I would leave them strong enough to take my little gift, maybe take it all the way back to Bernshulme to poison their water. So stand fast! Stand strong! Stand for Lucky Meas!"

And the call came back, strong and proud.

"For Lucky Meas!"

"Gullaime!" he shouted. Before him on the deck, the brightly coloured figure stood tall within a circle of white-robed acolytes. Its feathered mask turned to him. "Are you ready to bring me the wind, Gullaime?"

The Gullaime opened its curved predatory beak, lifted it to the sky, raised its wingclaws so its coloured robe became flashing wings and it screamed, and Joron felt the familiar pain in his ears, the heat across the deck as it took hold of the weather. Clouds appeared above the ship, first white then darkening and it felt as if the Gullaime's scream never stopped, as if it reached out across the water and Joron imagined the crew of those approaching ships hearing it, wondering what it was that could make such a noise. Seeing the clouds that gathered around *Tide Child*, and he knew they must feel fear. Brave deckchilder, he thought, to still come on. Brave officers, to face the Black Pirate despite the noise they must hear, despite the clouds they must see, despite the savage reputation he had.

A crack of lightning. His ship writ out in stark white lines. A rumble of thunder.

"Hold there, Gullaime!" he shouted. "I'll not have them run from us in terror."

"Sea sither spirit," shouted the Gullaime. "In the air. Angry."

"Then calm it, Gullaime," he shouted, "we want to put up a good fight and run, not blow them from the sea."

"Foolish, smash bad humans." The gullaime yarked to itself and those in its circle nodded their heads, all except Madorra who hissed at Joron as the storm calmed, the clouds paled and the wind fell to something more manageable.

Two ships advanced and Joron Twiner, shipwife in all but name, smiled to himself.

"Open the bowpeeks! Crew the gallowbows, we'll fight both sides as we pass!" At those words he heard the slap of bone on bone as the bowpeeks on the underdeck were opened. Two ships, approaching fast. The two-ribber less of a threat, only ten small bows on its deck and *Tide Child* was far taller. The smaller ship could not sweep his decks with stone, or fire into the bow crews. All the two-ribber's shot would be straight into the hull and Joron knew *Tide Child* was sturdy enough to take it.

"Untruss the bows!" Farys, her voice cutting through the song of the wind. Gavith the bowsell nodded and the crews went to work, bringing up and over the firing arms of the heavy bows so they stood ready for their bloody work.

The four-ribber was his problem: not as big as *Tide Child*, unlikely to do enough damage on one sweep to stop them – though there was always the chance of a lucky shot, a spine coming down, the tiller shot away – and then it would be boarding and hand-to-hand and real hard and harsh work.

Though it would be harsh whatever.

One pass — four great bows, probably loaded with rocks, ten smaller bows loosing directly into the underdeck. He foresaw it, the slate awash with blood in the blue glow of the corpselights, the way the gentle blue made it look the deepest purple. The screaming. The agony. The endless churn of the longthresh in the water as the dead went overboard and he again saw that flash, that moment long ago that never truly left him; *his father crushed between two hulls.*

He felt his hands shake. Not fear, not quite. Or maybe it was but he had become so used to it he no longer recognised it, felt it as excitement, felt it as anger, felt it as a burning fury for what he believed was right. Inside, where there had once been fear, and then hate, there was now only an empty place. When he did feel fear, it was often the fear that someone would see the hollow within him, or that the lack of direction and purpose was a symptom of the rot eroding his mind. He needed Meas back.

Shaking hands behind your back. Stand straight.

Get them ready.

"Today," he shouted, ignoring the closing ships, not thinking of the damage a bolt could do to him, "my women and men, my loyal girls and boys. We fight a quick fight, once through and we'll be off. Put on a good show, hurt 'em bad but not too bad. We want them to feel like they've won their prize!" A glance forward, the ships large in his view. In his mind counting down the grains of sand in the glass before he gave the command.

Ships growing.

Water rushing.

Ships growing

Rigging singing.

Ships growing.

"Wind the bows!" he yelled, Gavith shouting the same, the bowsells echoing him. Furious work on the deck, women and men winding back the cords on the gallowbows. Shouts going up of "Ready! Ready! Ready!" all along the slate as the cords locked in, the warmoan of tightly stretched cord sang out. "Load the bows!" The bolts going into the grooves.

The ships growing.

Water rushing.

Rigging singing.

He could make out the keyshan skulls on the front, so much smaller than on the creatures he had seen. For a second he wondered what it had been like, in the days of the great bone-ships, the skullships that must have had crews of thousands. To crew such a ship now would empty Bernshulme.

What was it all for?

"We'll not go the Hag today!" he screamed into the air. "We shall not hear her call!" A roar from the deck.

The ships growing.

Warmoan loud in his ears.

The sound of *Tide Child*, hungering for blood.

"Loose as they bear!"

Into the maelstrom.

Into a storm of shot.

The bows on either side of the deck loosing. The two-ribber's shot angled up, trying to cut *Tide Child*'s rigging, punching through wing and bouncing off spar and spine but not strong enough to smash through it. The four-ribber loosing its shot, sweeping the decks of *Tide Child*, cutting through his crew. Saw Chelvin have her legs ripped from under her. Saw Hotston lose his head in a pink spray. Saw Kitgon's torso seem to just vanish, arms legs and head hanging there for a second. Shards of bone were smashed from the rail and the hull, piercing and bludgeoning and cutting. Blood hanging in the air as the storm moved down the deck to surround him with noise and screams and violence. And all the time, that thing that was not fear and not anger and not hate growing within him. A bolt ripped through the circle of gullaime, killing two of the white-robed windtalkers, but the rest did not waver and despite the violence the wind kept coming and the ship kept moving and that dark empty place within Joron kept growing until they had passed through the storm.

The order was there, in Joron's mouth. *Bring him round*. So easy to say it – his Gullaime, his friend could work the wind like no other. Vengeance for the pain they had just suffered could be his, swing the ship round, loose into the rear of his enemy. So vulnerable now. Fire his wingbolts with hagspit. Watch them burn and die.

"We're clear, D'keeper!"

Deep breath. Blood on the decks. Bodies to seaward and landward. The ships behind them the same, a faint haze of bonedust about them both. Swallowing air as if to fill the empty place within him, suddenly aware he had been holding his breath.

"Full wings! Gullaime, give me more wind, let's get out of here." He stepped forward, "Farys, I'd know the price we paid the Hag if you would."

"Ey, D'keeper," she said, and turned to relay the order to Solemn Muffaz, who took it gladly, even though she was half his age and third his experience, for he had taught her all he knew and was well proud of the woman she had become. And all around them the deck was cleared of the dead, and the wounded were dragged below to the hagbower.

"D'keeper? D'keeper?" He found Gavith looking up at him, holding out a rag.

"Ey, Gavith?"

"For your face, D'keeper,"

"My face?" he said.

"The blood."

He raised a hand, touched his cheek above the scarf, found wetness, blood flowing from a cut below his eye. Recognised a cut that would need stitching, would leave another grey scar on his dark skin. Took the rag from Gavith.

"Thank you."

"You should go to Garriya, have it stitched, D'keeper."

A scream from down the deck as a man was lifted – *Chariff*, he thought, a good deckchild, his leg broken, white bone showing through flesh.

"Others need her attentions more than I right now, Gavith." The boy nodded.

"Ey, D'keeper," he said, bowed his head and glanced across at Farys, gave her a shy smile that she ignored. Solemn Muffaz arrived, a spray of drying blood across the light brown skin of his face.

"D'keeper," he said, his voice as sonorous and serious as ever.

"What news from the Hag?"

"None good, D'keeper. Twelve lost to shot as we passed, another four we will lose, three we may and if we do not they will be poor deckchilder from now, on account of not having an arm or leg." He paused, glanced down at Joron's spur. "Although, I suppose one can learn to cope with anything, ey?"

"Indeed, Deckmother; in truth I worried it would be worse."

"It is worse."

"And how is that?" The big man rolled his shoulders.

"Colwulf, the bonemaster, she only says the mainspine caught a bolt." An immediate cold shock through Joron and he stared down the deck, all too aware of the tower of wings, catching the wind and straining the central spine of the ship. "Says it ain't about to go yet, but we should be careful." As he finished speaking, Colwulf, a small thin woman swathed in bandages, appeared from below with three of her fellows, all carrying spars of hardened varisk.

"What goes, Colwulf?" said Joron, striding down the slate accompanied by the deckmother. "Does my ship ail?"

The woman paused in directing her helpers up the spine.

"For sure it does, as it will indeed if you insist on taking him into the range of other's bows, and who has to fix it all with dear old Coxward gone to the Hag? Colwulf, ey. Colwulf does." She turned away and spat on the deck, and Joron swallowed his annoyance. The bonemasters were an odd lot, afflicted with the rot, just like him, and Meas had told him to treat the good ones well and Colwulf was as good as they came, trained as she was by Coxward.

"How does he ail, Colwulf? Should I bring down the wings?" She sucked her teeth, or on what she had left of them.

"If I thought that I would not have brought up the bracing, no. Caught a glancing blow further up, took out a chunk but it seems strong still. I'll have my women and men up there, tying on the varisk around it. I'll leave old Chiff up there to watch for any sign of splinters."

"Good, now—"

"While we is talking, D'keeper, the spine is weakening, so you go do your ordering them that need it about and I will do my job, ey?" Joron nodded, suddenly feeling no more a commander than the day he stepped aboard *Tide Child*.

"You do that, Colwulf," he said and turned back to Solemn Muffaz. "There is something I would speak with you of, Deckmother, privately." He walked the big man to the rail.

"How can I help, D'keeper," said the deckmother.

"Farys," he said, "and Gavith." Solemn Muffaz nodded. "I have noticed."

"The Bernlaw, Solemn Muffaz, it is strict on such things. Lovers of the same sex only, a child must never be brought onto a ship of war." Joron stared out over the sea. "I am only a deckkeeper, Muffaz," he said. "If I went against the Bernlaw for my crew there are those in our own fleet who would use it against me, and many who would agree." He turned to look at Solemn Muffaz. "You must speak to Farys and Gavith, I have no wish to find Farys with child and then be forced to pronounce sentence of death upon them. None at all, I could not stand it."

"I will speak to them, Deckkeeper," he said, his voice so low it was little more than a growl.

"Thank you," said Joron, "such an order is likely to cause less resentment coming from a friend than a commander." Solemn Muffaz nodded and turned away, to be about the clearing of *Tide Child*'s decks.

For a moment Joron wondered if he had made a mistake, if

he had simply pushed away a task he did not wish to do onto another. But the decision was made so he took out his nearglass and stared behind them. The two ships he had fought were making good time away from him, all their wings raised and full of wind as they sped toward the corpse of the arakeesian and all that had in store for them. He allowed himself a little smile at that, wondered if right at that moment they were jeering him, calling him out for a coward that he ran from them. Then the larger of the two ships moved a little and Joron saw the third ship, the one that had been on the horizon. Too big to be one of his. It also had full wings raised, a tower of billowing white and six blue corpselights glowed above it. But it was not heading toward the massive corpse, it was heading toward him. As he watched it an arrow was launched from the tops. Up and up it went, a flame burning brightly and when it reached the zenith of its climb the arrow burst into a dirty black smear against the blue, blue sky.

"A signal," he said to himself.

"Could be ruse though, D'keeper," said Farys, coming to join him, "to scare us away from the corpse, like?"

"Could be, Farys," he replied, and put away thoughts of his conversation with Solemn Muffaz, "but we cannot afford to treat it as such. We must presume there are those out there watching for such a signal, and now they will be coming."

"A chase then?" she said.

"Ey, a chase, and with the mainspine weaker than I would like we must be canny about it. Call Aelerin, have them set up the table in the great cabin. Our pursuers will know we head back to the Gaunt Islands and I would not fly straight into a trap. Let us see if we can outthink them."

"If they pursue us," said Farys.

"Ey, if, but no one ever died from being over-prepared, as the shipwife always said."

"Indeed," she said and turned away, heading toward the underdeck with the name of the courser already on her lips.

8

A Well-observed Plan

Aelerin's map table was constructed on two wide varisk
boards. It had been made by the courser and Mevans,
scavenging all they could from around *Tide Child* – old clothes
and rags, broken bones and pins – until they had amassed a
collection of objects quite as eclectic and useless-seeming as
anything the Gullaime had gathered within its cabin-nest. Then
they had set to work making a recreation of the Hundred Isles,
or as near to one as they could – a recreation which, every
time they set it up, Aelerin was quick to point out was "not
to scale, and not correct in every way." Nonetheless, Joron
thought it an amazing thing, to stand within the great cabin
and look down upon his world, the Hundred Isles and the
Gaunt Islands, split by the black line that represented Skearith's
Spine. *I did not build the Spine as it would obscure the rest of
the map, and take too many materials, but I could . . .* He
mentally waved away that echo of the courser's voice as his
mind made its way around the map and through the islands,
drifting across the lines where the gion was dying, down and
through where it was growing, and from there along the frac-
tious winds of the Northstorm, blown up toward the Eaststorm,
grabbed and thrown toward the Weststorm and then, once

more, gently drifting down to the Southstorm in the eternal circle of air currents passed around the walls of cloud that encircled the world he knew.

And for a moment, he thought of the impossible, the unmentioned, the question that was eternal but never asked. Was there something beyond the storms? Every deckchild knew someone who claimed they had travelled through them, to rich and fabled lands of comfort. And every deckchild knew them a liar, for the storms were impassable. They ripped up any ship that approached; even their edges were fierce enough to tear the wings off a ship's spines. No, those who talked of passage through were liars and fools for they were as impenetrable as any wall.

"Deckkeeper," said Aelerin, "my apologies for the map but . . ."

"It is a thing of wonder, Aelerin, no apologies are needed."

"But I could . . ." He saw Mevans move forward, gently touch the courser's arm and smile and the courser, cowled and hidden, gently nodded and took a step back. The once-silent courser had become positively loquacious since the mutiny, as much part of Joron's command crew as any other on the ship, though Joron could not shake the feeling they were always slightly embarrassed to be speaking out.

"A boneship follows us," he said. "We need to avoid tangling with him."

"Unlike you to run from a fight, D'keeper," said Mevans, "and that'll be two in one day." A look shared at Mevans's gentle teasing.

"Oh, it is all I can do not to turn around and bloody our pursuer's nose, but we took a pounding early on, and Tide Child trails a lot of weed on his bottom. We need to careen the ship and clear it off if we are to have best speed and movement."

"We could still take him," said Solemn Muffaz, the huge man speaking quietly as he slipped in through the door. "Nothing on the water that Tide Child cannot put under it, no matter how ill he feels or how far to landward he pulls."

"You noticed that too," said Joron. "I fear something struck the tiller below the water. I am thankful for your belief in the ship, Solemn Muffaz, but the time for battle is not now, and my decision is made."

"I hear, D'keeper, and what you say, well, that will be done, for it is no doubt the right course you set." Beneath his mask Joron smiled; it touched him, this simple belief strong women and men had in him. But at the same time something dark within him called, something that could, with just a little more persuasion, give the order to turn the ship and wreak havoc on those behind. To rend and kill and strike back at those who had taken his shipwife, his leg, his Dinyl.

A deep breath.

"Aelerin, I want to get back to Sparehaven in the Gaunt Islands as quickly as possible. We have weakened the Hundred Isles beyond anything that could be expected, and if they take that keyshan corpse back to Bernshulme it will weaken the Hundred Isles past even what Tenbern Aileen and all her Gaunt shipwives dream of."

"Then we move against them," said Mevans.

"Ey," said Joron quietly, "then the Tenbern can move against them, I care naught for that, though we may have to commit ships from our fleet to help them. What interests me is the shipwife. They will take Bernshulme and I will find Meas if I have to burn the whole place to the ground and kill every woman and man there to do it."

"Some of our crews will have family there, D'keeper," said Solemn Muffaz, and Joron caught the warning in his tone. Nodded, for Solemn Muffaz kept his crew in line, and a large part of that was done by ensuring they had no wish to step over the line in the first place.

"We will do all we can to protect families, Solemn Muffaz, you know this, and I would have you make that known across the deck and through underdecks." He took a deep breath, then added quietly, "But do not let them forget, Solemn Muffaz, that this will be war, and people will die. War is like the Northstorm, the Hagsbreath, it cannot be controlled."

"True, D'keeper," he said. "I will make sure the crews know the way the currents drift."

"Thank you, Solemn Muffaz. Now, to the business in hand."

"Eames's Passage is nearest." Aelerin, pointing at a slit in the black lines of Skearith's Spine.

"But almost definitely patrolled," said Mevans.

"Ey," said Joron.

"Word among the Gaunt Islands coursers, afore we left, was a line of ships and watchtowers in the waters above the centre-line." Aelerin pulled a piece of string across the centre of the map. Then placed a small model boat, a simple piece of carved varisk, behind it. Then they placed another. "The first is us," they said, "and we head up toward the patrolled line and calmer waters. I dream gentle winds."

"We could slip through at night," said Solemn Muffaz.

"That ship following would alert them, we would be swarmed."

"Then we try and slip through Eames Passage? Or one of the lower passes?" said Mevans.

"We turn around and go south," said Aelerin. "To here," they touched the map, "Wilson's Cut."

"South?" said Joron.

"Ey, the cold times there are coming and the Southstorm bears its teeth. And the route is longer, right enough."

"But unlikely to be patrolled."

"The ice," said Solemn Muffaz, "it is as dangerous as any ship. Not like the north where it stays still, the ice in the south wanders."

"And that is why they are not likely to follow us," said Joron. He stared at the map, knew the danger of ice, the great floating islands that could be seen, and the low sitting ice reefs that could not. Knew the way the cold bit into the bone of a ship, made it brittle, how ropes under tension could weaken and snap, cutting an unlucky deckchild in half. How hard it was to work the ship in the freezing air, the way flesh could blacken, fingers and toes could be lost. He scratched at his shoulder where the sores on his body were at their worst.

"D'keeper." Farys, walking into the room.

"Ey, Farys?"

"Topboys report another ship, coming for'ard of us off the seaward side."

"Size?"

"Too far away to tell for sure, but they think another four-ribber." Joron stared at the map.

"Well, that is decided then," he said. "I do not rightly want to fight one ship our equal, never mind two. We will head south toward the ice, and hope the Hag favours us."

"Ey, D'keeper," came the call from all about the room.

"And Farys," said Joron. "You came yourself to give me this information?"

"Thought it important, D'keeper." She said. "Gavith has the deck." *Ah*, he thought, *of course he does*, and he noticed a similar frown upon the face of Solemn Muffaz to the one that must be on his.

"Thank you, Farys, but Gavith is not in a place of command, you are. Next time send him to me with the message." She nodded, her burned face flushed with the admonishment.

"Ey, D'keeper." She swallowed. "Should I turn the ship now?"

He shook his head. "No, Aelerin must chart a course for us and I would try a little bit of cleverness out on our shadows. Steer us on a course away from the two ships for now, as though we intend to continue north and pass through their line of lookouts.

"Ey," she said quietly and he felt her disappointment. Not with him – with herself, for leaving Gavith in charge? Maybe, but just as likely for not pre-empting his decision to keep to their current course, as near as possible during the daylight hours.

"And, Farys," he said, "send me Bonemaster Colwulf. I have in mind a fine trick to play on our pursuers."

Colwulf had looked ill at Joron when she was told what must be built. And in the manner of bonemasters throughout the fleet she had moaned and complained, "'Tis a waste of good varisk, and all my best gion spars on this thing; for what use is it?" And when the bonemaster had finally stopped her complaining, then it was the turn of the wingwrights, who grudgingly gave up their tired cloth, worn by the winds and the seas and barely holding together, though they had assured Joron it would hold long enough for his purposes.

And while the women and men of *Tide Child* put together the slowly growing construction on the slate deck, the ship himself had tacked back and forth as he moved north against the wind. A course of huge zigzags and hard work, though in such a currently pleasant climate it was no great task for this crew, this well-practised and fleet crew.

"Arse!" shouted Black Orris from his perch on Joron's shoulder. And Joron raised his nearglass once more, in an action that had become repetitive enough over the long hours he stood on the rump that it sparked an ache in his shoulder. One ship, there. Turn a little, find the other, slightly bigger ship. Both converging on him, both slowly gaining on him. He looked up at Skearith's Eye, marking its slow progress across the blue sky, interrupted only by lines of thin and feathery cloud, and wished he could speed its passage a little.

"Arse indeed, Black Orris," he said, and ruffled the black feathers of the bird's throat.

"They catch us, ey?" said Jennil.

"Indeed they do." He walked to the rail and looked over the side, long streamers of green weed waved at the side of the ship as he cut through the water. "You were right all those weeks ago, Jennil, and I was wrong. We should have careened the ship and cleaned the hull when we last had chance."

"But then we would have not caught the *Foolish Maiden* before it hit Landhulme and many lives would have been lost. Or been in time to hit Windhearth before the southern ice started to move."

"True," he said, and the weed waved and the water rushed by. "But now it may cost us." He stood back, put the nearglass to his eye and watched the ships gaining in increments. What to do? He could make out a gullaime on the deck of each ship; that was where they got their speed, they did not need to tack the way he did. Should he bring up their own gullaime? He should, to not do that surely looked suspicious when he was running. But he may need them later and it had been too long since they had visited a windspire. The weaker ones he could push no more, the stronger he must hold in reserve. He saw a flash on the nearest ship, the larger four-ribber, and knew that across the water someone watched him as he watched them. Did they know what he built, were they near enough to see detail? He touched Black Orris's feathers once more.

"Jennil," he said, "who is good with a paintbrush?"

"Zarif and Azar-lis."

"Have them paint some of that spare wingcloth with the image of a gullaime. Then raise it as a shield to hide what we build. I would make it look like we have gullaime on deck."

"They are hardly of the standard to grace a Bern's bedchamber, D'keeper," said Jennil.

"They need only create an impression to those looking from afar, get them to it."

With that he went back to watching the ships and their slow chase of him. He noticed that they were in no great hurry, no flyers out, and they did not drive their gullaime too hard, for which he was grateful. If they got too close he was sure they would not fall for his trick as he was sure they would recognise what he built, and though Zarif and Azar-lis had already set about painting Jennil was right about them, the Mother had blessed them with far more enthusiasm than skill.

"They could catch us quicker," said Farys, coming to stand by him, squinting against sunlight reflected back from the glass surface of the sea.

"They do not have to, Farys."

"Why?"

"They are like longthresh hunting a shoal of fish, they simply herd us toward a place where their fellows wait."

"And when we do not go the way they wish, D'keeper?" she said.

"With any luck they will be far behind us, and we will be far away from them." He wondered if she was also thinking, *and if luck is not with us?* But she did not voice it, and no deckchild ever would, so afeared were they of bringing bad luck down on the ship. He stepped a little closer.

"Were you thinking, 'what if our luck is bad', Farys?"

"No, I . . ."

"You are an officer, now, Farys," he said in a whisper, "and my job was always to question Meas when she needed those questions asked. That is your job now, for me. An officer has no need of luck, Farys, for we plan, we do not leave it to chance." She nodded, slowly, the burns on her face stretching and he saw confusion in her eyes. When she spoke, the words came slow and hesitant like the first breeze coming to the becalmed.

"So, D'keeper, if they do not fall for your trick?"

"Then we run, and hope their gullaime tire before ours, and make sure we fly our ship sharper." She stared at him.

"Does that not, well, trust to luck, a little?" she said. Joron shrugged.

"A little, maybe. Now, let the wings run a little ragged, Farys, I'd not have them think too much of us. Even though we have a reputation we're still not fleet to them and it's a hard idea for them to accept, that we could be their equals in any way. The sloppier they believe we are, the easier they will be to fool."

"Ey, D'keeper," she said, and left him to contemplate the sea, and the ships and the weed that slowed *Tide Child* down, a green and living staystone.

Skearith's Eye closed and her blind eye rose as a crescent bowl of light, a shining smile against the scattered points of light that were the Skearith's bones, the patterns that pointed out the paths of the sea to the coursers. *Tide Child* rode the waves, sliding through gentle rolling water that was as kind and warm as the seas of the Scattered Archipelago could ever be. All around the ship the gentle rituals of night were carried out. The bell rang out the passing time and deckchilder moved around the slate and the underdeck with tapers, lighting the softly glowing wanelights along the decks, and in the main cabin Mevans lit the brighter lights that allowed the study of charts late into the darkness, and stared out the great windows as that light was reflected back at him from the water below. From above he heard the rasp of saws and the thud of hammers as the bonewrights constructed a lifting rig, just as the deckkeeper had ordered. Mevans leaned out of the open rear windows to light the landward of the two large lanterns that hung from the rear of the ship and smiled to himself.

"Clever as a hungry skeer," he whispered into the sea air, "the shipwife would be proud."

In the night air above, Joron watched the lifting gear, a huge A-frame, as it was completed. He watched his deckchilder swarm over it; practised hands tied knots and soon a complex web of rope surrounded the A-frame. From the top of the frame another rope ran to the ship's central windlass, around the buffers and bollards worn smooth by years of use and back to the ungainly looking construction the bonewrights had worked so hard to construct.

From the central hatch came the Gullaime, followed by Madorra and a procession of its white-robed and feathered followers, until the ship's Gullaime turned on the windshorn, hissing and spitting.

'Away go! Away!'

Madorra bowed low to the ground, looking subservient, though Joron did not believe it for a second. The windshorn had shown itself to be anything but, and although it rarely directly challenged the Gullaime it had a way of wearing the windtalker down.

"Not go," said Madorra, "not go. Help. Only help."

"Enough! Enough!" squawked the Gullaime. Behind Madorra the heads of other gullaime rose above the deck like strange fungi, masked and yet still managing to orientate themselves on the confrontation. "Not slave! Not yours. Gullaime officer." It raised itself to its full height, stretching out the wings beneath its colourful and ragged cloak and it let out a stream of high-pitched song, occasionally croaking and cawing as it fluttered and danced. Behind Madorra the acolytes drew back and Madorra shrank down before it. Giving a little nod of its head.

"Away go, then," it said, but Joron could not help thinking that if the windshorn had been human he would have seen a glint in its one good eye, like that of someone with a plan, and a plan he may not rightly like. "Madorra away go." It backed away, staying low. "Go. Gullaime go. See friends. See humans." Slowly the Gullaime came down from its threat posture, the colourful feathers that had raised in a ridge on its head smoothing down. Its head twitching from side to side as it studied Madorra, first from one side then the other. To all about in the world it would have looked as if the Gullaime regarded the windshorn with eyes hidden behind the mask. Of all the people in the small world that was *Tide Child*, only Madorra and Joron knew that it did, that unlike every other gullaime this one still had its eyes, and that they glowed with the same fire that a keyshan's eyes had, and for that reason Madorra called the Gullaime Windseer. Joron shuddered, more familiar now with the prophecy of the Windseer that saw the Gullaime's people freed in fire and death, and unsure of his place within it as the caller. Uncomfortable too, ey, that was true. And maybe he had not spent the time with the Gullaime he should have because of that.

"Gullaime," he said, "welcome to the deck."

"Yes, yes," it said, hopping forward, the confrontation with Madorra seemingly forgotten. It stopped at the rail, beak pointing at the ocean, then up at Skearith's Blind Eye before it turned on the spot in a whirl of colourful cloth and tinkling trinkets. Then it paced across the deck, stopping to squawk something at a deckchild who was polishing one of the handles on the windlass.

"Ey, Gullaime," she said, "I'll be sure to do a good job, don't you worry yourself," and the Gullaime moved on while behind it the deckchild smiled to herself and thought of what an odd and wonderful ship she had found herself on, and thought on when she would eat next and if the good d'keeper would allow them an extra ration of shipwine this time after working so hard on whatever that Hag-forsaken thing they were building was. From there the Gullaime hopped over to another deckchild, watching them working their way up the wanelights and checking each had enough oil.

"What do?" said the Gullaime and the deckchild – lost in thoughts of when the bell would ring and his watch would be over so he could go to the depths of the ship and meet up with Collun, for they were new shipfriends and much in the tides of passion – almost dropped his oil.

"Filling the wanelights, Gullaime," he said quietly. "So we can see what we do."

"Good, good," said the Gullaime. "Good job is." Then it hopped on towards a third deckchild who had paused momentarily in untangling a knot within the rigging where it attached to the side of the ship and was staring into the darkness, far over the sea where you could just make out two dim lights. And she knew they were the ships that pursued them, and the memories of earlier action were fresh in her head and her hands shook a little.

"Good night is? Good night is?" said the Gullaime, and the deckchild turned.

"Ey, good night it is," she said and she took some comfort from the windtalker, for sure the battles may be dangerous but their Gullaime was more powerful than any other, and hadn't it come to the d'keeper? And wasn't the d'keeper the son of Lucky Meas herself? And wasn't Meas the greatest shipwife who had ever lived and the favoured of the Hag? The

Gullaime moved away and she returned to her work, if not entirely happy, then at least a little more at peace.

"Keep it free, keep it free," said the Gullaime to a deckchild who greased the gimbal on Savage Arrin, the rearmost seaward gallowbow, and was lost in his task, aware of little more than the pleasant feel of the grease on his fingers and the smell of it, which was not a million miles away from a stew, a stew gone a little rancid maybe but a deckchild ate what they could and maybe he should taste it?

"I'll keep it free, Gullaime, worry you not, don't want old Savage Arrin locking up on us," he laughed and the Gullaime moved off and he carried on with his task a little lighter of spirit. Lastly the Gullaime came to Joron, overseeing his construction as it was put into position beneath the A-frame.

"What is this? What is this? Ey? Ey? What is? Looks right Hag's arse. What is?" And Joron turned to the windtalker, a gleam in his eye and a smile beneath the mask that covered his face.

"It is not good for an officer to use such belowdecks language, Gullaime," he said. "But to answer your question, it is a decoy."

"What what what?"

"A model of the ship, Gullaime, and I will lower it behind us and set its wings and let it float off, and hope those who chase us follow it, not us. We may need your wind soon, though in truth this blow currently favours us well." But the Gullaime was not listening, it was moving around the model, brushing against it with its wingclaws, then it hauled itself up the side, crawling around and over it, inspecting and feeling it until it ended up on top, where it stood for a moment before leaning over at what appeared an impossible angle, its long neck extending so its head was above Joron's and he had to look up into its face with its mask that, just like his own, hid a secret from those around them.

"Is very bad," it said quietly. "Not look like ship."

"No," and Joron coughed, found himself laughing after what

felt like a lifetime of dour feelings, bad news and cruel acts. "Not in the light, it does not, and not up close either, you are right."

"Why do?"

"Because under Skearith's Blind Eye, Gullaime, magic can be done." And the bell rang, marking the centre of the night when Skearith's Blind Eye was as high as it would get at this time of year, and Joron smiled to himself for now was the time. "Mevans!" he shouted. "Kindly put out the lights in the great cabin, for it is time I was asleep."

The shout came back of "Ey, D'keeper!" and Joron smiled to himself.

"Now, Gullaime, I will carry out my trick, and win us some much needed time." He did not add "hopefully", though he thought it. Because, though he denied the title and would not take up the two-tail, he knew that to all on the deck he stood as shipwife of *Tide Child*, and a shipwife never said hopefully, a shipwife simply knew what was and what was to be. "I hope the Mother looks kindly on us, Meas," he whispered under his breath, "and I will be freed to find you." He turned, looked at the crew, and every one of them, on watch or not, was awake. And all those who did not have some job to do in the bowels of the ship were waiting for the d'keeper's trick, for his magic. To see what his strange contraption was, for had he not been so very particular about it, ey? And had he not been so very "no this here and that there", though all could see it looked like nothing more than a big square of varisk and gion with a clumsy wing. And this all built atop the ship's smaller flukeboat and if any woman or man knew what he was about then none had spoken up. But he was the d'keeper, and he was the child of Meas and none doubted he knew what he was about.

"Farys," Joron said, and she was there, at his shoulder.

"Ey, D'keeper?"

"I'll have every wanelight aboard the ship out if you will, leave only the rear lanterns."

"Ey, D'keeper," she said and she was gone, into the quiet

throng of deckchilder that stood behind him and he heard the order spread through them, a slow whisper, like a wave on a beach of shingle. He watched as the lights on the deck went out, and the familiar faces and bodies, twisted by the many hardships of the Hundred Isles, gradually vanished and, when his crew were no longer burnished by the light and had become a huge, amorphous shadow, as much a part of *Tide Child* as the wings or the spines or the gallowbows, he turned back to the A-frame and the crew around it. Those he trusted most, Solemn Muffaz and Jennil each leading a small team of hand-picked women and men, and below them in the great cabin Mevans waited with his own people. And here he stood, Joron Twiner, every soul aboard waiting for him, waiting for this plan he had dreamed up to work. He lifted the nearglass to his eye, found the place where Skearith's Bones washed across the sky and met the ocean. Drifted the circle along the line of darkness below the tiny colourful pinpricks, the wash of misty light. Found another light in the distance, a ship, blinking on and off as it rolled with the waves. He kept going along the horizon, nothing. Went the other way, that same ship again, then he found the other. No doubt watching him watching them. Catching him by increments.

Now or never.

"Lift," he said.

"Take the strain," said Jennil. Ropes tightened.

"Pull," said Solemn Muffaz, and though all knew it unlikely the pursuing ships could hear, voices were quietened and soft singing began.

> My true love on a ship away.
> Ship away, ship away
> Left me all alone today.
> Ship away, ship away
> I'll drink my sadness far away.
> Ship away, ship away
> And sink into the brine.

As they sang they hoisted, pulling on the ropes and lifting the contraption from the deck of *Tide Child*, and more than anything Joron wished he could join in that song, for to sing had been his great joy. But a shipwife called Gueste had taken his voice with an order and a garotte, and what came out of his mouth now provided him no pleasure. But worse than that, twice he had sung and that had brought a keyshan and Joron was not fool enough to think he controlled such beasts, merely woke them somehow, got their attention at best.

"It's up, D'keeper," said Jennil, little more than a tall shadow in the night.

"Bring it forward then," he said. And the ropes holding the A-frame were played out until the contraption was slowly spinning in the empty air over the rump of the ship.

"Tie it off and bring out the gaffs!" said Solemn Muffaz, his voice carrying in the quiet night. Deckchilder ran ropes around tie-off points, others ran forward with the long hooked sticks to steady the ungainly pyramid dangling behind them and once the light from the rear lanterns showed it was steady he felt Jennil's hand on his jacket.

"Lower it, D'keeper?"

"Ey, lower it, but don't put it in the water until I give the signal."

"Bring it down, my girls and boys," said Jennil, "down till it kisses the waves soft as you kiss your shipfriends and no further." All around him grunts and sighs as the weight was once more transferred to those holding the ropes, and he heard the shuffle of feet as they found purchase on the slate and his machine began to slowly make its way down to the sea.

"Steady, steady," he said. And further and further down it went, dropping below the level of the deck and Joron was leaning over the side, using the light of the rear lanterns to judge its fall. Below Mevans leaned out of one of the open windows.

"It's near, D'keeper," said Mevans from below.

"Ey, a little further though, I want as little to disturb it as possible when it drops."

"Ey," said Mevans.

"Hold fast!" hissed Joron. Then he turned to Farys at his shoulder, behind her was Cwell, a literal and lethal shadow that he had become so used to he barely even thought about. "Steady it," he shouted as it started to swing with the motion of the ship, "or I'll have Solemn Muffaz cord the lot of you." The gaffs came up and the swinging stopped. "Gavith, Chadir!" he called. "Bring your lanterns." Gavith came up with Chadir, the youngest member of the crew, both with covered lanterns. "Now listen, the both of you, when I give the order you are to uncover your lights, and not before and if you do I will feed you both to the longthresh, you understand?" They nodded. "Now get in position." The two deckchilder were quickly over the rail and clambering over the mass of spars so that each sat at the furthest corners from the ship, leaning over as they hooked their lamps over the construction, then lashed them on.

"Ready!" they called, almost in unison.

"Loose its wing," said Joron. And the two deckchilder pulled out the makeshift wing, designed to keep the thing straight and little else; he knew it would barely make headway but it did not have to. They lashed the wing in place before returning to their hooded lanterns.

"Mevans?" shouted Joron, leaning over the side of the ship.

"Ey, D'keeper, we're ready." Below, two of Mevans' chosen were leaning out with snuffers, ready to put out the lamps on the rear of *Tide Child*.

"After three," said Joron, "all ready?" A chorus of "ey" in return. "Then one, two, three, now" And the lights on *Tide Child* were snuffed, just as Gavith and Chadir lifted the covers from their lanterns and those very few among *Tide Child*'s crew who had not worked out what their d'keeper had planned suddenly smiled in the darkness, and whispers were exchanged as Gavith and Chadir clambered back aboard the ship, grinning like children having carried out some prank. Joron wondered if on those following ships they had seen a momentary blink, and if they put it down to tired eyes, or if they were suspicious that some trick was being played. But he could not know, so he put it out of his mind. "Enough whispering!" shouted Joron. "To your places, get ready to bring us about and we do it in total darkness. I'll not have any hurt themselves simply because of that; I'll have you cleaning the bilges if you do, for you should all know this ship better than you know your ship-friends' bodies. Get to it!" And all was action as Joron turned back to those at the A-frame, waiting with boarding axes. "Well then," he said, "cut it loose." The axes fell, the ropes were loosened and with barely a splash Joron's makeshift recreation of *Tide Child*'s rear fell into the water; then the great ship started to come about in a gentle circle until his wings caught the wind conjured by the gullaime, filled out and pushed him onto his new course to the south.

As he watched the lights of the decoy recede Farys came to stand by him.

"How long do you think it will fool them D'keeper?" she said.

"Until they catch it, or until it is light enough for them to see what it is. Let us hope it gives us enough time to get over the horizon."

"Ey," said Farys. And Joron did not reply, lost in contemplation of the two lonely lights, slowly receding into the night.

9

The Open Sea

Tide Child flew before the wind for six days, his black wings full, flags flying and hair whipping around the faces of those on the slate. And on each day, when Skearith's Eye opened, Joron took to the deck and scanned the sea with his nearglass, and when Skearith's Eye closed, Joron scanned the sea with his nearglass. And when the ship's bell rang Joron scanned the sea with his nearglass and when he did not scan he walked up and down the deck and he found Aelerin and asked how they dreamed the winds and he found the answer always the same.

"Brisk, the air clear."

And the air was clear, and the winds were brisk and did he imagine it or were they already becoming far colder?

But *Tide Child* flew before the wind, and Joron found tasks for his eager crew, set them moving stores, the better to fly the ship. Set them with long gaffs to scraping at the hull from precarious rope swings, to remove as much weed as they could, and as they worked they sang and Joron closed his ears to the sound, concentrated on the sting of the sores on his face and shoulders, concentrated on the line between grey sea and blue sky and on how he hoped and hoped that the line would remain empty of all but lonely islands and soaring seabirds.

On the seventh day, Joron began to believe they had done it, that they had misled their pursuers, and found enough speed to escape over the horizon and leave their enemies searching the seas in vain for *Tide Child* and his crew.

But they had not.

"Ship rising!"

When the call was made, Joron felt it was his fault. That by starting to believe they had escaped he had somehow vexed the Sea Hag, and she had sent an errant wind to their pursuers. If it was the same ships. He did not know if it was. So he climbed the mainspine. His bone spur part of him now, the ache where it met his flesh like a familiar but unwelcome deckchild appearing on the rump. Up and up he went, around the billowing wings, feeling his ship through vibrating ropes, having his breath stolen by the wind as much as the height. Still, after so long, he felt the muscles of his thighs weaken a little when he looked own. Then he was in the tops with the topboy.

"Where do you see him, Bearna?" She pointed behind them, and his eyes could pick out nothing, but when the horizon leapt at him through the circle of the nearglass, he found it quick enough.

"Can't tell his size, no I can't for sure," she said.

"Four-ribber, a big one," he replied, the words a gentle sigh. "I would wish it were the other, the smaller, but what care the Hag for wishes." A movement caught his eye, little more than an errant dark dot upon the waves, could have been a seabird, or something of the deep coming up for food. But it was not, he knew that. It was the second ship, no doubt the smaller four-ribber that had previously been with the larger ship. He closed the long lens and placed it in his coat. "The answer, Bearna, is that the Hag cares nothing for the wishes of women and men. Keep an eye on those ships for me."

"Ey, D'keeper," she said.

With that he was down the spine, working his way through the nets of rigging until he felt the hard slate beneath him once more.

"Jennil! Farys! Mevans! Solemn Muffaz!" he shouted, striding up the deck. "We have been making good time up until now, but not good enough. Use every trick, take every shortcut, put up every wing we have. Our ruse did not buy us the freedom we hoped for, but it did buy us time. If we can make Wilson's Cut before we are caught then they will not follow us into Gaunt Islands territory, so we fly fast while the winds are good, ey, my crew, ey?"

And a shout of "Ey" returned, and if any woman or man felt the same dismay he did then they hid it well, as well as he hid it from them and each and every one resolved to keep that worry hidden deep within.

"Farys," he said, and she appeared at his arm, as calm and quick as if she had been expecting him to call at that exact moment.

"Ey, D'keeper?"

"Have Aelerin and Mevans set up the map table, let the Gullaime know I will wish to consult with it also. Try and keep Madorra and its Hag-cursed entourage away."

"Ey, D'keeper," she said and was gone, leaving him on the deck to watch as his crew found new tasks to get themselves busy with, each and every one knowing their place and purpose and he did not need to call out, to say they needed every drop of speed that _Tide Child_ had, did not need to ask for ropes tightened, for wings checked, for the hull scrapers to push themselves to reach that little bit further down to scrape off more weed. For these were the women and men of _Tide Child_, and they knew their ship as they knew themselves and he was naught but proud of them.

Time passed, the bell rang and Joron paced the deck. He felt the nearglass in his pocket and fought the temptation to constantly stare through it, knowing such a thing would make him seem nervous and be unsettling for the crew. When he did once more raise it to his eye, he could not lose the feeling that the ships chasing them were gaining. Did they use their gullaime? Was that where they got this turn of speed from?

For if so they could not keep it up. Their gullaime would tire, they would have to stop.

In his heart he knew the winds favoured them the same way they favoured *Tide Child* and that their greater speed was simply that of well-run ships, fresh out of a port and using the advantage that gave them. He called a passing deckchild.

"Reyan, kindly ask the courser to the rump, if you would." And he barely heard the returned call of "Ey, D'keeper," or saw the smile that passed on the face of Reyan, who was one of the newer crewmembers and felt a rush of pleasure not only that the d'keeper knew his name, but that he trusted him with such an important order.

It seemed no time before the courser was by him on the deck of the rump, though enough time had passed for Joron to feel even more sure those two ships were gaining.

"D'keeper," said the courser. "I have left Mevans grumbling that he must set up the map table alone." That gentle reproach at taking the courser from their beloved map brought a smile to Joron's face, one that made the sores around his mouth sting.

"Look at the ships chasing," he said, passing over the near-glass, "I think they gain on us." He waited, enjoying the play of the brisk wind around his face, the way it got under the scarf and cooled his skin.

"I think they gain also," said Aelerin. "It is hard to tell as they move and we move, and I need more time to take better measurements. If we change course to pass nearer that island to the east of us then that would help, a static marker is always good and—"

"Could the wind favour them more than us?" He suppressed a smile, that the once so quiet courser now had to be stopped from talking too much.

"Unlikely, D'keeper," they said, "but not impossible. The storms can play strange tricks, they favour the Maiden that way, but I have dreamed no strangeness, seen only clear skies around us at this moment, so I think it safer to say we share the same winds."

"Mother give me a clean hull and we would vanish like the gion forest in the dying time," he said under his breath, as he took back the nearglass and once more stared at the following ships. But the Mother did not magically make the weed fall from the bottom of *Tide Child* and Joron did not expect it to. Her children had disobeyed her long ago, when Hassith threw the spear that killed Skearith the godbird, and now they must help themselves. "Right." He closed the nearglass and placed it in his jacket. "We should go and see if Mevans has your map table up yet."

"And that he has not damaged it."

"Indeed," and again he smiled; that the courser could sound testy about anything was something he would never have believed, upon a time. He turned, two deckchilder stood, waiting their turn at scraping the hull. Each had a scraper, the wide blade on the end polished to a mirror sheen, and he caught glimpses of a figure in the shining blades: black clothes, tall, a missing leg, a masked face with many grey scars on the dark skin. He did not see Joron Twiner there, he saw his creation, the Black Pirate. *We all change*, he thought, *but not all of us for the better*.

Down into the underdecks, the gloom lightened by open bowpeeks, the crew almost absent as all were on deck or below trying to eke a little more speed from the ship. From there into the great cabin, where the floor was dazzling white and Aelerin's table sat on the desk and Meas's chair sat to one side, with her hat hooked over the back.

"D'keeper," said Mevans, and he took a step back as Aelerin hurried forward, checking the map table was set up to their specifications.

"Mevans," said Joron. "if you could bring Jennil while Aelerin sets out our positions. Tell Farys she has the deck until I return."

"Ey, D'keeper."

She vanished and Aelerin set out her ships on the board, black for *Tide Child*, white for their pursuers. "It is not . . ."

"To scale, I know, Aelerin." He walked forward, staring down on the Scattered Archipelago as Aelerin lay a piece of string before the model of *Tide Child* and along the map, showing the course they intended to take toward the southern icefields and Wilson's Cut.

"You wanted me, D'keeper?" said Jennil as she entered.

"Ey, Jennil. You were once a fleet officer, you and Mevans know as much about the sea as any other on the ship. Aelerin has set out our course, we are pursued by faster ships. I would hear what ideas you have to offer us."

Jennil stepped forward, staring down at the map with Joron, and it was clearly all Aelerin could do to not once more call out, "it is not to scale," but the courser held back as the woman and the deckkeeper and the hatkeep studied the undulations and dark seas of the archipelago.

"How is the weather for the next few weeks?" she said.

"Aelerin said clear skies."

"Not quite, D'keeper," said the courser, "I said that for now, regards the ship that follow. My dreams though, they have been troubled by thoughts of storms from the west coming toward us."

Joron's brow furrowed. "Rare the Weststorm speaks," he said.

"But furious is its voice when it does," said Jennil, parroting the words of deckchilder the sea over. "At the rate they have caught up with us so far, then I give us at least another two weeks before they are near enough to loose their bows. Will the storm be on us by then, Aelerin?"

"It is a tricky business to predict a storm, Jennil. I think not; I think three weeks before the winds come and the waves rise. But it could come quicker, or it could veer off and go another way entirely. Such is the way of the Weststorm, it is as if it acts to frustrate my arts." Jennil nodded as she stared at the table.

"How near are these islands?" She pointed at a set of islands that looked only a palm's breadth from *Tide Child*. As Aelerin was about to speak Farys entered the room.

"I have come to see if I can be of any help, D'keeper," she said. "Solemn Muffaz has the deck and there is no great need for me there." Joron was about to chastise her but held his voice in his gullet – unlikely she could help, ey, and she knew it. But well likely she could learn, and that made her presence here worthwhile and if Solemn Muffaz had spoken to her about Gavith then maybe best she was allowed some time away from him.

"Good choice, Farys," he said, and he saw tension leave her like it left a gallowbow cord when it was unstrung. "Carry on, Jennil."

"We could turn for those islands in the night, then hide among them while these ships pass."

"They are numerous, these islands," said Aelerin, "but very low."

"We could take down the topspines," said Farys.

"It's half a day's work, to get them fully down," said Mevans, "then half a day or more putting 'em back up."

"The crew are not afraid of work," said Farys. Joron could hear the hurt there, at her idea being knocked back.

"Oh no, we do not doubt it. You have fashioned them into a good crew, Farys," said Joron. "They work as well and as hard as any, but if we were found we would not have half a day to put the spines up. That would leave us without recourse to half our wings, we would be caught immediately."

"Oh," said Farys, bowing her head, "of course."

"But every idea is worth hearing, Farys." He turned from her. "The islands are out, Jennil, anything else?"

"Skearith's Spine, D'keeper?" She looked about her. "We double back again, a black ship against the black rock? Would be terrible hard to spot from a distance."

"It is true," said Mevans, "and if we can find a cove where Skearith's Eye does not reach then there's a chance they fly right past us." Jennil nodded, looking at the map table. Silence while Joron considered it. First they would have to find a cove, and though Skearith's Spine was full of such places they would be searching in the dark, and the water at the edges of the spine was full of rocks that could rip open *Tide Child*'s hull and end their escape there and then, sending every soul aboard down to join the Hag.

But if they could find a place? Surely if any crew could then it was Meas's crew. But of course, and he smiled to himself, it was also true to say that he knew no other crew at all.

The smile fled as he imagined what it would be like, to have *Tide Child* and the crew moored at the staystone, to sit for days on end, all but the topboys hidden in the underdecks to ensure no movement gave the black ship away, no splash of colour. He could dot the ship with white paint as an offering to the Hag, and to make it look like guano-covered rock. All so possible. Yet, all aboard would know that it would only take one alert topboy to spot them. The tension on the ship would rise, fights would happen, not even the best crew could take such enforced idleness under stress. But still, it may be worth it.

Though what then? Run back north, hoping to slip though the line of ships and lookout towers, and maybe find themselves in the same situation but with the wind against them?

"Call the Gullaime," he said, and the Gullaime was called, quick to appear as Farys had already let it know it would be needed. But it was noticeably quieter and, despite Joron's request, Madorra was in tow.

"Why bring Gullaime," said Madorra, its voice wheedling as it hopped into the room. "Gullaime tired. Gullaime need rest."

"The Gullaime is an officer of *Tide Child*, Madorra, which you are not, and the Gullaime can speak for itself." The wind-shorn regarded Joron from its one good eye and hissed at him before hopping back to sit by the door, a pot-bellied figure squatting down, a bundle of ratty feathers, filthy robe and bare pink skin. The Gullaime, in its finery, seemed to grow a little at Madorra being put in its place, then hopped forward, predatory beak opening.

"Jo-ron Twi-ner," it said, and it was almost like their first days, he was struck by the alienness of that scratchy voice coming from the open beak without lip or tongue moving. "How help, Joron Twiner?"

"I only need answer to a question, Gullaime. That is all. Be truthful when you speak and let me know where I stand."

"In cabin. Joron Twiner stand in cabin." A round of gentle laughter.

"Indeed I do, but I would know from you how much wind you, and your fellows, have. For we are chased by . . ."

"Bad boats."

"Ey, bad boats." It was easy to forget, with their alien ways, that the gullaime were just as attentive and understanding as any human. "I would know how long you can push us on for. It has been longer than I would like since we last visited a windspire."

The Gullaime crowed, opened its mouth and set up a great racket, lengthening its whole body out as if to project the noise into the cabin.

"Bring wind for ever," it said. "Wind and wind and wind. Push big ship."

Hyperbole, Joron knew, was not unusual from the creature and it was something he always tried to take into account when it spoke. It would also speak to annoy Madorra whenever possible, though why it did not simply dismiss the windshorn he had no idea.

"Thank you, Gullaime." He gave it a nod of respect, a thing he knew it enjoyed. "But remembering your fellows are not as strong, we want no windsickness, and must have some of your power to call on should we need it another time. So how much wind can you safely bring? Tell me lower rather than higher. I value surety above hope."

"Joron Twiner," the Gullaime said, then made a dismissive sound, blowing air out through its nostrils before reaching up and touching its mask with a wingclaw. "Gullaime strong," it said, slowly swaying from side to side. "Others not, must help yes yes yes . . ." It seemed to lose interest in him, fixing its masked face on the map for a moment. "Two weeks. If gullaime bring soft wind. Two watched each day. Yes. Harder wind. Less time."

"Thank you, Gullaime. You may return to your nest." But there was something there, some feeling in the back of his mind that he had mis-stepped in saying that. The Gullaime nodded slowly and Joron wished he had given it leave to stay longer, for as soon as it was time to go Madorra was up once more, and the Gullaime seemed to shrink as they shuffled out of the great cabin. Inwardly, Joron swore to find out what was going on there, what strange hold the windshorn had over the Gullaime. Not the first time he had sworn it, but as commander of a ship the tasks were always piling up, and time was seldom something he had.

He put Madorra out of his mind and stared morosely at the map. He knew, as they all did, that what the Gullaime could give was not going to be enough.

"The shipwife," said Mevans, "I met her first on a two-ribber called *Tailor's Cuffs* and we were once in a similar situation to this, chased by two Gaunt Island ships when we'd already tangled with a four-ribber after raiding an island. Down on crew and the ship in a sorry state, we struggled to outrun them. All seemed lost to me and every other on board, but not to Meas."

"What did she do, Mevans?" said Joron.

"She emptied the ship, threw everything overboard; all but water and food went down to the Hag."

"Even the bows?" said Jennil.

"Ey, even the bows," said Mevans.

"But we'll be defenceless," said Joron.

"True," said Mevans, then he grinned. "But we'll be fast."

10

The Wait

A cold brisk wind. A hard grey sea.

In the time they had been in the great cabin, Joron was sure the ships pursuing them had grown, felt it was impossible. They had not been stood over the map for that long, and though he had done his rounds and various tasks it did not seem like enough time. Or did the shipwives of those beautiful, tall white ships with glowing corpselights flog the last life from some poor gullaime to catch them?

He walked down the deck, dipped a finger in the paint pot by the mainspine and turned, leaned against the spine, his booted toes on the edge of a familiar crack in the slate as he stared back through the ropes and past the rearspine at his far away pursuers. He placed the image in his memory then returned to the rearspine, smearing blue on the bone where the nearest ship was, at what he was sure was about that ship's current height in his nearglass. Then back to the place by the mainspine, nearglass up, studying his handiwork and finding himself pleased with it as the small blue smear of his fingerprint was almost the exact size as the ship on the horizon.

"Now I will know," he said to himself. "Now I will know."

"D'keeper?" He turned to find the purseholder. Mevans had

skipped the duty given to him and handed it to a man named Hedre, who had little understanding of the sea but a good head for numbers. He waited on Joron, head bowed and with his ledger open and ink on his long thin fingers.

"I have made a list of the goods in the hold it will cost us the least to lose as you asked." Hedre licked the end of his quill and Joron thought how odd it was, that the features of the man should be as long and pointed as his writing tool.

"I only need to know how much food and water we must keep to see us safely back to Sparehaven," said Joron. He walked down the deck followed by the purseholder.

"The Gaunt Islanders short us on all we bring them, D'keeper, and inflate their prices on all we buy from them. We are likely to find ourselves bankrupted and having to sell our ships to them if we—"

"Hedre, as I said earlier, we are likely to find ourselves dead if we do not outrun those ships." The purseholder's eyes widened. "So do as I ask and I will have Mevans rope off those supplies."

"And the rest goes into the sea?" It was almost comical how miserable he looked, and if Joron had not been able to see the white dots of their pursuers on the horizon he may have smiled beneath his mask. But he could and he did not. The purseholder's fondness for the material goods in *Tide Child*'s hold and the coin it was worth was something Joron prized as much as the crafts of the sea in his deckchilder. Hedre fought for every coin that could be saved in stocking the ship's hold, and those coins were precious indeed for he was right and the Gaunt Islanders gave them no quarter in trade, despite they were allies. But penny-pinching served no purpose now.

"Ey," he said sharing the purseholder's sense of regret, "I am sorry, Hedre, but the rest goes into the sea." The purseholder nodded, and Joron searched for some way to soften the blow for the man. "But if you can organise goods by weight, the heaviest can go over first and we shall see how he flies then. Maybe we will not throw all over right away, ey?"

"A wise course, D'keeper," he said, a smile on his face. "I will make sure Mevans is aware." He scuttled off, nose deep in his ledger and Joron went back to watching the pursuing ships. No growth against the blue smudge in the moments of that conversation. No shrinkage either. Then he folded up the nearglass, placed it in his jacket. Straightened his shoulders and tried to shed the worry the way the gullaime shed loose feathers.

"My women and men," he shouted, "gather you round, for I have a task and one that you may right enjoy." All knew that task already, for nothing but fire travels as fast as gossip on a boneship, and every woman and man aboard knew what was afoot. For the purseholder what was to come was a painful exercise full of loss, and for Joron it was a difficult but necessary task that must be carried out; for the crew it was no such thing. For them, for the dead, for the women and men whose lives were forfeit to the whims of the Scattered Archipelago's waters, the ships behind them were easy to forget and little more worrying than clouds, for was not the d'keeper sure to get them out of this? For sure he was. So when the first objects on the list were carried up from the hold, and the crane was set up for the heaviest objects to be lifted from the hold, the atmosphere on the slate of *Tide Child* was almost one of carnival, of gaiety. Songs were sung and they danced and capered as if they crossed the centre line of the world and they expected deckchilder dressed in the guise of the Circle Dragon to appear and hand out rations of anhir. A deckchilder, a woman called Vara, who he had barely spoken to since she had come aboard, stopped in front of him, a shy smile on her face and a sheaf of hard varisk for mending the wings in her hands.

"Seems wrong that we should be the ones to start this, D'keeper. On my old ship, *Skeerpath*, was always the shipwife'd throw over anything if we 'ad to. So I reckon'd you might be the most likely to start." He stared at the sheaf of stiff cloth, oddly touched by this nod to a tradition he had known nothing about.

"Thank you, Vara." He took the cloth, aware that all eyes were suddenly trained on him. At the back of the crowd he saw Mevans, and the sheaf of varisk reminded him of something he had overlooked. "Before I throw this over, Mevans, make sure the soft varisk and warm weather clothes are safe. I would not outrun our pursuers only to have the crew freeze to death in the south." Could they hear the smile in his voice, hidden as it was beneath a mask? He was unsure until he saw smiles and nudges, heard gentle laughter. "Now, let us start our task, and unhobble *Tide Child*, let us see how he really flies!" And he threw over the bale of cloth, watching it splash into the grey sea, move along the hull, bobbing and buffeted by the curling white foam of the ship's wake as the crew cheered and the bonerails became crowded with deckchilder, excited as children as they threw the ship's precious stores and cargo into the cold, cold sea. "The ship is yours, Farys," he said, and retired to his cabin to study charts and the cost to his small fleet of the goods they were throwing overboard. All the while he pretended not to hear the raucous laughter above him.

Time passed, he did not know how much. It was remarkable how easily he could vanish into charts and the filling-in of logs – a thing he did meticulously now as he knew Meas would check them when she returned – so when there was a gentle knock on his door he was surprised to find that a gloom was falling, that the long shadows of his body fell across the desk as Skearith's Eye had dipped toward the horizon behind them.

A coldness passed through him. Had he really been so busy time had ceased to have meaning, or was this another symptom of the keyshan's rot that scoured his body? He shook his head.

"Enter," he said. Aelerin slipped into the room.

"D'keeper," they said. "It will soon be time to put fire to the lamps, you have been working hard."

"Ey," he said. "Though I should go up on deck before full night, see if those ships still gain," Aelerin looked away and from that small action he guessed that the ships did. He sighed.

"I do not think we will be lighting our lamps tonight. I'll keep them out, let them think they have lost us, maybe they will change course in case we do the same in the night." Aelerin nodded.

"It is only . . ." Their voice tailed away.

"Only, courser?"

"That I thought you should know, in a week, we will be running along the old keyshan migration routes."

"And?" he said, though he felt small and cruel for it, for making Aelerin ask. But the courser surprised him, did not waver or become meek, stood straighter.

"There is talk among the crew that you steer us that way so you can sing one up, D'keeper, if it gets truly dire. I thought you should know." He stood, let out a small laugh.

"Thank you for telling me," he said, and wondered at his foolishness in believing any of them thought it was Meas that raised the keyshans. How would they, when there were those in the crew that knew the truth and gossip ran quick as water along the hull aboard a boneship? "In truth, I am not surprised to hear it. But no one will be singing up a keyshan." He made to walk past the courser and they spoke again.

"Joron," they said, and he stopped. He could not remember them ever using his first name before. How did he feel about that? Was it right? Should he be angry, discipline them? He did not know. So he waited, let them speak. "I know why you do not sing the keyshans to you, D'keeper," they said. "I know you are sure our enemies will kill the shipwife if they think it is not her with this power."

"They will," he said.

"Ey, they will," said Aelerin, "but if we die, she dies too."

"I know," he said quietly, and thought it odd that this had come from Aelerin. He had expected those words from Garriya, the hagshand, not the courser. But apart from the dressing of his wounds he had not seen her for days. "I will think on it, Aelerin."

He waited for the courser to leave, then left the cabin himself, and was sure he saw the ragged, bent figure of Garriya recede into the darkness as he did. Despite himself, he could not help a small smile crossing his face. "Clever old hag," he whispered into the darkness, "but bring your messages yourself next time." No answer.

On the slate the sky was awash with blood and the sea capped with lines of gold as Skearith's Eye, magnificent and hazy with sleep, met the ocean. *Tide Child*'s path across the waves was marked with a hundred bobbing pieces of flotsam, cast aside.

"Do we have new beakwyrms?" he asked to the air, knowing a reply would come.

"No, D'keeper, just the six we already carried." He did not see who replied, though he knew the voice. He tried to hide his disappointment. He found the crack in the slate by the mainspine and stood on it, took the nearglass from his coat.

"Gavith, take a wanelight and stand by the rearspine for me," he said, and Gavith jumped to his task and stood right in Joron's line of sight. "Other side, if you will, Gavith," he said and smiled to himself as the man moved across. The boy they had found on the harbourside had become a good deck-child, would make officer one day he had no doubt. If they survived of course. He put his mind back on course, found the blue paint he had placed on the rumpspine earlier, and stared at the ships so far behind them and felt a certainty within as cold as the air. Still gaining, no doubt about it. "Hedre!" he shouted.

"Purseholder's asleep, D'keeper," came the shout.

"Then wake him," he said. "I will be on the rump waiting his pleasure." He did not wait long, Hedre appeared, still fighting to wake from sleep, ledger held tightly in his long thin fingers.

"D'keeper?"

"You have done well, Hedre, I see the signs of your work drifting away behind us." The small man bobbed his head in acknowledgement. "And, though I know it pains you, we must lose more."

"I have made a list," he said, "of what is heavy, and of what is needed." He passed over a sheet. "I thought you should look it over before any decisions are made." Joron let his eyes scan down the list, so much that was important to the running of his ship: spars and rope, spare boneboard, sand, caulking, boneglue, nails and a hundred other things a ship could be lost for want of. He took a deep breath. He wanted to keep it all, knew its import.

"Have the wingbolts put over the side," he said, knowing the crew would be displeased at the loss of the feared ammunition. "That weight of stone should . . ." Hedre scratched his head under his hat, caught an insect and crushed it between his fingers as Joron spoke. "No, not the wingbolts, lose all the spare spars but one, and also all boneboard but one stack. If we lose a spar to misfortune we may still stay ahead, and fix it while under way, but if we lose more than one then we will have been slowed too much, and have no choice but to fight anyway." The purseholder nodded and Joron handed back his list. "Take this to Mevans and tell him to consult with Fogle, I had hoped one round of losses would be enough but now I see it is not. I want a further list of goods and supplies, prioritised by weight and by what use to the ship they are so we can start putting them over if we are not making headway on these ships by the morran. Then get some sleep; Mevans and Fogle are to sleep too." He turned, found Jennil waiting patiently behind him.

"I have the evening watch, D'keeper," she said.

"Good to hear it, Jennil, keep him straight and true, and throw a bit of paint that the Hag gives some misfortune to those who pursue us." He nodded to her and headed to his cabin.

Once in his hammock – still unable to sleep on a bed aboard ship, even after so many years – he felt the weight of the pursuit on his spirit. Brekir had been right, he had over-reached this time, taken his ships too far from safety in his desperation to weaken the forces of Thirteenbern Gilbryn. They had a long way to run before they could find safety. Sleep eluded him for a time, but the familiar rock of the ship and the ring of the bell and the soft sound of feet on the bones above him worked their spell and eventually, he slipped away into the deep.

And dreamed.

He was massive and weightless. He was dangerous and playful. He was hunger and fire and an internal roaring. He was awake. He was one of many. He heard the slow song of the sleepers. He heard the fast song of his people. Some songs filled with need, others with fury, others with confusion. Behind it all another song, a song so quiet and fast he could barely catch it, but it was full of promise, of rebirth, of fire, of empty seas and long migrations without the fear of death from the world above. He moved through the deeps with lazy flicks of his tail, he opened his mouth to catch the life within the water, a million specks of it washed down his gullet and through his system.

The coldness of the water was a comfort.

The coldness of the water.

The coldness.

Cold.

He awoke to the window at the back of the great cabin banging against the frame. Cold air blowing through and around him in the early morning light. He tumbled from his hammock to close the window before the glass smashed. The catch had come loose and he fought with it, being thwarted again and again as it refused to stay in place. Eventually he pulled a ribbon from the braids of his hair and tied the window shut, swearing and cursing the Hag for this small misfortune.

Then he saw the ships, triangles of white wingcloth, noticeably larger than the day before; he could pick them both out easily with the naked eye. He wanted to run up on deck, set the crew to once more throwing all they could over the side.

He did not.

Panic would not help. He imagined how Meas would react

before wrapping the black scarf around his face, then called for Hedre. "More must go over," he said to the purseholder, who nodded sadly. Then he called Mevans, had water brought. Removed the mask. Washed and let Cwell shave him, sitting still and trying not to think while she moved the blade carefully around the growing red and white sores on the dark skin of his chin and cheeks. Never mentioning them, never speaking to him about them. Clothed himself and walked up onto the deck. Found Farys at the rear, Barlay on the steering oar and made as if it were a day like any other.

"The weather is fine again, Farys," he said. "The wind cold but brisk."

"Ey, D'keeper, could not be finer for flying if'n it tried."

He turned and lifted the nearglass to his eye.

"I do believe those ships have gained a little overnight; well, we are still experimenting, are we not?" he said, his voice as light and as conversational as he could make it. "Kindly consult with Mevans and Hedre as to what comes next on their list. *Tide Child* is the fastest ship on the water in the right circumstances, we must concentrate on making them more to his liking." He raised the nearglass once more. "Then we'll see those fellows behind shrinking fast, no doubt."

"Ey, no doubt," said Farys and she sounded a fair bit surer than Joron felt as the orders were given. Then the deckchilder ran down the ramps and set up the cranes to once more start bringing cargo and stores up from the hold. Mevans came to stand by him.

"We still have some spars, and board, D'keeper," he said.

"I gave orders for them to go, Mevans."

"Ey, but Hedre is more of the rock than he is of the sea, was hiding away the valuable stuff and I had to explain some things are worth more to a boneship than coin. So we had a little re-jigging of his list."

"Very well." He stepped closer, so none but Mevans could hear his whisper. "It is dealt with?" Mevans nodded.

"No need for you to mention it, I reckon."

"Good," said Joron. He leaned in a little closer. "Do you think we will outrun those ships today?"

"I dare say, D'keeper, we'll have to put a lot more over the side afore we are quicker than those ships. They fly them well, and I bet they are clean out of harbour."

"Ey, said Joron. "That is what I thought." He raised the nearglass once more and stared at the towers of wingcloth in the circle, seeing the wink of light on lens as someone on the larger ship stared right back at him.

11

The Weight

Time and distance passed in that deliberate way time and distance will when you become aware that neither are well disposed toward you. As if in solidarity, the weather also turned against them. The air became colder, the sea became greyer, the waves higher until *Tide Child* was lurching forward, a steady rhythm of rising and falling punctuated by sprays of freezing water breaking over the beak.

Tide Child's precious supplies and stores continued to go over the side.

The ships behind them continued to increase in size. First they had been specks, only identifiable through the nearglass. A week later they were ships, their details only distinguishable through the nearglass. Now they were fleet for all to see and to count the corpselights bobbing above them. When Joron lifted the nearglass to his eye he could see the individual crew, officers and deckchilder. See the shipwife – a man, which surprised him; he thought his depredations upon the Hundred Isles would have earned him more respect from Thirteenbern Gilbryn than to have her send a man after him.

He could even make out the ships' names now. The smaller called *Keyshanpike*, the larger called *Beakwyrm's Rage*. As the ships had grown so the atmosphere on the deck of *Tide Child* had changed, as he knew it would, it became tighter, no slip in discipline, not in the least, and pride swelled within him at that. But he knew worry was setting in, noticed how when the deckchilder worked they would glance behind at those ships, look them up and down. Heard talk in low voices of how heavy the jointweight of shot they may be able to launch would be. But always behind it was the simple and constant belief that the d'keeper would get them out of this, for he was the child of Lucky Meas, and how could he fail?

How could he fail?

How?

It had seemed, for a time, that *Tide Child* gained; indeed, he had watched the ships shrink against the paint on the spine that he placed there to measure them. He had felt his crew's spirit lift. Then watched, dismayed, as the ships followed his lead in another way, and started to throw cargo over the side. Once more creeping up on *Tide Child* and his crew, and the pressure aboard ratcheted up once more.

If it was just one ship this would have been so much more simple, he thought, and had thought day after day after day. If it had just been the big four-ribber he would have turned and taken his chances, confident in his crew and their ability, their ferocity. But that was no longer an option. Four days ago they had put all of the wingshot over the side and thoughts of taking on that ship had sunk to the Hag at the bottom of the ocean, along with the lovingly carved ammunition. Still, he thought, he had plenty of long bolts left, and if he could weather a few rounds of loosing from them and get his ship in near enough to board, well . . . His crew would make short work of them, it'd be bloody work, and no mercy given.

But it was not just one ship. It was two, and they both better supplied and in better condition, and if he turned to confront them, to release that constant pressure of knowing they were there, that constant feeling of them at his back even when he stared into the clear sea before *Tide Child*, then he felt sure his ship and his crew would be chewed up between them.

"What I would give for a sea mist," said Joron, folding the nearglass away and placing it into his jacket, feeling foolish, for this must be the third or fourth or fifth time he had said as much.

"I'd ask the Mother," said Solemn Muffaz, "though I doubt she would listen to one such as me." And Joron had no answer to that, as Solemn Muffaz had murdered his wife and few in the Hundred Isles were as cursed as a man who murders a woman, no matter how much they may be haunted by regret. "Though if the Mother don't look upon us well, D'keeper," continued Solemn Muffaz, "then maybe the Maiden or the Hag 'as something in store for us." Joron turned to look out over the side of the ship. Far in the west were the first signs of a growing storm. It had, of course, been promised to him by Aelerin, two weeks ago now. Joron both dreaded and welcomed such a thing. The danger in a storm was ever present, and *Tide Child* no longer carried enough spares should their wings or spars be damaged, as all but the great gallowbows and the lesser bows and their bolts had gone over the side. *But a storm*, thought Joron. A storm could be just what he needed, for whatever danger was there for him was also there for those following, and he knew from experience how hard it was for two or more ships to stay in convoy when foul weather hit. If they were fools they may stay close and more likely than not one ship would ram the other. But they had given no sign of being foolish, so he was sure they would keep their distance and more like than not find themselves separated. And, if that were to happen, who knew, maybe his crew would get their red day after all.

But not today. Today they would fly on and fly on and eke every bit of speed out of *Tide Child* that they could get from the ship and, as if feeling Joron's need, he seemed to heel over just a bit further, cut the waves just a little cleaner, smash through them just a little more fiercely. Joron put out a hand, touched the rumpspine and said a silent prayer of thanks to the Mother and to Meas for giving him charge of such a sturdy and speedy vessel, for he was sure that any other craft would already have been caught by those well-flown boneships behind him.

"Magnificent, really." He turned to find Jennil staring at the ships. "The big four-ribber, I mean."

"Ey, a beautiful ship, and he would be a fair sight more beautiful if he were not chasing us." Jennil nodded and Joron raised his nearglass to watch some commotion on the deck of the smaller ship. "The crew of *Keyshanpike* are throwing over more cargo to keep up with *Beakwyrm's Rage*; a rough sea always favours a heavier ship." *Beakwyrm's Rage* loosed more wing, the cloth billowing out as it caught the wind and as the larger ship smashed its way through the waves in a spray of white water Joron found himself nodding to the enemy ship-wife. *You slow to or speed to keep convoy with your consort,* he thought, *you are careful and do not take chances.* He turned from the rail, wishing it were any other shipwife chasing. Careful shipwives were the best to work with, and the last he wanted to face in a fight.

"Jennil," he said, "tell Mevans to unload the next items on Hedre's list and put them over the side." He stared at the gathering storm, the slowly growing towers of black cloud on the western horizon. "Have him also move some of our heavier stores into the bilges, when the storm hits I'll have *Tide Child* be as stable as possible. I want our weight held as low as we can get it."

"Ey, D'keeper," she said and started to turn away.

"Jennil, have Mevans put aside some barrels and plenty of rope."

"You have a plan, D'keeper?"

"Maybe, though not much of one."

"It'll work," she said, as if the simple act of him having thought of something was enough to settle her.

As the day went on the contents of the hold went over the

side, and word that the D'keeper had a plan must have spread as he noticed a lessening of the tension, fewer glances to the rump of the ship, a generally more happier demeanour among the deckchilder and he wondered at this small miracle.

Time passed, the air continued to get colder, the three ships raced toward the ice islands of the south as a storm gathered around them. Sometimes *Tide Child* had the advantage and made better speed, and sometimes *Keyshanpike* and *Beakwyrm's Rage* were the faster. More often than not it was their pursuers that had the upper hand. They continued to grow and Joron began to wish the storm would hurry and close around them. A cold rain had started, a thin rain, enough to make a woman or man close their eyes against the thin icy slivers of water, but not enough to cloud the vision of the pursuing ships.

Thunder rumbled, the voice of the Weststorm uttering its threat, giving fair warning to those who flew the sea of what was to come.

"It is a way off yet." He turned to find Aelerin. The courser leaned in close as the wind set the rigging to whistling. "It will hit us just as night falls, I believe," said the courser. Joron glanced behind them. Had they been friendly those two Hundred Isles ships were now near enough to give the appearance of travelling in convoy. He could see deckchilder, busy on the front of *Beakwyrm's Rage*. They were raising a frame and women and men in the white bandages of the bonewrights directed the construction.

"What are they about, D'keeper?" asked Aelerin.

"I suspect they move a gallowbow to the front of the ship. It is not a bad idea and I think they will be in range before the storm hits." He stared over the rump, counting the beats of the wind against the wings. "Have Mevans come up here, and the Gullaime."

"Ey, D'keeper," they said and vanished belowdecks. For a moment he wished he could do the same. He was not wearing the right clothes for this weather, was still dressed for the morning which had been dry, though still cold, but to go below and put on heavier clothing would appear weak. He would order the deckchilder to change soon, then give it until the next ring of the bell before he allowed himself that luxury.

"D'keeper," said Mevans, coming to stand by him, "you should be wearing a thicker coat so I brought one. Put it on, cannot have the deckkeeper getting a chill, not with those great luggers behind us." Joron shook his head, affecting the air of a man much put upon while shrugging into the coat.

"Solemn Muffaz," he shouted, "I cannot have Mevans force me into a wet weather coat and leave the crew shivering. Those who wish it may go below and put on stinkers." And Solemn Muffaz gave the order that all on deck were to "dress for poor weather" and the crew, his good and fleetlike crew, organised themselves in such a way that small groups went below and the ship was never left without enough hands to cover each and every much-needed task that kept them heading toward the storm. Joron leaned in close to Mevans, raising his voice, aware that now it took just a little more effort to be heard than when he had talked with Aelerin only moments before, feeling it hard on his damaged vocal cords.

"Set the bonewrights to taking the windows out of the great cabin and boarding them over."

"The board'll not stop a bolt."

"No, but it is better than glass flying everywhere, ey?"

"There is that."

"Have them reinforce the rear as much as they can. Then get a team to set up an A-frame and move one of the rear gallowbows, Savage Arrin I think, to the rump. They intend to loose at us, it would be rude for us not to return the favour."

"Ey, D'keeper," grinned Mevans.

12

The Sea Hates a Thief

The underdeck had been cleared as if for battle, though every gallowbow remained trussed and every bowpeek shut against the rising seas. Joron staggered his way along the floor and down into the hold, his missing leg making already treacherous footing worse as *Tide Child* lurched, seaward to landward and beak to rump, in an uncomfortable corkscrewing motion as the storm grew. The crew who waited in the gloom for him moved with the motion of the ship, an unconscious movement of the knee and hip that they were barely aware of, this was simply part of their life, their world. The bone cases of their ships often moved in most disconcerting and unpleasant ways, and the cold and the damp that he felt through his clothes was simply the way it was.

"Getting in to blow," said a shadow, and Joron squinted, saw Oast, one of the seaguard, standing by one the many of the barrels arrayed like soldiers behind him, grunting and groaning as they slid against the floor and rubbed against one another.

"It'll blow worse yet, mark my words," said Joron, and laughter from those gathered as they regarded this simple truth, as if he had said something witty at a Bern's high table. Over the laughter he heard the percussion of the bonewrights' hammers as the windows in his cabin came down and the A-frame was raised above. "Now, you must wonder what we are about, ey?"

"Ey, D'keeper," came one reply from many mouths. Joron smiled beneath his mask and used his voice to convey his pleasure to the crew gathered in the gloaming.

"You all know I was a fisher once?" A mental image of his father's face – *and what have you become now my boy?* – Nods and eys returned. "Well, a fisher's life is a hard one, I reckon many of you know that as true." More eys. "See, when I flew with my father, you know what he feared more than beakwyrms, or toothreaches, or even a fabled keyshan rising from the deep?" No reply. He had not expected one – those who knew would keep quiet to let him tell his story, and those who did not would not speak to the d'keeper without good reason. "Nets," he said. He held up a hand to stop any questions, filled his voice with bonhomie. "I know, what strangeness, ey? A fisher afraid of his nets. But you listen to me well. A fisher needs speed, for he steals from the ocean and the ocean hates a thief. So every beast of the sea is out to get a fisher, and he has no great gallowbows, no sharp curnows and no seaguard to protect him. Speed is his ally, speed is what he must rely on. But a net? Well that is there to catch the creatures of the sea, and if he is not careful, if the fisher turns too quickly upon himself, or crosses the net of one his fellows, then he is caught as much as any fish. The net will wrap around the keel or rudder of his ship, it'll drag in the water and slow him as sure as any seastay, and then he is prey for whatever may choose to take him."

"You want us to make a net?" said a confused voice from the back of the stacked barrels, the question almost lost in the sound of shifting varisk.

"No, we shall make a trap, but use the principle of the net. Take a length of rope, long as five women with their arms outstretched. Tie a barrel – secure, mind – on either end. Then do the same with three more barrels. Is Solemn Muffaz here?"

"Ey, D'keeper," came the familiar deep voice from the back of the hold, "for someone must keep charge of this rabble."

"How many barrels do we have, Solemn Muffaz?"

"Twenty-four, D'keeper."

"Then make four strings of five barrels, and one of four, Muffaz. We'll throw them over the rear once it's dark and see if we can catch us a ship."

"He'll need to be near us to tangle him up, D'keeper," came Solemn Muffaz's voice.

"Ey, he will, and we'll take shot from the bow on his front, though we'll answer it too. But if we can catch him in our net the rope and barrels will create drag and slow him down. He'll have to stop to cut them off, which will be a Hag of a job, and that should give us time to get away."

A moment's silence, but for the creaking of the ship and the barrels and the hammering of the bonewrights and the sound of the waves battering against the hull.

"Well," shouted Solemn Muffaz, "are you waiting for the rope to measure itself, you useless slatelayers? Get to it!"

Joron smiled to himself once more and left Solemn Muffaz in control, returning to the deck. The light was not noticeably better there, and the storm was noticeably stronger, wind howling, freezing spray washing over the slate. Farys and Aelerin stood on the rump, watching the A-frame lower a great gallowbow into position as Colwulf guided it down to the slate where it would be secured with bonebolts that ran right through the deck. Behind them towered the *Beakwyrm's Rage*, *Keyshanpike* falling further and further behind as the seas became higher. *Beakwyrm's Rage*'s greater jointweight gave it an advantage in the high stormy seas, making it a more stable platform, allowing it better passage through the waves. He lifted his nearglass, lowered it, wiped spray from the lens and looked again. There on the rump of *Beakwyrm's Rage* was his shipwife. Joron glanced forward; the storm was near now, huge towers of black cloud, shot through with skewers of light. It would not be long before those towers of cloud came crashing down on *Tide Child*. Water would be the only thing in their world – in the air, beneath them, filling the ship. The pumps would have to work constantly, tiring the crew, and every moment they were in the storm the bigger ship would have the advantage.

Once more he looked at the bigger ship, white and beautiful in the driving rain, corpselights glowing above it. Knew it would fly them down, catch them if his plan with the barrels did not work.

Would it work?

He had never heard of anyone doing such a thing, maybe it would be a wasted effort. But the importance was in the striving. In the knowing that you worked to live, and were not simply standing still and waiting for death to come upon you, for although the Hag revelled in death, she was never glad to see someone at her fire, and she rewarded those who fought to stay away.

The storm fell upon them like a predator on prey.

"All but the top wings down," shouted Joron into driving rain. The ship crashing through waves, beak raised high then smashing back into furious seas. Figures moving, seen as the Hag must see the women and men above, through a veil of water. Vague and formless shapes running over the slate of the deck, carrying out his orders before he gave them for they knew the ship carried too much wing for such a blow, only the smallest would remain to give the ship steerage and allow Barlay, bent over the steering oar in a thick stinker coat, to control the ship. Waves swelled, great slabs of water coming at them. "Keep him head-on!" Joron shouted; needless, of course, needless. Aelerin dragged themselves over to him.

"How long will it blow, Courser?" shouted Joron, one hand on his hat to hold it to his head, the other around the courser's shoulders to draw them near.

"All night, D'keeper," they shouted back, "and well into tomorrow."

"Then we'll weather it tonight, *Beakwyrm's Rage* won't come too close in the dark, can't risk a collision in weather like this. In the morning we'll see what we can catch in our nets, ey?"

"Ey, D'keeper."

The night was hard and sleepless, the storm ferocious and the crew unable to rest, always a wing needing adjusting, help needed on the steering oar. Their ballast needing constant adjustment so *Tide Child* flew true. The ship straining to climb massive waves, racing down the other side barely under control. Gullaime constantly on deck, fighting the winds, trying to soften the hardest blows, but even together, and with their leader, this storm was sapping their strength and Joron had them give up.

"Save your energy, it may be better spent later."

Behind them *Beakwyrm's Rage,* relentless, smashing through the seas, his lights vanishing as *Tide Child* careened into the troughs between waves, then reappearing as he climbed once more.

Not even Garriya could rest, and she was known to sleep through almost anything. Through the night a steady stream of injured was sent down to her in the hagbower: crushed fingers, turned ankles and a couple of broken arms and legs. To add to this, Joron had reports of at least three bodies gone overboard when the waves smashed over *Tide Child*, soaking every woman and man to the skin in freezing water that chafed the skin where it was not already chafed, and stung where it was. Icy watery hands pulling the living toward death.

And so, when Skearith's Eye rose – though it was hard to tell, so dark and thick were the furious clouds of the Weststorm – it was a tired, damp, cold and demoralised crew that stared over the rump of the ship, squinting into driving rain.

"There!" shouted Farys, as there was no other way to be heard above the storm. She pointed to landward and Joron saw *Beakwyrm's Rage*. It had dropped back during the night, but not far, and he knew that it would catch them today, its weight would tell and it would plough through the waves in a way

Tide Child never could. Already Joron felt it was gathering speed, closing the distance on them.

"Where is the other?" said Joron, staggering a little as a wave hit *Tide Child* from the side and the boat moved in a sudden, sickening and unfamiliar way. He heard a creak from behind him and saw that their flukeboat, tied between the mainspine and the frontspine, had moved. "Stow that boat better there, you useless slatelayers! If I lose one of you for want of a tight knot then Solemn Muffaz'll be taking the skins off some backs tonight." Women and men ran, struggling through sheets of furious water to the boat, tying it down more firmly while Joron stared into the storm. Ropes screamed in the wind as he squinted into the storm.

"Five points off seaward to the rear, D'keeper," shouted Farys, "I think that's *Keyshanpike*?"

Joron raised his nearglass, scanned the shifting horizon, wiped the glass free of water and then lifted it once more, protecting the end as much as he could with his hand.

"Ey, that is him and it seems the Hag smiles a little on us, he's lost a topspar so he won't be keeping up."

"You think *Beakwyrm's Rage* will hold off until his consort catches up?"

Joron wiped his nearglass once more, lifted it. Saw *Beakwyrm's Rage*, saw its shipwife, sword in hand, pointing at *Tide Child*.

"No." Then the ship was lost to him as *Tide Child* was lifted on a wave, and with it tiredness washed over Joron. He fought it down. No time for it.

"D'keeper," he turned, Aelerin there once more, soaked through and miserable.

"Ey, Courser?"

"I only thought that when we throw over your barrels and ropes, we will have to let that ship get awful near, or he can steer a little to the side and we waste our work."

"I know that, Courser." He bit out the words, started to limp away, annoyed that the courser did not think he had considered such a thing. He stopped. "Sorry, Aelerin," he shouted over the wind, while trying to make his words gentle as he could, "I snapped and I should not, I am tired."

"We all are, D'keeper," said Aelerin, "and you work hard, it is only that I have had an idea."

"Then speak it, Courser." He felt his voice cracking, damaged vocal cords complaining. "In my cabin, it is quieter there." He turned, shouting as loud as he could into the weather. "Farys! Tell me when that great thing behind us approaches loosing range!" She replied but the storm whipped her words away.

Below, in his boarded-up cabin, the only illumination was from wanelights, the glowing eyesockets of the skulls staring out.

"What is this plan, Aelerin?"

"It is a gamble, in truth, but I have watched the waters as they swirl around us, they sing their own song, and it is not that different to the winds. It seemed to me, that where the enemy may see us putting your barrels over the rear there may be another way. We could put the barrels over the side nearer the beak. If I read the currents right, and we time it well, they may not even see them coming or know what they are. They will think we simply throw over more cargo." Joron stared at the courser and Aelerin pushed back their hood, rubbed their shaven head, smiled at him. "What do you think, Deckkeeper?" they said.

"How sure are you, that you can read the currents of water?"

"Not entirely," the smile faltered, "maybe I should not have said . . ."

"No, you are right to." He lowered his voice. "One wingbolt gets past the Gullaime in this weather, and it will . . . Well, if it gets into the rigging and takes a spine or spar we are lost. It is with little hope I set this plan in motion. More to give us something to do when *Beakwyrm's Rage* gets near enough to do real damage. But if what you say is true, it may give us enough room to be safe; and you are right, they would think nothing of barrels in the sea until it is too late." He stood, thinking. "How sure are you? No false modesty, Aelerin."

"I have been throwing over bits of wood, painted red, during the storm, and where I have been able to follow them – or Gavith has, as I had him help – four out of five times I have predicted where they go."

"That is enough for me to risk it, Aelerin, better odds than letting *Beakwyrm's Rage* come near." He made to stride past, to go back into the teeth of the storm but the courser put out a hand, a gentle touch on his arm

"D'keeper, I will not lie to you. There were many pieces of wood we simply lost in the churning water."

"Aelerin," he said quietly, "I will not lie to you either. Tell no other this. I wake every day surprised we are not lost already. And if that ship gets near enough that the Gullaime cannot shield us, then all that awaits us is the Hag's fire." Then he walked away, unable to bear the sudden empathy he saw in the courser's eyes, the pity. Of all the people on the ship, the courser knew most what it was to be alone. And Joron, as Meas had once said, had found command was the loneliest place of all.

13

A Slow and Stately Terror

"What is? What is?"

The Gullaime was hanging on to the rear rail of *Tide Child*, squawking, clacking its beak and repeating those words between each soaking, freezing wave, and for the life of him Joron could not decide what the creature meant. It did not mean the gallowbow, untrussed and ready, as the windtalker was more than familiar with the weapons. And it did not mean the ship behind them which towered over *Tide Child* as it rose and fell on the waves, before vanishing into the troughs, only the topspines showing, for again, ships it knew well.

"What is? What is?"the Gullaime cried, and it was in such a state of excitement, whirling around, so that its colourful robe made a circle in the air, suddenly untouched by the howling wind or the driving, freezing rain and waves. "What is! What is?" it screeched, hopping onto the rail, back down and spinning in a circle again. Black Orris fluttered down, like a black rip in the air, a fractured part of the furious clouds hovering above them, the faint echo of the bird's voice heard above the wind – "Arse!" – and then the black bird was gone once more to play in the howling air.

"Please, Gullaime!" Always shouting in the screaming wind.

"What is what?" And it turned on him, masked face focusing, colourful feathers beaded with rain ruffling in the wind and catching any stray shaft of light from Skearith's Eye that squeezed through scudding clouds.

"What is what? What is what?" and spinning and spinning and spinning.

"What is this, Gullaime, this mad and unseemly shouting and whirling?"

"Is anger, is fury."

"With me?"

The Gullaime froze, mouth open and so still it looked like a statue in the pouring rain, a statue against the rising and falling sea, and the threatening white boneship that pursued them.

"Why you?" it said, sharp head tilting, puzzled.

"I see nothing else for you to be angry with."

"Windshorn." The word fell from its mouth, somehow quiet and cutting through the howling wind, the whistling rigging and booming wings.

"Madorra? What has it done?"

"Bad windshorn," said the Gullaime, and it turned away from him as if that put an end to conversation about Madorra. "Blow big ship away?"

"Could you?" The Gullaime hunkered down, shook itself.

"Maybe, hard. Maybe." It hopped forward two steps, staring blindly at the huge ship as it smashed over the top of a wave in an explosion of white froth. "No," it said, and it felt strange to Joron, to hear that small admittance from the Gullaime. Had it ever said no before in such a way? Oh, it had blustered and bluffed about its strength, played dead or sick when it did not want to do a thing, but this simple admittance that it was unable to help was, Joron felt sure, new.

"No one can do everything, Gullaime, and there is no shame in admitting it. All I ask is when that ship starts sending wingshot towards us that you are here to blow it off course."

"Do that," it said, and before he could speak more to the

Gullaime, quiz it on what had made it act so strangely, they were no longer alone: Farys was there, with Gavith the bowsell, Reyan, who he marked as his best aimer, and the rest of Savage Arrin's team gathered around the bow.

"Won't be long now, D'keeper," shouted Farys, almost hidden beneath a massive stinker coat. "Nearly in range."

"Ey," said Joron, "that he is. Do you think he'll aim for us or the rigging?"

"Rigging, for sure," shouted Gavith.

"No," shouted Reyan back, "he'll want the bow gone, no doubt about it."

"I say rigging too," said Barlay from the steering oar.

There followed a quick conversation, verging on argument, between the bowcrew on what was tactically best. Joron smiled to himself about how his crew could be so very unconcerned about the danger and lifted a hand. "For my money, I reckon they'll try both, but those who chose right where the first wingshot is aimed, I'll give an extra ration of shipwine to." At that sly smiles were exchanged, for each was sure that they had chosen right, and each looked forward to the warmth an extra ration of shipwine would leave in their throats and bellies, and not a one gave a thought to death, or being smashed and broken under a well-aimed rock.

Though Joron thought of little else.

"Not long now," he said to himself, raised the nearglass, cursed and lowered it. Wiped the end and covered it with his hand. Did he never learn? Raised once more. There was *Beakwyrm's Rage*'s shipwife, staring back at him. Threshing water and howling wind between them. The gallowbow by him loaded and taught. Ship rising, rising, rising. And at the apex of the wave the shipwife shouted something, the trigger was pulled and a wingbolt soared out into the storm. He tried to follow the trajectory of the bolt but it was lost in squalls of rain and water whipped up from the roiling sea before ever getting near *Tide Child*. Laughter and mocking from those around him. *You loosed that one to give your deckchilder a thrill, is all*, thought Joron. *The next though, the next time you loose a bolt you will be in range.*

"Ready yourself, Gullaime," he shouted through the wind. "Gavith, don't you string that bow yet, we'll keep the cord dry as long as we can." He turned, found his shadow. "Cwell, I doubt you can protect me from a gallowbow bolt, so bring Aelerin if you will."

"Ey, D'keeper," she shouted back. A moment later back with the courser, cowl hidden beneath a stinker so they looked like every other deckchilder running along the decks or crouched against the howling wind.

"Where is best for you to be, Aelerin," shouted Joron, "to read the currents of the sea?"

"Here, at the rump, I reckon, D'keeper."

"We may take some shot, Courser."

"It is what we do, ey, D'keeper?" they said and Joron smiled beneath his mask. How far the crew of this ship had travelled, and maybe him the most among them, but the courser ran him a good race.

"I'll have the barrels and rope hidden behind the flukeboat," he yelled. "You tell me seaward or landward and when. Solemn Muffaz here can relay the orders. Mevans can lead the team throwing the traps over the side."

"A good plan, D'keeper," they replied, and left unsaid that it was the only plan they had. Joron raised the nearglass. Then swore as he saw nothing but the wetness on the end of the instrument.

Cleaned and raised once more.

There, rising in the storm. *Beakwyrm's Rage*, and his shipwife calmly watching him. Waiting, judging the moment the larger ship would be in range of *Tide Child*.

Waiting in the screaming storm.

Waiting.

"Gullaime," he said. "Be ready."

"Ready, ready. Always ready."

Watching over the tumultuous waves.

Watching.

"Not long now, D'keeper," said Barlay, "he has the wind."

"Ey, not even bringing Gullaime up to help him out. He'll regret that."

"Regret," squawked the Gullaime. "Regret!"

The deckchilder spinning the gallowbow, the arms coming back. The loaders struggling against the wind with a wingbolt, the stone shaped to catch air adding to its weight and making the deckchilder stagger as the ship shuddered with the surging water.

"String ours, D'keeper?" shouted Gavith.

"No, he's taller, gives him range. We'll need him closer or we just waste what bolts we have."

The shipwife, watching the crew at his gallowbow. Raising his arm.

"The barrel traps are on deck, D'keeper." This shouted by a scuttling deckchilder Joron could not recognise under their cold weather clothing.

"Good, we'll have to weather this first loosing." He turned, "Aelerin, put yourself behind the spine, I'll not lose you to a stray boneshard."

The arm falling.

"Now, Gullaime!"

Did he see it or did he imagine it? The Gullaime screeching and gesturing with its wings and bright robes to landward. The grey, winged bolt of stone, flying so straight and true for the rigging of *Tide Child*, snatched from the air and thrown, tumbling and twirling through storm-tossed rain and zephyr to splash harmlessly into the sea. Did the other shipwife smile? He definitely nodded, made some remark. Joron lowered the nearglass.

"Aelerin, get ready." The courser ran forward, leaning over the rear rail, staring into the sea, occasionally raising up their body to stare into the howling air. "Gavith!" he shouted to the bowsell stood by the gallowbow. "Grab Aelerin by their stinker, I'll not have a rogue wave heave them overboard."

"Ey D'keeper." The bowsell reached out, taking hold of the courser's stinker coat. A brief look over their shoulder, a smile exchanged between the two.

Black Orris fell from the sky, painful points of his claws digging into Joron's shoulder where he perched, feathers ruffling in the gale.

Joron raised the nearglass, view obscured again by rainwater on the lens.

"Arse!" said Black Orris.

"Indeed," he replied, and cleaned the lens once more. Saw the shipwife, watching the gallowbow crew, waiting, waiting. Then a gullaime in sodden white robes joined them on *Beakwyrm's Rage*'s deck. "They have brought up a gullaime."

"Be ready, be ready," squawked their gullaime, shifting from foot to foot.

"Nothing you can't handle, ey, Gullaime?"

"Nothing nothing."

"Arse," said Black Orris.

"Arse," said the Gullaime, as if in agreement and there was laughter, split by Aelerin's voice.

"Landward side!"

"Landward side ready!" shouted Joron and he heard Solemn Muffaz boom out the order and then it was lost in the teeth of the storm "Now!" And the order echoed through those three throats again, Aelerin to Joron to Solemn Muffaz. Joron dearly wanted to look back, to watch the barrels go over, ensure they were free of snags, make sure that the ropes held. But to do so may signal that something was up to the other shipwife. So he let the nearglass down and stared at the huge white bone-ship, while trying to scan the sea behind them. Did he see a string of barrels, momentarily lofted past on the crest of a wave? Did he see that in the moment before *Beakwyrm's Rage* vanished behind another wave and *Tide Child* began to rise on one?

"Gavith, string the bow. I think we have range now. Aelerin, get behind the spine."

"Ey, D'keeper." The same acknowledgement from two voices.

Ship rising, ship rising.

Ship falling, ship falling.

Starting to raise the nearglass.

"Arse!" from Black Orris and Joron smiled to himself, wiped the end of the nearglass before looking through it.

"Ready yourself, Gullaime."

The shipwife's arm falling.

"Spin!"

The bowcrew spinning the bow.

"Load!"

The enemy gallowbow loosing. Dropping the nearglass from his eye, a spray of seawater making him squint. The Gullaime screaming into the wind, pushing its wingclaws forward into sodden air. The feel of something smashing into the sea to landward.

"Loose on the uproll, Gavith," shouted Joron. "We don't have any wingbolts or cutters so stay off their rigging, aim for the bowcrew."

"Ey, D'keeper," and Gavith grinned for there was little a bowsell liked more than the warmoan of a taut bowcord in the wind. And the ship rose and rose. "Aelerin, back to your place at the rail; Cwell, your turn to make sure the courser doesn't join the longthresh."

All running to act and the ship rose and rose and as it hit the highest point he heard Gavith shout, "Loose!" Felt the concussion of the bow as the arms sprung back to their rests. Felt the tension and the hope as all eyes followed the bolt as best they could through the stormy air. Saw the bolt aimed true but fall short.

"Spin it up, Gavith. We'll hit him next time, just getting our eye in is all," said Joron.

Wiped the nearglass, raised it to his eye.

"Seaward, D'keeper," shouted Aelerin, and another order passed down the deck. This time he did see the barrels, tossed on white-topped waves, looking like no more than flotsam lost overboard, and in among them a lone figure, arms outstretched for a moment before the sea took them under and he had to restrain himself from asking, *who was that?* Who had they lost? Felt guilty that he looked around for Farys, for those who had been with him longest. *Watch the other ship, Joron. Not ready yet. Not getting ready to loose.* What trickery did *Beakwyrm's Rage's* shipwife plan? More white-robed gullaime joining him by the gallowbow.

"Seaward again, D'keeper, be quick!"

The order given, the barrels going over. Shouldn't he notice something by now? Shouldn't that great ship be slowing just a little with all that buoyancy wrapped around its keel? Had they missed? Was the courser wrong, was the storm simply too chaotic, had the Hag withdrawn her blessing? He swallowed, lowered the nearglass. Took a breath.

"He's brought up more gullaime," he said to the windtalker by him. "Can you handle them?"

"Handle, handle," chirped the Gullaime, no hint of worry.

The bigger ship was near enough now that he did not need his nearglass, could see the crew spinning the bow, loaders waiting.

"Aelerin, behind the spine if you will." The courser retreated, Joron stood a little straighter. "Gavith, spin, load and loose at will. See what damage we can do now he's a little nearer."

"Ey, D'keeper," cried Gavith as the other shipwife's arm fell. The Gullaime screeched in anger. The feeling of something rending the furious air. The crack of a rope snapping and he knew the bolt had come near that time.

"Solemn Muffaz!" he shouted. "Have that rope fixed or I'll stripe someone's back!" Then he turned to find the courser. "Return to the rail, Aelerin. Cwell, keep them safe." Actions repeated as *Tide Child* loosed a bolt; it leapt out, missed *Beakwyrm's Rage's* bow but raked down his deck. "Good aim there, Reyan," said Joron. Then leaned in close to the Gullaime. "You said you could handle our defence?"

"Gullaime make wind hard each side. Hard to fight. Hard."

Joron leaned in closer, so he could share his words with only the Gullaime; even though he knew no one on his crew would disagree, the words he spoke felt like betrayal.

"If it is a choice between the rigging and wings or the ship, Gullaime, drive the bolts into the ship's hull or along the deck. If we lose a spine we all die. So if we lose some lives, then that is what must happen." The Gullaime did not reply, only made a soft cooing sound and locked its masked face on Joron. Then Aelerin was shouting.

"Landward, D'keeper, to landward!" More barrels went over and *Beakwyrm's Rage* rose before them, wingbolt being loaded on its gallowbow as it crested the wave.

"Behind the spine, Aelerin."

"But I—"

"Do as you're ordered!" Barking the words out, and the hurt on the courser's face reminded him why he could not have friendship, why he must be alone in his command. The courser scuttled past him and the Gullaime screeched. A moment later, a crash, a shudder, a scream. Joron was on the floor. Shaking his head to clear it. Lying facing the beak. He sat, turned, behind him part of the bonerail gone. Reyan lying on the deck, her body rolling and slack with death. The gallowbow crew scattered around her, one other – Chafin? – dead, one wounded. Gavith sat on the deck, looking stupid and dazed. Joron pushed himself up. Where was the Gullaime? Sudden and sickening panic. But the Gullaime was fine, squawking and flapping on the other side of the deck. Then Cwell was there, pulling him up. Gavith getting to his feet, helping up the wounded of the bowcrew. Joron touched his shoulder and found the corpsebird missing. If Black Orris was lost, the crew would . . . But the familiar black shape touched down once more by his ear.

"Arse."

"Farys!" he shouted. "Farys, where are you?" She came running, took one look about the deck.

"Seems he has his eye in now, D'keeper."

"Ey," shouted Joron. "Get that bow crewed! Get the dead

overboard and the wounded to the hagshand." He looked around him, "Aelerin! Where are you?" The courser pushed past, stopped for a moment when they saw the place where they had been standing was destroyed, the rail entirely gone. "Find somewhere safe to look over the rump, Cwell will help you."

"D'keeper," they said. "You are bleeding." He reached up and touched his face by his eye, aware of the sudden stinging where the seawater met his skin. Found an open wound, pulsing warm blood.

"It is a poor commander that doesn't show a few scars, Aelerin. How many more sets of barrels have we to go over?"

"One," they said, which he knew of course; he only wanted the courser to stop thinking about how close they had come to death. "You would think that ship would have slowed by now."

"It will, Aelerin," he said, though the same worry shivered within him. "Be quick, they spin their bow, we should get another set of barrels in before they loose upon us again."

The courser ran, standing in front of the bow as the new crew spun it up, shouted on by Gavith.

"Landward!"

The order rushing along the ship's rocking and bucking deck. A repeat of all that had gone before. Though this time when *Beakwyrm's Rage* loosed, the wingbolt did not hit. With a scream of fury the Gullaime raised its wings into the air and Joron was sure he heard it shout, "Over!" Then it sat back on the deck as if pushed, managing, despite being wet through and windblown, to look immensely pleased with itself. Aelerin rushed to the broken rail, Cwell holding on to them in the roaring wind as they watched the last of the barrels pass *Tide Child* to landward.

And, and, and . . .

And nothing.

The wind roared. The gallowbow spoke and the Gullaime shrieked as Joron stood, trying not to flinch as wingshot thudded into the hull, or skidded down the deck, or smashed into the sea by them, and *Beakwyrm's Rage* got bigger and bigger. He knew that it was only a matter of time now. The frontspar of the enemy four-ribber was pointed at them, like a promise, like a finger, like a threat. *I am coming for you and there is little you can do to stop me.*

"I am sorry, D'keeper." He turned, found the courser.

"Sorry, Aelerin?"

"That it has not worked."

"We have done our best," he said, then raised his voice, "and we must simply think of something new, for the Hag loves—"

"D'keeper!" He turned at Farys's voice, saw her pointing over the smashed rail.

The frontspar of *Beakwyrm's Rage* was, very slowly, moving away from them, ceasing to point directly at their prey as if the shipwife had taken pity on *Tide Child* and broken off his pursuit. But from the action on the beak of the ship it was clear to Joron it was not so. The shipwife was pointing down the deck, shouting orders. Arms waving. Women and men running down the length of the ship toward the steering oar, the gallowbow abandoned. Then, as if the Hag herself had lifted her hand and taken *Beakwyrm's Rage* in her grip, the huge ship was wrenched around to seaward, a turn far too tight for such a big ship, for any ship in the midst of such a savage storm.

"Mother's love," said Joron quietly to himself, "for I only meant to slow them, truly I did." Because he knew what must come next, what was inevitable in such high seas. The ship, this giant of the waves, was coming down. A collapse of slow and stately terror. Its top spars reaching for the water, raining deckchilder into the furious sea. His deck slanting sharply, spilling more crew into the water. Could he hear the screaming from here? No, it was the cheering of his own women and men, joy at the misfortune suffered by their enemy. Joy in *Beakwyrm's Rage*'s certain doom as the spines, with a few sparse wings rigged for storms, smashed into the seething water in a froth of white; and the sea, the furious, angry hungry sea, rose up and threw itself across the stricken ship. Farys turned to him, a fierce grin on her face.

"Wrecked, 'im, D'keeper, we wrecked 'im good and proper! Must have fouled the rudder, ey?" She glanced back to the ship, then to him. "Shall we put the flukeboat over? See if any survive?"

"No, Farys," he said, watching as another huge wave covered the white ship, and saying the words he must, that all knew he must. "For we are still pursued by the enemy." He turned away. "Four hundred and probably more souls gone to the Hag in a moment," he said to the air, then took off his hat, saluted the air. "They flew their ship well, ey?"

"Ey," said Farys, and he found the screeching and celebration had stopped. His crew stood behind him, heads bowed at the sacrifice, the terrible but necessary sacrifice, that had been made to the Sea Hag on this day.

He took a breath.

"Back to it!" he screamed. "The storm still rages, would you join them in the sea?" The deck all action while Joron returned to his cabin, dark and shuttered off from the horror outside, as the Weststorm smashed the remains of *Beakwyrm's Rage* to shards of white bone, floating on black and angry waves. There he sat at Meas's desk in its familiar groove in the white floor while he dripped blood from the cut on his face, and tried to stop the shaking of his hands.

14

Leviathans of the Deep

It was as if the wrecking of *Beakwyrm's Rage* was the sacrifice required to appease the Hag and the storms that served her. When Joron woke, from dreams of gliding beneath the cool water, fearless and hungry and sharp, *Tide Child* was free of the twisting and groaning and creaking that had been his passage through the storm. Instead Joron heard the familiar rhythm of the ship as it smashed through breakers. Heard the familiar sound of deckchilder set to cleaning the decks.

Mevans brought him food, hard bread and brackish water to soften it. As Joron dressed and ate, Mevans talked of putting the glazing back in, and though Joron was sure he had ordered the glass put over the side he said nothing of it. Mevans often made judgements and Joron let them pass, for they were generally good ones and, if he was honest, he was sometimes glad that he did not have to carry all the weight of the ship.

"Blue and clean out there, D'keeper," said Mevans as he ran a cloth down the shining blade of Joron's straightsword in preparation for sharpening the already keen edge.

"Good. How many did not live to see it?"

"We lost only eight, two from the bowcrew, Reyan and

Chafin gone. Sarlin was bad hurt and will probably die, Garriya sat and held her hand all night."

"I will go down to the hagbower before I go on deck," said Joron.

"Then Camran, Brookes, Mchoo, Soori and Karlee are all missing; Jennil says she saw Camran get caught up in the barrel ropes, and I reckon the waves took the rest. Still a small price compared to that paid by *Beakwyrm's Rage*, ey?"

"Indeed it is," and he could not eat or sit any longer, he needed to be doing, to not be thinking. He stood, heading for the door.

"D'keeper," said Mevans. Joron stopped.

"Ey?"

"Your scarf." Joron reached up, touched the raw and burning flesh around his mouth and hissed.

"Of course." Mevans held out the cloth to him.

"They would not care," said Mevans as Joron tied the mask on. "They are as loyal to you as any crew I ever sat among. So they would not care."

"It is good of you to say that, but the rot brings madness and we all know it. I look at some of the things I have wrought and wonder whether it has already taken me."

"'Tis only the aftermath speaking there, D'keeper, many who live through an action feel the melancholy after. I say a third time, they would not care."

"But others may," said Joron, and he opened the door to leave before he spoke the real truth, before he said, *and I do*.

In the bowels of the ship he found Garriya, sat in the hagbower with Sarlin's hand in hers and her head bowed.

"I came to speak to Sarlin," he said quietly.

"Too late, Caller," she said, "girl sits with the Hag now, and all her pain is over." Garriya raised her creased and scarred face, stared out from between bars of filthy hair. "Would it were for all of us, but I fear it's just beginning. The worst is yet to come, I say."

"A ray of light as ever, Garriya." The old woman stood,

gently placing Sarlin's hand on her chest. She had been not much more than a child, really. Barely past her laying night and yet she came here, to die slowly and painfully on the water from a boneshard to the gut. "I do not want any of them to die," he said.

"But they will, and many more yet I reckon. You could always fly away, become a fisher once more, boy, aye? Sit somewhere in the Gaunt Islands with a new name, cause no more deaths, raid no more settlements."

"Leave Meas in her mother's clutches?"

"Maybe Meas would wish it for you, did you think of that? Maybe you've already gone further than she ever would. Never heard of her laying waste to a village for supplies, taking those she needed as crew. She dreamed of peace, and do you bring it? Would she approve?"

"If she does not, old woman, she can tell me that herself." He took a deep breath, turned away then stopped as he heard Garriya's low chuckle.

"Matters not, and I jest with you." She stood, groaning and pressing a hand against her back where it ached. "There is no peace for you, Joron Twiner, from the moment you sang a keyshan from the sea your course was set. Your journey is a red one, boy." He turned, ready to be angry, to tell her to keep her old mouth shut, to stop burying him under her talk of what he "must" do or what he "was" or where he "must" go. She was there. Right in his face. "Never doubt, Caller, what is done is needed. Harsh, and hard it may be, but these seas are harsh and hard, and they ever will be if none rise. So steer your great boat well, and if it is what you need then find your shipwife." She nodded, more to herself than to him. "Now I must tend to the sick. Surely you have some rope to tie or some other shippers' thing to be about?" The woman pushed past him and although he was commander of *Tide Child* it was difficult for him not to feel that he was the one who had been dismissed. So he sat his one-tail harder on his head and wound his way up through the dark ship to the deck.

On the slate of *Tide Child* it was as if the storm had never been. Farys stood on the rump and the wings were full, for a brisk wind pushed the black ship merrily through the water. Stinker coats were gone, instead the crew wore lumpy cold weather coats stuffed with down, lethal in high seas as when soaked they became heavy quickly, but warm and perfect for a clear day when the winds were cold.

They flew south on winds Aelerin called the dancers, promising all would remain clear and fast for at least a week. Joron found himself forgetting the seriousness of their situation. On their second day a call went up, a call once heard often, then not at all and now becoming more common once again.

"Keyshan rising!" A thrill went through him at that, and he tried not to notice how the crew looked to him at those words. How smiles were exchanged, how deckchilder nudged one another and he tried to pretend he knew nothing of their belief that the keyshans came to him, though he knew he had not called this one. But the childish excitement within him was the same as that felt by every other member of the crew. Up the rigging he went, past the booming and cracking black wings until he found himself in the tops with Bearna.

"Where is it, Topboy?" She pointed off to seaward, four points off the shadow and Joron followed her gaze. Seeing the first chunks of floating ice out in the blue, blue sea. He didn't see the keyshan at first, a matter of scale more than anything. The keyshans he'd seen before had been huge, as big as islands. This one was smaller, the smallest he'd seen though still far larger than *Tide Child*. Maybe three or four times as long as the ship, and thinner than the larger keyshans. Even from here he could see the burning white eyes on the long thin head as it breached, not jumping from the water, only lazily breaking the surface, head first, jaws open. It was a deep and luminous blue colour, like the heart of an ice island. He watched it as it rolled, a flipper out of the water in an arc of white froth, bright blue belly showing, colours flowing down it, second flipper out the water and then, as if pleased to have showed off for him, the keyshan vanished beneath the waves.

"Sea sither happy." He turned to find the Gullaime next to him.

"A young one, do you think?"

"All sea sither old." The Gullaime hopped across the tops, catching on to the rigging with a wing claw and hanging there. Opening its predatory beak. "Some not big old." From the deck below he heard a squawk of outrage and looked down to see Madorra spinning round on the slate. Snapping at any deckchilder that came near. "Bad windshorn," said the Gullaime quietly, then let itself drop, catching a rope on the way, swinging to another and seeming to almost float its way down to the deck where Madorra screeched and chattered and snapped at it before chasing it to the hatch and into the belly of the ship.

"There'll be an extra tot of shipwine for you, Topboy," said Joron. "Keep your good eyes open." Then he made his way carefully down the rigging, the stump of his leg aching where it met the bone of his spur.

He had taken the sighting of the keyshan to be a good omen, though maybe it was presumption. They flew on undisturbed for three weeks until a cry from the topboy came. He was in his cabin, rubbing one of Garriya's foul-smelling salves into the stump of his leg while Mevans cleaned the socket of his spur and Cwell sharpened his sword.

"Ship rising!"

"Hag's breath," said Joron. "I would pay my other leg for that to be Brekir, or some other friend to us."

"Given how you complain about having one leg, D'keeper," said Mevans, "I am not right sure anyone else would agree with that." Cwell supressed a laugh and Mevans pushed the cushioning more securely into the spur. "Now, let me strap you up." The strapping done, his warm coat on, Joron went up to the deck and found Farys and Jennil on the rump, talking with Solemn Muffaz.

"Report, Farys," he said. She turned, gave a brief salute and passed him his nearglass.

"Ship rising, D'keeper," she said. "Almost directly behind us, three spines of a four-ribber."

"*Keyshanpike*, you think?"

"I reckon so, D'keeper," said Jennil. She had a new cut on her cheek, deep and sewed neatly with black thread by Garriya. Had taken the wound during the storm and he knew it must hurt when she spoke but she did not seem to care. "Either that or we are fair unlucky to find a different Hundred Isles ship."

"Hag's breath," he said. "I had thought we lost him in the storm."

"Well, he still has a lot of water to cover to catch us."

"Ey," said Joron, raising the nearglass to his eye and tracking along the horizon until he found the ship. "But if it is the same ship that chased us before then we know he flies well." He closed up the nearglass and passed it back to Farys. "Keep watch on it, let me know how quickly he gains." He looked around and did a mental tally of what they had left in the hold. "I will need to speak to Aelerin but there is no great hurry yet. I'll do a round of the ship first."

"I'll have the map table set up," said Cwell quietly from behind him.

"Did it not go over the side?"

"Mevans says he forgot all about it and Hedre claims to have never even seen it before." Joron nodded.

"Probably for the best," he said. "I will see you in my cabin." Though of course he rarely truly saw her, she was simply always there. His shadow, as much a part of him as his hand. A thing he only gave thought to when he needed her and sometimes he thought it strange, that this once rebellious woman, so eager to stamp out her place in life, had found some measure of peace in barely existing at all. Stranger still how completely he had come to trust her.

So he did his rounds, found all was as good as it could be:

the smashed rear rail had been fixed by his bonewrights, a small miracle considering how few supplies remained, and the gallowbow, Savage Arrin, had been returned to its customary place on the deck. He complimented those he saw working well, frowned a little at those he thought slacking – it was rare that more was needed – and finished his walk around the ship in slow order, better to give Mevans and Cwell and Aelerin time to set up the map table. When he no longer had any reasonable excuse, and began to think his presence there may affect the authority of Jennil, he went below into the darkness, navigating sleeping bodies by wanelight, to think about his next course of action.

In his cabin – the windows back in place, light streaming in – if he squinted, he was sure he could see the boneship following them as a dot on the horizon. Farys, Mevans and Cwell waited patiently behind the map table while Aelerin bent over it, their small models of ships set out.

"Do you have good news for me, Aelerin?" he said.

"Maybe," said the courser. "The weather dreams true for the next few weeks, blue and clear."

"Benefit to them, not us," he said, glancing out of the window at the barely perceptible dot between sky and sea. Did he really see it, or just feel it as a pressure between his eyes?

"We could turn and fight," said Farys. "One on one there are none on the sea can match us."

"True," he said quietly, felt Mevans's eyes on him. "But *Tide Child* suffered in the storm and our mainspine is still weak, Farys, we all know it. Mevans has a list of repairs longer than a keyshan and we take on water more quickly than I would like. Colwulf says the bonewrights struggle to keep up with the leaks. And, of course, most of our spares and supplies went over the side." He looked around the table at those gathered. "We must run, like it or not." Farys nodded, stepped back, disappointment on her face. "Aelerin, can we make Wilson's Cut before we are caught?"

"If our pursuer was damaged by the storm, maybe. But if he weathered it well and can make the same sort of speed he kept before? Then he will catch us."

"Well, Farys," said Mevans, "seems you may get your fight."

"It'll not go well," said Cwell. "We have precious little ammunition for the gallowbows."

"We cannot fight," said Joron. "It is that simple. We need another option."

"There is another option," said Aelerin, "but none will like it."

"What is it, Courser?" said Joron.

"Spantonnis Bank." They pointed at the map table. A moment of silence in the cabin. He heard feet on the deck above, the brushing of the slate as it was cleaned, women and men shouting to one another.

"Bank is haunted by the Hag-cursed," said Farys quietly. "All know it, none will want to go there."

Aelerin nodded.

"That is what is believed," said Mevans, "'tis what all aboard will say, but they will follow you there if you tell 'em to, D'keeper, like it or not."

"It will be a near run thing anyway," said Aelerin, and they touched the map, a line of blue in the south. "We'll run from him; it's three days at least with the wind as it is. We're making poor speed with all the water we take on and even if we slow no further we may still have to push the gullaime until they're good for nothing but crying in their nests."

"D'keeper," said Farys quietly, "I do not want the ghosts to take me." Then she spoke even more quietly. "Can you not sing that keyshan we saw to our aid?" She looked up, and he saw fear in her eyes like he had not seen since she faced fire for him, long ago now.

"I cannot bring the keyshans, not the way you think. And if I could, then to do it would put the shipwife's life in such danger that it must be the very last thing I do."

Farys stared at him, her burned skin tight across her face, fear in her eyes.

"I heard tales of the bank, D'keeper, ships vanish. Others float out but with nothing living on board. They say those taken will never know the warmth of the Hag's fire, 'tis well known."

Joron's words stuck in his throat; he knew what he wanted to say but the same fear that gripped Farys squatted in his damaged vocal cords.

"It is not ghosts, Farys," said Aelerin gently. "The bank is where the cold water meets a warm current coming from the east, the same current we ride now. That and the air brought with it creates a fog bank that never moves."

"Ey, well, I do not know what coursers know," said Farys, "but what then of these ships that vanish, or come out with none left alive on 'em?"

"I know why they vanish," said Aelerin, more forcefully. "Behind that bank of fog, and hidden within it, is where the ice mountains start. Great floating islands of ice. Ships go in under full wing, too fast to stop and then wreck themselves as they are not fully prepared. Too afeared of ghosts to go slow they try and speed through and pay the price."

"Don't their coursers warn them?" said Farys.

"Not all shipwives listen," said Aelerin, but Joron could tell Farys was not placated, she wrapped her arms around herself, staring at the line of blue-painted bone that represented Spantonnis Bank.

"And what of the ships that come out empty, ey?" she said. "What of them?"

"I do not know," said Aelerin quietly, and Joron wondered whether this course they set was just too much for Farys, so brave and true in the face of so much.

"I know," said Mevans, smiling but strong and sure in voice.

"You do?" said Farys.

"Ey," he said, "and so do you."

"I do?"

"Ey, you who would charge a line of deckchilder armed with wyrmpikes and think nothing of it. You who will balance on the tip of the mainspine and laugh at those who fear heights. You, who will fight your way across a deck awash with fearsome water simply to tie a needed rope, ey, you know why those ships come out empty. For you show us right now, and you shame yourself with it, lass, for I thought you better." She stared at him, and Joron thought that if she had a curnow at her side she would have drawn it. She reminded him so much of Meas in that moment that it made his heart ache. Not just the desire to answer an insult with strength, but that she took that extra moment to think it through, to follow Mevans's line of thought and come to her own conclusion.

"You think," she said slowly, "it is fear emptied those ships?"

"Ey," said Mevans. "For not all are as strong in heart as you, Farys. A fearful crew throws over its shipwife 'cos it thinks the ship haunted by a bit of fog. Takes to the boats in frozen seas and becomes prey for every longthresh that ever swum the bloody waters."

"Ey," she said, and swallowed, "I can see how that could happen. But not to a ship like *Tide Child*, ey?"

"Never," said Joron, "and not with women and men like you aboard him, Farys." She nodded.

"Well then," she said, and stood a little straighter, "if the courser plots a course I will go let the crew know where we head, for I reckon there will be some soft hands need held, and some heads need knocked together when they find out, and I am just the officer to do it." She nodded. "And you can spray a little paint on that, ey."

"Ey Farys, that would be time well spent," he said and watched her leave. When she was gone he turned back to the map, stared at the blue mark of Spantonnis Bank.

"Let us plot our course, then," he said, and did not speak a word of ghosts, for like every deckchild he feared that to mention them was to invite their attention.

15

In the Deeps, the Most Blue Ice

He dreamed of the cold.

He dreamed of it enveloping him as he moved through the deep darkness.

He dreamed of the songs of his sisters from far away, a haunting melody that echoed around him, surrounded him, informed him. He heard the counterpoint roar of his massive heart as it spread fire throughout his body and chased away the icy touch of the deep water.

He dreamed of a hundred thousand hurts, all over his body from the cruel oceans and all that lived within it, all shaken off with barely a thought and a flip of his powerful tail.

He dreamed of a terrible hunger that gnawed within him, a hunger that only grew. That filled him with cold the same way his heart filled him with heat, and in the song of his sisters he heard that hunger sated, of hunts completed, of wounds taken, of joy in battle, of flesh in jaws.

He dreamed of a warmth to come. Of fire and change and warm oceans. He had dreamed for so long that nothing was clear any more; his dreams were memories of other's dreams, and theirs memories of others, and he half remembered a time when the water was not full of hate and the sithers moved in vast schools through air and water alike.

He woke to the damp and the cold of his cabin and a vague sense of disappointment in his own small and broken body. A moment of confusion, of worry that his mind was going. Then who he was asserted itself. There was a duty to be done, tasks that must be carried out, a truth that must be confronted. He rubbed his face. Carefully slid himself over the side of the hammock, feeling that familiar disappointment when he saw his missing leg.

Mevans had left out water and a rime of ice covered the surface. He hopped over to it, using the walls of his cabin to balance, never looking out the windows. He splashed water on his face – shockingly cold, making him gasp, then gasp again with pain as the cold water set the sores around his mouth aflame. When the pain had receded he reached for his bone spur, lovingly cleaned and maintained by the steward, found Cwell already there with it. She helped him strap it on. He felt more whole then. More himself. Then he dressed, one boot on, his tunic and fine fishskin jacket. Cwell shaved him and wrapped the scarf around his face that hid the marks of the rot. One-tail hat upon his head. Only then did he feel ready and whole enough to turn and look out of the windows.

There he rose, *Keyshanpike*, white as fear with corpselights dancing around his rigging. The shipwife on the beak, leaning into his direction of travel, pointing at *Tide Child* as the ship smashed through the waves.

"You fly your ship well, shipwife," Joron said to the figure. "But I hope to fly mine better."

He went up on deck. Never once letting his eyes stray past the rump of *Tide Child*. The cold air bit, bringing a flush to his dark skin, and all around him deckchilder were busy salting and brushing the slate to keep it free of ice. They had crossed into climes where ice became a real problem, a creeping, slow weight that hampered the running of the ship, that solidified ropes, snapped wings, made fingers numb and climbing the rigging dangerous. *Tide Child* sparkled with it, icicles hanging from spars and rails, and the clearing of the ice was a constant job, unpleasant and tiring. A thin line of smoke escaped the galley to be whipped away by the wind. A welcome sight for most on deck as it meant there would be warmed shipwine to hold in freezing hands and to fire the body from within.

A call of "D'keeper" came from behind him and he turned, careful not to acknowledge the chasing ship, not yet. Yerffoeg, one of the wingwrights, held out a cup of steaming shipwine in hands wrapped in rags against the cold. "I thought you may need this to warm 'ee up a little, ey?"

"Thank you, Yerffoeg," he said. She was shivering, and no doubt needed the drink more than him, but to reject this act of kindness would be to insult her and he recognised that. Besides, he was truly thankful as he closed his hands around the warm stone cup. "Been up the rigging this morran?"

"Ey, 'tis foul slippy up there, we been chipping ice all night and it won't stop until we're well north of this place."

"Well, get you to the galley for another drink, and spend some time before the fire to warm yourself through." Yerffoeg nodded, though it was difficult to tell – like them all she was a strange-looking human now, her body a series of ungainly lumps where clothes had been stuffed with whatever rags could be found to keep away the cold. "Solemn Muffaz!" he shouted, and the deck-mother made his stately way down the deck, to stand before him.

"Your orders, D'keeper?" Joron stared out over the sea before him, Skearith's Spine to landward, a distant line of black teeth on the horizon. Before it a hundred smaller teeth of ice, all white as bone and all sharp and hard enough to tear the hull from beneath them. Each one floating, directionless, and far bigger below than above. On the horizon before them he could see a line of white fog, the edge of Spantonnis Bank. He tried to estimate how far away it was and how long it would be before they breached the ghostly mist, but knew how confusing it could be to judge distance by eye. Better to wait for Aelerin. Joron turned his gaze back to Solemn Muffaz.

"A lot of floating ice out there, Solemn Muffaz," he said.

"Ey, and it will only get worse as we go further south. I worry about the speed we carry."

"Well," said Joron, and now he glanced back at the white ship chasing them, "I worry also, but I am disinclined to slow any and, right now, would add more speed if we could." He smiled and Solemn Muffaz almost did the same, almost breaking his countenance. "However, I would keep our women and men as safe as we can. Two hour watches from now on, I think. And I want some sort of rota so all get time in the galley where it is warm, and order them to share beds for warmth, but not with their shipfriends; I want them rested not tiring themselves out."

"They will moan, D'keeper, a deckchilder fair loves their own hammock."

"Let them moan, Solemn Muffaz, let them moan. I am sure that will stop when they wrap themselves in another's body heat." The big man nodded and made his way along the deck to roar out his orders, and Joron made his way to the rump of the ship to study *Keyshanpike*.

Aelerin appeared at his side.

"He catches us," they said.

"Ey, and I do not have to be a courser to know it." He coughed, to rid his voice of harshness and worry. "How far to Spantonnis Bank, Aelerin? I reckon we can be there by nightfall, but I also reckon that he'll catch us before then." He let out a sigh. "I am all out of barrels and all out of tricks. No storm to stop him boarding or ramming us, though he'd be a fool to board when he can stand off and throw wingbolts at us as we have no real answer."

"At our current rate, D'keeper, he'll catch us before twilight."

"Not even the veil of night to hide within," he said quietly. "Very well. We have ten gullaime aboard, although they are tired; even our gullaime tires though it will not acknowledge it. We will have to ask them to push."

"No doubt *Keyshanpike*'s shipwife will have gullaime too,

D'keeper," said Aelerin, "and he will push them more cruelly than you ever will."

"Ey, but we have to try." He took a step forward. "Bring up the Gullaime. Bring me Mevans and Hedre too." With that the call went back and down into the bowels of the ship. "We just need to get into the mist before him, that is all, Aelerin. If we get into the mist we have a fighting chance to either lose him or, if we must, get close and board him and fight it out. He may even balk at entering the bank if his crew are as scared of ghosts as ours were."

"No crew knows less fear than yours, D'keeper, or fights as hard," said Aelerin. Joron looked up into the rigging, saw his women and men hard at work chipping away ice, knew they had been at it for long, long hours while he slept. That they had journeyed for long, long months without rest.

"Ey, Aelerin, but no crew is as tired either."

"D'keeper," said Mevans. Joron turned; behind Mevans was Hedre, and behind him the Gullaime was studying the frozen paint pot at the base of the mainspine, accompanied by a slinking Madorra.

"Ey, Mevans, I must know what we have left that can go over the side."

"Little, D'keeper," said Hedre.

"True," said Mevans, "we've been throwing over what we could all day and there is little more we can spare unless you wish to gamble on rain and throw over our water." Joron turned, glanced down the deck at the great bows, trussed and silent on either side of the deck, and the thin line of mist in the distance that promised, if not safety, at least the chance of it.

"Gullaime," he called. The windtalker's masked head shot round to look at him and the predatory beak opened.

"Jo-ron Twi-ner," it said and hopped over, closely followed by Madorra who regarded Joron suspiciously from its one good eye.

"I need an answer from you, and a truthful one, not a boastful one."

"Not lie!" squawked the Gullaime and it shook its whole body, the brightly coloured feathers on its head rising and falling. "Not lie!"

"I do not say you lie, Gullaime," said Joron, keeping his voice low and calm, "only that on occasion you may get a little excited."

"Excited," it said, and the feathers on its head slowly flattened as its outrage subsided.

"How much strength is left in you and the other gullaime? That ship," he pointed over the rump, "is catching us, and we need a burst of speed." The Gullaime fixed on him with its masked eyes and clacked its beak slowly. "How long can you give us wind for?" The windtalker nodded its head.

"How long, long, long," it sang. Then span in a circle, its bright robe brushing the deck. "Other gullaime weak, foolish. Hours maybe. All push together." Then it screeched, stretching out its neck and pushing the harsh noise out through its open beak. Loud enough to attract the attention of all those about them, though they quickly turned away again, for it was only the Gullaime being the Gullaime, and what else could a deck-childer expect of it?

"Give longer," croaked Madorra, moving forward, its one good eye blinking. "Other gullaime will work to death for Windseer." At the mention of "Windseer" a few heads turned, a little notice was taken and Joron bit back his anger. The windshorn had become less and less careful of talking about the prophecy it believed the Gullaime was part of – a prophecy that promised death and destruction for all, and not one Joron wanted spread about his ship.

"None die for me," hissed the Gullaime at Madorra, "none die."

"All who die reborn," croaked Madorra, and before it could continue Joron interrupted.

"The Gullaime is right, I'll not run its people into death for this," said Joron, and what of the many of his own he had run to death, ey? What of that? But he shut those thoughts down and let them be carried away on the winds that pushed *Tide Child* through the sea. "Now, Gullaime, you know the strength of those with you better than I do. Bring them on deck, set a rota that'll keep wind in our wings and push us forward, we just need to make the mist before *Keyshanpike* does." Then he leaned in close. "And save your own strength if you can, Gullaime, for I'll need wind to manoeuvre on the bank to avoid ice, and maybe to avoid that ship. I trust none to bring it as accurate and fast as you." At that the Gullaime cocked its head and purred a little, then, as Madorra approached it snapped at the one-eyed windshorn and bustled off to go below and bring its fellows.

"Aelerin," said Joron.

"Ey, D'keeper?"

"That thing you did, where you read the currents in the storm to send the barrel traps over the side?"

"Ey?" Beneath the cowl bright and inquisitive eyes considered him.

"Do you reckon you could do the same with floating ice?"

"I don't understand," they said.

"Well, the ice must affect the currents, the way a rock or island does, ey?"

"Possibly, if it is big enough."

Joron smiled, and pointed at one of the huge floating ice islands in the distance.

"What I want, Aelerin, is to go into the mist at full speed, as sure as I can be that I will not run us straight into an ice island." The courser stared at him, he saw their tongue come out, run along lips, the saliva left behind freezing into a silvery rime.

"That is all you want?"

"Ey."

"Well, I can try, D'keeper."

"And I can ask no more." He waited for the courser to move away but they stayed. "You have more to say?"

"The gullaime, it will not be enough," said Aelerin quietly, and they nodded at the ship behind them. Joron turned, saw what the courser had seen. The shipwife of *Keyshanpike* was bringing up his own gullaime.

"So," he said, "it is to be a straight race."

"And there is nothing left for us to put over," said Aelerin. "He will catch us, I think." Joron stared for a moment, a war going on within him.

"There is something else to put over, though it saddens me more than I can say," he said, then turned and shouted, "Solemn Muffaz!"

"Ey, D'keeper?" came the reply.

"Call up the bonewrights, Solemn Muffaz, it is a sad time, but a needy one. Put the gallowbows over the side. Both the great and the lesser for we need the speed." At that moment, the hull of *Tide Child* creaked alarmingly, as if the ship itself felt the pain within Joron, within Solemn Muffaz, within Aelerin and Farys and Mevans and Jennil and every other member of the crew at pulling the black warship's teeth. "It must be done," whispered Joron, putting his hand on the hard black surface of the rumpspine. "I am sorry, *Tide Child*, but it must be done."

16

The Ghosts in the Fog

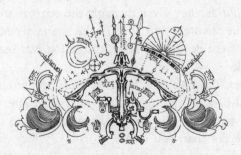

Skearith's Eye dipped toward the horizon, turning the mist of Spantonnis Bank a deep red shot through with streamers of gold.

Tide Child had run before a gullaime-assisted wind all day, the windtalkers coming up in pairs and standing before the mainspine until they began to shake and Joron, despite Madorra's cursing and dancing and calling them weak, sent them down before they became windsick. There was little point running them to death when Aelerin had done the calculations. With the bows gone they had enough gullaime to run before the wind without killing them doing it.

They just didn't have enough speed to make escape a surety, and killing the gullaime with work would make little difference.

Now they were in a straight race, and unlike the bigger ship that had chased them before, *Keyshanpike* had not moved a gallowbow to its beak. An error, Joron thought as he watched the shipwife on the beak of the ship, who in turn watched him. Or maybe they were just supremely confident that her ship would overtake him. He could not blame them. They must have felt a little leap of joy when they watched *Tide Child's* great bows splash into the sea.

Well, he thought, folding up the nearglass and putting it in his jacket, *I think you are overconfident. Let us hope I am right*. He turned, staring at Spantonnis Bank; the glowing mist filled him with trepidation and he well understood Farys's talk of ghosts. Well understood the strange mood among the crew of *Tide Child* as they flew through the sea toward the fog. "Aelerin," he shouted, and already the sound seemed strange to him, as if the deadening effect of the fog was reaching out of the bank.

"D'keeper," said Aelerin, but they were not looking at him, they stared back at the four-ribber as it sped after them. "It will catch us before the bank," they said. "She drives her gullaime harder than you will."

"It will not catch us," said Joron. "I will enter the bank at full speed. We will not slow as they expect us to, and we shall see who blinks first. I am sure it will be them."

"But D'keeper," said Farys, and she wrapped her hands around herself, "there could be an ice island right behind the mist. We could . . ."

"Calm, Farys. Aelerin can read the currents of the sea, they know where is safe to enter the bank."

"And if they are wrong?" said Farys, glancing at the courser.

"Then we will not have to worry about being caught for long, Farys. But I trust Aelerin." Farys turned away, to stare at the golden fog once more.

"What is to stop them following us in at full speed?" said Jennil.

"Fear, Jennil. Fear of ghosts, fear of bad luck. They have already lost a topspar in the storm and their shipwife does not move her gallowbows for'ard as *Beakwyrm's Rage*'s did. I think she is inexperienced. I think she will choose safety. I think she will blink." Jennil stared at him, then looked back to the pursuing ship, the metal prow of its beak lifting from the waves, and she nodded.

"If you say it, D'keeper."

"The work starts in the icefield, Jennil." He glanced for'ard, the mist growing by the moment, and then behind him, where *Keyshanpike* also grew. "When we enter the mist, Aelerin says we go hard to one side, then come to an almost full stop. From then it will be little more than walking speed through the ice fields. I'll not escape this ship behind us just to run into an ice island and sink."

"What if they—"

"If they follow us in then they will do the same and it will be a game of cat and mouse. I want you and Solemn Muffaz to ensure the crew are silent, every single one of them. If any of 'em so much as breathe loud I'll have the skin corded from their backs, you understand?"

"Ey, D'keeper."

"Then get the crew ready, we'll be making a hard turn before the next bell rings."

Then back to watching as the ship behind them grew and grew. The deckchilder lining its rails. The gaggle of gullaime huddled at its mainspine. The white wings billowing with wind. Back to watching as the mist bank towered over them, racing nearer and nearer. Watching Aelerin at the beak, the subtle raising of their hands as they guided *Tide Child* forward, relaying those orders quietly to Barlay, massive and calm at the steering oar. Knowing, moment by moment, that if he was wrong about Aelerin's ability to read currents they may smash into a towering ice island at full speed, and then all would be over, Meas would be lost to whatever fate awaited her and he would have failed. And if he was wrong about *Keyshanpike*'s shipwife then the other ship would overhaul them before they made the fog, and without gallowbows there was nothing he could do.

"Solemn Muffaz," he said quietly. The deckmother turned from his place before the mainspine, walked up to the rump. "Watch Aelerin for me, relay their orders quietly, Barlay will keep us on course." Solemn Muffaz nodded and Joron turned and took out his nearglass. His sores itched, his stump ached, his head throbbed. He watched *Keyshanpike* cutting through the water, gaining all the time and near enough that it seemed as if one of their deckchilder could, if properly motivated, run along the bowspine and jump the distance between the two ships. "Blink, Hag curse you," he said. He felt *Tide Child* alter course slightly beneath him and looked back to *Keyshanpike*. Nearer and nearer. "Blink, curse you," he said. Looked back, found the slate of *Tide Child* slowly filling. Every deckchilder coming on deck, some shivering as there were not enough cold weather clothes to go round. Garriya among them hunched over, bustling about and pushing those ill-clothed deckchilder to huddle together for warmth. The ship's crew of gullaime, around the colourful figure of his Gullaime, all shepherded by a hissing Madorra. All here without being asked or ordered, as if they knew that this was the moment, that now it could all end and they had decided, without speech or coaxing, to face it together. In front of them the massive wall of fog, the sky darkening. Behind them the ship. "Blink, Maiden curse you," he said. And they rushed toward the mist together. Rushed and rushed and rushed. Water hissing along hulls. Spray crowning their beaks. "Blink, Mother curse you!" And still they rushed on. "Blink!"

And as if in answer.

They blinked.

He heard the order go out on *Keyshanpike*'s deck, as clear as it if it had been on his own, when the shipwife's nerve broke. "All slow! Hard to seaward!" *Keyshanpike* heeled over, a huge wave splashing up and over the rump of *Tide Child*, soaking Joron and the crew in freezing water as the ship changed course to run along the edge of the fog bank, wings bowing inward as its gullaime reversed the direction of the wind to slow the big warship. Before he could feel any triumph, any joy in calling his opponent correctly, the fog swallowed *Tide Child*. The world shrunk to little more than a few armlengths in any direction and all the everyday noises that he took for granted – the creak of the hull, the crack of the wings, the whistle of wind through rigging, the jingling of fittings – became stilled by clinging air.

"Landward!" shouted Aelerin.

"Now, Gullaime!" he shouted at the top of his voice. He felt a wave of heat pass over *Tide Child*, and his ears hurt with pressure as the Gullaime set to work. The ship heeled over as Barlay leaned into the oar and Joron grabbed the rearspine, hoped all those gathered on the slate had the sense grab on to something. A moment of dizziness, feeling like he would slide down the tilted deck and into the freezing sea. Then the ship straightened, a blast of freezing air howled around the ship and the spines creaked alarmingly.

Tide Child coasted to a slow stop and Joron Twiner – the Black Pirate, most feared man upon the sea – realised he had his eyes tightly closed.

He opened them. If any had noticed none said a thing. He looked to the front of the ship. The Gullaime's blast of air had driven away the fog and he saw Aelerin. Gave them a nod and salute. To seaward of them was a huge mountain of ice; if they had gone into the fog just a little further along . . . If they had turned just a little less tightly then . . . But he could not think about that. He looked round, saw Jennil near him.

"Find out if any were lost overboard during the turn," he whispered. "Get the flukeboat over the side and ready for towing, I do not doubt that *Keyshanpike* will follow us in eventually."

"Ey," said Jennil. Then she moved away to be lost in the encroaching fog.

"What now?" said Farys, her eyes wide with fear, no doubt at the thought of ghosts, though her voice did not betray her.

"Now, Farys," he said, "we play a most dangerous game of hide and seek."

As quietly as possible *Tide Child*'s remaining flukeboat was taken from the centre of the deck and put over the side. Then tied on to the front of the ship. That done, Barlay and seven of her strongest took to the oars and started to row, pulling the big ship slowly forward while Jennil stood in the front of the flukeboat with a line and weight to measure the depth of the water. By her stood two deckchilder with keyshanpikes, ready to fend off the smaller ice islands that floated about them and, though of no danger to *Tide Child*, would hole a flukeboat. Beneath them in the blue water the lethal tubes of beakwyrms, denied the bow wave of *Tide Child* to race, span angrily away before vanishing into the depths. Deeper, the vague shapes of longthresh waited for any accident that would bring them food. On the beak of *Tide Child* stood Joron and Aelerin, the deckkeeper squinting through the thick mist, the courser studying an unrolled chart.

"You should thank the old man back in Bernshulme for these documents," said Aelerin.

"If Yirrid still lives I will. What have you found?"

"This chart was buried at the bottom of Meas's chest, it is very old. Fascinating, really. I . . ."

"Does it help us, Aelerin?"

"Ey, I think so. It speaks of seven channels through the ice fields."

"But if it is old and the ice moves, what use is that?"

"These are channels of flowing water, D'keeper, they will keep themselves clear of ice. If we can find one then we can use it to leave."

"But *Keyshanpike* may also find one," he said, "and they may get out of here before us."

"Or they may make their way slow and careful," they replied. Joron stared into the mist, thinking about the decisions he could make now and all the destinations those decisions must have them travel to: some to Meas standing on the slate once more, some to the bottom of the sea where the Hag's fire burned and all those Joron had lost on his journey so far waited. Go fast, or go careful?

"How far from the other side of the bank to Wilson's Cut?"

"If *Keyshanpike* finds a way out before we do? Too far. They will catch us for sure."

"Then there is little choice, we find a channel and we take it." He looked out into the fog, well understanding the talk of ghosts. One second the haze was so thick he could barely see Aelerin, the next it cleared and he could see a landscape of vast islands of ice before the fog closed in once more. "Are there clues as to where they are on that?" he asked, pointing at the chart, and Aelerin nodded, showing him the parchment.

"We are here, I think." They pointed at a space about two thirds along the bank. "*Keyshanpike* most likely came about and tried to enter near as it could to us, but we travelled a fair way before coming to a full stop. The nearest channel is behind us." Aelerin traced a blue channel with a finger, he noticed their nails were bitten down to almost nothing. "But that way, we are likely to run into *Keyshanpike*, so it is better that we make for this channel here, further up the bank."

"And then we make our way out."

"Ey, but not too fast, D'keeper. I think from the script on this – it is well faded – that the channels are freer of ice, but not completely."

"Forward then," said Joron and *Tide Child* began to move off, making his painstaking way through the ice. The night was long and stressful as they were, slowly and carefully, towed through the icefield, the world about them a cage of fuzzy lights. Joron found, during that long slow night, that talk of ghosts felt all too real and it was all he could do not to start at every odd sound in the darkness. As morning broke, he turned to find Mevans standing behind him, enveloped in a blanket of thick air.

"Ey?" said Joron.

"The topboy wanted to know how she should alert you if she sees something, she is loath to shout when we are trying to hide."

"And wise to ask," smiled Joron. "Though I doubt she will see much in this." He held out his hands in the freezing mist.

"Bearna says that fog is low-lying in some places, and in the tops she sometimes gets glimpses much further out through the mist. Almost right over the bank."

"Has she seen anything?"

"Big ice island two points of the for'ard shadow; she thought she saw the tops of another ship behind us an hour ago but it was dark and she could not be sure."

"But she did not report it?"

"Did not want to come down, lest she miss it again. Did not want to shout for fear of alerting them." He leaned in closer. "I think her decision canny, D'keeper, not one needing stripes."

"Of course," said Joron, and wondered how his crew's opinion of him had changed that Mevans needed to tell him not to cord a deckchilder for making a good decision. Did he appear so hard now? "Find some small bone offcuts, Mevans, I am sure the bonewrights did not throw over everything they had. Bearna can drop them on the deck to get attention. Even if it is heard by another ship it will hopefully be taken as ice falling."

"Ey, D'keeper."

"Nothing too heavy, Mevans, I do not want one of my deckchilder's heads dashed open for attention."

"Of course not," said Mevans, and vanished into the mist.

It felt almost as if time was suspended within the bank; the glass turned and the bell rang but it was curiously disconnected from the usual steady, repetitive running of the ship. Faces loomed out of the fog, oddly distended, caught mid-expression and made alien by the sudden lack of context. *Tide Child* moved slowly through the day, the only sound the splash of oars, the ship's wings furled into black lines as the rowers strained in the flukeboat and the giant ice islands slowly passed them by. Sometimes Joron was not sure if the ship moved or if the islands did. He saw strange animals on the ice, unlike anything he had seen before, neither fish nor bird, fat and round with wide flat heads and covered in thick small feathers. The beasts watched *Tide Child* pass, curious as to what this strange creature was, and Joron wondered if they had ever seen such a thing as a ship before, and if they were good eating.

"Look!" He recognised the shout – Farys – and strode over to the mid rail where the sound had come from. He found her pointing out over the misty water, into the thick fog.

"Keep your voice down, Farys," he hissed, "you are an officer, not an excitable stonebound on their first journey."

"Ey, D'keeper, 'tis only what I saw surprised me so much."

"And what did you see?"

"I thought it were a woman, I reckon, though a strange one. But the mist, it plays tricks." He was about to tell her not to be foolish when the mist cleared again, and he saw something he had not expected. A row of small boats, no wing on them, and each one with a single oar in it. Up from them a group of strange people like no others he had ever seen. They were abnormally round, and he did not know if it were thanks to thick clothing, maybe made out of skins, or how they were made by the godbird. Each held a stick and he could hear them chattering to one another in a strange and guttural language.

"Ice men," said Solemn Muffaz from beside him. "I came up here on the *Wyrmtooth* and the shipwife knew about them, fair unnatural they are. Let their men rule them and I do not know why the Hag lets them live." One of the ice men raised the spear in his hand and ran forward, dancing backwards and forwards and shouting in his strange tongue.

"I do not mind them being unnatural," said Joron, "but I wish they would be quiet."

"Had we a gallowbow we could shut them right up."

"Ey, but we do not. So we must hope no one is listening." As Joron finished speaking the ice man launched his spear at *Tide Child*, though it fell fair short, and then the mist swallowed them up. "A belligerent bunch," said Joron, "and I suspect, Farys, there is the answer to your ghosts and empty ships." She nodded.

"D'keeper," his name whispered as the courser appeared. "The water at the beak has changed, deeper and darker it is. I think we have found the channel."

"At long last, this creeping along is no good for the nerves. Solemn Muffaz, Farys, get the deckchilder up the spines ready to unfurl the wings, and get the flukeboat ready to go in tow. When we hit the channel I intend to use more speed than is wise. Bring up the Gullaime too, I'll want its wind in case we need to change direction suddenly."

"Ey, D'keeper," came back in unison.

Free at last, he thought. *At last.*

17

The Fog and the Ghosts

They did not move as quickly as Joron wished, the treacherous ice was too ever-present for that, and even this "clear channel" was no such thing. The hugest ice islands did not fill it right enough, bracketing the black ship as it cut through the water, but smaller chunks floated within the channel. Those deckchilder that were not lookouts for ice floating just below the surface were engaged in chipping off ice from the rigging, deck, rails and wings. Extra topboys were put aloft, one on each spine rather than just the mainspine, and each of these given a mate to relay urgent messages. The Gullaime stood ready at the side, shivering miserably despite its heavy, colourful cloak, and refusing to speak to anyone. Only coming alive in those moments where it was required to help *Tide Child* veer off his path to avoid floating ice.

They saw more of the ice men, though these were less belligerent than the first they had seen, and only stood and watched as the ship passed. Joron wondered if they thought *Tide Child* some great beast, tamed and trained to carry women and men on its back. He did not know, would never know what they thought. Plainly they were not a people who would welcome his approach, and he did not intend to put his own people in harm's way for no other reason than his own curiosity.

His hands were burning, as he had stood for so long gripping the landward rail that the thin sheen of ice had melted and refrozen around them. When he pulled them free it felt like he removed a layer of skin.

"D'keep." He turned, found Larin, one of the topboy's mates.

"Word from Bearna in the tops?"

"Ey," said Larin, looking at the deck, unwilling to meet an officer's eye. "Ship wising, D'keep," she said, the deformation of her lip stopped her saying the letter "r".

The cold within him matched the cold of his hands.

"She is sure?"

"Ey, D'keep," she said. "Is diwect off the seawad side wight now."

"It keeps pace with us?"

"No, D'keep." She shook her head. "Ship is stopped, it is."

"Stopped?"

"Ey, D'keep." Joron looked around the deck, wondering why that would be. Did they wait for him? Did they somehow know they had got ahead and planned some trap? It made no sense.

"Has he seen us, Larin?"

"Beawna says there is no one in the tops."

Joron waited, as if the air could give him some answer. Then made his way to the mainspine.

"Farys, slow *Tide Child* by half, you have the deck while I am in the tops."

"Ey, D'keeper," came the reply and then the deck was lost to him, swallowed by the swirling fog as he climbed the rigging, followed by Larin.

In the tops Bearna was waiting; without speaking she pointed out to seaward and Joron brought out his nearglass. Found the ship quickly enough, the tops floating above the mist between two huge ice islands, but a trick of the mist made it hard to be sure of distance.

"No one in the tops, D'keeper. Something is off, right?"

"Ey, it is," he said, and closed up the nearglass, deep in thought. "Keep watching, send Larin down if there is any change." Then he made his way down to the slate, to be once more wrapped in mist while trying to think of a reason why the ship pursuing them would come to a dead stop in the middle of the ice fields. By the time his bone spur hit the deck he had no more answers than when he had first spied the ship. "Mevans, Solemn Muffaz, Aelerin, and Jennil, come to me on the rump," he said. "Farys, have the seaguard armed and bring weapons up on deck for the crew, then you join me also." He stared out into the mist. "Full stop, and put out the seastay." He ignored the puzzled looks of the deckchilder around him and walked to the rear of the ship, where some trick of the mist seemed to play him back the terrible sound of *Beakwyrm's Rage* going over in the storm. When he was joined by those he had called he nodded to them. He felt a tightening of the tension on ship as the weapons were given out, like a rope under strain. He straightened his warm coat around himself, let out a breath of air in a puff of mist. "A ship is out there," he said, "I can only think it is *Keyshanpike*."

"And yet we stop," said Jennil.

"*Keyshanpike* is stopped, and has no one in the tops."

"Ghosts," said Farys.

"Enough of that," said Joron, voice as cold as the air.

"We should take advantage," said Solemn Muffaz. "If he is foolish enough to stop and post no lookouts we can take him."

"Strange that he stops though," said Mevans.

"Ey," said Joron, "I thought that. Now I try to think of a reason why he would."

"You think there is an ambush ahead?" said Jennil. "Is that why you have armed the crew?"

"I think it is a possibility," said Joron. "But you are all knowledgeable of the sea, so I ask for other possibilities."

"An ambush makes most sense," said Jennil.

"But no one in the tops," said Joron, more to the air than those gathered.

"Could have hit ice," said Solemn Muffaz. "Most likely has the crew working in the hull to stop them sinking."

"But no one in the tops," said Joron, more to the air than those gathered.

"Mutiny," said Mevans. "Weak shipwife and fear of the ghosts."

"But no one in the tops," said Joron, more to the air than those gathered.

It made no sense, to leave a ship unguarded so. Joron could tell no one but he was haunted by the loss of *Beakwyrm's Rage*, by the loss of so many in such a way. In battle he had no qualms about taking life, but to see that great ship upset by the power of the sea and to do nothing felt wrong somehow. If some calamity had also befallen *Keyshanpike* and he could help then he felt he should. To leave the crew stranded here in the freezing mist did not sit well. Perhaps if they were stricken and he helped, then the officers of *Keyshanpike*, in the spirit of cooperation, might give up information of Meas to him; and if not, he was sure they would do what honour required and give him a head start, as if he had never stopped. Maybe offer him supplies. He knew it was more sensible to simply carry on, leave the ship to its fate, but some deep-seated core within him, that boy who had listened in awe to his father's stories of the fleet and the honourable behaviour of the best shipwives, would not let him. "I would know more of what has happened," he said, "if for no other reason than what befell them may befall us. Solemn Muffaz, put a thin rope on the flukeboat, so it does not get lost and if needs be we can haul it back." He wanted to go himself, to get sight of this mystery, but knew he could not stray so far from his ship with the crew so jittery and talk of ghosts still among them. "Mevans, take a small crew and get sight on *Keyshanpike*, nothing more, no matter what you see. Then return here and tell me all you can."

"Ey, D'keeper," he said, and left to make preparation.

"And the rest of us?" said Farys.

"Well," he said, "we have little to do but wait."

And the waiting was always the hardest part: first to wait while the flukeboat vanished from vision, then wait while the gentle splash of its oars was swallowed up by the mist and then there was only the lap of water against the hull and the bite of the cold against his skin.

Time.

Time slowly passing with little regard for feelings. Time felt no discomfort, anxiety or worry. Time was little more than a slow tyrant whom they all must obey.

So Joron stood on the rump and watched the sand go through the glass, and he walked up and down the ship while his crew did their jobs with what enthusiasm they could muster in the sharp and freezing air, for they all felt it. The strangeness. That a ship should stop in the middle of a chase was odd enough, that it should post no lookouts even stranger. Usually, his crew would simply work on, he knew them as a fleet and steady lot. But talk of ghosts had spread cold and clammy hands over them, and they were not as the women and men he knew. Wide-eyed and wary they worked and he wondered if he had that same look, if his dark skin was a shade paler with cold and fear of the unknown.

And all he could do was wait.

All they could do was wait.

Eventually, time passed as time does and he heard, with much relief, the gentle splash of oars. Then saw Mevans emerge from the mist at the beak of the flukeboat, gently gathering up the line attached to the front of it so as not to foul the small ship. When it bumped against the serrated sides of *Tide Child* Mevans was quick off the mark, up the side of the ship and over to the rump of the deck, where Joron stood, looking as calm as he could and not at all like a man desperate for news.

"D'keeper."

"Report please, Mevans," he said.

"Were a most curious thing, D'keeper," said Mevans. "We approached the *Keyshanpike*, and when we got close the mist vanished, like they had gullaime set to keeping the area around the ship clear. So I took the flukeboat off around the sides of this clear part, I did, not wanting to be seen. And so I found an ice island where we moored the boat and old Anglan and I made our way to the top of the isle, fair hard going that were."

"And?"

"Well, we saw some of them ice men but it turns out when they're close up they are not ones for a fight, and as soon as they saw us they made for their little boats and were gone into the mist. So we reached the top of the isle and had a right good view of *Keyshanpike*, the mist being thinner higher and all, and with that strange clear patch about it – though the clear patch I am sure were getting smaller."

"And what is your report, Mevans?" The smaller man grinned at him, for he knew that Joron knew how much he liked to talk, and Joron, like the shipwife before him, was wont to indulge Mevans in that love of talking, for few aboard the ship were as respected and liked as Mevans.

"I do not right know what to make of it, D'keeper." He reached up and scratched at a louse bite on his bald head under the heavy hood. "*Keyshanpike* were at his staystone there, but he were all outfitted for war, wings furled and sand across the deck."

"To be expected, Mevans, they were hunting us."

"Well, ey. But also their bows were untrussed, and strung too. And no one keeps a gallowbow under tension for any length of time for it ruins the cord, as you well know and like to tell us. Worse in weather like this of course." Joron nodded, willing the smaller man to get on with it. "But D'keeper," he said, and it was difficult not to get the impression Mevans was relishing the telling of the tale, "there were not a woman or man on the slate. Not a one. And I sat there for long enough to get my arse numb on the ice, listening, for a ship can never be truly silent. I heard nothing. As far as I could tell the ship was empty."

"And that is all?"

"I think there may have been blood on his decks and down the hull, but could have been dirt, hard to tell without going closer."

"You did not go aboard."

"You ordered not, so . . ." He grinned. "But I can go back?"

"Not alone." Joron shook his head, called Farys and Jennil over. "*Keyshanpike* sits at staystone just over there," he pointed. "To all intents and purposes he seems abandoned. If so, all we put over the side we could reclaim from him, stores, gallow-bows, everything."

"Could be a trap, D'keeper," said Jennil.

"Ey, that it could. I cannot think why they would do it in such a way though. There was no guarantee we would see them as we passed. The mist could have obscured them." He stared out into the fog. "I think we must chance it," he said. "Refitting *Tide Child* in the Gaunt Islands will take every coin we have; if we can do it for free here, all the better. If it is a trap, well, crew on crew, even tired, I back us over them," he said this with a piratical gleam in his eye. Though within he quailed at the thought of a trap, for his women and men were thin and worn now from too many days at sea without proper rest and food. But he could not for the life of him work out the other shipwife's thinking. If it was a trap it relied entirely on luck. It needed the topboys of *Tide Child* to see *Keyshanpike* in the mist, and for Joron to feel the need to investigate. "Set the wings, bring up whichever gullaime have any strength left," he said, "we'll take *Tide Child* over there and drop the staystone opposite. I'll lead a boat over myself to have a look around."

"Should we not simply come up alongside?" said Jennil, as Joron stared out into the mists. "If there is trouble then it is easier for us to get across the rail to help."

"Easier for them too," said Mevans. Joron looked from one to the other, two experienced deckchilder; both had been on boneships longer than he had, far longer. Yet he was expected to decide, to know.

"Ey, we'll do that. come up alongside," he said eventually. "Easier to take across what we need and we won't be running. If it's a trap then we'll have to fight anyway, may as well make it as easy as possible on us. We'll use grapples to tie on and keep the staystone up, but have deckchilder ready with axes in case we need them to cut us free. We'll come up on *Keyshanpike* from behind, only tie on the beak of *Tide Child* to their rump, that way we'll never pass their bows, just in case they have them ready for us. Solemn Muffaz!" shouted Joron. "Get us under way!" As the orders were given and women and men ran to the great bone windlass to bring up the ship's staystone, Joron had a second thought on an earlier order. "Keep the wings furled. Tie on the flukeboat and put rowers in it. We'd need gullaime wind to move anyway, better to make our way slow and steady. Get pikes up front and keep measuring the depth, I don't want the bottom ripped out of *Tide Child*. Mevans, you already know the way, you can pilot us in."

"Ey, D'keeper," said in unison, and the action on the slate doubled. Ropes were tied, rowing crews readied and once more *Tide Child* moved off, creeping through the fog. Moving forward no faster than a sick man would walk to the hagbower for surgery that would most definitely be painful, and likely end his life.

But still, he went.

Moving through fog, the flukeboat's rowers calling back measurements to the ship, their voices seeming dislocated from the world around them. The fog thickening once more, and it looked as if the taut rope at the beak of *Tide Child* vanished into the air; if not for the voices calling out the stroke it would have been easy to believe in the ghosts so many of the crew believed in.

Joron paced, he wanted to run, to run around the deck, to hear the slap of his boot and the tap of his spur and within him a madness arose. He was shipwife, he could do what he wanted, he could run and keep running, away from the fear and the pain and the anger and the things he had done, the things he would do. The things he must do, if he wanted to bring Meas back. Then it passed, like a moment of giddiness passed when he looked down from the top of a spine to the swaying world below.

He found he was by the mainspine, leaning his head against it, willing away the sudden weakness running through him.

"Caller," he turned, found Garriya, staring up at them. "Stop that."

"What?" he said, and as he said he knew what she talked of, for the ship was vibrating with song; all around him his crew were singing in low voices, from below he could hear the gullaime's discordant chants twisting around the melody and he knew he had been lost, joining in without even knowing. His mouth moving. His heart beating. His blood whistling through his veins.

"You know," she said.

"Yes," he replied, "I know."

She stepped closer, almost half his height, as ragged as he was proper in his black uniform. "Guard your dreams, D'keeper, I have felt the movements in the deep. I have felt ancient minds turn their eyes toward the surface."

"What do you mean?"

"Guard your dreams," she said again, then stepped back. "I have to go deal with those you've put under my care. Send no more today."

"I will try," he said.

"You've proved mighty bad at that so far." She chuckled, spat on the deck and walked away. Leaving him confused, his mind a turmoil and he knew that all he could do to clear it was work. Was put his mind to the ship and the movement through the fog. To check on those sounding out depths and watch, brow furrowed in worry, as women and men used keyshanpikes to push chunks of ice away from the hull, and all around was the constant tapping of ice being removed from the ropes and the bonework. A hot drink was pushed into his hands and he sipped it thankfully as the burn of the cold was chased from his fingers.

Eventually, there came a shout from the front and the mist around them began to thin. He saw the corpselights first, all the blue of firstlight, slowly drifting through the tops of the ship. *Keyshanpike* was rump-on to them at a slight angle and through the thinning mist Joron could see his four landward gallowbows. All were untrussed and ready to loose, just as Mevans had said. And, just as he had also said, the ship appeared quiet as death.

"Jennil," said Joron, "have the flukeboat detach and the crew come around the rear. We'll coast in the rest of the way." She nodded and walked down the ship to give his instruction. "Gavith!" he shouted, and the man appeared, shifty looking as if he did not want to be called. "Get to the beak with your grapple, you have always been the best with it."

"Ey, D'keeper," he said.

"And gather those you know throw well. I want to bring *Tide Child* to a stop with our beak against the rear, and if we overshoot Solemn Muffaz will cord the lot of you," said Joron, and he meant it as light-hearted but Gavith did not seem to hear that and nodded his head seriously.

"I expect he would," said Gavith and Joron turned away for the business of war beckoned, and he must give it his all.

18

A Mystery Resolved in Blood

It was a nerve-wracking business, tying *Tide Child* on to *Keyshanpike*. Every moment expecting an attack; either women and men boiling up from belowdecks, or flukeboats coming out of the mist. Wary-eyed deckchilder stood by the ropes holding axes, flexing their hands around the hafts in readiness should the black ship need cutting free. Sand passed through the glass and the crew stood still and silent, straining every sense, always expecting to hear something. Anything. And time passed, as time does, Joron, and Farys, and Jennil, and Mevans, and Solemn Muffaz and every member of the crew began to feel more certain they would hear nothing.

"Ain't natural this," Joron heard from a deckchild behind him, made no comment. Let them talk if it eased their mind a little.

"'Tis the ghosts, just as we knew."

"Truss that talk!" he shouted. Ey, let them talk, but not too much. "There'll be no ghosts here, you mark it. For those who doubt it, well, I shall lead us onto *Keyshanpike* and any ghost that awaits us will answer to my blade." He thought of drawing it, did not. Was sure if he did his hand would shake, and so he stood still, unmoving apart from his eyes, which roved along the deck; and in turn, the crew saw that lack of movement as bravery, as surety, as not shrinking in fear, as not even needing a weapon and they took some comfort from him, for was he not Meas's son? And was she not the greatest shipwife who had ever been?

"Shall we all go, D'keeper?" said Farys. He stared at the white ship, so perfect, the sort of ship Meas should have been on. Quick and strong and unmarred, unshamed. It was so perfectly white he could pick out the splatters of paint at the base of the spines and around the gallowbows, and he wondered what prayers to the Hag had been made as the paint had been thrown.

Whatever they had been, they had clearly gone unanswered.

"No," said Joron, "not straight away. I want Jennil and some of her seaguard with me, and our best eyes ready with bows and crossbows. I'll take a small party across first."

"You go yourself, D'keeper?" said Mevans. "But—"

"Have I not already said I will? I'm near enough Tide Child for you to see me, Mevans, don't fret." He grinned beneath the mask. "I'll add Gavith, Yerffoeg, Solemn Muffaz and Zafar to the seaguard, and Cwell will have my back. Enough bodies to get me back here if we have good cover from the bows. Now set a plank across to Keyshanpike. Let us be on our way. All this standing about in the cold is good for no one's health."

Then they were making ready: bows and crossbows were brought up and strung, pots of arrows set out along the deck, though the supplies were measly, and a plank was run across from Tide Child's beak to Keyshanpike's rump and Joron, with a deep breath and a sure step, led the way for his small party onto the deck of Keyshanpike.

What an odd feeling he had then, standing unopposed on the deck of a white ship. To feel the soft glow of the corpse-lights on his face. To not have a sword in his hand and hate in his heart. To step forward, sand crunching beneath his foot, without meeting resistance. To not smell blood and bodies.

To be alone.

"What first, D'keeper?" said Solemn Muffaz.

Or alone as he ever was.

"Forward," he said. So they moved, spreading out across the deck.

"Where are the flukeboats?" said Solemn Muffaz. Joron saw no boats stacked in the centre of the deck, had noticed no boats tied on behind either.

"Curiouser and curiouser," said Joron, "you think they left their ship?"

"Why leave a good ship out here in the mist and ice?" said Jennil.

"Blood here," said Gavith, pressing his hand against a patch of red ice.

"And here," said Yerffoeg. Joron walked to the nearest, Gavith, crouched near the mainspine holding up a hand to show red on his fingers.

"Blood here too," said Jennil from further down the deck.

"Look!" said Oast of the seaguard and he bent over, coming up holding a shipwife's two-tail hat.

"Mutiny then," said Solemn Muffaz. "The fear got to them."

"But where are the crew?" said Joron.

"Hiding below maybe?"

"We should go look," said Joron. "They may join us." They moved slowly along the deck, sand crunching underfoot and Joron saw how ice had been allowed to build up on rope and rail. Found more places where blood had been spilled to freeze upon the deck. Gavith pointed to seaward and Joron wondered what at, then he saw it, a curl of smoke rising from the galley's chimney which stuck out the hull to the side. Joron nodded and then they headed down. The underdecks were brighter than on the black ship, all painted white with wanelights glowing along the sides. Flickering, dead eyes considering them. Light flooded in from open bowpeeks and all the hammocks were stowed away, as if for action. But the long table the crew ate at was up and even had food on it. Bone knives were scattered on the floor and the cabin walls that would usually be stripped down for action still stood. Joron's little group picked their way through the underdeck, splitting up to examine the detritus strewn across it.

"Whatever happened here," said Jennil, "it happened fast. Time to strew the decks and untruss the bows, but not to clear for action." Joron nodded, watching Solemn Muffaz pick up a knife from the floor.

"Oast," said Joron, "take the seaguard and go through the hold; Jennil, and Gavith, look to the hagbower and the armoury and all else on the lower deck. I want lists of anything useful to us. I will go check the shipwife's cabin. Solemn Muffaz, check the other officers' cabins and the gullaime nest."

A chorus of affirmatives greeted his orders and they parted. Joron could not suppress a shudder, there was something very wrong about this quiet, still ship in the mist. Farys's talk of ghosts echoed loudly in his head as he entered the shipwife's cabin. Found it neat, food on the desk and the shipwife's logbook lying open on the floor, dropped but never picked up. The rear windows had been shattered and he reached out, saw blood on the glass. Beyond the broken windows *Tide Child* sat, his reflection shimmering upon the water. Farys stood on deck, saw Joron and gave him a nod; he nodded back before turning to look through the shipwife's belongings. Nothing special, nothing out of the ordinary. Clothes he could take and have sewn to fit, a good sword – he would give that to Farys, she needed one. But all that was for later, for now he picked up the log book, written in code as he expected. He would have the cabin searched for books. The code may be breakable back in the Gaunt Islands.

What had happened here?

"Deckkeeper!" Solemn Muffaz from outside. Joron left the great cabin, found the big man peering out of a seaward bowpeek.

"Ey, Solemn Muffaz?"

"Thought I saw a flukeboat out there."

"Where?" Joron took out his nearglass and crouched, looking out the bowpeek.

"Straight ahead, but it is gone now." Joron raised the near-glass, scanning the flat water, finding nothing. "Maybe it was just movement in the mist, ice or somesuch," said Solemn Muffaz. Joron was about to lower the nearglass, when he too saw something.

"No," he said, "you were right." He altered the focus. "Wreckage, flotsam, a few sheets of varisk, it looks like."

"You think it was the ice men?"

"I do not know," said Joron, "but I think we should get on deck and start loading *Tide Child* with supplies. I do not believe in ghosts, Solemn Muffaz, but I do not like this place either." The big man nodded and they headed up.

Threads of mist were invading the air above the slate. Silky feelers making their way onto the deck, unwelcome stowaways reaching out icy fingers. In the back of his mind something lay, some remembrance of his father, some words that he could not quite reach. He turned, saw his small party moving back toward *Tide Child*.

"Farys!" he shouted. "This ship is empty, get a crane rigged and our people ready, we'll take everything from *Keyshanpike* that we can, then take the ship in tow. It will fetch a fine price and we need the coin."

"Ey, D'keeper," said Farys, almost lost in the thickening mist. He was uncomfortable; that memory hanging in the back of his mind remained unreachable, but only just. It felt like a simple nudge would take him to it. Felt like he should pay it more attention. Mist and ships and ice. What was there?

"Deckkeeper." He turned to find Jennil waiting. "This ship is well stocked, Deckkeeper, everything we need, from ammunition to food to stores."

"I thought they threw over half their hold while chasing us."

"They must have been stuffed to the gills, fresh out of a port." He nodded. Wondered for a moment what it must be like to command a ship so secure it could fly for months without coming in to port or stealing what it needed.

"Jennil," he said, that stray thought still worrying at him, "does anything about this seem familiar to you, from stories?"

"Plenty of stories of ghost ships, Deckkeeper, found drifting like this."

"Yes, but the mist, gone then returning. I find it familiar. I hear my father's voice. He told me so many stories, but they fade like the memory of his voice."

Jennil shrugged. "We never had time for stories when I grew up," she said. "My father was a tailor and had too many children for his job to feed. I went straight to the ships at eight, never even got a laying night." He wanted to apologise to her for some reason, but could not. It was not done, and he knew that if he did apologise it would only serve to discomfort her. Her face twisted, he could see the thoughts breezing across it. "Though, when I were just a runner on the *Howling North*, I remember a story. Old woman call Aishline used to tell it, of mists gone and then returned in the cold places." She paused.

"That is what I remember, Jennil, the mist."

"Oh," said Jennil, and her face changed – shock, fear? Realisation? "No."

Then she was gone.

Not walked away. Not run off in fear. Not hidden by the mist. Just gone.

His face above the mask felt wet. He reached up, confused more than afeared, touched the skin around his eyes and took his hand away. Fingers red. Blood? Like when a gallowbow bolt struck a deckchilder, and bodies were completely destroyed. But this was no gallowbow bolt. He would have heard it, felt it. There had been no noise, no disturbance of the air.

"Jennil!" he shouted her name which brought his party running.

"What happened?" said Solemn Muffaz. "D'keeper, you are bleeding."

"I do not know," he said. "And it is not my blood. Jennil

was there one moment and then gone the next." He glanced down at his boot and spur upon the slate. And something else: a darkness worming its way across the deck, a single line of movement between Solemn Muffaz and Yerffoeg, and the story his father had told came flooding back. He knew what had happened here, knew the terrible danger they were all in. Those on the deck of *Keyshanpike* and those back on *Tide Child*. The black line moved, whip-fast. A tentacle that curled up and around Yerffoeg and before he had time to scream it pulled him from the deck. As it happened, Joron gave sound to the horror. Shouting out a warning the top of his voice.

"Toothreach!" he screamed. "It's a toothreach!" And he didn't know what to do. Was frozen in that moment by the terror his father had imparted in him. The toothreach: the great eye of the sea, the snatching tentacles that ate you slow and alive, always hungry just as the sea was always hungry, and death to ship and crew alike.

"Form a circle," shouted Solemn Muffaz and all jumped to his order. "Weapons!" Curnows came out and were brandished at the encroaching mist and it all came rushing back, his father's voice: *"Clear air, Joron my boy, for them to watch for prey, then mist to hunt in. They watch and wait and plan; a malign intelligence they are."*

"So you must run?"

"No, boy, for that is what they want."

"Then how do I escape one, father?"

"If I knew that, boy, I'd be shipwife of a boneship not a fisher in a flukeboat."

And his father's laughter floated away, vanishing into the mist for there was no laughter here.

"We need to get to *Tide Child*, run for it" shouted Gavith.

"Hold!" shouted Joron, grabbing Gavith by the arm before he moved. "The beast wants us to run."

"Hag's breath," said Mastir, one of the seaguard. "It's a beast, it is not clever." And he broke from the circle of weapons, running for the gangplank and this time Joron saw it, the black whip in the mist. One second Mastir was there and the next he was gone. But the creature must have known it was seen now, and Mastir did not die silently like Jennil and Yerffoeg, his screaming carried through the mist. Joron and his small circle stood breathing hard and hot, weapons extended.

"Never seen nothing so fast," said Oast.

"Ey, the deckkeeper'll get us out though," said another voice.

"No beast'll put down Meas's boy," said a third voice and Joron felt a tremendous weight on his shoulders, as though he coasted through the ocean and all the water in the world pressed down on him.

"Toward the ship's gallowbows," he whispered, his heart beating within his breast, breath coming fast. "They are untrussed and primed, step as I call it." Then he raised his voice. "Toothreach, Farys!" he shouted. "All aboard *Tide Child* be wary!"

"Deckkeeper!" came the call from *Tide Child*, "are you hurt?"

"No, Farys, but we have lost Jennil, Yerffoeg and Mastir. Defend yourselves and watch well, for this beast is quicker than the Hag when she's hungry. Get the gullaime to blow this mist away. If we can see it, we can loose on it."

"As you say, Deckkeeper," then he heard her voice again, as she spoke to the rest of the crew. "Bows out, keyshanpikes too, form into groups, protect each other. Shut all our bowpeeks!" And he smiled to himself despite the fear that filled him, and his sword leapt left and right, looking for a target that could move so quickly he would be lucky to see it.

"Seaward or landward, D'keeper?" said Gavith. "Where do you think the Hag-cursed thing is?" Joron did not know, could not know. He only knew it was out there.

"We should get to *Keyshanpike*'s for'ard seaward bow," said Solemn Muffaz, "has the largest arc of target of all the bows, best chance for us. And had bolts stacked by it."

"Mastir died to seaward of us," added Cwell, "I'd put coin on it."

"But is it furthest from *Tide Child*," said a voice behind him. Vud? Or Yancy? One of them, he thought.

"Stow that panicky talk," said Solemn Muffaz. "'Tis nothing worse than waiting for another ship to loose is all. You listen to the d'keeper, we have Meas's luck with us."

"Step," shouted Joron and they took a step across the deck, heard a scream, from *Tide Child*. "And step," he said and they moved. A scream and Vud was gone from behind Joron, nothing but mist there until the circle closed. Terror now, of a different kind to that in battle. He heard it in his crew's breathing. Knew this was becoming close to too much for them, that after so long running this may be what broke them. Then he felt the pressure on his ears that told him the gullaime worked, and a cold wind blew across him, picking up the mist and shifting it.

"Run for that bow!" he shouted, for now was the time for running. That part of him that understood command knowing that his party needed to act.

They ran.

Pell-mell across the deck, fast as they could for the for'ard seaward bow. As they ran Joron was sure he could feel the air being split by tentacles, hear the crack as they cut the thinning mist apart. At the same time he heard the twang and hiss of crossbows and bows loosing arrows. Then he was at the gallowbow and that part of his mind that was fleet took over. He forgot to be afraid. Forgot anything but duty and the rote words that would arm the weapon in front of him.

"Solemn Muffaz, load it. Gavith, loose it, Chirot and Alsa, on the spinner. Oast and Cwell organise the rest to protect us."

A chorus of "Ey, D'keeper," as familiar routine overtook them. This was better. Better than standing in fear, this was doing something, getting ready to strike back.

"Mist is thinning further, D'keeper!" shouted Chirot as she worked the spinner.

"Good, Spin the bow!"

"No!" screamed from behind him. He turned, and another

of the seaguard vanished. But the mist was truly clearing now, *Tide Child* was visible as a black mass and he could see the rumpspine of *Keyshanpike*.

"Ready, D'keeper!" shouted Solemn Muffaz and Joron turned back.

"Load!" As the gullaime's wind took hold more mist was blown away. Solemn Muffaz handled the heavy bolt into the weapon and for the first time Joron saw the creature that attacked them.

"Hag's breath," he said. He had heard tales of the toothreach, met some who said they had come across them, but each description of the beast was wildly different, and now he knew that each was wildly wrong. A mass of writhing flesh rose from the sea about four shiplengths out from them, difficult to judge how far with the remains of the mist still confusing his sense of distance. The creature had no real form, was only a churning knot of ever-moving blue-black tentacles and within it was a single yellow eye, with a black pupil that twitched and moved from side to side, seemingly without focus — though Joron had no doubt the creature knew they were there, had seen the evidence of it. "Aim," he said, his voice quiet, but no one responded, all of them staring at the creature." Joron took a deep breath. Was it his imagination or did the air stink? "Aim!" he shouted again, and the bow was pushed around. No need for him to help, his deckchilder were well trained. "Loose as you will! Pay that thing back for those it has taken!" They cheered as Gavith pulled the cord and the bow let out its terrible bark and the bolt shot across the distance between the ship and the beast, vanishing into its twisting body. The toothreach let out a scream, a painful wail as if from a hundred mouths. A great roar went up from those around the gallowbow.

"Hold!" shouted Joron. "Spin again!" And as they tensioned the bow he watched the toothreach. If their loosing had damaged the creature it showed no sign of it. The tentacles still writhed, the eye still jerked and twitched. It let out that high pitched, teeth-grating scream again, and spraying from its sides came thick clouds of mist.

"The mist," said Gavith, "the creature makes the mist."

"Don't be foolish, boy," grunted Solemn Muffaz as he lifted the bolt into the gallowbow. "Too much mist here for that." Then, as if it heard Solemn Muffaz, the creature screamed again and the water at the beak of *Keyshanpike* erupted.

"Another one!" shouted Gavith, as a wave of stink, worse than the smell of *Tide Child*'s bilges, washed over the deck, a choking, retching miasma. "Another one, Deckkeeper!" screamed Gavith. "There's another one!"

"I see it, pull the bow round," shouted Joron. "We'll put a bolt in the near one's eye!" They swung the gallowbow around just as tentacles shot out from this new toothreach and it let out that vile scream. Black ropey tentacles from the beast wrapped around the spines and the rails of the ship. One of the seaguard stepped forward and brought his sword down, hard, on a tentacle wrapped around the rail as the ship groaned and began to list. The curnow cut through the tentacle and it fell to the deck. Laid there, still writhing, and Joron saw that along the inner edge of the black rope of flesh were twin rows of tiny round mouths, sharp triangular teeth still working as if the last thought going through the dying flesh was one of hunger.

"Loose!" Joron shouted, though he could not take his eyes from the pulsing mouths, even as he fought against gravity to keep his balance on the rapidly tilting deck. With a cough the bolt was loosed and he saw it flash past, down the ship and into the toothreach, and whether this one was quicker than its sibling or had watched and learned from beneath the freezing water he did not know. He only saw that it caught the bolt in a mass of black tentacles, then tossed it away. As it did, Gavith pointed, shouting something, and a tentacle shot out, wrapping around his arm, pulling him forward. His head crashed against the arms of the gallowbow and he went limp. Only the quick reactions of Solemn Muffaz saved him; the big man grabbed his body, holding it tight and the toothreach pulled, Gavith and the deckmother falling to the deck. Solemn Muffaz jamming one foot on the rail, one on the gallowbow's base.

"Hag's sake," he screamed, "cut the tentacle!"

"I cannot reach!" shouted Chirot, and just as she finished speaking tentacle wrapped around her and pulled her screaming from the deck. Joron looked down, saw Solemn Muffaz struggling not to let go of the unconscious man, saw Gavith's arm stretched across the bonerail and knew there was only one thing he could do, or both Gavith and Solemn Muffaz would be dragged off the ship. He brought his sword down on Gavith's upper arm. The sharp blade cutting through flesh but not right through, white bone showed in the second before blood started flooding from the wound. Joron raised his sword once more and struck again, screaming as he brought the blade down as hard as he could on the arm. Once, twice, three times until he severed it completely and the lower arm was whipped away, the tentacle claiming it and the boy's unconscious body fell back onto Solemn Muffaz.

"Bind the wound if you can, Deckmother," he shouted, then turned, pointing his blade at the toothreach as it pulled once more on the ship, dragging it down with a jerk that unseated them all and pulled the beak of the ship beneath the water. Joron fell to the deck and luckily so, for he saw a tentacle shoot over his head and then withdraw.

"Loose!"

He heard Barlay's voice, loud and clear, and a rain of burning arrows shot out from *Tide Child*, landing on the toothreach, but if it noticed or cared he could not tell.

"Deckkeeper!" Farys's voice shouting from *Tide Child*. "Get back here! We'll put fire to *Keyshanpike*!" It was a good plan, Joron knew it. More tentacles, waving across the deck above Joron's head. Grasping whatever they could, the ship, the spars. With a screech of aching bone the top spars of *Keyshanpike* were wrenched away.

174

"Do it, Farys! Burn it!" he shouted, looking around, only four of them remained – him, Oast, Solemn Muffaz and Gavith, who was in no state to help. "We will never make it back!"

Did she reply? Did she scream out "No, Deckkeeper"? Did she fear for him? Did she fear for her crewmates? Joron did not know, would never know. For the words that rang out next seemed miraculous, and strange and yet utterly inevitable, as inevitable as the visions of moving through the depths that haunted Joron's dreams.

"Keyshan rising!"

19

The Leviathan Returns

He had not called it up. Had not brought it to them. Had not gathered the Gullaime's song around him like a cloak. Had not wished it nor considered it in his fear and panic. Yet knew he should have expected it. The dreams had been getting stronger ever since they had sighted a keyshan. The dreams of soaring through the deeps, of incredible pressure on his shoulders, of the blue light, filtered through an uncountable watery distance.

Dreams of hunger.

It came, of its own bidding and to feed its own desires and he knew that even before he saw it. Felt the water cut apart by the sharp beak, felt it run along the vast body, felt it beaten into swirls by flippers as big as boneships. The toothreach must have sensed it too, the black tentacles slipped from the spines and rails of *Keyshanpike* and the ship began to right itself.

"Grab Gavith!" shouted Joron. "Back to *Tide Child*!" Solemn Muffaz scooped up Gavith and flung the boy over his shoulder and Cwell helped Joron up. As they turned they saw the rapidly advancing hill of water in the distance that marked the keyshan's approach. Glancing back to see the toothreach behind them, venting mist, the air filling with a new sound, an unpleasant basso hum, and then they were running across the slate. The plank between *Keyshanpike* and *Tide Child* lost, ropes were flung, hands outstretched, and still the hill of water came upon them, and *Tide Child* rose and rose, *Keyshanpike* following it, the sudden tilting of the deck scattering Joron and the deckchilder before they made it to their own ship. A deckchild fell from low in *Tide Child*'s rigging, hit the deck of *Keyshanpike* and tumbled past Joron as the deck tilted further and further. He reached out, hand grabbing at cloth, a momentary wrench on his shoulder, the deckchilder swinging round. The face of the bonewright Colwulf staring up at him, her mouth open in an "O", and then he could no longer hold on and Colwulf tumbled away down the crazily tilted deck, body smashing into the bonerail, bouncing over it before it fell into the water.

Below them passed the vast body of the keyshan: long beak, fiery white eyes, ice-blue body in the ice-blue water, almost a part of it. As it passed beneath the two ships the hill of water pushed before the sea dragon passed and the two ships fell into the trough, screaming and moaning as hulls were forced together, the sound of smashing varisk and gion as the spines entangled, rigging and spars falling from above in a heavy lethal rain, cracking the slate; and yet Joron did not raise a hand to try and protect himself, he was mesmerised by that body passing beneath and by the huge tail propelling the arakeesian through the water.

It dived. A twist so quick it made the thing seem small, a turning of its body as it went into the depths. The toothreach let out their mournful basso call.

"D'keeper, we must get to *Tide Child*," said Solemn Muffaz, once more picking up the limp body of Gavith.

"Ey," he said, stumbling for the rail, touching his temple and finding his fingers bloody. *Tide Child*'s deck's was havoc, the for'ard rail ripped away and hanging from the hooked and serrated hull of *Keyshanpike*. Rope hanging from above like vines in the gion forest in full growth, deckchilder gathering up fallen spars under the eye of Farys.

"Don't throw it over, you fools, we have little enough stores as is!" she shouted. Broken material piling against the base of the spines. Then Joron, Solemn Muffaz, Cwell and Gavith, still unconscious and held by the deckmother, were being shouted at to cross the gap between the two ships, to time their leaps for the moments when the two ships were closest, the ocean seeming to breathe in and out as if recovering from the passage of the great beast that had vanished into its depths and distracted the toothreach.

"D'keeper, jump!" Hands held out to him as the ships came together, some missing fingers, some gnarled with the Hag's Kiss, some brown some white or of the many colours in between and all beckoning him on to their safety. He threw himself across, grabbed by many, pulled onto the deck. Turning as the ships once more parted. Leaving behind Cwell, and Solemn Muffaz with the limp body of Gavith over his shoulder. Behind them the sea. Rising once more and within in it a writhing black shape, a bilious yellow eye. A toothreach. Tentacles wrapping round *Keyshanpike* once more.

And the keyshan returned.

The ocean a flowering bud, splitting apart around the rotten fruit of the toothreach, the beak of the keyshan as a white stamen, the water as petals. The ear-splittingly loud sounding of the keyshan as it rose beneath the toothreach, burning white eyes closed against whipping tentacles. The *hoooom* of the toothreach taken within the jaws. More tentacles, ripping through the air, wrapping tightly around *Keyshanpike*, pulling the ship away from *Tide Child*.

"Catch!" shouted Solemn Muffaz. "Catch the boy!" And with a great heave he threw Gavith across the widening gap, limp body flopping through the air like a dead fish, crashing down among the throng waiting on *Tide Child*'s deck as *Keyshanpike* was pulled away by the water. Bones groaned and complained as the tangled spines and spars of the two ships pulled apart and crashed back together. Once, twice, three times. He saw Gavith taken below. Deckchilder staggering down the deck tossed about by the sudden violent movement of the sea between the ships in the moment before they slammed back together again.

Like his father's body ground between the hulls.

"Cut those spines loose!"

Beak open, rising and rising, pulling on the ships. The terrible grinding of bone on bone.

"Cut us loose, Hag curse you!"

Deckchilder running up the rigging with axes and curnows. On *Keyshanpike* Solemn Muffaz stood, ready to meet his fate when the boneship was ripped away from the black ship. Behind him the Keyshan started to fall back into the water, shaking its massive head as black tentacles crawled over its body, ripping away clouds of its thick feathery coating that fell around them like snow.

"Muffaz! Cwell!" shouted Joron. "The ships will crash together again, be ready to jump!" Cwell jumped, made it just as the keyshan smashed down into the ocean, but the tentacles of the toothreach, anchored around the spines of *Keyshanpike*, refused to let go. With a further scream of protesting bones *Keyshanpike*'s for'ard spine was ripped from its mooring, the tops of the rear and mainspine also ripped from their places, and then the giant wave of the keyshan's landing hit the side of both ships.

"Brace!" shouted Joron, "Brace for your lives!" Rigging, spars and deckchilder rained down on the deck as *Tide Child*'s own topspars, tangled once more with *Keyshanpike*'s, were ripped away. The ships pulled apart, crashed together again, and Joron saw Solemn Muffaz thrown to the deck of the stricken ship. A howling wind sprang up and battered the two ships as the waves of the keyshan hitting the sea crashed over *Keyshanpike*, shoving it against *Tide Child*. "Get up Muffaz! Mother curse you!" he shouted. Joron heard the cracking of bone, the screaming of women and men. Saw Solemn Muffaz push himself up, take his jump and Joron thought he would not make it until a huge wave rushed over *Keyshanpike*'s deck, picking the big man up and throwing him onto the slate of *Tide Child*. Behind him the keyshan twisted in the water, the currents created dragging the two ships apart again. Behind the keyshan the second toothreach's massive body seemed to dissolve into something long and thin, elongating and stretching its tentacles out, writhing through the water at alarming speed toward the keyshan.

"Call the Gullaime!" shouted Joron. "Raise whatever wings we can, if we don't get away we'll be crushed as they fight."

"Ey, D'keeper," was shouted from a hundred throats as the ragged *Tide Child* was thrown around in the currents, directionless. Joron ran up the heaving slate, shouting for Barlay and the Gullaime. Finding the big steerswoman already there, fighting the steering oar with Farys, soaked to the skin by waves of freezing water. The keyshan sounded again, deafening, a hundred thousand different tones that caused the toothreach in its mouth to go limp, its tentacles to let go of *Keyshanpike* – though the boneship was beyond help, half below the water, leaning so crazily Joron knew it lost.

The second toothreach attacked the keyshan just as the first of *Tide Child*'s wings fell into position. Joron saw the tentacles open, imagined thousands of tiny pulsing mouths latching on to the keyshan at the moment the massive sea dragon was about to bite down on the toothreach in its mouth. Instead the keyshan opened its mouth and screamed, a different sound, one full of pain, or maybe outrage, that woke the toothreach held in its jaws, vicious tentacles reaching out.

"Wind," shouted Joron, "we need wind! Where is the Gullaime?"

"Here here." The windtalker waddled down the deck, seemingly unaware of the carnage and chaos and screeching as three vast bodies churned the water around them into froth.

"Quickly Gullaime! Wind! Our need is fierce!"

The windtalker stopped in front of Joron, the mask covering its eyes fixed on him.

"Bring wind," it said, then yarked and croaked and whirled

before shouting into the air. The wind came at its call. The familiar pressure in Joron's ears, the heat crossing the deck and the gale following it. *Tide Child*'s wings caught the wind and the ship's beak came around to face the way they had come and the mist was blown from their course.

"For'ard!" shouted Joron at Barlay and they set the steering oar. Behind them the keyshan lurched from the sea, water falling over the black ship as it shook its massive head from side to side. Two writhing black shapes wrapped around the sea dragon, one around its middle, one around the head. Blood ran from where the tentacles were locked about it. For a moment Joron thought the great beast would fall on *Tide Child*, killing them all, but the keyshan fell to landward of them, its huge body crashing onto on an ice island, sending up a wave that pushed *Tide Child* toward the ice island on the other side of the channel. The keyshan shook its head back and forth, smashing the toothreach in its jaws repeatedly against the ice so hard that more waves sprang from the bottom of the ice island and buffeted *Tide Child*.

"Gullaime," shouted Joron, "blow us away from the shore!" The wind changed, counteracting the waves as the toothreach went limp in the keyshan's mouth, though the great sea dragon continued to smash the beast against the ice until something burst and black ichor spattered over the black ship, burning where it touched skin.

"Onwards!" shouted Joron, pointing forward. "Onwards!" *Tide Child* shuddered and the wind renewed, howling over the deck as the massive body of the keyshan behind them rolled off the island, still wrapped in the searching, biting tentacles of the second toothreach. "Brace!" he shouted and the keyshan hit the water, the resulting wave forcing *Tide Child* sideways again, crashing into the ice island to landward, and the hull screamed and screeched as it scraped along the ice. "Gaffs! Push us off the ice!" he shouted, fighting to keep his feet as the ship was slammed once more against the island and he feared for the hull, feared for the underdecks. Had visions of giant holes in the boneboard, of the keel snapped in two. "Someone go below and check the hull, make sure the pumps are crewed!" Before the gaffs could push *Tide Child* away the backwash from the waves did the work. Crew stumbled at the erratic movement but the ship was loose, though a sorry sight: missing topmasts and all the crew that had been in them, bonerails smashed, trailing rigging and rope, but he still moved, still floated. The keyshan and the remaining toothreach were locked in an embrace as the sea dragon gulped down the remains of the first beast.

"Look to for'ard!" came the shout. Joron did, and where the two ice islands were closest a third toothreach blocked the way, venting mist and staring forward with its baleful yellow eye.

"Gullaime," shouted Joron over the rending and screaming and howling wind, "give us as much wind as you can, the ship is the only weapon we have. We'll ram that Hag-cursed thing."

"But D'keeper . . ." began Farys.

"We have no other choice!" The Gullaime shook its head, lifted its bright crest and then made a noise so loud it hurt Joron's ears. A harder, faster, stronger wind came. *Tide Child* creaked and groaned alarmingly and the beast before them vented mist and let out a low, disturbing *hoom*. "Ready!" shouted Joron and the toothreach loomed above the deck of the broken ship as they sped toward it. "Ready!" Then, at the last, in the second when *Tide Child* would have crashed into the beast, it used its tentacles to climb the walls of the ice islands to each side. Screaming and *hoom*ing it passed over the ship, a mass of writhing tentacles, each one covered in small, grasping mouths. Thinner tentacles fell from it, writhing over the decks, and there were screams as deckchilder were grabbed. Shouts of fury as others hacked at the black ropes, and then the thing was gone, ten crew with it and it dropped into the water behind them with a great splash and made a direct line for the keyshan, joining the fight between the titans behind them.

And *Tide Child*, broken, smashed and limping, made his escape.

The Song of Lucky Meas

She worked her way to shipwife
A child of tide and wa-ter
Hard and bold she rose
The sea it was her sither.
But her mother tret her cruel
Said, "The babe, it should have died."

Thirteenbern called out
"Give the child to the ships!"
And the sea came to her rescue
As word left the Bern's lips.

PART II
THE SHIPWIFE

20

Those Who are Cursed to Know the Future

Waves as monuments. Vast and cold, brutal, and ugly. Waves washing over all sound and sight and sense. Waves leaving you breathless. Waves leaving you gasping. Unstoppable, agonising waves.

The hands coming closer and she tries to shy away, turning her head, straining the muscles in her neck, pushing her cheek against the hard wood of the chair. The desperate need to escape the coming pain meeting her own stubborn need to deny this woman anything. Waves crashing in her throat, they drown any sense. The noise that comes out of her mouth is a guttural "Nnn, nnn, nnn" as she stretches and the bindings holding her tight dig into her wrists and ankles.

"Come, come, Meas," says the hagpriest. "Do not worry, do not fear. I will not hurt you today." Words that mean nothing. Nothing.

How many times has she said that before, only to change her mind and bring out the wrap of tools and cast Meas into the sea of red, drowning in the agony of pincers and blades and hot metal? "Come, Meas, be good and do as I ask." So gentle and soft and yet she cannot. Only when the last word comes, a harsh bark – "Behave!" – does she stop struggling. Give in. Let her muscles relax and her body sag in the wooden chair stained dark by what feels like a lifetime of shed blood. Her blood.

Gentle hands unwrap the bandages around her head. The woman talking all the while.

"I only wish to look at the cavity, Meas. To ensure there is no infection." A smile. "It would not do to be losing you now, would it? When we are so close to our goal?"

"I've told you everything I know." Beaten words fall from her lips. The bandage pulls away from her face, skin sticky with dried blood and the unguents they have treated her with after . . .

Just after.

"It's remarkable really, how well the socket is healing. Losing an eye has killed more than one who I've been through it with. But they were weak. And you were not weak, were you? You were a strong woman." The hagpriest sits back. Smiles at her. "You've been a real challenge."

"I've told you everything I know."

"The other eye though," she says, "that's where the real truth lies." She sits up straighter on her stool. "Because you know the pain now, but you not only have the pain to fear. You have the fear of being completely blinded." She leans forward. "You must be frightened that I will take the other eye, surely?"

Is she?

Maybe. But pain no longer holds any fear, it is her life now. Her every day and maybe it always has been. And a life of darkness? Well, what does she have to look at here? She knows the hagpriest wants her to say yes but she isn't really frightened, not any more. Fear has passed, been burned away along with the hope of anyone taking pity or turning up to save her. She is nothing now, a husk. A dead woman without even the comfort of a black ship's slate to stand on or the Hag's fire to warm her.

"Yes," she says.

"Good, that fear will save you a lot of pain." A hand takes her hair, pulls her head back. A knife point wavers in front of her eye.

"Now, unless you want to join the gullaime, stumbling blindly about with a leaf mask over your face, then tell me the truth. How do you raise a keyshan?"

A tear runs from her one good eye.

"Joron Twiner. Joron Twiner and the Gullaime aboard *Tide Child* – the one they call Windseer – they have that power, not I. It is the truth, I can say nothing else. You must believe me." A moment, the pressure on her hair increases until she expects the hagpriest to tear it out. The knife comes closer.

Then it is gone, her hair released.

"I do," says the hagpriest, and she picks up a damp cloth, cleans her slender hands with it. "I do believe you. So we won't be meeting quite as often." She puts the cloth down. "We still will be meeting, don't you worry about that." She leans in close and puts a cold hand on Meas's cheek.

"Just end this," says Meas. The hagpriest's face twists in confusion.

"End this? Now? Oh Meas, you are too important to be ended." She leans in close, to whisper like a lover into her ear. "There are people who will do anything for you. Anything. Such loyalty, such love." She leans back and turns, picking up some clean bandage and wadding. "And that makes you important to us. I will be taking the best care of you now. The best. And who knows, Meas, maybe soon you will have some company?"

21

No Safe Harbour for the Dead

Joron sat with Brekir on the great grey blocks of Sparehaven harbour in the Gaunt Islands, both as miserable as a pair of shipwives could be. *Tide Child* sat before them, propped up by bone and stone on the dry dock, and if ever a ship had looked sadder than *Tide Child* Joron had never seen it.

"He looks," said Brekir, "as though you fought every ship the Hundred Isles had then found some others to fight afterwards, and came off worst in every battle."

Joron smiled to himself beneath the cover on his face, felt the sores sting. There was both humour and truth in Brekir's words. What she said was true; poor *Tide Child* had sprung bones in his hull, his three spines were cut down by half, his wings ripped. It had taken all they had to limp back to Sparehaven, leaking and wallowing, creaking and snapping, and not one member of the crew ever getting to rest for long days and longer weeks. Now the ship sat there, black paint flaking away to expose the yellowing bone below, awaiting permission from Tenbern Aileen, leader of the Gaunt Islands, for work to start on him to restore some of his glory.

"I tell you, Brekir, I would face every ship in the Thirteenbern's fleet with my bare hands if it meant I never saw a toothreach again. I have never seen such a thing. I would rather have faced the ghosts of the dead that Farys was sure waited in the mist."

"But now all are talking about how a keyshan saved you, Joron. So long you have tried to keep your secret but now it is out." Joron let out a short laugh, almost a cough.

"How unfair, Brekir, that I have spent so much time guarding my secret, never singing to the keyshans when they may have helped, and now the secret is out by pure bad luck."

"You did not call it then?" she said, and he shook his head.

"For truth, I did not even consider it. I was so scared I could barely move. I think the creature was simply hunting."

"Or watching out for you."

He shook his head. "No, I do not think it even knew we were there. Had it rolled a little to landward, breached and fallen a little to seaward then I would dine with the Hag now and *Tide Child* would lie in pieces at the bottom of the sea." They sat a little in silence, listening to the skeers call. "But that will not matter, word will get out."

"Well, Joron, let us put keyshans aside and look to our present predicament," said Brekir. "Do you wish the good news or the bad news?"

"What news could be worse, than that bad luck may have doomed the shipwife?"

"Joron," said Brekir, putting a hand on his arm, "remember, any talk of a keyshan's rising on your word must escape Sparehaven first, then make its way across the sea to Bernshulme."

"Ey," said Joron and he picked a bit of grit from the stone they sat on, threw it at a scavenging kivelly which ran from them squawking its dismay, causing panic in its flock which swiftly followed it down into their burrows. "We have a little time, that is all. But I have heard nothing that will help us find Meas from those I pay, and the Tenbern will not see me. Word will get back."

"Then," she said, "should we not concentrate on what we

can control, rather than peer into the mists of the future and worry about what we cannot?"

"Huh," he nodded to himself. "What does it come to when gloomy Brekir must cheer me?" He stretched aching muscles. "Well if you have bad news then I would have that medicine sugared, if you will, Shipwife," said Joron.

"The good news is we can afford to refit *Tide Child*, and supply our fleet."

"And the bad news?"

"It will cost us every coin we have taken from every raid and every battle; there will be nothing left after. The Gaunt Islanders know we have nowhere else to go and charge accordingly." Joron lifted his one-tail and scratched at his forehead where some insect had bitten him.

"We can always take more."

"Taking has become harder and harder, Joron, you know that. Our fleet has gone from twenty to twelve in the last four raids. We must go further to find targets, and those targets are better protected. Thirteenbern Gilbryn makes a ring of hard bone around what she has left. If we continue as we are, we will break upon it."

Joron sat up a little straighter on the rock they perched upon. Let out a sigh at this unpleasant truth. He almost spoke, almost said something then realised there was little to be said and changed the subject.

"How are our people?" he asked. Brekir shrugged.

"As expected. The Gaunt Islanders treat them with suspicion, overcharge them for food and choose them last for employment. Even when they find work it is the jobs no one else wants. There have been fights between them and us, and we must be harsher with our people than they are with theirs, as we are guests. There is growing resentment on both sides." She leaned in closer to him. "Until now, we have eased that resentment with money, but to refit our fleet and fix *Tide Child*, that will leave us no longer able to do so."

"Meas once told me there are only hard choices for a shipwife."

"Then you will finally take up the two-tail?" she asked, and he felt a sudden shock, a sudden coldness. A sudden shame at his words, that he had put himself in Meas's place.

"No, Brekir, a figure of speech is all." She nodded her head, but didn't look at him. "There must be ways we can save money."

"There is one main one."

"What is that?"

"*Tide Child*," she said.

"What of it?"

"That is where the bulk of our coin goes. We could buy a new ship for two thirds of what they will charge us to refit him."

"There are no new ships," he said.

"Not yet," said Brekir, and she did not look at him. "The other option is not to fix him fully. Make him watertight, ey. But you can move your command to another ship. Take Chiver's vessel, his crew can barely stand him and would welcome it. Then we move our people onto *Tide Child* and use him for transport."

He thought on that. Knew it sensible and stout advice. He watched the harbour front. Four other ships sat in dry dock, all surrounded by Gaunt Island bonewrights finding and fixing their faults. Out in the harbour were twenty boneships of various sizes, all busy with crew and women and men. But around *Tide Child* was a circle of silence. He was becalmed. A haven of inactivity born out of the unwillingness of their hosts.

"I have been here before, Brekir," he said, pointing at the broken ship. "Meas brought him back to Bernshulme with his keel broken. Most would have written him off then, I think. Written the crew off. Written me off. But she did not." He took a deep breath. "She rebuilt him." He pointed at the sorry ship. "She rebuilt me, Brekir. He rebuilt the crew. And when she returns, she will return to the slate of her own ship, not find him some sorry hulk full of stonebound using his bilges as a dump for their filth and rubbish."

Brekir smiled at him, a flash of broken teeth in her face. Then she ran a hand down her face, from her forehead to her chin.

"I knew you would say that, but I at least had to try and talk some sense to you."

"Will you tell me Meas is probably dead next?"

"Of course not," she said, "for I know you would not listen." She smiled again. "You must get in to see the Tenbern, Joron."

"I will try again this evening," he said.

"Do not simply *try*; take Solemn Muffaz, Barlay, Farys, Mevans, and some of your seaguard. Turn up as if you intend violence if she will not let you in."

"She could crush us," he said. "She has enough soldiers on this island to do so without thinking."

"She will not," said Brekir. "Our people may be unpopular interlopers, but you are becoming a legend. The Black Pirate, the rock upon which the Hundred Isles breaks its ships. Tenbern Aileen is not foolish, she will not want to kill you in front of her people while they still hold you in esteem."

"What about when I am no longer in front of her people?"

"Well, then she may kill you," laughed Brekir, "but at least you will have got in, ey?"

"Ey," he said, and stood, brushing sand and grit from his trousers and causing the small flock of kively that had returned to once again go running back to their holes in the sea wall. "And what is life for us if we are not lurching from one life-or-death situation to another?"

He left Brekir sitting by the harbour watching his ship and made his way to the drinking hole his crew had taken over and occupied in shifts. The rowdy room quietened as he entered.

"Will no one bring me a drink?" he said, and one was brought and he sat in the corner alone, thinking of what he would do and what he must do and how no course seemed like a good one. Little by little, he became aware that he was dampening the mood of the place. That the usual rowdiness he heard in passing was gone. Oh, his women and men still drank, still talked, only more soberly and less freely. A game was afoot at one table, Black Orris perched above them, and bets were being taken on whether the corpsebird would say "arse" or "Hag's breath" or one of his other foul-mouthed utterances when a scrap of food was offered up to him. Joron knew it for a rowdy game, usually, but this was verging on polite and it seemed barely any fun at all was being had. His fault, he knew it. He stood.

"When Skearith's Eye dips beneath the high peak," he said to the room, "send Mevans, Barlay, Farys, Solemn Muffaz and ten seaguard to my quarters."

"Ey, D'keeper," said a small woman – Vinsa, one of the best up the spines. She had a scrap of bread for Black Orris in her hand and had taken the bet on Orris saying "arse". "I will do that."

"Thank you," he said. "I will leave you to your games now." He left, and as he did he heard Black Orris call out, "Arse!" And though he was saddened that his place meant he must always be alone among his crew, he was glad, at least, that Vinsa had won the coin.

Later, he met his small party.

"Where is Farys?" he asked Mevans.

"Took sick, D'keeper," he said.

"Very well, best she stay abed then," he said, and they headed up to the Tenbern's bothy. Twilight had descended and the warm air was full of the strong, heady fragrance of night flowers just opening. They did not call their larger buildings bothies here, they called them "stonehouses" but he could not stop himself thinking of them as bothies, it was ingrained in him. He found the Gaunt Islands strange, so similar to the Hundred Isles in many ways, and so different in many others. The buildings, for instance, were not rounded as he was used to, with no rising tenements of soft stone and varisk. All was grey. The Gaunt Islanders had access to stone islands, like Sleighthulme, but many more of them. They quarried a hard grey stone and they built hard grey buildings, rising tall from the harbour and up into the hills. The buildings had small slits for windows, the architecture of the colder north where the Gaunt Islanders had originally had their capital, built to stand against the Northstorm. Sparehaven was definitely no Bernshulme, no mad riot of streets here, not organic and untrammelled. Bernshulme architecture was created by Hundred Isles people without thought or plan as they explored the island and the places to live on it. When the Gaunt Islanders had moved their capital they had done it with a ruthless efficiency and Sparehaven reflected that. Its streets were built upon a grid pattern; wide roads led from the grand stonehouses at the top – which held their fleet training, Bern, Kept and hagpriests – down to the harbour, allowing easy transport of goods and stores and people through the town and into the market squares. The lesser people lived in tenements that were simply smaller versions of the grander buildings.

Joron did not like the place, he found it as cold and hard and unforgiving as the people that lived there.

Though, of course, now he counted himself and his people among them. Though they did not truly live in Sparehaven; the majority of those who had run from the Hundred Isles, or declared for him in the Gaunt Islands, made camp on the other side of the island, together with a flock of about a hundred gullaime – thirty windtalkers and seventy windshorn – in addition to those that served on his ships.

"Do you think it is right to walk through Sparehaven armed, D'keeper?" said Mevans. "It will win us no friends."

"We need answers, Mevans," he said. "And we need to be moving, doing something. It is even more important now that the rumour I called a keyshan to us is out. It will fly from here to Bernshulme quicker than a brisk south wind, and it will doom Meas." Mevans nodded.

"We will follow you then," he said, and they did. Joron led them through the streets, and the people of Sparehaven – more mixed than Bernshulme, not quite as pushed into strata by their deformities as Joron was used to – regarded him and his party with suspicion, though also with some excitement too: he saw how they pointed and whispered at him. The Black Pirate, striding through their town, swathed in scarf, dark clothes and hat, bone spur clacking on the cobbled roads. Not one of them knew that he worried with every step that he would slip and make a fool of himself. That he worried he would slip constantly, whether on land or sea, though less physically and more in his duty. Always waiting to fall.

They arrived outside the Grand Stonehouse. The Tenbern's seaguard barred their way – women and men in her seaguard, another small difference to how the Hundred Isles was, though his own seaguard were mixed now. The Gaunt Islander seaguard's leader, a small woman with a missing hand, would never have had such a place in the Hundred Isles.

"What do 'ee want 'ere, Black One?" She spoke with a strong accent, often affected here by those with position in society.

"What I want every time I visit, Seaguard, to speak to the Tenbern."

"Tha usually comes alone; a see tha now brought friends." She gestured with her missing hand at his party.

"Ey, I do. Merely so the Tenbern understands how serious I am, that I intend to see her today."

"You threaten blood?"

"I ask to be seen, I think it is the least I deserve for the havoc I have wrought on the sea for her."

"For her?" chuckled the seaguard. "There's some'd be fooled by that, Black One, not I. Tha wait 'ere and I will speak with my lady." She looked over his crew. "Trouble not my guard," she said, "for thar only act on my word. Be patient." With that she vanished into the gloomy building.

"What happens, D'keeper," whispered Mevans, "if she comes back with fifty more seaguard and a thirst for blood?" He could hear the grin in Mevans's voice; like all the crew, he had an odd lust for violence. Joron also felt that draw on occasion and he knew it for foolish, as no doubt Mevans did.

"We die," he said. Mevans's looked about, at the cold, grey angular stone, and the hard-faced guards pointing spears at them. A drizzle was falling, and the smell of night flowers had been replaced by old fish.

She came back alone, appearing from the blackness of the building's interior.

"She will see tha, Black One," said the seaguard, "but only tha, the rest must wait here." She pointed at the floor with the arm missing a hand, in case he was unsure where she meant.

"Of course," he said, "and do you want my weapon?"

"Forward, that is." She leered at him and grinned, making him feel uncomfortable. "Would be good to say I sheathed the Black Pirate's weapon, ey?" When he didn't answer she chuckled once more, letting it die away when he did not join her ribaldry. "Not one for humour is tha? No, Black One, I do not think I need to take tha sword, keep it. If you try to unsheathe it in the Tenbern's presence tha will not live to bare the metal fully." She turned away from him. "Now come."

He followed, into the darkness, through a small false hallway that opened out into a reception hall far bigger and more airy, lit by thousands of wanelights. Glowing eyes surveying him as the seaguard led him up a wide staircase that curved around, it was far less utilitarian than the rest of Sparehaven, not pretty, but some effort had gone into it. On the second floor, more seaguard eyed him warily. On the third floor a pair of large gion doors waited, seaguard before them with burning lanterns and pikes. They opened the way into the presence of the Tenbern. He took a deep breath; though Joron would never admit it, the woman frightened him.

Like the room of the Thirteenbern in Bernshulme, the Tenbern's receiving room was almost empty, though it lacked the light of the Bernshulme bothy. This was a dark place, lit by flickering torches and dim wanelights that peered through the gloom. The Tenbern sat at the end of a path of torches on a simple and unornamented chair, not for her the showy misery of a throne carved with the images of dead children. Hers was an austere authority. She dressed in very little, despite that it was cold in this room. A simple skirt fell over her knees to cover her feet. A fur coat fell around her shoulders but left her stomach and chest bare to show the marks of her battles and all the scars and wounds of childbirth. Her hair was cut to hang so it only brushed the fur of the cloak, straight and grey, and the face beneath it was unornamented with paint or expression, stark as the grey rock. He took off his hat, held it in his hands.

"Joron Twiner," she said quietly. "It has been a while since we spoke, aye?"

"Too long, Tenbern."

"And yet, tha repays my hospitality by bringing arms to me door."

"That was not my intention, Tenbern. I simply walked with a retinue as befits my station."

She smiled then, a real smile, that lit up her face like storm-light – golden, beautiful, and threatening.

"Tha plays politics and brinkship, man, and I knows it. But I 'ave played that game far longer than tha has and I know it too. I reckon also, man, that I play it better and harder, when my hand is forced."

"Then," he said slowly, "I apologise for any insult you may imagine I brought to your door."

"Used tha popularity, and it was a clever thing to do." Then she sat forward, her bird-of-prey eyes on him. "Tha is popular, among my people. Brought us victories with little loss of life, and though my shipwives curse you, I think thar are glad of it also. But jealous too. And, should tha die, Joron Twiner, do it out there." She pointed straight out the building, through the walls and over the horizon. "Do it about and on the sea, for then I will make tha a legend. But push me, and die on the swords of my fellows, then tha popularity will not last, and them raggedy people tha chose to protect will be cut adrift and sure to drown. Understand?"

"Ey, Tenbern."

"Good." She sat back. "It is good to be sure where tha stands in a place, Shipmother Twiner."

"I am not—"

"I do not care what tha thinks, I will call what is. Tha leads a fleet and tha commands a ship, tha is Shipmother. Tha is shipwife."

"It is about my shipwife that I come." She shrugged, leaned to the side and rubbed her face.

"Do not a hanker after what is lost, when tha has power in tha own hands."

"She is not lost," he said. "We know where she is – Bernshulme, if not exactly where in the town. I know you have spies throughout the Hundred Isles, surely they have reported something by now."

"Little sign or speak of her. Thar either hide her good or thar have killed her."

"No," he said, too sharp, and the Tenbern's head shot round, skewered him in her gaze.

"I had wondered why tha was so sure she lived. I have heard rumour and talk of thar who raise keyshans, put it down to fancy and foolishness. But then I hear one comes to tha rescue, and maybe I put one or two things together Joron Twiner. 'Tis it, that the Thirteenbern think tha shipwife can raise the beasts? 'Tis that why she lives still? But is the truth that it is tha who has the power?" It seemed to Joron that the temperature in the room rose a little. And in the corner of his eyes he saw movement in the gloom, realised there were seaguard there, waiting, watching. Had they been there all along? He had been too intent on the woman before him and the aura of power and beauty around her, as obvious as her fur cloak. *Step careful, Joron,* he thought, *or your journey could end in a cell in Sparehaven.*

"There are those in the Hundred Isles who believe a woman or man can raise keyshans and they are hungry for that power. Meas simply used that hunger against them so her fleet and people could escape Sleighthulme, she offered herself as sacrifice. A keyshan turned up in Spantonnis Bank and that saved us, it is true. But it had no interest in us, it was interested in filling its belly, that is all. We were lucky to escape its wrath. Hold me here if you must, but you will reveal yourself as gullible as Thirteenbern Gilbryn if you do."

She stared at him, rubbing her chin with her hand.

"Maybe, Shipmother, it would simply be careful of me, to hold tha here?"

"But, Tenbern, if you imprison me and I can call the keyshans, what would stop me calling them for help? And what would happen to Sparehaven then?"

She continued to stare at him. Then laughed.

"Hag-cursed if I do, Hag-cursed if I don't, aye?"

"No," he said, took a step forward, became more aware of the shapes in the corners, more sure of them as seaguard. The Tenbern held up her hand, stilling her soldiers. "You told me if I weakened Gilbryn, you would move against her. Now is that time."

"I did, aye," she nodded. "But in truth, Shipmother," she made the title sound mocking now, "I did not think tha would survive past a couple of weeks." She chuckled, then pointed at him. "All credit to tha for doing so." She sat back, set her fur cape more firmly around her shoulders. "We will move in, take what islands we can. But Gilbryn is no fool, she has withdrawn her ships, made a ring of stone around Bernshulme and what else she knows is valuable. I'll not throw my ships against stone, Twiner. I am no fool."

"You promised me."

"Well, mayhap I did, but now I must break that promise, I am afraid. Not only cos I have no wish to waste my ships, tha understand. I have given much thought. And truthfully, I were tempted to beard Gilbryn in her lair, even knowing the cost. But my spies tell me a plague has hit Bernshulme and I have no wish to bring it here. So I will let thar wallow, Twiner. And maybe, if the plague weakens them to the point thar have so few ships that ring of stone crumbles, I will take action then. But until then, my fleet and my people take precedence, does tha understand?"

"You promised," he said again, the anger within him burning, but he knew to unleash it was to die. Tenbern Aileen leaned forward.

"Tha does not understand our ways, pirate. A promise to an outsider means nothing here. Even less when it puts my people in danger."

"You have—"

She raised a hand, silenced him.

"Tell me, Shipmother, that tha would do different? Cast tha people unto death when there is no real need nor benefit for tha, bar request of a rot-pocked stranger?" He stared at her. His anger eaten up by the cold shock of finding out that she knew his carefully hidden secret. And he knew she spoke true. He risked his people only when he must. "You should leave, Twiner," she said, "afore tha says something tha would regret." He stood there, unwilling to move, wanting the last word but having nothing in his mind, no clever turn of phrase to turn her to his cause. Meas would have, he was sure. Meas would not slink away with her tail between her legs.

But he was not Meas.

He placed his hat on his head, and made to leave.

"One thing, Shipmother," said the Tenbern, "I would not have tha think I am ungrateful. If tha can bring Gilbryn's fleet out from her ring of stone, and away from her plagued island, then I will meet it head-on and smash her pretty ships into shards for tha." She stared at him. "Is that enough for tha to feel less slighted?"

"I suppose it must be," he said.

"Ey," she said quietly, "tha suppose right."

22

The Solitude of Command

Joron sat in his room above a rowdy drinking hole, his meagre possessions – he had sold almost everything he had to re-outfit *Tide Child* – lit by two guttering wanelights. He felt cast adrift, lost. All he had done had been in pursuit of finding Meas. Either getting good intelligence, and freeing her that way, or having the Tenbern lead her fleet against Bernshulme and finding Meas through strength.

Now he had neither option.

A knock on the door.

"Ey?" he said quietly, and tried to hide his despair.

"It is the courser, D'keeper," said Cwell from outside.

"Let them in, Cwell," he said. He pulled up the mask to cover the sores on his face, even though of all the crew, Gullaime apart, the courser was the closest to anything he could call friend and equal. They both existed outside the usual groups and cliques. The door opened and Aelerin slipped in, robe as pristine white as ever, hood covering their features.

"Deckkeeper," they said.

"Courser," he replied, "how may I help?" No answer came, but in every line and movement of the navigator he could read their discomfort. It was clear that whatever course the words they had would set, it was not a comfortable one to Aelerin. "The crew have sent you, to find out what was said by the Tenbern, have they not?" The hood moved as Aelerin nodded, their posture relaxed a little now that Joron had chosen to broach the subject, rather than being forced to bring it up. "Well," he said, and shut his logbook, "I do not blame them for their curiosity, I understand it. Though," he let his finger trace the keyshan worked into the birdleather of the logbook's cover, "I do not think they will be glad to hear what I have to tell them."

"The Tenbern has let us down?"

"Ey, and I cannot blame her, she has done what is right for her people. Why send them to die for just one woman and a crew of criminals and rogues?"

"Powerful people, Deckkeeper, simply throw away those such as us when we are used up. She has no wish for the war to end, it is how she holds her power."

"You would not say that if you had met her, Aelerin. I think she has no problem holding on to her power." He scratched at his scarf and the sores underneath. Had a sudden irrational desire to lash out at someone, but not Aelerin. They did not deserve it, and his words would hurt them more than most. He dug his nails into the palms of his hand. Was that desire for violence simply frustration, or was the rot reaching his brain, twisting his thoughts? "She has told me, if I can get Gilbryn's fleet out of the defensive ring she has set up in the Hundred Isles, she will bring everything she has against it."

"And that is why you sit up here, to plan?"

He nodded. "But it is all for naught, Aelerin," he said. "How do I draw out Thirteenbern Gilbryn, ey? What do I have that she wants?"

"Us," said Aelerin.

"A few ships will not draw her out."

"What about all of us? Our brownbones, our boneships, everything?"

"She may consider it then," he said, eyes flicking to a place in the future where his ships sat at sea trying to tempt out the Hundred Isles fleet. Then he shook his head. "No," he said, "the trap is too obvious. Why would I parade my fleet for her to see if I did not want her to come out? She will suspect something and depending on how much she has learned from . . ." He let his voice tail off when he realised what he was about to do. To acknowledge what all thought, that after so long in her mother's unkind company Meas would have cracked by now. That she would have told the truth. "If rumour of what happened in Spantonnis Bank has reached her, then she would not come to meet me for fear of a keyshan rising and dashing her fleet to shards."

"Then you must take the only other thing she desires from her, and make her chase you."

"And what is that, Aelerin?"

"Meas, of course."

He stared at the courser, then laughed.

"And how do you suggest I do that?" They shrugged. "I hardly think Bernshulme will welcome *Tide Child* into their harbour so I can look around."

"I am no tactician, Joron, but there is talk of plague in Bernshulme. Such things create confusion. Set your fleet to tempting the Thirteenbern from her town and all eyes will be on it. None will expect you to come into the town."

"But we do not know where she is," said Joron, and as he spoke the door opened.

"D'keeper," said Cwell.

"Ey?"

"I could not help but hear what you talked of, and if I may make a suggestion?"

"Of course, Cwell."

"If you wish to know where the shipwife is," she said, "then ask her mother."

Joron laughed, so taken aback he could do nothing else. Then he realised that Cwell was deadly serious.

"You mean it," he said.

"She will not expect it, and if all is lost, as you say, then a desperate gamble is the only play to make. For we are desperate." He stared at her, then looked to Aelerin, expecting them to waver a little but they held his gaze as well.

"You agree with this, Aelerin?"

"If we have no other option," they said.

He looked from the courser to the small fierce woman in the doorway, and back again. "How I would get in to see her, I do not know."

"I am no stranger to getting into places where I am not wanted, Deckkeeper," said Cwell. "In my other life, anyway." He stared at her, wondering if she mocked him but she did not. She offered her help in a desperate moment, and did it in all good faith.

"Very well, we can at least consider it. Bring me Jennil—"

"The toothreach took Jennil, D'keeper," said Cwell.

"Of course," he said, and for a moment wondered whether his mistake was a symptom of the rot, eating at his brain as well as his body. "Well, we must make plans and hope there is some way to do what we wish. Find me my shipwives, not all of them though. Bring Brekir, Coult, Adrantchi and Turrimore, that will be enough for now. We will talk among ourselves and decide if this is possible."

"Perhaps," said Cwell, "it may not be best to discuss this here, D'keeper," she said. Joron glanced around at the thin walls of his rooms.

"You are right," he said, "Tell Brekir to ready her ship, we will meet aboard *Snarltooth*."

Aelerin left, and Cwell returned to her place guarding his door and he could do nothing but wait and worry and listen to the rattle of rain against the windows and try not to think about the ache of the sores on his face or the ache of the stump of his leg or the tightness in his hands where the Hag's Curse was beginning to take hold and swell his joints.

"I am not even old," he said quietly to himself, "and yet the sea takes its toll." He stood, walked to the window, and something uncomfortable in the cup of his spur made him wince, but he did nothing about it. There was always something uncomfortable in the cup of his spur. Grey clouds scudded across the seascape outside and the sea beneath was blue, cut with white breakers as it rushed in toward the land. That land was not yet the riot of colour it would become, the growing season had just started and the night air was cold, like a memory of the sleeping season. The gion and varisk was only beginning to make its tortuous way out of the ground, and those first steps were always the hardest, he supposed. The first growth the most painful, when the plants were most likely to die; the strength that would hold the plant up through its life was not yet there. Did the pain of growing ever really stop? Or did you simply become used to the stress and hurt and strain of every day until it became normal to you? A background buzz of constant worry cut through with moments of transcendent joy, or terrifying fear?

There had been little joy in Joron's life since his shipfriend, Dinyl, had died and his shipwife had been taken.

Sometimes, when he closed his eyes, he saw the flaming projectile fired from Sleighthulme that had sunk Dinyl's ship, but he did not see it as he had at the time, did not watch it arc over *Tide Child*. Instead he watched it as if from Dinyl's eyes, felt what Dinyl must have felt. The triumph at finally being shipwife of his own ship, the joy of a new command. A shipwife's calculating curiosity as he saw the projectile launched from the great mangonel on the island. His mind working with the wind and the trajectory to decide where it would land and how he should steer his ship. Worry, at first. Then concern. Then fear – not for his life, not yet, fear for his ship, that it may land near. That his ship would be swamped and he would be tossed into the sea, and a deeper, darker fear, that his ship would catch afire and he would burn, for all deckchilder, from the lowest stonebound to the shipmothers who controlled the fleets, feared the bonefire. Then, at the last, the realisation that all was lost. That he was a dead man and all those who flew aboard *Bonebore* with him were dead too. The terror of death, of the unknown, not enough time to accept it and find peace and no doubt, knowing Dinyl as he did, his last fleeting thought was that he had let down Meas.

At least it had been mercifully quick.

Joron opened his eyes and stared out at the miserable sea. Though these images of Dinyl filled him with terrible sadness he was also thankful for them; their time together had been short, too short due to the strictures and straightenings that duty put upon them. Even a dream where he shared that last moment was a small gift, that he could be with him again.

"Joron," he said to himself, "you become melancholy and it is no good." He walked to the door and grabbed a waxed coat from the hanger, wrapped it around himself. "Cwell!" he shouted, and the door opened, revealed the woman who had started as his enemy and become his protector. Another bound up by duty to become something she had never expected.

"Ey, D'keeper?" Her voice, always just the right side of insolent, made him smile.

"I cannot stay in here and stare at four walls wondering on what may be or what will be. I shall walk; let us go the lamyards and find the Gullaime. We shall take a walk up to the wind-spire and make sure it is happy."

"Madorra will not like that."

"That Hag-cursed windshorn will do as it is told, it is under my command and must learn its place."

"Good luck wi' that, D'keeper," she chuckled as he swept past her pretending not to hear her words. She wrapped herself in a stinker coat and followed, still chuckling to herself.

They made their way out of Sparehaven town and wound among the low hills surrounding it. The growing vegetation had yet to take on its most violent hues and was a mixture of washed-out pinks and purples. If not for the breeze Joron knew he would have been able to hear the vegetation creak as it grew; still, he fancied he could see it growing, and knew that if he put a finger and thumb around a stalk and closed his eyes and counted to one hundred then when he opened them the new growth would have pushed his fingers a little further apart. Out of the shelter of the town the wind was stronger, plucking at Joron's clothes and pressing the coat against his body. He could see children in the fields around the town, there to keep the varisk and gion from overrunning the food crops. It was hard, backbreaking work, he had done it himself as a child when the fishing had been poor and his father had needed money.

Further along the road they came to the lamyards where his fleet's gullaime had settled. He heard them first, their squawking and hissing and singing. Once he had found them unnerving but now he heard only music, a beautiful, turning, spinning, forever-mutating song. But that song was shot through by a sadness from the Gaunt Islands lamyards just around the hill, for their gullaime remained as all gullaime, blinded and caged. His fleet's gullaime were free, or as free as the Tenbern would allow. There was a fence around their settlement, though the gullaime continually found ways to bring it down. Inside they had built their own dwellings. Their structures were strange to Joron's eye, ramshackle, and they fell down as often as they stayed up, but Joron felt sure they were never meant to be anything but temporary. The gullaime disdained walls and each "nest" was under a crude shelter of old gion leaves. Many leaked when it rained, though this did not seem to bother the gullaime any. The roofs were held up by sticks. A haphazard selection of many different sizes so they leaned at odd angles, and under each roof was a nest built of more sticks and whatever oddments the gullaime had managed to collect. The gullaime village was not only noisy with their song, it rang with bells, and tinkling and chiming and clacking as they had collected all manner of things that made noise, from bones to bits of metal, and strung them across the encampment. It was a merry sound when set against their own singing. *Tide Child*'s Gullaime had a nest building set apart from the others, and Joron was unsure whether this was because they revered it or feared it, or maybe it was both. In the centre of the village was what Joron could only call an altar – no nest under that roof, only a crudely pecked-out model of a bird, and Joron could see Madorra there, its back to them, and around the one-eyed windshorn were gathered a gaggle of gullaime, both windtalkers and windshorn.

As he approached the Gullaime's building the wind died away a little, and Joron felt warmer, and smiled to himself. What point in controlling the wind if you did not use it for your own comfort now and again, ey? The Gullaime sat in its nest, huddled down in its brightly coloured robe. The leaf mask turned toward him.

"Joron Twiner?" it said.

"Ey, Gullaime," he said. "I find myself restless and in need of something to do. I wondered if you would walk to the windspire with me?"

"Walk walk," it said, rising from its nest. "Like to walk."

"Then we would like to walk with you."

They turned, only to be interrupted by a fearful noise, the squawking and hissing and spitting of a gaggle of gullaime. Madorra approaching, flapping its wings and spitting.

"Not take! Not take Windseer." They found themselves surrounded by Madorra's white-robed acolytes, predatory beaks open, long claws unsheathed. Cwell went for the blade at her hip but Joron stopped her.

"We are not taking the Gullaime anywhere, Madorra, only going for a walk."

"Not ship," hissed the windshorn. "Not order gullaime here."

"I have ordered nothing."

"Go away, man," said Madorra and advanced on him; the rest of the circle of gullaime began to sway backward and forward, as if readying themselves for violence and Joron felt a tremor of fear, for he knew how fast gullaime could move when they wished, and that he and Cwell could not stand against them. Then he was pushed out of the way by a bundle of feather and bright colour and the Gullaime landed in front

They wound their way up the hill, the cobbles making way for grit and the grit making way for dirt. On a plateau they came to another area set aside for fields, and a group of women and men were working, pulling vines so the crops before a small house of varisk were not overrun. They were dressed like deckchilder. One of the workers noticed them, pointed. The others stopped their work and Joron felt eyes upon him but ignored the attention. He was used to being watched. It seemed as there was no place he was trusted, and could he blame them? He was the Black Pirate – raider, murderer – and they may toast him when he was not here, when he was doing their dark work for them. But by the same count they did not trust him when he was among them. He may work with them but he was not of them, and he had given sanctuary to those of their people they did not trust or like. It was hard to find blame for the sidelong glances and he thought it a strange course for him to be upon here, one where he was both lauded and hated in the same breath.

"I do not much like the look of them," said Cwell.

"You do not much like the look of anyone," said Joron. Cwell did not reply and the farmers did not move against them, only watched as they made their way up around the path toward the windspire until they turned another twist on the path and the farmers were lost from sight. Not much further along and the windspire came into view, at the same time the Gullaime started to make a cooing, happy and content noise. It was a sound Joron had heard only a few times before; in fact, he felt sure he had not heard it since Madorra appeared.

"Good, Joron Twiner," said the Gullaime. "Good be here. Good be here."

"Do you hear the song, Gullaime?" he said, and he stared at the spire. This one was huge, almost entirely straight and bright white, though it had a gentle twist to it when he looked more closely As he stared the Gullaime started to hum a gentle tune, and that tune twisted up around him, filled him. Set him feeling warm and tall and strong and he wanted to give voice to it. Did he imagine it? Or as he opened his mouth did the soil tremble beneath his feet, did the windspire sway slightly? Did he hear a voice? No. Not a human voice, not words of any description he was capable of. It was more a feeling of longing, a desperate, lonely and sad longing. *Let me wake*. Did he feel the itch of parasitic tunir, moving across his skin? Did he feel the weight of the rock and soil above him? The almost imperceptible sound of small creatures moving upon it? Did he long for freedom with all his heart, long to tear and rend and . . .

"Gullaime, stop," he said. Found himself on his knees before the windspire. The Gullaime before him, similarly prostrated, and he felt Cwell at his back. Saw Madorra from the corner of his eye and knew the creature to be full of delight. "Hag's teeth," said Joron, "I almost . . ."

"Not do, not do," said the Gullaime, and it sounded frightened, terrified. "Not Windseer."

"Is Windseer!" screeched Madorra. "Is Caller! Is almost end! Is almost fire and almost blood!"

"No!" said the Gullaime. "Not yours, give back, what not yours!" It sounded so furious Joron expected the Gullaime to fly at Madorra but it did not, only sat there meekly. Joron put his hand to his waist, found the handle of his straightsword.

"Does Madorra hold something over you, Gullaime? Have something you need? For you are a friend to me, and I would not have that." As he finished speaking, Madorra hissed at him, spread its stubby wings apart and the fighting claws on its feet extended.

"Not hurt!" screeched the Gullaime at the moment Joron was about to draw his blade. "Not hurt!" Joron watched Madorra, and did he see a shine of triumph in its eye when the Gullaime put itself between it and Joron? He cursed the day they had brought the creature aboard, and he was tempted, in this quiet place, to strike it down anyway. But the Gullaime was his friend, and it had asked him not to, and their ways and society were not his. So he would honour its wishes. He removed his hand from his blade.

"Do you wish to stay a little, Gullaime?" he said.

"Yes yes," it said, and went to squat in the hollow at the base of the spine. Joron and Cwell sat at the edge of the clearing, which the growing gion and varisk yearned to fill, but which they could not as some strange power of the spine held the vegetation back. Joron sat, enjoying the slow encroachment of night as the Gullaime rested within the windspire, but the enjoyment did not last. He began to fancy he could feel the shifting of the great beast entombed within the rock. A horror slowly growing within him, at the thought of being stuck beneath a mountain. He remembered clawing his way through caves with Narza, the shipwife's shadow, and the terrible feeling of rock pressing down on him. He tried to shake that thought, of the slowness of time passing while held within the island, as if in a tomb. How long had those keyshans been there? For time beyond thinking; these islands must have existed when Hassith the spearthrower had killed Skearith the godbird, and given birth to a strife that had persisted ever since. They had been witness to the Maiden, Mother and Hag, who watched over the archipelago, being gifted the gullaime. To be stuck for so long, it was beyond bearing. He took a deep breath. Distracted himself by wondering where Narza was now; she had left the ship soon after they had been forced to leave Meas. Quietly slipped away in the night and Joron had hoped, each time he docked *Tide Child*, that she would be there with news of the shipwife, but it had never happened. No doubt Narza was either out there now, trying to free Meas, or dead in the same endeavour.

"Windtalker has finished its sleep," said Cwell. Joron looked up, saw the Gullaime emerging from the windspire to the attentions of a fussy Madorra.

"We should make our way down to the harbour, no doubt the shipwives are gathered by now and waiting on my appearance." He stood, brushed dirt from his trousers and coat. "Let us make our way back then." They walked down the hill, and much to his chagrin in places the slope was steep enough that

Joron had to take Cwell's arm to ensure he did not overbalance. "I can stand straight on heaving deck, Cwell," he said, "but gravel and mud are no place for a one-legged man."

"Land is not our place, D'keeper," she said. Then raised her head. "Reckon we're not the only ones thinking it."

In the field that women and men had been clearing earlier was now a group, huddled together around a small fire. When they saw Joron, Cwell and the two gullaime they stood, left the field and spread out across the path. Joron counted eight. Five women, three men; the woman who stood at the fore of them was well dressed and wore a hat. In the gloom Joron was not sure if it was a one-tail or two-tail, though he was sure they were an officer.

"May the Hag never see you, Shipwife," said Joron, for if the officer was not a shipwife he complimented them, and if they were he was merely correct.

"The Hag is always watching, pirate," said their leader, and a little nearer Joron could make out they were a deckkeeper, grizzled and scarred – much older than Joron. He recognised her as a type, the type who would never rise above deckkeeper, maybe didn't deserve the rank but had been about so long they had finished up in it. Bitter and angry, he had met those like her among the deckchilder of his small fleet. The ones who had been officers but had been too cruel, or lashed out at those above them and ended up as deckchilder on the black ships. They seldom lasted long without the uniform, and when they had the uniform they were wont to gather around them similar souls, like skeers flocking to carrion.

"My rank is deckkeeper," he said politely. "I would thank you to use it."

"Is that what tha Tenbern calls tha?"

"She called me shipmother, though I think her too kind." He saw how it wrong-footed the woman, how it was not the answer she expected and how this simply wound her tighter within.

"She is one for sarcasm," the woman said, grinning to those

around her and Joron knew there was little point in civility now. This deckkeeper had set a course and meant to fly it.

"I am surprised you have met her," said Joron. "Few rulers invite aged deckkeepers to their table." A stillness fell upon the woman and her group.

"Careful with tha words, foreigner," she said, "for tha is a guest on our island, and tha is not welcomed by all." She took a step forward and Joron noticed she wore her sword. Those with her too were armed and he thought that strange for a group out doing farm work.

"I am needed in the town, by the Tenbern as it happens," he said. "So if you would kindly let us pass." He made to walk past but two of the deckchilder, blocking their way.

"Tha have done our islands a service," said the deckkeeper, "is true. But tha also brought tha Hundred Isles vermin to us, and picked up the flotsam and jetsam that we would have let drown were it our way."

"Women and men are reborn on the black ships," he said. "What is your name, Deckkeeper?"

"Togir," she said. "Deckkeeper Togir."

"Well, let us pass and I shall not mention your rudeness next I speak with the Tenbern. I am sure you have no wish to take up the black armband."

"Tha people are not wanted here," she said. He stepped up to her.

"Have you been ordered to tell me that?" She met his gaze, unafraid, a woman used to violence, the type to enjoy it, and Joron felt his heart racing within his chest. For he longed for the violence too, and then all the anger and the hurt within him could be released through it. But eight against four, and two of them gullaime, was poor odds.

"There is a feeling in the town," said Togir, "that were something unfortunate to happen to tha, it would be no bad thing." Joron put his hand to the hilt of his blade, slipping off the strand of kivelly leather that kept it secure as Togir's people moved to surround them.

"And you and your fellows, are you that unfortunate thing?"

"We may well be," she said, and stepped back, smiling all the while.

"Eight of you, against four of us. And me a cripple, and two of us gullaime." The gullaime also sensed the violence in the air, and Madorra had put itself before their gullaime, head cocked, one bright eye watching. He noticed that its fighting claws were not extended. Wondered if the creature saw this as a way to get rid of him. Though that made little sense, as it also seemed to think it needed him.

"Tha may be crippled, and there may only be two of you, but tha are still the Black Pirate," she said. "I do not discount tha skills, pirate. Tha are not needed, and tha people not wanted."

"Then why waste any more time?" said Joron, and as she drew her blade, those around her did the same. Joron brought his sword out and swept it around to his side. He did not lunge for the deckkeeper as she expected. His blade bit deep into the thigh of the deckchilder meant to take him from behind and the man fell, screaming and grasping his wound. He felt Cwell stand against his back, knew she would have her twin bone knives out. But there were too many still. Then the Gullaime lifted a foot and pushed Madorra out the way. With a screech it punched its wings forward and a blast of wind knocked the group of deckchilder from their feet. "Into them!" shouted Joron, and it was quick and filthy work. Two down before they could stand again. Now five against Joron, Cwell and the two gullaime. Madorra struck out, opening a man's guts and his entrails looped around his feet as he stood there, watching open-mouthed, silent in his shock as agony. Cwell ran in among them. Though she held the same position as Narza she had none of that woman's balletic skill in killing. Her fighting was dirty. She threw a handful of mud in a woman's face and rammed a blade into her gut while she was blinded. Kicked out at a shin and when her kick missed, rather than backing out of the way of a sweeping curnow she threw herself onto her attacker, taking them both to the ground where their fight degenerated into grunting and swearing in the mud.

Joron faced Deckkeeper Togir, their fight apart from the rest, as was often the way with officers. He was no born swordsman, and his missing leg hampered him, made him wary of his balance on the muddy ground. Swords clashed, not with great anger, not yet. Simply a test of each other. Joron practised every day, had done since the shipwife set him to learning the straightsword. He was quick enough to parry Togir's second lunge and push his own sword into the space created. Togir parried back and they stepped away from each other, circled. Togir smiled at him. A confident smile. She had reason to be sure of herself, no doubt she had practised the straightsword from the moment she was strong enough to hold one, where Joron had only ever learnt what every Hundred Isles child learns, the rudimentary moves of the curnow, the quick and the brutal ways of the harboursides and of the deckchilder. Had this been a fencing match, Joron would no doubt have lost, but it was not. As they circled he studied Togir, saw that her straightsword was old – the blade gleamed, but the guard around the hilt was rusted, and the basket hilt broken in places. When Togir closed again, and lunged, he danced to the side, delivered a clumsy looking thrust and saw Togir smile, thinking in his panic he had thrust wide. She intercepted his attack easily.

But that was her mistake, not his.

The hiss of metal on metal as his blade slid down Togir's, over where the basket would usually catch the blade and protect her thumb. Neatly slicing into the flesh there, cutting the tendon and making her drop her sword. A foul and lowborn move, no doubt. But Joron cared nothing for such things. He was the Black Pirate, he cared about winning and he cared about staying alive.

Togir jumped back, holding her bleeding hand and saw that her entire group was down and either dead or screaming in the dirt.

"I yield," she said. "I yield." Backing away from him as he came upon her, bloody sword held low.

"I care not," said Joron and the damage to his voicebox, done long ago, made it come out as a growl. And at that, Togir turned to run. Found Cwell stood in her way.

"He said," grinned Cwell, "that he cares not." And she drove her blade through Togir's throat and stepped back. Watched her bleed and choke to death. "Filthy business," said Cwell. "And needless too."

"Ey," said Joron, and he knelt to clean blood from his blade on the muddy ground. "Is it not often the way, though."

24

Down Among the Desperate

He sat in the great cabin aboard *Snarltooth* surrounded by his shipwives and wondered why any of them should answer to him. They had eaten, not well but better than most in his fleet, and now he must speak and say of the courses to be taken and the winds to be flown upon. How had this situation arisen? That he was the anointed of a woman who many of them believed was dead, and yet they did not move against him. They knew he was not Meas's son, that he was only the child of a fisher and condemned to death like any other. Yet they hung upon his words as if the seniority was his and not theirs.

But he could not hold that weight, not yet. He walked to the windows of *Snarltooth*, looked out upon the dark sea that gently lapped against the black bone of the hull. Out there, sitting beyond the confines of Sparehaven's harbour, he could make out his fleet. The lights of nine fighting ships were reflected in the water – though no corpse light glowed above them, no children died for Meas's fleet – with two more ships out on the seas in search of plunder and *Tide Child* on the dry dock for at least one more week. And two brownbones, empty now, as their people were camped on land – as unwelcome there as the ships were in the harbour.

How strange, he thought, that a fisher's boy should end up cradling so many lives in his hands. He had an image of his father, smiling at him. *If you knew what I had done*, he said to himself, *you would not smile so*. That thought soured him, and he turned away from his ships and the sea and back to those in the room: Brekir, standfast and serious; Coult, as vicious and angry looking as ever; Adrantchi, without his deckkeeper Black Ani, who had been lost earlier in the year, and something of Adrantchi had died that day too; Turrimore, dark skinned and all fight, waiting upon his pleasure and words.

"A woman tried to kill me earlier," he said. Four pairs of eyes watched him until Coult spoke.

"As you stand afore us, I reckon they failed in that task," he said, picking at his metal tooth with a fingernail.

"And what was this?" said Adrantchi quietly. "Some argument over drink? Some matter of honour you settled with them?"

"No. An ambush," said Joron. "Had it not been for Cwell and the gullaime I would never have returned from Sparehaven's windspire."

"We should tell the Tenbern," said Brekir.

"No," said Joron.

"You think she knew?" said Turrimore, her hand touching the knife at her side.

"I do not, as it happens, but I also do not think she would be too sad were I to be killed in a brawl. We must face facts, shipwives. We are not popular here. We are not wanted."

"Then," said Adrantchi, "the sooner the Tenbern helps us get Meas back the better, and we can be off her apron."

"The Tenbern will not help us take Bernshulme," he said. All but Brekir looked shocked.

"We are betrayed?" The look of anger on Coult's face was a warning to how narrow the ledge he must walk was. These were his people now, they felt no loyalty to the Gaunt or Hundred Isles, and it would not take much more than an angry shipwife to send a crew of women and men, just as angry as those who had ambushed him, in search of a vengeance that could turn the entire Gaunt Islands against them.

"Not betrayed, no," he said. "Not as such." He sat back down. "She will not attack Bernshulme directly; the defences on the isles that surround it are too strong." He sighed. "Truthfully, I cannot disagree with her. She may break most of her fleet upon Thirteenbern Gilbryn's defences and lose all the advantage we have fought so hard to win her."

"Still sounds like a betrayal to me," said Turrimore.

"It is not," said Joron, words hard. "She has said that if we can bring out the Hundred Isles fleet then she will take it on with her own."

"So we should smash our ships upon Thirteenbern Gilbryn's defences instead of her?" said Adrantchi.

"We cannot survive that," said Coult. "We have barely survived our last few hit-and-runs. We have no choice now, Deckkeeper. Sing the keyshans to us and let us fly in at the head of an army of the beasts."

"I cannot do that, Coult, and even if I could the Thirteenbern would kill the shipwife the moment she became sure she did not need her." He sat back down in Brekir's chair. "And then our whole reason for attacking is wasted. We do not do this for revenge, or hatred, we do this to get her back."

"Ey," said Brekir. "So what do you suggest?"

"We take all of ours off this island," he said. "They are not welcome here anyway. We load the brownbones with those who cannot fight; all those who can, we put on our fighting ships. We offer up everything we are as bait to bring out the Hundred Isles fleet for Tenbern Aileen." He looked around the table, trying to read faces.

"It will not be enough," said Coult. "Even if Gilbryn knows we have every soul loyal to us aboard, she will not risk what is left of her fleet. The damage we have done has been too grievous and she is not foolish."

"You are probably right," said Joron. "That is why we will give her something else worth chasing."

"And what is that, pray tell us?" said Adrantchi.

"Meas."

"You said you did not know where she is," said Turrimore.

"And I do not," he said. "But I know she must be in Bernshulme. So I intend to go there." This caused such an outburst, such a shouting and braying that Joron was quite taken aback and held his hands up. "Peace, my shipwives, peace."

"It should not be you," said Coult. "Send any other of us, with a force of arms. You are needed."

"I understand why you do not wish me to go," said Joron. "But it must be me. If Meas has been mistreated then it must be a face she knows that comes for her. And I will take Mevans with me, he knows the island well, and I will take a couple of others who I trust and Meas knows." A babble of voices once more, raised and arguing across him. Telling him his place, his responsibility, what they needed, what was best for their fleet.

"He is right," said Brekir, smashing her hand down on the table and standing. "The deckkeeper is right!" she said again, looking round the table, meeting every eye.

"Even if he is right," said Turrimore, "and I will take you at your word for it, Brekir, as we have flown together many a year, it seems a terrible risk. He is the Black Pirate," she said. "He is us."

"He is us, it is true. But," Brekir looked down at Joron, "and forgive what I say here, Deckkeeper – he may be our leader, but we are bound together by Meas. By her name, and more, by the legend we have made her into." Her eyes scanned those gathered, meeting every face, a nod for each at the table. "Every woman and man has her name on their lips when they work and when they fight. They ask her protection as often as they ask it of the Mother. They swear vengeance in her name as if she were the Hag. She is more than a person now, she is a figurehead."

"She may not even be alive," said Coult. "And I say that with no pleasure for I respect her as much as any."

"No," said Joron, "she may not. But I believe she is. I believe they keep her for what they believe she can do."

"If news of Spantonnis Bank reaches them though . . ." said Adrantchi.

"Yes, and that is another reason for us to act quickly," said Joron. "For me to act quickly."

"Meas knows me, you know," said Coult. "I could go. She would recognise my face."

"Ey," said Brekir, "but who wants the first friendly face they see to be yours?" Gentle laughter at that. "More seriously, how long would a man with the accent of the Southern Gaunts last in Bernshulme?"

"I could keep my mouth shut," said Coult. "Besides, the deckkeeper is hardly likely to walk the streets of Bernshulme unrecognised."

"It has to be me," said Joron, quietly. "It is not just about who she will know, it is about the myth of it, Coult. The idea of it." Now he met every eye around the table. "We have a people, and Meas bade us look after them, they are ours. And all we have done is in service to her. But lives such as ours? They are not long lives and we all know that. Many have fallen."

"Too many," said Brekir quietly.

"Ey," said Coult, "we have dipped paint for too many, and will dip paint for many more."

"That is just it," said Joron. "What Meas is, what I have become, as Brekir said, it is something more than a commander. Joron Twiner is not the Black Pirate, and you all know that. I am just a man. But to so many of those we protect, the Black Pirate is more than human. And . . . and . . ." His words faltered. He closed his eyes. Then he lifted his head. "And there is this," he said, removing his scarf and revealing the marks of the rot on his face. He did not know what he had expected from them. Fear? Revulsion? But he saw none of it. And he saw no pity, which warmed him inside for it was pity that he had feared the most.

"I am sorry, Joron," said Brekir.

"Do not be," he said, then replaced the material over his

mouth and nose. "I have known I would die from the moment I set my feet on the slate of the Tide Child. Truthfully, I have lived far longer than I expected. But I do not want to go down to the keyshan's rot. Those on Tide Child saw how it took Coxward, saw his decline. You have seen it in others." He tapped his fingernails on the table and when he spoke next he spoke quietly, staring down at the table. He watched the liquid in the glasses of those gathered as it gently moved with the motion of the ship at its staystone. "I know you all believe Meas is dead. I know it is likely true, though I refuse to believe it myself." He looked up, "But it does not matter. Meas ties us together, as does the Black Pirate. All we have is names and the stories we have created, that is all. We make myths for our people to bind them together. But if the Black Pirate dies of keyshan's rot, raving and screaming the way Coxward did, then what kind of story is that? All the victories, the last-minute escapes, they will be forgotten."

"Much of what have we done should be forgotten," said Adrantchi.

"Do you think I do not know that?" bit out Joron. "Do you think I glory in anything we did? The raids, the deaths?"

"No," said Adrantchi, and looked away. "Of course not. I spoke out of turn."

"And I do not resent you for it, Adrantchi, you have lost much, we all have."

"Ey," said Brekir. "Throw paint on that for truth."

"The worst of what was done will be forgotten, my friends. It will die with me. It will be blamed on me, and that is right. But if I die going to rescue Meas . . . If I simply vanish?" He looked to Brekir, for understanding.

"Then you leave your people with a legend."

"Our people," said Joron.

"Ey, our people," she said. "And what better legend to give them? That Meas's son died going against impossible odds to save her?" There was silence then. Coult picked up his drink and took a sip.

"I can think of a better one," he said. All eyes to him. "That he brings the shipwife back." There was a moment of silence.

"Well," said Joron, "I must admit that is my preferred option."

Gentle laughter around the table.

"What of us, Deckkeeper?" said Turrimore. "Do we parade our fleet out there for nothing? If you do not come back, what of your people then?"

Brekir laughed to herself.

"You are a clever one, Joron."

"What have I missed here?" said Coult.

"Joron is a threat to the Tenbern, our fleet under him is a threat to her. But without him, we are just a bunch of criminals. She cannot give him what he wants, but she can take pity on his lost people, I reckon. Give us an island, somewhere harsh, no doubt. Unfriendly. Probably demand we give all our ships to her."

"We become Gaunt Islanders once more," said Coult.

"Those that can bear it, ey," said Joron. "It is not what I wished for us. But it is more than the Hundred Isles would offer. Brekir can arrange it, she is still on good terms with the Bern of the Gaunt Islands."

Coult shook his head. "I came here to plan war, and it has turned into a wake." He took a drink.

"All Meas ever wanted was peace," said Brekir into the silence.

"And a poor job I have done of that," said Joron.

"Enough pity," said Coult. "You have done what you must and we have still not answered the biggest question. If you are determined to sacrifice yourself so that we may scrape out a life somewhere arid and lifeless, how do we get you into the Hundred Isles?"

"Trade," said Joron, glad to be away from the subject of his choices.

"Trade?" said Adrantchi.

"Ey," said Joron. "Mulvan Cahanny's organisation controls

all crime in Bernshulme. With the Hundred Isles under such pressure, from both us and from the Gaunt Islanders, smuggling will be rampant and profitable."

"So what, we raid a smugglers' lair and steal their ships?" said Coult.

"Won't work," said Brekir, "there'll be all manner of code and signals pre-arranged to get ships through. We need to take a code book as well, that's if they have one. A lot of them just memorise what they need to know. So we'll have to take someone important alive and persuade them to tell us what we need."

"That will be hard," said Turrimore, "most of Cahanny's people would rather die than betray him and face the consequences of it."

"There is another way," said Joron.

"Ey?"

"Tenbern Aileen knows all that happens on her islands. She gave me the locations of the islands black-market goods are run to Bernshulme from months ago, in hope I raid them."

"And?" said Brekir.

"We find Cahanny's people and ask them to smuggle me in."

"And you think that likely, that smugglers can be trusted?" said Brekir. "You are the most wanted man in the whole Hundred Isles. They'll betray you in a loosing and live like fifteenbern on the ransom."

"Oh, I know that," said Joron. "So Joron Twiner will not be going. Someone far more important will be, someone they will be more than happy to give passage to, along with her servant."

"And who is that?" said Adrantchi. He looked genuinely puzzled.

"My shadow, Cwell," he said. "She is Mulvan Cahanny's niece." Then there were smiles around the table, and drinks were raised at this clever and fleetlike idea.

"Well," said Brekir, "in that case, let us drink to successful family reunions."

25

The Woman and the Servant

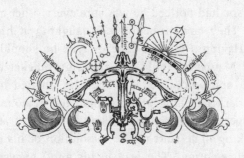

It was hard to leave *Tide Child* behind, hard to leave his people behind and hard to become a simple traveller on another shipwife's ship. To walk the slate with Brekir and see a rope not wound just how he would have his deckchilder do it, a wing not furled just so, a gallowbow trussed in a way that was slightly unfamiliar to him, and yet he could not give voice to it or correct it. For the long weeks of the journey, guided by the fair hand of the east wind, he had bitten his lip beneath the mask. Though he knew Brekir a solid shipwife – one with far more experience than him – in truth, he felt she could drive her ship, small as it was, more quickly. Could raise more wing, could be more daring when the winds tore at it, could push harder during the night.

But he said nothing.

One morning, walking the deck through a soft mist, the water chuckling along the side of *Snarltooth*, he saw a loose flap on the material spread over the flukeboat in the centre of the deck. He almost spoke, ordered a nearby deckchilder to deal with it. But instead bit his lip, held his council and Brekir – at that moment passing – laughed quietly to herself.

"I do not mind if you give the order, Deckkeeper," she said.

"I do not even mind if you wish me to step aside so you may command. In truth, it may be easier than watching you fight with yourself every day." He did not quite know what to say, embarrassment that he had been so transparent was foremost in his mind, then annoyance that Brekir had said nothing – because if she had noticed he was sure every other among her crew had. They had probably been laughing at him behind his back. Having a fair old joke. Maybe he should take her command? Maybe he could run this ship quicker and faster and harder and, and, and . . . Then he laughed to himself. Though a darker feeling lurked behind the humour. Was this sudden anger with someone he liked to think of as a friend the rot talking? The start of the dissolution of his mind into nothing but emotion? The wall in his mind between feeling and action being eroded the way the rot eroded the skin of his face? But he did not do anything, only shook his head and walked down the deck with her. He knew that Brekir was fleet, more fleet than he had ever been, and she had flown this ship throughout the archipelago, fought it, beaten bigger ships than *Snarltooth*, taken bigger ships than *Snarltooth*. If anyone knew how to fly this ship quickly and efficiently it was her.

Not him.

"No, Brekir, this command is nothing but yours and I am sorry for my ill spirits. The Hag dogs my every footstep lately." She came to stand by him, gently leading him over to the rail so they could watch the water. Having to provide support for him as he no longer wore his bone spur, too much a symbol of the Black Pirate – now he had only a varisk peg and found balancing with it hard so was forced to practise.

"We run eight beakwyrms at the front."

"A good speed, Brekir, I know that."

"I am maybe gentler with my people than you," she said.

"It is your ship."

"Ey," she said, "but I say again, I would rather have you comfortable and—"

"No, Brekir," he said. "I must travel with Cwell to Bernshulme and if I am not to raise suspicion then I must learn not to act like I am used to ordering around all those within earshot." Brekir turned to him, her long, dour face full of hidden amusement.

"I fear you must try a lot harder, Twiner," she said. And he nearly bit at her, for not using his rank in front of the common deckchilder. Then laughed to himself.

"I fear I must, Shipwife," he said, "you are right."

"We will be there by tonight," she said. "Jirton's Isle will dock any ship that has trade, but it is riddled with spies and ne'er-do-wells." Cwell came to join them at the rail.

"D'keeper," she said, "I know it pains you, but you must no longer wear the mask."

"It is common, for those afflicted to cover the sores," he said.

"Ey, D'keeper," she said, "it is. I will get you a headrag, to wear over your hair, it changes the look of someone, as does a different hat. But the sores on your face, D'keeper," she said, "I know you hate them, but so do others."

"It will draw attention," he said.

"Ey," she said, "but it will also deflect it, for none think the Black Pirate has the rot. They will think you some poor afflicted soul and want little to do with you. Faces will be turned from you. In the Hundred Isles, we like not those we think are sick."

"She is right, Twiner," said Brekir.

"It is hard," he said. "I like not who I see below the mask I wear."

"Few of us do," said Brekir.

"That is true, D'keeper," said Cwell.

"Twinder," said Joron.

"What?"

"You cannot call me D'keeper if I am your servant. So call me Twinder, it is near enough my name for me to answer without thinking." Cwell stared at him.

"I cannot believe we had not thought of that," said Brekir, "what fools we are."

"Not fools," said Cwell. "'Tis just the way of woman and man to inhabit the world they live in. Not to think about the one they shall inhabit tomorrow."

"I have never taken you for a philosopher, Cwell," said Brekir.

"I am not," she said. "Merely a realist. And Twinder is too near, far too near. Too good as well," she said. "For a woman of any means, which I am as Cahanny's niece – well, you are either an old servant who I have liked and trusted and taken pity on now you have become sick, or I have fallen upon hard times, and a rot-kissed servant is all I can afford."

"There is little pity in the Hundred Isles," said Joron.

"True," said Brekir.

"Then I will call you Servant," she said and turned to walk away, stopping a few paces down the slate. "And you are dressed too well, Servant," she said. "Your jacket cost more than everything I wear. Your sword is nothing a servant would wear, you should give it to me." They stared at one another for a moment. A memory shared between them of when she had taken the sword from him once before. Then Joron unhooked the straightsword. Passed it to Cwell. "You are not worried I may steal it?" she said.

"Not after all the trouble it caused for you to bring it back the first time." She nodded.

"Ey, that is true, Servant," she said. "That is true."

They made port at Jirton's Isle just as night was falling and the gion and varisk jungle, now rampant over the islands, was painted as black as Brekir's skin. The ship was quiet as it glided in toward the island, and Joron watched the merry lights of the port, heard the sounds of song and laughter drift across the bay toward them from the town. He stood watching, felt someone come to stand by him, glanced across to see Mevans.

"We are slowing, Mevans."

"We cannot fly right in," said Mevans. "Brekir says they have a chain set across the harbour mouth, will wreck the ship that tries to force entry. So we must wait for their pilot to come out and guide *Snarltooth* in."

"It is set up like a military harbour."

"Cahanny runs this place and he is no fool," said Mevans. He heard Cwell step up from behind him.

"Mevans is right. My uncle always had contacts within the Grand Bothy, and with the Hundred Isles squeezed by our actions he will have become more powerful, I imagine."

"So," said Mevans, "this place exists with the help of the Thirteenbern, you suspect?"

"It is likely," said Cwell. "And maybe the Tenbern also, as we know, such places are useful."

"They could just pull up the chain behind us, trap us in there," said Joron.

"They will not." He turned to find Brekir behind him. "I have been here many times before," she said. "And Cahanny is, at heart, a smuggler. If he shows his hand once, locks us in, he loses the trust of all those who would trade with him outside the law, Hundred and Gaunt Islanders. I have no doubt he reports all our movements, but his lieutenant, Broom, will not trap us here if he wishes to carry on with his trade. There are always others who would host the smugglers."

"And you are sure of this?"

"As sure as I can be, Servant." She grinned at him.

"Something comes," said Cwell, pointing towards the island.

"The red lantern, it is the pilot boat coming," said Brekir. "She'll ask us to come in by flukeboat, say there is no room in the harbour at Broomstown." Joron squinted into the night.

"It does not look full."

"It is not. She simply expects her palm to be filled with coin." And so it was, greetings were exchanged. Much *umm*ing and *ahh*ing over whether the harbour could fit in a ship of the size of *Snarltooth*, and whether they would indeed trust a ship of war, and a ship of the Black Pirate's no less, in their small harbour. Then more talk was made, back and forth before a price was agreed on – one quite exorbitant to Joron's thinking – and ropes were thrown over so *Snarltooth* could be slowly towed in through the gap between the moles of the harbour. As the ship passed the towers on the end of the harbour walls Joron saw they were tracked by two massive gallowbows, as big as any he had ever seen.

"They's keyshan hunters," said Mevans. "*Arakeesian Dread* mounted two when I first joined him as lad. They were too slow to load for battles between ships, more for show than aught else. But if they put a bolt in us, we'll feel it."

"Let us hope Brekir was right about Jirton's Isle not wanting to sully it poor reputation, then," said Joron as *Snarltooth* was brought to a full stop and the staystone dropped, all in full view of the two huge gallowbows.

"It is for show," said Mevans, "they cannot be kept under tension for long, and it takes ten deckchilder to spin the Hag-cursed things up."

"Well, that is a comfort." He turned at a call from Brekir.

"The pilot has offered to take us ashore to Broomstown, Mistress Cwell," she said, and there was a strange moment of dislocation for Joron, that Brekir should not be addressing him. "If you would wish it."

"The sooner I am away from you, the better," spat Cwell, and Joron put a hand to his face, to hide his smile at the pre-arranged subterfuge, but the smile fell away as soon as he touched the skin of his ruined features. He had no doubt that the words served their purpose, that reports of friction between Cwell and the shipwife of *Snarltooth* would run ahead of them in the small port. When they boarded the flukeboat, and once more had to pass over coin for the privilege, Joron and Mevans joined Cwell on the rump and Brekir and her deckkeeper, Vulse, went to sit upon the beak, and both small groups glowered at one another until Brekir broke the silence.

"Tell me, Pilot, is the Mother's Pot still a good place for a shipwife to stay?"

"Ey," said the pilot, a small woman, old and sturdy with a scar down her face and only three fingers on the hand which grasped the steering oar. "I can put in a word with Ostir who runs it."

"For a price?" said Brekir. The pilot grinned, showing a mouth with more gum than tooth.

"Is always for a price."

"Then," said Cwell, "tell me where a woman may stay if she wanted to avoid a good place for a shipwife to stay." Cwell glared down the boat at Brekir. "And name your price."

"That would be in the Maiden's Skirts . . ." The pilot left a gap for Cwell to fill in her name.

"Cwell," came the reply, "Cwell Cahanny." She leaned over, holding out a coin but the pilot held up a hand.

"That's a known name," she said. "You keep your penny, bonny lass, and remember my name is Huld and maybe one day you can do old Huld a favour, ey?"

"I have a good memory for names, Huld, and am well disposed to them that treat me well."

"Well, you remember old Huld then," she said, and sat in the boat with her back to Brekir as they rowed toward shore, the oars beating the black water, sending silver ripples out into the harbour and stirring up angry clouds of tiny luminescent creatures. Joron turned to watch the glow die away in the black water behind them. *That is where we all go*, he thought, *that is all we are. A brief light in the darkness, destined to be swallowed up by the sea.*

26

The Passage

They spent four days on Jirton's Isle. Cwell was put up in the Maiden's Skirts, living in luxury while Joron and Mevans stayed in the servants' quarters, little better than an animal shelter. During the day they walked through Broomstown with Cwell, and a number of loud and cruel-sounding altercations were had with Brekir, including a fight between Mevans and one of Brekir's deckchilder, which was not entirely planned but something Mevans said the woman had coming to her and her beating was well deserved, though he hardly escaped unscathed himself. Joron was unsure who, exactly, had received the worst of it.

The approach was made on the morning of the third day. A woman came to Joron while he tried to sleep and fend off the cold of morning; she had stayed the night and lain near him in the shelter.

"Servant," she said. "You listen to me, servant."

"Ey," he said, and the day was still bleary, still unfocused and he awash with his own tiredness. "Who would speak?"

"My name don't matter none," said the woman, and she wiped at her face with her sleeve, sniffed up mucus from a growing season cold. "Just that there are those in this town who may well have noticed your mistress and that shipwife don't get on none too well." Sleep, still a fog between him and his thoughts.

"Water," he said. More to buy time than anything. He must not appear desperate, must not give away their need or desire. He yawned, hissing in pain as the skin around his ulcers stretched and the scabs that had formed overnight on his broken flesh cracked once more.

"The rot brings a thirst," she said, "I've heard others say it." She walked away and returned with a mug. He reached out for it and she pulled it back. "I'll pour it into your mouth; if it touches your lip no other will drink from it." He nodded, and opened his mouth, let her pour in water.

"Thank you."

"My father took bad from the rot, died raving and screaming. I'll not touch ee, but I'll not be cruel either." Joron nodded.

"What do you want?"

"Where is yorn other fella?" Joron looked around, saw Mevans's blankets empty. Shrugged.

"He sleeps badly, often gets up and walks around. He is not a servant, merely another traveller and offered to keep the mistress safe in exchange for passage." He tried to smile at the woman. "You have seen how it is between her and the shipwife."

"But she still travels with her?"

"What choice do we have, ey? She served the Black Pirate, see, but they fell out. Now she is to be exiled. I think she plans to find some way to return to Bernshulme."

"A risky destination, for someone who crewed with the Black Pirate," she said. Joron pushed himself up, looked around at the other sleeping bodies. Wondered how many pretended sleep and lowered his voice – though in truth, the more spies heard the better.

"It is," he said. "But the mistress is related to Cahanny, see. She's been trying to get off her ship for as long as I've known her." He smiled to himself, for it was almost true.

"Mulvan Cahanny?" said the woman, her show of surprise poor.

"Ey, that's him." The woman shuffled nearer, she was missing two teeth from the side of her mouth and the rest were black with either rot or staining from some foodstuff. Her breath did not smell of rot and he wondered what tasted good enough for someone to choose such a disfigurement. "I am deckkeeper on a brownbone, name of *Keyshan's Eye*, see," she said. "I am Mrin, and my shipwife – well, let us say we have reason to visit Bernshulme, and a belief that we will be let in if we do. Should your mistress want to make passage, then we leave tonight. But my shipwife would speak to your mistress first."

"They can come to her rooms."

"No, I reckon that Brekir has them watched. Meet us behind the old flensing huts, to the west of town when Skearith's Eye looks straight down upon us all."

"Very well," he said, and the woman nodded, looking around before leaving. When Mevans returned he found a quiet place to tell the man what had been said. Then they waited for Cwell to appear, for though Mevans was allowed in the Maiden's Skirts, Joron, due to the rot, was not. Mevans had been so incensed by this that he had almost come to blows with the woman who kept the place and had since sworn to never set foot within it. So they sat, and Mevans put a mark upon his bone knife and held it up so he could see how fast the gion and varisk grew.

"Best way to know the season's weather," he said. "For good or ill."

"News?" They looked up. Cwell stood above them, dressed well in red fishskin and purple feather sashes hung with crossbows.

"Meeting at High Eye," said Mevans. Cwell glanced up, squinting into the blue sky.

"Not long, should have come in and got me."

"You know my feelings on that place."

"Ey," said Cwell, "though I think the woman reckoned you my lover and was jealous. She knows better now."

"I'll still not go in."

"Please yourself, the anhir is good though."

"We have a meeting to get to," said Mevans without looking, and Joron had to suppress a laugh for he saw the war on the man's face between his pride and his love of good alcohol. He held up his knife, ignoring Cwell and checking the growth of the jungles squirming up around the town.

"Come then, servants," she said, and they set off.

The old flensing yards, as ever for such places, were deserted and it took them longer than they had imagined to get there, the gion and varisk blocking every path and having to be hacked down with curnows and brute force. When they arrived the huts were barely worthy of their name, a few old uprights were all that remained. The woman he had talked to earlier was there with another taller and better-dressed woman.

"Well, it is indeed Cwell," she said, looking her up and down. "Looks like life has treated you better than I thought."

"Ansiri? I had thought the sea would have taken you long ago." Cwell crossed the space and clasped hands with the woman.

"Take more than the sea to kill me," she said. "We all thought you had put in your lot with the Black Pirate."

"I made myself useful, is all. But have fallen from favour I must admit. He has had a good run, but cannot survive much longer and you know me, Ansiri, I am a survivor." Ansiri nodded. "My uncle will pay you well, if you can return me to Bernshulme," she said.

"He may," said Ansiri. "He may not though, you can never tell and much has changed. I will require upfront payment for your passage."

"I would not expect any less," said Cwell. Then the two women fell to haggling, eventually agreeing a price that Joron found exorbitant as it was almost all of what coin they had, but he could say nothing about it.

"One other thing," said Ansiri, "the rot-cursed one, you can't bring him. I'll not have someone running mad on my deck. A madman aboard brings the Hag down on a ship, all know that." Joron felt colder than the day warranted. Cwell glanced at him and smiled but it was not a friendly smile, and though he had sworn never to doubt her, he found that oath hard to keep in the moment.

"He is Hundred Isles born," said Cwell, "and I owe him my own life, see. I have promised he can be laid to rest in the soil of his birth and you know how important Cahanny believes a promise, ey?"

"Your promise, not mine."

"I will add to the price, by one tenth," she said. "And I give you my promise, Shipwife Ansiri, if he shows any signs of madness I will throw him over for the longthresh myself." Ansiri glanced at Joron. Then back to Cwell.

"Very well then. Pack your bags, then go for a walk around the town and I will have my people remove your belongings to my ship. Be at the docks when Skearith's Blind Eye is over the shoulder. My flukeboat will bring you aboard." She took off her hat and rubbed sweat from her brow. "Do you think the shipwife is likely to give chase?"

"She may," said Cwell. "I know much of the Black Pirate's doings. But I think it more likely she will be glad to see the back of me."

"Well," said Ansiri, "*Keyshan's Eye* is not as fast as a fleet ship, but I know enough tricks to get us away quick, and the harbourwoman will delay them as much as possible, of that I am sure. So we'll be over the horizon afore that black ship is after us if we do it right. You get back and pack." Cwell gave the shipwife a nod.

"Come then, Servant," she said, "there is work to do."

"I think, D'keeper," whispered Mevans to him as they made their way back to the forest path, "she enjoys saying that a little too much."

"Ey," said Joron with a smile, and he drew his curnow and hacked at the forest, starting the task of clearing the path back to Broomtown, "but we get little enough joy in this life, let her get her pleasure where she will."

When they were back in the town Cwell returned to her rooms, to gather her few belongings and put on the clothes they had sewn money into to keep it safe. In the servants' quarters Joron and Mevans put together their own few things and tied scraps of red material round those they could not carry with them. That done Joron wrote a note for Brekir and they made their way to one of the drinking houses frequented by the shipwife's crew. There Mevans got into an argument with a woman named Fontir, and Joron had to drag him away before the two came to blows. The owner of the house had them thrown out, with instruction never to come back again.

"You passed over the message?" whispered Joron as he dragged away Mevans, shouting abuse at the closed door behind them.

"Hag take you all!" shouted Mevans. Then turned away and let Joron see his smile before whispering, "Ey, Fontir will pass it to the shipwife."

That done there was little else they could do but wait by the door of the Maiden's Skirts for Skearith's Eye to dip beneath the horizon. Joron watched the shadows slowly lengthening, creeping toward his feet while Mevans continued to measure the jungle with his knife. When night finally fell Joron looked to Mevans.

"How fast does it grow?"

"Fast," he said quietly. "As fast as I have ever seen."

"Bad news," said Joron, "you always say that."

"Ey," said Mevans, "'tis a savage season coming, a savage season like no other." He looked away and Joron wondered at that, for it seemed since he had come to the deck of *Tide Child*, every season had been savage.

They waited in the darkness, and soon Cwell joined them.

"They not here yet?" she said. "If the Hag-cursed wastrels have done nothing but steal our chest I'll hunt every one down and feed them to the longthresh."

"There'll be no need of that," said a voice from the shadows and Mrin appeared. "Come, we have to trek over the island and it will take us an hour."

"Your shipwife said we would take a flukeboat," said Cwell.

"Ey, but yorn black ship is there, and no doubt watching," said Mrin. "So she changed her mind. This way they will not even know you are gone. *Keyshan's Eye* is waiting, and your goods are aboard."

"'Tis a good place for an ambush, the gion forest," said Cwell.

"Ey," said Mrin, "it is. But if we wanted your goods we would just leave with 'em."

Cwell nodded. "There is that," she said, "but I am not a woman given to trust, so if I think you betray us," she took a small crossbow from her sash and cocked it, "you die first."

"That is fair," said Mrin. "Now follow me." She led them through the small town and at the edge of the gion forest a small group waited. "Three of our deckchilder, two fellow travellers," said Mrin.

"This was not mentioned."

"'Tis not yorn business," said Mrin. "Now, do you come or not?" Her deckchilder started hacking at the edge of the forest and Cwell glanced back at Joron, who shrugged. Cwell nodded in return and led them into the darkness.

It was louder in the night, the beasts of the forest more aggrieved by this intrusion into their territory, their life. Joron shuddered, images of the tunir filling his mind. Such beasts would be impossible to see in the night and, as he swung with his curnow, cutting through the vegetation, he found he was doing it in a rhythm, starting to hum. As he hummed he heard a song starting up behind him, Mevans joining in and then Cwell. One of those they travelled with looked at them, a strange look, a worried one, and Joron felt as if some vast eye was suddenly turned on him. As if some great creature suddenly realised he existed. He stopped humming, his mouth dry, he coughed.

"Mrin," he said, "does this island have a windspire?"

"Ey," she said, "a small one mind, but it does. Why, have you suddenly grown feathers instead of sores, and wish to commune with the winds in your madness?"

"No," he said. "Was just idle curiosity."

"Good," said Mrin, "would be a trial for me if I had to put out your eyes, ey?"

Joron did not reply and they broke from the forest at that moment. Two flukeboats were drawn up in the sharp sand before them and Joron, without boots as befit a servant, felt the sand cut into the sole of his foot as he made his way across the beach. He climbed into the flukeboat and the deckchilder around him pushed off. He turned from the island and looked to the brownbone waiting on the placid sea. *Well*, he thought. *Once I set foot on that boat, there is no turning back*. They sculled across placid black water, to an old boat that stank of rotting bone and ill-kept gion and varisk, and when they hauled him aboard, he left bloody footprints on the deck behind him.

27

The Deckchilder

The kindest thing that Joron could say about the passage from Broomstown on Jirton's Isle to Bernshulme on Shipshulme aboard the *Keyshan's Eye* was that it was shorter than he had thought it would be. He spent the long weeks of the passage as deckchilder, Cwell was found a cabin and Joron became what he had thought he should have been all his life. One of the common women and men, part of the muscle mass that propelled a ship across the ocean. Working to stay afloat and keep them safe from the creatures of the sea that would rend and chew and rip and tear whatever warm flesh made contact with the water, staining the blue red with spilled life.

Much to Joron's dismay he found out he made a very poor deckchild. He lacked the strength that was common to crew, common to women and men who spent every waking moment pulling and heaving and twisting and brushing and mending. He tired quickly, found himself stumbling while those around him had no trouble carrying on. His peg was not the same as his bone spur – it made him slow, it ruined his balance and climbing the rigging of *Keyshan's Eye* was an impossibility. Though Cwell had said he was a man rated as deckchild, it had quickly become clear to all that he was not. The ship's deckkeeper, Mrin, had taken great joy in berating him for his slowness, for his slovenly ways, for his inability to do the simplest of tasks. The deckmother, a woman called Jimry, had followed him round the ship for an entire afternoon picking at every task he had attempted, telling him just how he had failed, though Joron was sure he had done at least some of them to a competent level, if not an expert one. But he was not fast enough, not exact enough, and in the end he was simply not enough. Had he been actual crew of *Keyshan's Eye* he would have had the skin corded from his back, and only Cwell's intervention had stopped him being put on punishment rations by a frustrated deckmother who, he knew, wanted nothing more than to take out her frustration on him with her fists.

Keyshan's Eye was not a happy ship either, even if he had to grudgingly admit it was a well-run one. The crew seemed to exist in a state of near terror; even on the first day when they were fresh from port punishments were frequent, the deckmother carried a stick that she used often, rations were docked and the crew accepted this without a word, heads bowed as abuse was heaped upon them. His inability to keep up with them was met with resentment as the other deckchilder paid his price when he could not be punished. When they were fed lunch one of them spat in his food before handing it over, and Joron had worked so hard that day, been left so unbearably hungry by it, that he had simply spooned out the spit and thrown it to one side, gritting his teeth and eating the rest of the grain mulch that was served to them.

Some time in the third week it became clear that the *Keyshan's Eye* was sinking. Worse, its pumps were jammed and Joron was given the miserable job that he was told he would retain for the rest of the passage: he became a bailer. His days were spent with a bucket, part of a chain of those judged not worthy to work the more responsible jobs on the ship. He trudged from the slate of the deck, down the steep steps into the underdeck, down into the hold and from there into the stinking bilges where filthy water swilled around his calves while he filled his bucket. Then he made his way back up to the main-deck – for the underdeck was so filled with cargo it made the bowpeeks inaccessible – to throw the water over the side. Then back down and up and down and up and down, day after day, week after week. Mevans spent his time in the tops and Cwell spent her time strolling the decks with Shipwife Ansiri and Deckkeeper Mrin, commenting on the weather and the course of the ship – both of which were judged good. Had Joron not been weary, and pained from his constant battle against the water in the bilges – a battle the ship was slowly losing, though none wanted to hear that – then he may have pointed out that nothing about this situation was good. Instead he only trudged back and forth with his fellow bailers, the lowest of the low, all raggedly dressed, half-starved and with no more time for him than the rest of the crew. When he tried to speak to them they looked blankly at him from haggard faces, skin worn by weather and poor nutrition. So he went on with his up and down and down and up and fill and pour, and it seemed the days passed in the slowest possible increments. All he had to look forward to was poor food and his hammock where he had the brief and black relief of sleep.

He passed Mevans one day, who pulled him aside.

"D'keeper," he said quietly.

"Servant," said Joron, "my name is Servant."

"Ey," said Mevans. "You look poor, D'keeper, I could ask Cwell to have you declared ill and—"

"This ship, Mevans, is sinking. Three weeks of bailing and the water is now up to my knees."

"Oh, ey," said Mevans, "most of these short haulers are barely worth the name ship, but we should be at Bernshulme in three more. It will stay afloat that long." Joron nodded, so tired he could barely speak.

"Why do the crew put up with the way they are treated, Mevans? I know the ship is run well but the crew are near to breaking, full of fear and—"

"Slaves," said Mevans quietly.

"But that is . . ."

"This is Cahanny's ship, you think he cares about the laws of Bernshulme? Besides, they are technically indentured, working off a debt and that is legal under Bernshulme law."

"They will never work it off though." He turned to find Cwell by the rail, staring out over the sea as she spoke. "It is a trick, a lie," she said. "They give themselves into these contracts in hope of escaping debt, then they are worked to their deaths."

"All of them?" said Joron.

"Ey," said Cwell, "apart from the officers and a few of the strongest deckchilder."

"And yet they do not take over the ship?"

"No," said Cwell, "for as you have noted, the ship is sinking. Where would they go?" Joron stared at the small woman, thought it odd how, since they had changed their positions, Cwell had spoken more than he ever usually heard her talk. "I will speak to Ansiri, have them reassign you as my steward. She does not like you and demanded you do this work out of spite, but she has made her point, and I think she worries I may say something unpleasant to Cahanny when we make Bernshulme so I am likely to get my own way."

"Thank you, Cwell."

"Do not thank me, you are tired. We will need you awake if we are to find the shipwife, ey?"

"Ey," said Joron.

So Joron's following weeks were easier, simply fetching and carrying for Cwell, in a way that was expected of a steward. When she saw his leg was paining him she commanded he take some time to clean the stump, which was much needed, as the constant walking up and down stairs had worn away skin and created sores which were now weeping. Joron had to ask Mevans to coax some bird fat out of the ship's cook to coat his wounds and protect them. After that he spent a pleasant afternoon simply being out the way and resting his leg. So the journey continued until he heard the call go up: "Ship rising!" Then it was all he could do not to run up on deck, his heart beating hard in anticipation of action.

Though of course, this was neither a fighting ship nor his ship. Should they see action aboard the *Keyshan's Eye* it would be short and pitiful and most aboard would end up as food for longthresh.

A knock on the door.

"Ey, enter," he said, knowing it must be Mevans. Cwell would simply walk in, as would anyone on the crew of the ship.

"Hundred Isles two-ribber coming up on us," said Mevans as he slipped in. "Shipwife says all is fine but the mood on deck is noticeably tense, it is."

"They fear trouble with it?" Mevans shrugged

"I think not, 'tis simply the normal fear of criminals meeting with authority." He got down onto his knees and pulled out their sea chest from under the thin bed. "But it does no harm to be prepared, ey?" he said, and took out a curnow, held the blade in his hand. They stood together in the small and cramped cabin. Feeling the ship slow, hearing the shouts of deckchilder as they brought their ship alongside the Hundred Isles boneship. The back and forth of words shouted from one deck to the other and the frustration within Joron that he could neither hear properly what was said nor see what was happening.

"Can you tell what they say?" he asked. Mevans shook his head.

"No, but it does not sound as though any are ill-disposed out there."

"Well, that is good at least."

"Should we try and open a bowpeek?" Joron shook his head.

"I wager this kind of encounter has been done many times before, let us not risk anything that may disrupt it." They waited, Joron almost too worried to draw breath. For what if it all ended here? In the dark depths of a stinking, sinking brownbone? So easy for something to go wrong, so terrible to be at the mercy of others. The shipwife of the boneship could decide to impound the smuggler, a fair amount of coin to be made that way. Or the shipwife of *Keyshan's Eye* could decide to give Cwell up. Though as Cwell stood on the deck with them it would be the last thing they ever did; she would repay treachery with her blade in an instant.

That would not help him, or Meas, wherever she was and whatever she was being put through. And all he could do was wait.

The air in the small cabin seemed to still, to close in on them. The familiar sounds of the ship receding, the running of water, the jangle of chain and song of rigging and wind drifting away as the ship came to a stop. Waiting. Worrying.

Then he felt *Keyshan's Eye* shudder, heard a call and not long after a jolt as more wings were dropped and the wind gathered. The door opened and Cwell appeared.

"That shipwife did not like smugglers much," she said. "For all that, they had no option but to let us through. Seems the people of Bernshulme are hungry, or those with enough money to buy black-market goods are, at any rate." She spat on the floor. "Be pleased if we get to kill a few of them."

"Let us hope we do not have to," said Joron. "Nothing would give me greater pleasure than to get in and out unseen."

"We have not spoken yet," said Cwell, "about how we get the shipwife away." Joron nodded.

"It was not a thing I could plan for," he said quietly, and what was not said, of course, was that they all knew there was little chance they would ever leave.

"My uncle may help," she said.

"Ey, and if not him then I must search out Kept Indyl Karrad; he has a past with Meas, maybe he will feel he owes her enough to help us. He must, I believe."

"The Kept care about nothing but themselves," said Cwell.

"True, of most of them," said Joron. "But Indyl helped our

cause, he is part of it. We exist in a large part because of him."

"He has no love for you though," said Mevans. "He will never forgive you for killing his son in a duel."

"Well, that is true, let us hope his respect for Meas overrides his hatred for me." He stared at the filthy deck of the cabin, momentarily lost. "He may be the only friend we have in Bernshulme."

"Well," said Mevans with a grin, "I think this will be an interesting trip, if the only friend we have is the man who had you condemned to death."

"War makes for strange bedfellows and stranger allies."

"Is it not peace we fly for, D'keeper?"

"When we have her back it will be. Until then, it is war." He gritted his teeth, feeling the pressure in his gums. "I do not know another way."

"Well, we are fleet, Deckkeeper," said Mevans with a smile, "war is what we are good at. So let us go to our war, and bring home the shipwife. That will be an adventure for me to tell my children, and them to tell theirs for all the generations of Mevanses yet to come, will it not?"

"It will," said Joron, and he felt something rise within him, some bright hope. With deckchilder such as Mevans with him, how could he fail? Both he and Cwell were stout and strong and skilled. "It is not about numbers, you know, Mevans. A two-ribber can take a five-ribber, given the right conditions, the right wind, the right commander and enough luck." His rousing speech was interrupted by a chuckling, and he turned to Cwell.

"Luck," she said. "Strikes me we have had little of that since we lost the shipwife."

"Ey," said Joron, mood darkening again, "and that is why we must get her back."

28

The Effect

They saw the smoke before they saw Shipshulme. Twisting spires of greasy black, lazily climbing towards the clouds, and Joron thought himself betrayed. Thought that Tenbern Aileen had sold him a lie and sent him away so she could raid Bernshulme without him. But later, as they came close enough that he could just make out some detail of the town, Shipwife Ansiri disabused him of that.

"Still burning the bodies," she said to Cwell. "I had hoped the plague had run its course; we will have to go around the other side of Shipshulme to dock."

"Why?" said Joron and the shipwife shot him a look of such filth he had to fight not to recoil from it.

"You tread my slate as your mistress asks, and she has coin and currency in Bernshulme, but I do not give you leave to speak." Joron bowed his head, mumbled an apology. "Cross me again, servant, and I'll have you thrown over the side."

"No," said Cwell.

"You think your uncle will avenge a lost servant?" said Ansiri.

"He will not," Cwell laughed. "He casts life away like a fisher throws fish guts over the side." Then she turned her head, ratty blonde hair blowing in the wind. "But I will, Ansiri." And she stared right into the shipwife's eyes. "Do you wish to test me?" She grinned. "For I confess, I am become bored this journey and would welcome some action." Ansiri's eye flicked away, toward where Mrin, her deckkeeper, stood. "Bring her to the party too," said Cwell, "and your deckmother if you wish, for the three of you may even make it a challenge." Her voice became colder than the Northstorm, as sharp and dangerous as ice islands. "I would not want it said the fight was unfair." The two gazed at one another and all action on the ship paused, as if awaiting the outcome of the conversation. Then Ansiri smiled, and laughed.

"I would not be so rude as to fight my honoured guest," she said.

"Good," replied Cwell, but she did not cease in her gaze, did not let her eyes waver from Ansiri's face. "Then you will answer my servant's question. Why do we dock around the far side of Shipshulme Island rather than at Bernshulme? This was not the plan and I am suspicious when plans change suddenly." Ansiri leaned in close to Cwell and Joron had to strain to listen over the sound of the wind.

"It is the plague," she whispered. "Closed the harbour."

"Why have I not heard of this?"

"To speak too much of such things is to draw the Hag's eye, all know it." Joron listened, and the Tenbern's reticence in attacking Bernshulme became clearer. Why attack a place already crippled by plague when she could let it do her work for her? And why risk bringing disease back to her own people? Joron stared into the distance, wishing for his nearglass. He could make out the bright pink and purple hump of the island, and what looked like a few shipspines before it. And something else, something he could not quite understand. It was as if part of the island had collapsed and landed between the towers of the harbour on the ends of their long stone piers.

"Not many ships," said Cwell.

"No," said Ansiri, "most of the fleet are out in defence of

the inner islands. The rest are round the rear of Shipshulme. Those few you see are there to defend the plaguebringer."

"Plaguebringer?" said Joron. Ansiri shot him another foul look but Cwell had made her wishes about him plain and Ansiri continued, though she addressed her words to Cwell, not to him.

"That is what they call it, the keyshan." A darkness descended on Joron then, he felt a sudden need to sit, his one good leg felt robbed of all strength. "So much rejoicing when it came, towed in by three boneships. Their crews were the first to die, then the plague spread across the docks, through Fishdock, the old town, the tenements. It is a cruel sickness, much like the rot your man has but faster. Nausea, vomiting, seizures, the skin falling away like it is burned but there is no fire. And it is made all the crueller that it came in with such hope." Joron turned back toward the island, staring at Bernshulme. Now he knew what he looked at, the shape made more sense, and his brain could pick out the massive body of a keyshan, yet one greatly misshapen, not smooth and beautiful like the ones he had seen swimming through the waters. And he heard no song from it. Or did he? Was there something there? Something far away? Something cold and sad and lonely?

"We must turn now," said Ansiri. "Stay and watch the island if you will, though with this wind we will not get much closer." She walked away and started giving orders to her listless crew and *Keyshan's Eye* began to turn away from Bernshulme to catch the wind which would bring it around the island. Mevans walked over to join them.

"We should get ready," he said. "With this wind we will be in dock by the end of the day."

"We do not go into Bernshulme," said Joron, morose. "We fly around the island to the other side as there is . . ."

"Plague, ey," he said, for nothing seemed to surprise Mevans. "I heard talk of it in the underdecks."

"It is my doing," said Joron.

"It is our doing," said Mevans. Joron shook his head.

"No," he said. "Mine. My orders, my idea. I knew I sent a poison to them."

"You did not know it was a plague, mind," said Mevans gently. "We fight a war as you said, women and men die."

"True," said Joron, "it is one thing to give an order and make a plan, another to have it blossom and see the rotten fruit ripen before you."

"No point talking," said Cwell, "it is done now. We should get our things." So it was that they made their way into the underdecks and gathered together all they had brought, packed it tight and well in the sea chest and Joron realised that, despite his life being one full of action and travel there was little he called important. Meas, she had many things, the trinkets, books and rocks that still sat in the great cabin aboard *Tide Child*. He had a bone spur and a straightsword, but these were workaday things, they said nothing of him, of who he was. Did he even exist beneath the persona of the Black Pirate? Was it even him who gave the orders that took so many lives, or just a shell of a man?

Did it even matter in the end?

He took a breath. Let it out. No time for melancholy, no time for indecision. Even if the Black Pirate was a fiction he must be that fiction from the moment he set foot on Shipshulme, he must command, decide, plan. For now he was as near to his goal as he had ever been. He felt sure Meas was on that island and alive, as sure of that as he was that a keyshan slept beneath Shipshulme. He felt the great presence, felt the slow beat of its heart and he was sure that it knew, in some way, of its dead sither on the island and that knowledge infused its slow dreams, and maybe it dreamed of wreaking vengeance, of waking to strike at those it might think had killed its sibling. Or could it understand they had not, that the corpse on the shore was product of its own kin fighting? Or maybe it did not notice it at all, and Joron simply assigned it human feelings in a bid to understand something so vast it was unknowable. He did not know and it did not matter. Without the Gullaime the keyshan was beyond his reach, he was sure of that.

It was strange, that thoughts of the Gullaime were like a stab in the heart. He missed it. When they were back on land he would be commander once more and alone; Cwell and Mevans would look to him. Back aboard ship even Aelerin deferred to him, would never be truly what he could call a friend, the same with the other shipwives. The Gullaime was the only thing in his life that did not care who he was, treated him no differently despite his rank. It was rude, dismissive and somehow that was a comfort to him, and he felt in need of comfort. In need of direction as well, but that he would find with Meas, he was sure of it. Like a ship with a broken rudder he had gone far off the course she had set him, but he would find her and bring her back and she would set him right and straight and, somehow, fix their world. Find their people a place.

A sob broke from him.

What am I? he thought. *What weak creature am I? You judged me worthy of this burden, Meas, and all I wish to do is place it back on your shoulders.* Was that his real reason for being here, was it entirely selfish? Was all his talk of duty and promise simply a cloak with which to mask his cowardice? He did not want it to be, felt sure it was.

But if so, he must wear that cloak again, must stand tall and be ready. He was not finished yet. She was there, somewhere. He was so close. And whatever happened, find Meas or die here, the Black Pirate would end on Bernshulme, and Joron was glad of that, for his command was heavy, his mask was heavy, and his hands were heavy, weighed down with blood.

Joron had little to do but wait then, long hours listening to the sounds of the ship, and he took some sleep and used the time to pad the cup of the varisk leg he was using. Trying to make some better comfort of it until he was on land, and could once more strap on the bone spur his stump had learned the shape of in such a way it had almost become part of him.

On some days he did not even look down and feel surprise that his leg was not there. Just like on some days he did not look over the deck of his ship and expect to see old friends and lovers walking toward him. So much had been lost and here he sat, on the cusp of finding out if it was worth it.

"Servant." He turned. Cwell at the door. "We are coming in to drop the staystone," she said, "you and Mevans should bring up the sea chest and we will load it on the flukeboat to be taken ashore."

"Ey, mistress," he said, and moments later was joined by a grinning Mevans who took most of the weight while they pulled and pushed the heavy sea chest up the steep and slimy steps of the hold of *Keyshan's Eye*, the hatkeep cursing the thing all the while.

"I do hate a chest, damn things seem built to make life difficult for an honest deckchild," he muttered under his breath and Joron smiled to himself. At least some things were familiar.

On deck, Skearith's Eye was falling, dipping beneath the brightly coloured top of Shipshulme Island, and all around him were ships and boats of various sizes. Tall spines casting long shadows, reaching out across the sea like grasping fingers eager to close around him. He heard a splash as the staystone was dropped and *Keyshan's Eye* came to a full stop. It was poorly executed and he staggered a little with the heavy chest as the ship jerked at the rope. The deckmother shouted at someone and Joron heard the crack of the cord and a groan as it made contact with some poor soul's flesh. He would be glad to be off this ship, away from its crew of slaves and the constant reminder that no matter how hard he may sometimes think his life had been, others had it far harder. He looked back to the island. Shadows lay across the deck, making a cage of stripes around him and he thought how apt that was, for he knew deep down, in the depths of his mind, that he was unlikely to leave this place.

Then he was awash with guilt. What had he done? Brought Mevans and Cwell to this place to die. He and Mevans put the chest down by the bonerail and Cwell came over to stand with them. He lowered his voice.

"Listen, and listen well," he said. "I free you both, you understand? Cwell, your debt to me is paid in full. Mevans, you need not follow me as your deckkeeper; you are both free to stay on this boat and return to the fleet. Or go other ways, if that is your choice."

"Stay?" said Cwell. "On this leaky tub? I think not." Joron turned to Mevans.

"We have a job to do," said Mevans. "And I'll not leave it undone." Then he grinned. "Besides, I cannot bear to think what trouble you would get yourself into without me and her to look after you, ey?"

Joron stood a while. Then nodded, and a great tightness that was within his chest seemed to unwind a little.

"Thank you," he said, and had to fight to keep the emotion from his voice. He had not realised how much he wanted them to stay, how much he feared going to his death alone.

"Are you ready?" They turned to find Shipwife Ansiri stood behind them. "For I'd have you off my ship."

"Where will I find my uncle?" said Cwell.

"Bernshulme."

"He did not flee the plague?"

"At first, ey, but it seems the plague knows its place and it leaves the houses of the rich and powerful alone. If you see a rope go around it, they rope off the plague zones." She turned, watching as her deckchilder pulled up an A-frame and started to heave the flukeboat off the deck and transfer it to the water. "When you are on the docks," she said, "hire a porter is my advice; the way over the island is a hard enough walk without carrying a chest, the porters are strong and used to such journeys. Honest too, most of 'em."

"How do we know which ones are not honest?" said Mevans.

"Well, you'll have to judge that on meeting 'em," she said. With a splash the flukeboat landed, sending up a sheet of water that soaked Joron, Cwell and Mevans. Ansiri strode off, shouting at her crew and demanding the deckmother "teach 'em some lessons".

"I will be glad to be off this ship," said Joron.

"Ey, me too," said Mevans, "'tis a miserable place. But from what is said, Bernshulme is not much better. Now come, Servant," he grinned at Joron, "let us get the sea chest aboard the flukeboat and us off this tub before it sinks in the harbour. If I'm going to die on Shipshulme it would at least be polite to give the Thirteenbern a chance to do it."

29

A Homecoming

The makeshift port at the rear of Shipshulme was neither well planned nor comfortable. Merely a collection of gion and varisk huts connected by paths made muddy by their proximity to the sea and the constant wading ashore of deck-childer and their officers. There was no water deep enough for a true harbour on this side of Shipshulme, just a gently sloping shingle of sharp shells, and the ships were forced to sit far out in the bay and send their flukeboats to the island. In the bright light of morning Joron stood on the sand and watched as a snake of brown boats, painted with all manner of symbols – some familiar, some not – moved through the water bringing cargo and people. Behind him Cwell argued a price with a porter to take their sea chest over the island to Bernshulme. Joron felt faintly resentful at any price paid as the chest was more for show than anything else, and would be discarded once they reached Bernshulme.

That aside everything seemed so beautiful; the sea was placid, catching the light of Skearith's Eye and transmuting it into a lake of shining silver. The air full of the plaintive calls of skeers and the shouts of deckchilder going about their tasks – mostly happy, occasionally irritated, often singing. Beneath the sound of human voices, rising and falling on a warm breeze, he could sense the deeper song of the island. Joron felt more than heard that song, the call of the beast buried far beneath it.

"I have known your song all my life," he said to himself, and he wondered how many others heard it. If it was the constant background of their thoughts, and they never gave it a moment's more reflection than breathing or the flow of blood through their veins. Could they all do what he did? Could they all be what he was?

For a single, golden moment the world before him shimmered and he felt as though he looked through a glass at the same scene in almost the same place. But it was not. There were no ships, instead keyshans wallowed and upon their backs sat strange devices, as if woven of air, and women and men moved about within those devices. Above, vast winged creatures flew and the same devices hung beneath them, and all around him stood women and men but taller and fitter than any he had known, dressed strangely too. No sign of the sick, the lame or unformed. As if all were Bern, and none were Berncast here. Then, these strange and wondrous people heard some signal, silent to Joron but loud to them; they turned and looked to the sky and those beautiful, strong, healthy faces twisted in fear and all was brightness and heat and a cloud, rising and rising . . .

"Joron?" He felt a strong arm grab his elbow. "Are you all right?" He turned to find Mevans, dear, kind, worried Mevans. "You stumbled, and for no reason I could see."

"Tired is all, I think, Mevans," he said. "The bailing of that Hag-cursed ship took more from me than I realised and I still feel it." He tried to smile, but the after-images of that light were laid across his vision, ghosts of those beautiful faces, and he felt like he had the answer to some vast and great puzzle, but that the puzzle was so vast and great that he did not even know it existed. Had it existed? He grabbed Mevans by the forearm, holding him hard, feeling the solid muscle beneath the skin. The realness of him. "If I lose myself, Mevans, if I go like Coxward and the rot overcomes me, you will not let me suffer?"

Mevans, usually so stoical, so dependable and quick to joke, froze. For just a moment, a terrible sadness distorted his features, chased away a jolly reply, and he locked eyes with Joron.

"I would not let you suffer, D'keeper," he said softly. They stood there, locked together for a moment. Then Joron let go, stood back. Straightened his filthy clothes.

"Has Cwell agreed a price with the porter yet," said Joron, "or have they come to blows?"

"A price is agreed and the woman has already set off. Truthfully," he leaned in, amused, "I reckon they both enjoyed the verbal sparring."

"Well, Cwell has always loved a fight, it is true."

"You talk of me?" She approached them grinning, belting on her bone knives and holding a curnow for both Mevans and Joron. "I did not really want to trust your straightsword to that porter, they are all thieves, but I reckon she was the most honest of the lot and if I handed it to you now there would be talk."

"My spur too?"

"Even more talk with that." She spat on the shingle. "So I have put them both in Mevans's pack, if they steal the chest now it will be a favour to us. Do you wish more rest, D'keeper, or shall we make our way over the island?"

"We may as well start, the day is young so let us not waste it."

With that they set off into the gion forest, always making their way up as that was the quickest path over the island, and with every step Joron winced as his stump complained at the rough treatment meted out by the ill-fitting peg leg. *A day of this, at least*, he thought. *Maybe longer if I cannot make the pace.* Ahead of him Cwell and Mevans worked methodically, cutting down the forest, weaving a path around heirthrews and the more vicious vegetation, and all the time the air was full of the noise of the forest life, sounding out its fury at these creatures pushing their way through a domain that was not theirs. But the noise did not stop Mevans and Cwell, and biting insects did not bother them the way they seemed to beset Joron. About midday they strayed near the nest of a pair of birin and the vicious birds ran out of the undergrowth, wings outstretched and slashing claws at the ready. They reminded Joron of the Gullaime, their aggression totally out of proportion to their size, as they were no higher than Mevans's waist. The birin's desire to protect their nest only served to provide food for the pot and draw attention to their eggs. The two deckchilder cut the birds down out of hand, blades falling, squawking quickly stilled. Mevans swiftly gutted the birds, spraying blood on the base of a gion palm as if it were paint on a ship's spine. Then he tied the birds' legs together and draped the corpses round his neck. Cwell vanished into the bushes, returning with a clutch of eggs and the birin's nest.

"We shall eat at least, and these nests make fine sun hats," she said, placing the eggs carefully in her bag and then, after brushing what filth she could from the inside of the wide nest of braided stalks, she placed it upside down on her head. They stopped for lunch, more hard bread, eaten as they sat on rocks while Mevans plucked the birin, saving the primary feathers which Cwell placed in her bag as they were valuable. More than anything Joron wished to inspect his leg, but that would be to show weakness.

"You should check your leg, Deckkeeper," said Mevans.

"Ey," said Cwell. "The porter will meet us at the top of the island, they will set up a camp there and we'll cook them birds. The less damage done to you now the better, cos we may have to fight in Bernshulme." Joron nodded, oddly touched by her care for him; even though Cwell made her interest a gruff thing he knew it was more. Their silent relationship was as odd and as close as any other he had, and because he often simply forgot she was there she knew as much about him as any other alive. He undid the peg, unwrapped the stump and tried not to seem bothered by others seeing it. Mevans inspected it.

"Bloody," he said, "but clean, the cup could do with repacking." He gave Joron a smile. "I'll do it while we rest."

When they set off again, Joron felt much lighter, better; he was not pain-free but he was not as pained as before and the way seemed easier, despite it being steeper now. They walked through the afternoon, the heat of the forest slowly abating. As Skearith's Eye began to fall he smelled smoke on the air.

"Smell that?" he said.

"Ey," said Mevans, "that'll be the porter's camp. Will allow us a view over Bernshulme and some proper rest. Hag knows we are sore in need of it."

They stumbled into a clearing where several porters had set up tents, while around the edges of the clearing children were stationed with torches and behind them younger children were busily pulling up any vegetation that might trip the unwary. The air was full of a smell – something unpleasant and familiar yet also, and at the same time, alien and he found he could not place it. He wanted to hold his breath and he wanted to breathe it in. The strength of the smell waxed and waned with the breeze blowing over the hill.

"That's ours," said Cwell, pointing at a blue tent painted with the signs of the Maiden. Their porter, a haggard-looking woman with all the wiry strength of a deckchild, sat before a fire using their sea chest as a seat and turning a spit. She looked up, nodded at Cwell and returned to concentrating on the bird she was roasting. When they were near she looked up again.

"We sleep on the ground in the tent, it's covered so you shouldn't end up with a varisk vine growing through you." The porter chuckled to herself. "Keep your weapons by your sides; ever since the plague came there have been tunir in the heights, that's why we got the children round the edges, as lookouts. I don't reckon the fire scares tunir none, but it gives some comfort as to those as choose to believe it does." In the firelight Joron saw her eyes were different colours. "We'll eat then sleep; nothing to see in the night from here and tunir seldom bother sleepers."

Joron doubted that was true, and while he ate he found himself watching the edges of the forest, the vegetation writhing in the torchlight in time with the movement of his jaws. He did not sleep well either, and the thought of tunir preyed upon him. Mevans and Cwell and the porter showed that wonderful skill unique to deckchilder and fell deep into sleep as soon as they lay their heads down, but Joron found no rest. He felt as if he had somehow travelled back through time to the night after he was condemned to the black ships, felt the Hag standing at his shoulder, ready to pull him down to her domain in the depths of the ocean.

"Sentence is passed," he said the words used to condemn a soul to the black ships to himself, "only the day is undecided." He turned on his side, the sores in his face stinging and the night sounds of the forest filling his ears. The muscles of his face starting to ache as he strained to hear more. At some point exhaustion overcame him and he fell into darkness.

He woke to a camp full of happy noise, the industrious sound of women and men going about their work and knowing that at the end of the day they would get paid for their labours. Cwell and Mevans were already up and out the tent, he could hear Mevans talking with someone about the rate the gion was growing this year, faster than usual, and whether this was a good or bad omen. He could not hear Cwell but then he so seldom did. No doubt she was nearby somewhere, near enough to keep an eye on him. He sat up, rubbed his bleary eyes. Saw that a scarf had been laid out – it was red, not his usual black, but he understood that. The less he looked like the Black Pirate and the more he looked like some poor unfortunate who had contracted keyshan's rot the better.

And of course, that was what he was, Black Pirate or not.

He sat up, unwrapped the bandages from his stump and looked at his skin, raw and red where it was not hard and dry and cracked. Mevans pushed through the entrance to the tent with something wrapped in greased material in his hand.

"Here," he said, handing it over. His hand was covered in red lumps, as was his face. "It will help keep infection away." Joron took the wrapped package, smelt it before he opened it and then understood the welts on the hatkeep's body. Honey.

"Thank you, Mevans," he said, "it looks like you paid a high price for it."

"Not as high as the price I charged some of the porters for the rest, we done all right."

"He up yet?" said Cwell, pushing in behind Mevans and the hatkeep nodded. Cwell came around him and held out his bone spur, though it no longer gleamed.

"I got it from Mevans's pack, and painted it black so it will attract less attention." He took it from her.

"Thank you, Cwell." She nodded.

"You should come out," said Mevans, "look down the hill." Something in his voice that Joron could not place and did not like.

"You do not make it sound like I will enjoy the view," said Joron. Mevans shrugged.

"I will wait for you on the ridge to the east," he said. Joron nodded, then smeared the honey on his stump and re-wrapped it in bandages before strapping on his spur and standing. Testing his balance, finding the spur as welcome as a familiar friend, someone you could slip right back into conversation with after a gap of years. Though, hadn't Meas told him, an age ago now, that people like her, like him, had no friends?

He stood, feeling maudlin. Rubbed at his shoulder, missing the weight of Black Orris who so often came to perch there and he wondered how Farys and his crew managed, and how the Gullaime was; did Madorra's influence over it grow? Was it miserable without him?

"It seems I miss *Tide Child*," he said, grunting as he stood, "and those aboard, as much as I miss my leg." He made his way out, through a camp breaking down and women and men eating a thin broth that he found he had no stomach for; no doubt he would regret that later. More of the area around the camp had been cleared during the night, and now to the east the edge of a cliff had been revealed and it was there that Mevans stood. A black figure against Skearith's Eye as it rose from the sea. He walked over, wincing a little where the spur rubbed his stump – though it was a magnitude more comfortable than the peg leg he had used up until then.

"Mevans," he said as he came to stand by him.

"Deckkeeper," said the man and Joron looked out. From here he could see the whole inner curve of the island. The Grand Bothies, the tenements, the winding streets and the great deepwater harbour of Bernshulme. And slowly, and surely, the horror of what he had wrought sank into him. His first thought, whimsical, was *ah, now the smell makes sense*. He almost laughed, so light and frivolous was that thought compared to what was laid out in front of him.

Filling the deepwater harbour was the corpse of the keyshan. The head was pulled up onto the shipdocks, the huge beak slightly open to show long teeth. Behind it the body swelled and at the point of the two light towers on the end of the piers it blocked the harbour completely. The creature was rotting; bone shone on the head and at the centre of the beast, while between the piers, the flesh had rotted far more quickly, almost as if it had been burned away, and the massive curving rib bones, the same bones that would be straightened and bonded for the lower hulls of boneships, stuck out stark – not white, but yellowed on top, darkened below also as if burned. Through the harbour entrance he followed the vast body of the keyshan, hidden below the water, a pale shape that gradually vanished into the depths.

Within the harbour were four ships. They must have been trapped there when they towed the keyshan in. Now they floated empty, dead and spattered with a million dots of skeer guano, though no birds sat along the spars of the ships, or picked over the massive rotting corpse of the keyshan. Nothing moved at all. There was a huge three-quarter circle where something was not right spreading out from the harbour – it took in the drydocks, Fishdock and the tenements of the poorest. The circle's borders passed through some areas and took others in whole and Joron was not sure what it was that made this strange difference between one part of the town and another, what demarcation there was.

Not at first.

Slowly, he realised what he saw, or rather did not. It was a stillness, a halo of inactivity. He squinted down at the town and Mevans passed across his nearglass. Joron raised it, focused it. Found the edges of the still area and through the magnification of the lens he found another demarcation. Rags were tied on sticks and ropes, following a circular line through the streets. Outside those sticks he saw people moving around, though not many, but inside those lines nothing. He followed a woman carrying a heavy basket and watched her take a long way round, even though she was struggling with the weight of her cargo, rather than pass through the rag markers. He changed his focus to inside the lines, saw that upon the doors of almost every house and tavern and shop and building was the Hag's mark, the mark of the dead. Many of the buildings were boarded up, even the expensive ones, the best ones at the highest points of the circle. Then he saw his first body, a pathetic, sad rotten thing in an alley. Once he had spotted one he started to see more – some adults, some children, some women, some men, some poor, some rich, though he could only tell through their clothing as the bodies were so far gone as to be unrecognisable. But, just like the ships, they were not picked over by scavengers. They remained untouched by any life, slowly melting into nothing where they fell. He took the nearglass from his eye.

"I did this," he said.

"It is war," said Mevans matter-of-factly.

"But you wanted me to see what I have caused." Joron felt like the air had thickened, become almost unbreathable and the smell of the rotting keyshan, now he knew what it was, threatened to overwhelm him. Mevans looked at him, a flicker of concern moving across his open face. Then he realised how this must seem to his deckkeeper and shook his head.

"I do not blame you," said Mevans. "Only thought this a good place for you to see how the ground has changed is all. We must make our way through the town, but it is not the town it was."

"No," said Joron, and once more he looked at Bernshulme, once so busy and now laid low by his own hand, "it is not the town it was."

30

The Dying Town

The journey down through the gion forest took them all day though it was a far easier journey for Joron; with his bone spur once more strapped to his leg he felt more real, more himself.

"We should wait for true night to fall before we enter," said Mevans. Cwell grunted her assent behind him. "And I reckon it is more important than ever that we keep who we are secret. I had thought we could contact Cahanny but now I have seen the town . . ."

"Ey," said Joron, "there'll be little forgiveness for the Black Pirate here. But I still think we should try and reach Cahanny, if we can." He looked over his shoulder and beckoned Cwell forward.

"I know I slow you, Cwell," he said. "I want you to go ahead and find us somewhere to stay, see if you can make contact with your uncle."

"My place is with you," she said, glancing around at the porters. "Who knows if we can trust these people?"

"You employed one."

"Ey, and that one I trust, for she depends on us for her wage. But they gossip like stonebound."

"Mevans is with me."

"He can go into town," she said, and he saw that stubbornness that had made the woman hate him for so long, now twisted round into a fierce loyalty.

"We will need to speak to Cahanny if we are to find the shipwife, and there is no guarantee he will see Mevans, or if he does, no guarantee he will ever let him return."

"So you send me into danger instead," she said, and though she sounded sullen there was the ghost of a smile on her face.

"In my experience, Cwell, there are few more likely to come out of danger than you." She grinned at him and touched the bone knife at her side.

"Very well. Stay where the gion thins before the town outskirts and I will find you. If I am not back before morning then I suggest getting off the island as quickly as you can."

"You intend to betray us?" grinned Mevans, though the joke did not quite land; the trust was not as total between them as it had become between Cwell and Joron. Cwell shook her head.

"I mean to be real, Hatkeep," she said and that mocking tone that was almost a part of her was gone. She was serious, cold. "My uncle, he . . ." She stopped, looked up between the gion leaves to the sky. "Family counts for something, that is true. But his ambition counts for more. Should he decide that he wants you more than he cares about me, or that he holds a grudge for what we have done to the town . . . I am not a fool. He has people skilled in pain. If he wants information I will not hold out for long, no one can."

"That will not happen," said Joron.

"It won't?" said Cwell.

"No," said Joron, "why would your uncle waste time torturing you, when you are going to bring me to him anyway?" She grinned.

"If I do not feel I can trust him, I will not bring you," she said. Then she turned away and started to jog down the hill, taking a far steeper and more direct path toward Bernshulme than Joron could, or the porters with their heavy bags.

The rest of the journey continued in silence, Mevans occasionally having to help Joron. Eventually, they started to hear something that was not the noise of the forest, not the constant creaking and chirruping and chattering that filled the air, but a sound that had been absent from Joron's ears since they had left the *Keyshan's Eye* on the other side of the hill. Human voices, chattering and speaking and running together into a hiss of sound. For a second he wondered if a hoard of Bernshulme's people were waiting, vengeful and furious for the architect of their sorrow. But as the gion forest thinned he saw it was not the case, and felt foolish. How would they know? Gathered at the edge of Bernshulme, huge bothies rising beyond them, were hundreds of people, all the ragged and misshapen and broken of Bernshulme in a city of tents and lean-tos; and, for a people displaced by plague, for a people who had lost loved ones and homes and everything, the atmosphere was strangely merry.

"They seem happy," said Joron and their porter turned.

"It is market day," she said. "The days we come down from the mountain are always market day. They hope to trade with those who have goods and to fleece those who are desperate out of their coin."

"This is not good," whispered Mevans. "Since we had hoped to slip quietly into the city." He turned to the porter. "Is there another way?"

The porter shook their head.

"Only route in is through the ragged market." Mevans nodded at the woman and then took Joron's arm, slowing him.

"That place will be full of spies," he said.

"And the Bern's seaguard," said Joron. "I can see three from here."

"We can't go in that way," said Mevans.

"No," said Joron, "we can't." He took Mevans's arm, holding him still while the small line of porters and their clients walked onwards, then Joron sat in the mulch of last year's dying season and unstrapped his bone spur as the last of the travellers passed. "Here, take this," he said, handing the spur to Mevans, and he also unwrapped the scarf from his face so once more the sores of the rot were there for all to see. Then he took handfuls of the mulch from the forest floor and rubbed them on his face and on his clothes, much to the horror of the hatkeep. "No one looks at a beggar, Mevans," he said, "and none in Bernshulme would ever consider the idea that someone as grand and terrifying as the Black Pirate would lower themselves to beg for scraps in a market of the lost, eh?" Mevans grinned. "I will find a place over by the walls of the town and beg for what scraps these poor souls here can spare."

"They won't all be poor," said Mevans. "Where there is misery someone's always getting rich, and you can bet they'd be the last to throw scraps to the needy."

"Well," said Joron, "that is true indeed. I am thankful I do not really need scraps to eat."

He hopped forward, using Mevans as a crutch and feeling foolish and small and useless – though was that too bad, considering what he intended? Maybe small and useless would be a helpful mindset, since that was what he wanted people to see. "Go, Mevans," he said. "I would not have us seen together. Sell our chest and its contents, we may need the money," Mevans lowered him gently to the floor.

"What if you need help?"

"I am not incapable," snapped Joron. "Go." Then he sat there in the mulch, watching Mevans walk out through the edges of the forest to join the throng of people. As soon as he was among them he was surrounded by children, all holding up their wares and offering him the best prices for what they had, food and trinkets. Mevans must have said he had nothing and they swiftly vanished once it became clear he was not buying. When he was out of sight Joron counted to one hundred, letting the numbers move through his mind in the rhythm of waves lapping on the shore. When he had finished counting he made his own way to the bazaar of the lost and homeless, dragging his body along using his forearms. Unlike

Mevans he attracted no children with trinkets, and those who cast their gaze his way quickly found another direction to look in. To his right Mevans was once more assailed by those wanting to sell him things, his way blocked completely by a noisy gaggle of fish sellers. *It seems I may have the easiest job of all*, he thought as he pulled himself forward through stinking mud toward the edge of a bothy that had become part of the town wall. A pair of feet appeared before him and he looked up into the face of a woman. People seemed like giants from down here.

"Go around me, rot-cursed," the woman hissed, "we don't want your disease among us. We have enough to suffer."

"Ey, I will," he said.

"Don't speak to me, go around." He bowed his head and did as asked, all the time clenching his teeth for inside he wished nothing more than to lash out, that someone should dare speak to him so. But he could not, so he crawled, the muscles in his back and biceps complaining at such unfamiliar work. Arm over arm, dragging himself forward while people to seaward of him laughed and joked, no doubt many at his expense, to landward the forest continued pushing its way through aching land. Eventually, his journey ended and he found a place among the beggars sat against the wall, between an old blind woman and a man with only one arm and no legs.

"You have no cup," said the man with one arm.

"If you have no cup, none will give," said the blind woman. "I am not . . ."

"Here," she said, producing a cup from behind her and placing it in front of him.

"You are new to this, I reckon," whispered the one-armed man. "It is best not to speak, just sit here quietly, none take too kindly of being reminded they are uncharitable."

"Thank you," said Joron, and he sat back against the wall. Across the market Mevans had found a stall and was haggling over the sea chest and its contents. After a price was struck Joron watched as he found a place among a throng of women and men who stood near the largest street heading into Bernshulme. Occasionally someone would come out looking for workers and Joron watched as Mevans slunk to the back of the pack in an effort not to be chosen, though he need not have feared it – the women workers went first, then the largest of the men. There were clearly far more people looking for work than there were jobs. Bitterness was written large over the faces of those overlooked. Joron turned away. Had these people always been here, or had he brought this fresh misery? Certainly, he was sure he had done nothing to help.

He sat among the beggars for most of the day until a whistle made him look up, mostly because it sounded like Black Orris, though the foul-mouthed bird was far away with Farys on *Tide Child*. He looked for the source of the call and found Cwell, she gave him a nod and vanished into the shadows between two buildings further into Bernshulme. He waved at Mevans. As the hatkeep walked over Joron saw he had somehow acquired a bag slung across his back for Joron's spur. Joron took the four coins that had appeared in his cup in the hours he had sat there and gave two to the blind woman and two to the one armed man. "Thank you for your kindness," he said. Mevans lifted him up and helped him walk away from the ragged market and into the space between the buildings where Cwell waited.

"We have a problem," she said. Joron saw there were bruises across her cheeks.

"I can see." He pointed at the bruises. "Cahanny intends to betray us?" said Joron. She shook her head.

"I am sure he would be considering his angles, but he is in no position to. My uncle is dead."

"What?" said Mevans. "He was a clever man, I would not've thought his rivals could take him down." He put Joron down on the stone step of a building. Joron's stomach sank with the news.

"They didn't. Him and half of the gangs in Bernshulme were lost to disease. I saw one of his lieutenants. A woman called

Fedal, she is one of many fighting for the scraps of his organisation. She thought I was here to take over."

"I doubt she took kindly to that," said Mevans as he strapped the bone spur to Joron's leg.

"No, but she does not care about me any longer, and will be telling none we are here. And if we see Shipwife Ansiri again I'll leave her bleeding slow in an alley."

"Why?"

"She sold me out, warned Fedal I was coming."

"Ha," said Mevans, gesturing at Joron, "and here was us worried about 'im."

"I think the deckkeeper's secret is safe," said Cwell. "But I do not know where we go from here." Joron's thoughts raced. Contacting Cahanny had been his great hope. The man was well connected and cared for little but money and his family. He let out a deep breath.

"Then we have little choice," said Joron. "I do not like it and neither will you."

"What do you mean?" said Mevans.

"Indyl Karrad, the Kept. We must see him."

"If he will see you. He hates you," said Mevans.

"I do not need to be reminded. But he has seen me before and this is about Meas; he cares for her, deeply, I think."

"Hate is more powerful than love," said Cwell. "All who grow up in the Isles know that."

"We must confront him when he is weak. He does not know I am here. Maybe the shock will be enough to wrongfoot him and have him make us promises. If not, then I will offer him my life in return for Meas."

"No," said Mevans. The word coming out too fast, too hard.

"Our sentence has been passed, Hatkeep," he said, "only the day is undecided." Mevans shook his head.

"We need you."

"I will do what I must to get the shipwife back."

"She will need you," he said, words coming quick, urgent. "More than a year she has been in their hands now."

"Talking of the shipwife," said Cwell, "I do have a little good news. I found us some help, or rather some help found me." She pointed further down the dark alley. At first Joron saw nothing. Then a dark shape melted out of the shadows.

"Narza," said Joron. "Well, maybe all is not lost."

31

The Acquaintance

Narza, Meas's shadow – silent, violent, taciturn and absolutely loyal to her. More than anything, while he waited in the darkness, Joron wanted to ask Narza where she had been but he knew she would not say. "Looking for the shipwife," would be the most he could expect. Still, he felt safer that she was here, which was foolish of him. Four of them against a whole island was no safer than three, even if one of them was Narza.

"Guards are changing again," said Mevans.

"Still only two," whispered Joron as he watched the men outside Indyl Karrad's secret townhouse greet one another and two guards walked away. Down the street, the line of rags ended four doors before Karrad's building. He glanced up, saw the flickering light in a room far above them. "He works late into the night."

"You are sure he is in there, Narza?" She nodded, not saying how she knew, and he did not feel like he could press her.

"Do we go for it then?" said Mevans. Joron stared at the two men stood before the door, nodded.

"Cwell, Narza, take the guards down but do not kill them. We wish Karrad for an ally, not an enemy." The two women nodded and turned, vanishing into the shadows.

"Might be a bit late, D'keeper," said Mevans, "to ask for Karrad to be our friend."

"We can but hope," said Joron, and he touched the hilt of his straightsword for comfort. With that and his spur back he felt almost whole. Cwell and Narza reappeared from the night behind the two guards, putting the men into chokeholds and quietly lowering them to the floor then pulling them into the shadows where they were less likely to be found. Joron and Mevans hurried across the street, looking up and down for movement but this place, like all of Bernshulme, was unusually quiet even for so late into the night. When they got to the door Narza was already working on it, using a small rod and hook to manipulate the lock until, with a click, it sprang open.

"Are you ready?" said Joron, more to himself than those with him, but he was met with a chorus of "ey", nonetheless. "Then prepare yourself, and for the Mother's sake, none of you kill Karrad, he is our only hope." Nods, and they were in the building, going up the steep thin stairs in single file, and Joron hoped they would not meet more guards, that Karrad had not surrounded himself with soldiers. A steep stair like this could easily be defended, and no doubt the man had bolt holes and escape routes built into his townhouse.

But there were no guards, and as they ascended the stairs past the richly carved walls, no one came to stop them and they heard no noise. They stopped before the door of Karrad's rooms, quietly, but not quietly enough.

"I told you," came a voice from behind the door, "no matter what has happened, I am not to be disturbed." Joron smiled to himself. A little childish pleasure that he would get to upset the man who set him on the course that led him here. He opened the door. Karrad at his desk, head down, pen moving across a ledger. He looked up. Angry. Opened his mouth to shout at this intruder but no sound came from it when he saw those who had entered. To his credit, thought Joron, he recovered quickly. Did not falter or make a fool of himself by trying to escape.

He still wore all the trappings of the Kept, the leather straps, the oiled chest, long hair, but he looked noticeably older and more worn.

"I have no meetings scheduled," he said and sat back in his chair. "And I do not know you, so must presume you are here to rob me." He shrugged. "Hag knows the times are desperate. Take what you wish, only leave me to my work, unless you would see the Hundred Isles cleaved apart by the Gaunt Islanders and their Hag-cursed pirate." Under his mask, Joron allowed himself a smile.

"We are not here to rob you, Indyl Karrad," he said. Took a step forward, hand on the hilt of his sword. Looked down at the man who was the source of so much of his misery. "We are here to help you, and as for that Hag-cursed pirate . . ." Joron performed a bow, the kind he had seen the Kept do and which they spent many hours perfecting, and then looked up, arm outstretched toward Karrad, "it gives me great pleasure to introduce myself in person."

"I—" Now Karrad looked shocked, though not nearly as shocked as he did when Joron spoke again.

"Though you know me better as Joron Twiner, Indyl. I presume you have not forgotten me?"

For a moment, Karrad could not speak. His face a picture, pale with shock. He put down his quill. Looked away from Joron and picked up the sand shaker by his ledger, shook sand over his document and shut the book.

"I have heard no fighting in the streets, so I reckon you do not come at the head of your fleet ready to hang all those who will not give up their riches."

"I have come alone. My fleet remains at sea."

"Then," said Karrad, "I do not know if you are brave or mad."

"I reckon a little of both," said Joron, and he heard his dockside accent coming out, so very clear when compared to Karrad's High Bothy speech.

"You may get your vengeance, Twiner, if that is why you

are here," said Karrad, "but you will never escape. The island is surrounded and—"

"I am not here for vengeance, I am here for Meas," said Joron. Karrad froze at the mention of his old lover's name, but only for a moment.

"Meas?" he said. Did he take a breath? Was it hope, Joron saw? Was it calculation?

"Ey," said Joron. "All I have done, I have done in search of my shipwife," he said. "And I can only believe she is on this island somewhere." Karrad was staring at him; he had deep-set, intense blue eyes. The hair on his temples was beginning to grey. Joron took a deep breath, before speaking distasteful words. "You care for her, that much was plain when she brought me here so long ago. I do not expect you to like or want to help me. But you and her had a dream of peace. Help me find her and I will leave and none will be the wiser."

"Meas," he said. "All this, what has been done to my town, to my people, was for Meas?"

"All of it," said Joron.

Karrad put his hands on his ledger, splayed his fingers out and stared at them as if considering his position in the world. He let out a long breath.

"I thought Meas dead. But if not, there is only one person on this island who may know where she is," he said. "Her mother."

"So all I must do is break into the Grand Bothy; there are probably quicker ways for you to get me killed, Karrad."

"Undoubtably, but what I say is true. And Bernshulme is not what it once was, your depredations have tried us sorely. Then the keyshan plague came. The Thirteenbern is like me, she stays at her work until late into the night, and we do not have enough seaguard to crew our ships and command posts to waste on things like nightguards." He looked up and smiled. "A big show is made of taking her from the Grand Bothy to her home each evening, but the truth is she returns and rarely leaves until very late. The building is barely guarded at night."

He looked up. "If you are quick, and you go now," he said, "before Skearith's Blind Eye has waned, you may have the answers you are looking for, aye?"

"You cannot believe him, D'keeper," said Mevans. "They would never leave the Thirteenbern unguarded."

"She is not unguarded," said Karrad, "she is no fool. But her guard is smaller than usual and the Grand Bothy is large. Someone careful could slip in, that is all I say. The guards on the entrance to the throne room, well, you will have to deal with them, but as you have dealt with my guards I imagine that will not be a problem for you."

"Your guards are not dead," said Joron. "I am not a monster."

"I would be amused," said Karrad, staring at Joron, "to watch you try and explain that to the people of Bernshulme. They think you cursed that arakeesian, then sent it to us deliberately." Joron had no answer to that. "And I've seen the reports from the shipwives that brought it in – Hag care for them as they are gone now – so I know it is true."

"It is no curse," said Joron, "and your people would have brought it here whether I was there or not."

"Probably," said Karrad, "though it does not matter, now, because we have you to blame for our misfortune. It has been a help in managing the people's anger."

"The Thirteenbern would have blamed me for it anyway."

"No doubt," he said. "Or maybe, if they were not so in fear of you pursuing them, our shipwives would have taken a slower route, noticed the sickness and taken the thing to the old flensing yards. Or better, died before they brought it in." He stood, and Cwell went for her bone dagger. Joron held out a hand to stop her. "Only you really know your intent, the strength of your culpability," Karrad said, glanced at Narza and Cwell then sat again. "If you are to get to the Thirteenbern before the night is through you should leave now, though I would be happy for you to stay and talk with me of course. I would only be doing my duty and protecting the Bern after all; a few hours more and it will be day, the guard will be up to full strength. You and Narza may be able to hide for an entire day, but Cwell there, and Mevans, they are known to too many here. No doubt they are already recognised. Soon they will be sought."

"You should take us to her." Karrad smiled at that.

"Betray the Thirteenbern, and what use would I be then, Joron Twiner, ey? If you find Meas, you will need help getting off this island, Black Pirate or no," he said with a sneer. "And I am that help. I am the only one who can help you."

Joron stared at him. Realised he hated this man. Even though he offered to help he did not really; he could take them to the Thirteenbern if he wanted to. Could walk them through the Grand Bothy and no one would ask a thing about it. Could swear they forced him at the point of a crossbow, make any excuse. But to make Karrad take them unwillingly? Joron did not trust him not to give them up. What poor allies fate forced upon him.

"Very well," said Joron, "we go now."

"Someone 'as to guard that," said Cwell, pointing at Karrad. "Just in case."

"I'll stay," said Mevans.

"But I need—" began Joron. Mevans cut him off.

"You need Cwell and Narza, for something like this. Oh, I could hold my own, no doubt," he said. "But the shipwife has dealt with him before," he glanced at Karrad, no love nor respect there, "and I would not trust him. Someone must stay and keep an eye on him." The trickling of sand through a glass in his mind as the moments passed.

"Of course," said Joron. "You are right."

"I will be well, D'keeper, Indyl Karrad is a fine card player and we will amuse ourselves that way." He grinned at Joron. "I have a few coins from selling our sea chest, try and be back before he has taken them all from me." He put out his arm, offering it in the clasp of comrades aboard ship, something he had never done before. *You do not think I am coming back*, thought Joron. Then he took Mevans's wrist in his own, felt the man's rough hand grip around his wrist and he gave him a nod.

"I will be quick," said Joron.

"But not careless, ey, D'keeper?"

"No," he said, "never that."

"I never knew you two were shipfriends," said Cwell, "we should leave afore you start weeping."

"Only friends," said Joron quietly. "Be careful, Mevans," he said. Then they turned and left. Running down the steep stairs and out into the town. Through quiet streets, past houses that, even so late, should have had a couple of lights burning, but did not. *I did this*, thought Joron, and every step he took, every tap of his bone spur on the Serpent Road was weighed down by guilt. *I did all this*, he thought. *I knew what would happen and I did it anyway*. So lost in his thoughts he was that he barely noticed when they found themselves outside the Grand Bothy. He almost walked straight up to the entrance, for he had ceased to properly see the world around him and stared only at the yawning chasm within, created by his guilt.

"D'keeper." An urgent whisper from Cwell. Narza's iron-hard grip on his arm. He looked up. Four guards under the guttering torches of the Grand Bothy's arched entrance.

"He said there would be fewer guards."

"Usually ten," muttered Narza. "If we go back a while."

"Four bodies is more than I would like to leave in our wake," said Joron quietly. "It will bring attention."

"Other way in," said Narza.

"Where?"

"The side, through a culvert, can you swim?"

"No," said Joron. Narza gave him a look, as if he were the biggest fool in the archipelago.

"Then it will be hard on you," she said. "But none will see us that way."

"Very well," said Joron.

Narza led them around the building and down an alley, to a steep stair that Joron had never seen before in his life. At the bottom was a grate. A black, quickly flowing stream passed through it before tumbling down a steep fall and then vanishing into another grate further down the hill. Narza struck a flint and lit a small lamp, directing the light down toward the grate and Joron saw the bars had been cut just above the waterline.

"I been using it," she said.

"How deep is it?"

"Deep."

"And how far?"

"Far," she said. Then she turned to him, black eyes sparkling. "Be hard," she said. "Will feel like drowning. Long swim and you must lie on your back, and I will hold you. If you struggle, I will let go and you will drown. You understand? Shipwife needs me. I will not die 'ere for you." Joron nodded, looking down into the black water and feeling the same fear he had felt once winding his way through a tight cave, like he was being crushed.

"Take me first," said Cwell. "I swim, but have never been underwater for too long."

"Ey?" said Narza.

"D'keeper," said Cwell, "Narza only cares about the shipwife, that is her job and her honour. Mine is to care about you. So do as I ask, ey? Let me go first." She leaned in close to whisper in his ear. "Serin," she whispered, "was my mother's name. If Narza does not come back and tell you it, it is too far and I drowned. You must find another way." He nodded.

"Of course," he said. "You do not trust her?" Cwell grinned, swift on her face and gone in a moment.

"I trust no one," she said, then turned to Narza. "Let's get on, then," and started climbing down the stonework around the culvert. When she was in the water she looked up, as if to say something but she did not. Just waited as Narza made her way down, then swam over to her.

"Take deep breaths," said Narza. "Then relax if you can and I will guide you through. Remember, struggle and I let you drown." Joron watched as the two women breathed together, Cwell lying atop Narza and then Narza said, "Ready?" Cwell nodded and they vanished beneath the black water. He watched them moving beneath the surface, one of Narza's arms working, feet kicking and it was as if he looked down upon a keyshan from a great height as it moved beneath the seas. Narza's strength against the power of the water through the culvert, and for a moment the two women were moving but still, as the water and the muscle strength balanced each other, then they were gone, under the bars and through the tunnel and all Joron could do was sit and wait. He counted out seconds, closing his eyes and seeing a sandglass, the sand rushing through it. As he waited he tried holding his own breath for as long as he could. Found it impossible to hold for long and the space the sand in his mind filled was replaced with a deep, black dread of what was to come. To him, like so many deckchilder, water was a thing of the everyday, but also a thing of death, for to be lost in it was to be prey to the creatures of the sea which hated the creatures of the land, and hated woman and men above all others. The ability to swim was rare, as few ever chose to go in the water.

All too soon he heard a gentle whistle and opened his eyes, looking down into the water he saw Narza. "Serin," she said and he nodded affirmation at the code word. "Your turn now, D'keeper. Same rules." He climbed down the slimy wall, gasping as icy water closed around his good foot, then again when it hit the stump of his leg. He struggled to get air into his lungs when the water enveloped him totally. "It will pass," said Narza, "just breathe." He nodded. Concentrated on the in and out of air through his mouth as the water slowly turned from freezing to numbing. "Ready?" said Narza, those eyes, black as water. He nodded, and she span him around, placed one hand on his chin and let them both fall back in the water, the warmth of her body against his back. "Five deep breaths and we go," she said. "You struggle, you drown."

One.

Two.

Three.

Four.

Five.

He closed his mouth and felt her move beneath him, pull him into the water, the world above shimmering and shifting, bending and twisting and he wanted to fight. Wanted to struggle. This was not his element, not his place. His lungs told him this was wrong. This was wrong. This was wrong. This was wrong.

Dontstruggledontstruggledontstruggle

He was back in the box. Choking on broken vocal cords. Trapped beneath a mountain of rock. About to be taken on a ship with the sick and the dying and left there by Deckkeeper Gueste. It was so dark. It was so cold. It was so wrong. He was held. Trapped. Terrified. Back in the box. Choking on his own air. Under a mountain. He knew he must stay still to survive. But the panic was a tide, pulling at his good sense, unstoppable, powerful, and he could not control it. Could feel the energy building in his limbs. Feel the sparks in his mind. Wanting to kick out.

Dontstruggledontstruggledontstruggle

But some things were beyond him. Beyond his power. Sometimes terror was stronger than sense. Sometimes the unreality of memory stronger than the real, and the darkness in the box was overwhelming. The terror of the place it would lead too much and he wanted to scream to shout and to sing . . .

To sing.

To hear the song that spilled through the water and through his mind. To feel the water as no longer terror but comfort, something longed for, something desired. Something needed. The energy in his muscles bled away, the need for air receded to the back of his mind and was he drowning? He did not care. Because he was carried along by the song. By the deep, by the powerful body that propelled him through the depths and . . .

"Wake up!" A slap across his face. He opened his eyes. Cwell looking into his face. "You awake?" she said and he tried to answer but the words would not come, not yet. "Wake up!" She slapped him again. Harder, and this brought him fully back to life, coughing and choking. Cwell glanced over his shoulder. "Be glad he lives," she spat into the darkness. No reply. He coughed again, threw up water onto the ground.

"You should be glad." Narza's voice came from the darkness and he felt more than saw Cwell's hand go to the knife on her belt.

"I am glad I live," he said, "and glad Narza got me through the water. And in need of both of you, so if you must weigh your tits against one another then do it when we have got the shipwife out."

Chuckling from Cwell.

"Such belowdecks language," she grinned. "Swim must have knocked you more off course than I thought."

"Where are we?" said Joron.

"Deep in the hill beneath the bothy," she said. But he already knew it, he could feel the island breathing, feel the beast deep within.

32

And They Met One Late Night

The tunnels were thin, running around the side of the
island. Every so often they would come to a junction and
Narza would study the wall, plainly she had left some sort of
mark there but when Joron studied where she had looked he
found nothing. Had no time to look more closely as Cwell
pulled him on down dark tunnels.

"Not long now," said Narza, "this will bring us out by the
armouries."

"Good," said Cwell, "we can get you a sword."

"All I need is my knives," said Narza.

"If it comes down to fighting," said Joron, "then we will
never get out. Our aim is not to fight." Cwell grinned at him.

"And if the Thirteenbern calls her guard?" Joron shook his
head.

"It will not happen," he said quietly, "the Thirteenbern will
speak to no one once we have finished with her." The two
women glanced at each other, shared a smile and Joron felt a
twist within him. They were killers – loyal to him and to Meas
but killers. They knew neither mercy nor pity and felt little for
others. But that was what he had become also, how many had
died at his hand? Though when he thought of the Thirteenbern

it opened such a well of anger that it burned away all thoughts of pity, for others, or for himself, and he walked down the narrow corridor, grim and committed to his purpose. They came to a door, secured by a heavy padlock on the inside. Narza produced a key. Unlocked it and looked out through the gap. Then waved them on and out into the wider corridors of the Grand Bothy, though further beneath than Joron had ever been.

"You have a key?" said Cwell. "Seems odd."

"My lock," said Narza, "to keep others out." Cwell stared at her, then nodded.

"Let's get on," said Joron, and they moved along.

As they walked, Joron began to feel like he was high, jittery, his mind bouncing from thought to thought, his body full of energy and he knew it was the thought of action. Denied it for so long, forced to be someone else. But now he was the Black Pirate again, doing the things from the stories about him: sneaking in to a place where he was far outnumbered, only to outwit the enemy and leave triumphant. He knew those stories well, had started most of them and paid singers and strummers to spread them. All lies of course, he never knowingly went in anywhere outnumbered. He was no fool. Those who went in outnumbered eventually ran out of luck and out of life.

Even though he was fizzing, full of energy and ready for action he knew the truth. Knew the course he took, that his path most likely ended here.

"Cwell," he said, "Narza," and stopped. They stopped. Turned, looked to him. "Turn back, get out," he said, "you . . ." and words failed him. He did not know what to say, or rather did not want to say it. But had to. The words would not be denied. "You do not need to die here." Cwell stepped forward, looked at him.

"The sentence is passed, D'keeper," she said, "only the day is undecided." Then she put a hand on his arm. "I go where you go." He glanced at Narza.

"I owe the shipwife," she said and turned, walking along the corridor as if he had not even spoken.

Up and up they went, through a building so empty it was hard for him to believe this was the same place he had been to before. Then it had always been brimming with guards and hagpriests and Kept and Bern, all hissing and chatting and vying for power. Now it felt like a mausoleum, a memory, a place too big for the people it served.

"There should be someone here," said Joron as they came into the main hall, where paths spiralled up around the outside to give access to the higher levels, where meetings were held, where in the day there should be hundreds of finely dressed people. Even at night he expected to see tens of them, scattered about on business they would rather stayed quiet.

"Good there is not," said Cwell.

"No," said Joron. "It is not good. When things change dramatically it is for a reason. Hold here," he said. Cwell stopped. Narza slowed, then stopped. "There should be someone here," he said again. "No one at all makes me wonder if it is a trap." He wondered if somehow Indyl Karrad had managed to get word out, and if so what had happened to Mevans? But why would he?

"It's always like this," said Narza. "Busier in the day. But at night she empties it."

"You've been here before?"

"Every night."

"And yet the Thirteenbern still lives?" She studied him with black eyes.

"I do not know how to get information from someone, outside of using pain," she said.

"And you do not want to do that?"

Narza shrugged. "Do not mind it," she said quietly. "But the mother and the daughter are more alike than not. Would need more time than I would have in one night to break either of them."

"Then what use is this?" said Joron. "Why lead us in here?" Narza shrugged.

"Meas picked you," she said, "and you will free her." Then

she turned and walked toward the nearest ramp, and Joron's jittery, nervous state fell away from him, to be replaced by a fear of failure. What could he do? What would he do?

Up a level and up a level, nearer and nearer to the top where the Thirteenbern sat on her throne, held up by statues of children carved from keyshan bone.

What did he intend to do?

Up to where the one person in the entire archipelago who may have the answers sat, to the end of a quest that had seen him shed blood from storm to storm. So much blood, so many dead, so many lost.

And what when you have her back, Joron? What will happen then? What will she think of the things you have done in her name? This voice, his own in the back of his mind, was unwelcome. That question he put aside, because even if the Thirteenbern was so good as to tell him where Meas was, then he must still get his shipwife out, and he must still get her away and the entire island would be raised to stop him. Yet somewhere within him he still hoped, still believed, that it was possible.

Maybe he had heard too many of those songs sung about him to give up entirely.

Maybe they should have left Meas to her fate.

Maybe that was what she would have wished and maybe, just maybe, she would have the chance to tell him in person.

Oh that word.

Maybe.

Maybe.

Maybe.

And then before him stood the great doors.

He took a deep breath.

"Open them," he said. He meant it to be said proudly, but it came out a whisper. Cwell and Narza pushed the great doors open. Inside waited the great empty and dark space of the throne room. Dim lights all around it. No sign of movement, or people. He could not even see the throne in the gloom. "Wait here," he said, still whispering. "I hope I will not be too long."

And he stepped in, not trying to slip around the edge of the room. Walking forward through darkness toward where light bathed the throne. This, the end of the long journey, felt like the longest walk of all. At any moment he expected seaguard to boil from the hidden depths of the room.

None came, none delayed him, none stopped him.

And there she was.

Sat on her throne reading from a parchment, the carved bodies of the children beneath holding her up. He had seen her before, of course, her skin barely covered, better to show the stretches and scars of the birthings that made her the most powerful woman in the Hundred Isles. He saw her daughter in her, the same build, the same face hidden beneath her sagging flesh.

They shared so much, age could not dim them.

Yet, there was something different in Thirteenbern Gilbryn, some lessening of her, as if she were the living embodiment of the Hundred Isles, and his predations upon her domain had worn her down. In this moment, in this huge and silent place he felt that he caught a glimpse of the real woman, not the ruler but the person. Smaller than the ruler, sadder than the ruler.

She must have caught some movement in the corner of her eye, become aware someone was there, and any semblance that she may be a person like any other fled. She became what she was, the ruler of the Hundred Isles, as hard and unyielding as the black rock of Skearith's Spine. She looked up from her reading and at where he stood, in the shadowy centre of the room where the wanelights did not reach.

"Do not skulk," she said, in that skeer-cry voice. "Show yourself."

He stepped forward.

What did he expect from her? Shock? Fear? Surprise? He was given none of these things. She merely nodded to herself, as if she had known he would come, as if she had expected him all along.

"Joron Twiner," she said. He nodded. "The Black Pirate himself."

"That is what they call me," he said. She laughed quietly to herself.

"I had thought you more clever than to come here alone."

"But you knew I would come?"

"Yes." She looked at the nails on one hand. "Most thought it would be with the entire Gaunt Islands fleet at your back but I knew that, in the end, Aileen would let you down."

"Some people value power more than their word."

Thirteenbern Gilbryn leaned forward.

"People who have tasted power find it sweeter than any other drink, Twiner. You should know that by now."

"I live by my word." She sat back, nodded.

"Admirable," she said. "Impressive, that you got here too, though you cannot expect to leave alive."

"Most would say I would never get here at all."

"Ey," she said, "they would. But my daughter must have told you, a job half done is not done at all. It is for her you come, right? It is to her you gave your word?"

"Ey," he said, but the word, at this place in this moment with everything so close, was a struggle for him to push from his mouth.

"Meas was always the best of them," she said wistfully, then her voice hardened a little, "and though she could not admit it, always my favourite. Always given the longest leash, always given the most chances. Even after what she did." The Thirteenbern let her head fall so she stared at the floor then laughed to herself. "Any other shipwife I would have had drowned. But not her, one more chance. She always got one more chance." She looked up at him. "No wonder her sisters hated her so." He listened to her words unbelieving, knowing it for lies.

"You threw her out," he said, annoyed by the woman's self-pity. "She was raised in a sea cave by a hagpriest who hated her."

The Thirteenbern stood, and it was as if she pulled all she was to her – her voice became a roar, as loud as any shipwife's in a storm.

"A thousand years and more of tradition weighed upon me, Joron Twiner!" Her words echoed around the room. She glared at him and the sound died away slowly, as if the acoustics of the building were unwilling to let anything of her loose. Then she sat back down, looking at the floor as if she regretted the outburst. "The priests cried for her blood, and yet she was my child. The ocean gave her back and still they thirsted. The Gilbryn are an old family, strong, powerful, fertile, and so a compromise was reached. She would be cast away to the hardest of lives, and if she lived then she did. And if not, then the Hag had her price." The Thirteenbern looked up to the skies, beyond the roof of the bothy. "My firstborn, and each and every day I had to look out upon the town and know she was there, and that I, her mother, could not even touch her."

"You are powerful."

"Now I am, not then," she said. "Not then. Many stood above me then. It is the curse of the young, Twiner, to look upon how the world is and think it always was. I was just a girl, sick with grief for her lost child."

"You could have helped her."

"You think I did not? How do you think a girl raised in a sea cave by an outcast hagpriest could attend the Grand Bothy?" She shook her head. "I loved her, Twiner. Mothers are not meant to have favourites, but I watched her fight for everything she had, watched her earn every promotion, and I loved her more than the rest for it." She took a deep breath. "You are here because I let you be," she said. "You think we cannot guard a bothy? Think this place need be so empty? I have been waiting for you for longer than you imagine."

"Why? You cannot think I mean you ought but harm?" She stared at him. "There is a price that you must pay for the pain you have caused. You made hiyl poison to hunt keyshans from the bodies of your own people, from gullaime. You committed murder on a grand scale."

She stared at him, ice-blue eyes, just like Meas. Voice cold as the far north.

"I have done what I must to protect the Hundred Isles. I do not ask forgiveness, nor understanding."

"I would never—"

"Do the same?" She coughed out a laugh. "But you lie, Joron Twiner. You have raided and murdered. You sent back a creature you knew would poison half this town. Sentenced hundreds, maybe more, to death. Oh it was a clever ruse, to pretend you were ready to fight for the corpse, put the shipwives in a panic to get it back before you returned with more ships. They were brave too, my shipwives, thought they had some sort of plague, dropped seastays off the harbour and died on their ships while others brought the corpse into town. Our first arakeesian. More bone for the ships. We planned a grand celebration. Call me pitiless and cruel if you must, but do not pretend you are any better. You have seen what you did to Bernshulme."

He had no answer to that.

"Ey," he said quietly, "I have seen."

She nodded to herself.

"I have lost what I love most, Twiner, and if death comes upon me then so be it. But I wanted you here, so I could ask one kindness, that is all."

"A kindness?" He did not understand.

"Ey, give me it and I will not raise my voice and bring my guard running, I will let you leave this bothy, though I doubt you will ever get off the island." Her head came up, she stared directly at him. Grinned at him. "You intend to kill me," she said, "I see it in you. Well, I will ask anyway." She took a deep breath. "My daughter died fighting to get her fleet out of Sleighthulme. I have heard accounts from those that fought against her, but take pity on an old woman before you send her to the Hag, Joron Twiner, Black Pirate. Let me hear how she died, from the one who fought closest with her, not those who fought against her."

"What?" he said, suddenly confused, off-centre.

"Tell me of her death, pirate. They say she died a coward, begging to live, and I will not believe it. Tell me the truth of it. Tell me she died a hero to her people, fighting to the last."

"Tell you of her death?" he said, and it was as if the world spun around him. As if all he had known was turned upside down and when he spoke he stuttered over the words. "I cannot do that."

"You will not tell me?" she sighed. "I had thought you may be above such petty cruelties." She rubbed her forehead. "Meas would have been, and she chose you. Is it so hard to take pity? So hard to let me know the truth before you end me? It would be what she wanted." She leaned forward, and once more he no longer saw the ruler, but saw the woman beneath her skin. "I suppose you can learn to command a ship, but you cannot learn compassion."

"But she is not dead," he whispered, because she could not be. She could not be. If Meas was dead then everything he had done was for nothing. All that pain and death and suffering. For nothing, and what did that make him?

"What do you mean, Twiner?" A flash in those eyes, shock. "Not dead?"

"You have her."

"I?" Confusion. "Do you mock me?"

"No," he said. "You took her. The force you sent after us when we took Sleighthulme, they took her . . ."

"No," said the Thirteenbern. "You fought your way out and she died on the harbour. My daughter died at Sleighthulme."

"No," he said, "she did not die." The Thirteenbern stood, and he saw the confusion on her face, and could not deny that she believed she spoke the truth. He saw his words had shaken the powerful and strong ruler right down to her bare feet. He could not understand, and wondered, for a moment, if after all the pain and suffering he had been through in the run-up to taking Sleighthulme he had somehow remembered the events incorrectly. Had he simply imagined what happened there. Had he wanted her to be alive so much he had lived ever since in some dream? Had the rot damaged his mind so much, and none around him dared say? Was his entire world a dream? A figment of a mind coming apart, holed and sore like his skin? But no, he glanced down at the bone spur where his leg should be. Touched the hilt of the knife at his hip. Thought of dear Dinyl, now with the Hag with all his deckchilder and crew. Thought of Brekir and every other shipwife that served with him and their crews, all as committed as he to bringing the shipwife back.

"You lie," he said. But knew she did not do so knowingly. Knew from the look on her face, the grief in her body. "You must lie?" he said, and he tried to believe it. "She gave herself to your shipwives in exchange for her fleet being allowed to leave the island. There was no other way for us to survive." She stared at him, the shock had drained from her, and something else was there, something hard and something calculating.

"Even her life, Joron Twiner," said Thirteenbern Gilbryn slowly, "is not worth letting loose the whole of her raider fleet. Love her as I do, I would never agree to that."

"It was not her life they wanted," he said. "It was her knowledge. She raised the keyshan at McLean's Rock." A lie, he knew, one that tasted bitter in his mouth still. But he saw the effect it had on the Thirteenbern. Elation at first, that her daughter may live. Puzzlement, next. Then, was it fear? He did not have time to think properly about it before they were interrupted.

"D'keeper! D'keeper!" He turned, Cwell and Narza running toward him. "It is a trap, seaguard are coming up the ramp." He turned back to the Thirteenbern, pulled the straightsword from its scabbard.

"A trick," he said. "And Hag-curse me I almost believed you." He pointed the blade at her. "You will be the first to die."

"Take me as hostage," she said.

"What?"

"I swear, on the Mother, Maiden and Hag, nothing I have said is a lie and those coming are not of my doing. I will tell them to stand down, and you and I will talk more of my daughter. For something is wrong here." He could hear shouting.

"D'keeper?" said Cwell. The Thirteenbern walked down from her throne, holding her arms out to her side so he could see she had no weapons.

"Take me hostage now," she said, same voice as Meas, same commanding tone and he did it. Put his arm around her throat, his bone blade at her neck as Cwell and Narza came to flank him.

Seaguard ran into the room, all armed with spears, followed by men with crossbows. Then, walking down the centre of the room, came Indyl Karrad, strolling as if out for a pleasant evening along the docks.

"Send your guard away, Karrad, or he'll kill me," said Gilbryn, but he carried on walking and smiling.

"Truthfully," he said, "Twiner would be doing me a favour." He felt the Thirteenbern stiffen in his arms. He could not speak. The room before him blurred, his mind felt pierced, as if by a bone shard from a wingbolt hit. What was happening? How was Karrad here? Had Mevans let him go? Why?

"Seems I came in at just the right time to hear Joron saying Meas raised the keyshan." Karrad came to a stop and scratched at the side of his face. Yawned. "But she says it is him that raised it. That it is Joron Twiner who has the power." Karrad's chest gleamed with oil beneath the ornamented straps. "I had hoped to get to you, Twiner, before you had this conversation with the Thirteenbern, but subduing your man took longer than I had hoped."

"What is happening, Indyl?" said Gilbryn. She pushed Joron's sword away from her neck and he let her, for he no more understood this sudden turnabout than she did. He could not speak. Could not think. "Is what he says true?" She stepped around Joron, took two steps toward Karrad. "Indyl, does Meas live?"

"Yes," he said, still smiling. "She lives. I have her, and now I have him." He pointed at Joron.

"You have betrayed me?"

"Yes," he said.

"You will die for this," she said.

"I think not." He waved at the seaguard behind him.

"A few seaguard will not save you from my shipwives and deckchilder who—"

"—are all out at sea," he finished for her. "And every ship and soldier left in Bernshulme is loyal to me."

"Hag's breath," said Joron. "He means to take over. Curse me for a fool, Meas even said it at Sleighthulme, 'My Mother thinks so little of me she only sends her men.' We did not understand."

"Not her men," said Indyl. "Mine."

"The people of Bernshulme will not let a man rule them," said Gilbryn. "I will have you fed piece by piece to the longthresh for this, Indyl."

"You will not," he said simply. "Bernshulme would not usually stand for a man ruling, you are right. But in these times, with the ruin you have led them to? And if it is a man who can raise keyshans? Well, I think that will be a different matter." He raised a hand to the seaguard with crossbows and they lifted their weapons. "Twiner's appearance has accelerated my plans a little, I admit, but right now, I hold Bernshulme."

The Thirteenbern stared at him, this man who had once been her daughter's lover, and her own.

"Why, Indyl?"

"I have spent my whole life knowing I will be cast aside when I am no longer useful. You are raised to know that as a man. And knowing that, you must plan for when it happens."

"I would never have—"

"You would," he said. "If it was power or me, you would

and you know it." She lowered her eyes then. Unable to lie to him, for what was the point when all in the room knew the truth? "So I planned for that moment, only I planned with more ambition than most."

"You will not survive this," she said.

"Well, we shall find out." Joron could feel Cwell tensing, but she was too slow. Narza moved first. Stepping forward.

"Where is she?" she said.

"Safe," said Karrad. Narza drew her blade. Two of Karrad's troops raised their crossbows.

"That was not the agreement. I bring you Twiner, you bring me the shipwife." Joron's heart fell.

"You betrayed us?" said Joron. Narza shot him a glance, dismissed him. Cwell took a step nearer to Joron.

"Bring Meas," said Narza. "Or I swear I'll kill Twiner before you get anywhere—"

"I have no doubt you would try," said Karrad and gave a nod. The crossbows loosed. Bolts thumped into Narza, pushing her back. She stood for a moment, her face twisted into a mask of hate. She took a breath. A step towards Karrad. Blade held out. "Well," he said to his men, "finish her then." More bolts, one, two, three and still she stood. Breath coming in harsh gasps. She turned her head toward Joron.

"Save her," she said, and fell. Dead before she hit the floor.

"The other one too," said Karrad. But Cwell was already moving, she was behind Joron, and he was paralysed with shock. Still unable to believe it, betrayed by Karrad, betrayed by Narza. Cwell's arm came around him, her blade at his throat.

And he was betrayed again.

"Loose a bolt," she shouted, "and he dies. But I have an offer to make." Karrad lifted a hand, stopped his seaguard in their tracks.

"And you would trust me, after what I did to that?" He pointed at Narza's corpse.

"I trust two things only," she said, "ambition and coin. I reckon you are the same." Karrad cocked his head. Blinked.

"Speak then."

"I am Mulvan Cahanny's niece," she said. "Heir to all he built in Bernshulme, and I mean to take it back." Joron opened his mouth to speak but she placed a hand over it, he felt her rough skin even through his scarf.

"And why would that concern me?" he said.

"You wish to rule," shouted Cwell. "To do so you will need the people to accept you. With Cahanny's organisation ruled by me, as it should be, I can bring you the people." Joron watched Karrad as he weighed it up. Thought about it. "It is simple business," said Cwell. "Why do I care who sits in the bothy?"

Silence fell, Joron wanted to rage. To scream.

"Very well," said Karrad. He turned to his troops. "Sheathe your weapons." They did. He felt the pressure of the blade at his throat ease a little. "Take Gilbryn and Twiner down to my prison," said Karrad to his troops. "I will speak with Twiner later, and need to decide what to do with Gilbryn."

And, as they came forward, all Joron wanted to say was, "What have you done with Mevans?" But he did not, because he was heartsick and lost and, at that moment, he could not bear to hear the answer. How could he have got those around him so very wrong? Cwell's blade left his throat and, at the moment the heat of her body moved away from him, she whispered two words into his ear.

"Trust me."

Then they came to take him away.

33

The Woman in the Corner

He was numb. Numb and bound and stumbling forward between two guards feeling like life had outrun him, like he had jumped into the depths expecting to drown and been caught in a riptide which had thrown him up on the shores of a strange and foreign land. Everything had changed, and so quickly.

Numb.

The seaguard escorting him were not gentle, they laughed as he stumbled, not realising he was playing less able than he was, exaggerating his limp in the hope they would not take his spur from him, but maybe he worried too much. They showed no fear of him. Either Karrad had not shared he was the Black Pirate or they believed their power in this place was absolute. They walked him down through the bothy and into the tunnels toward the dungeons. Down here the walls wept moisture and those in the cells around him wept and moaned in misery. A door opened, he made to step through but one of the guards stopped him, undid his shackles and ripped the mask from his face. Turned him so they could look on him, immediately recoiled.

"We know what you are, who you are," the guard said, face

twisted in hate. "We know what you did to us and look at you, as rotten in your body as you are in your actions."

"So you will kill me?" He meant to sound defiant, instead he sounded resigned. "I had hoped to die at sea." The man laughed, his face was lined, older than most seaguard and Joron wondered whether that meant Karrad was forced by the plague to bring older, less capable seaguard into his forces.

"I would love to kill you, lost my boy and my woman to the pox the beast in the harbour brought." He took a step back. "But Karrad has said I must not, and besides, what he has in store for you is worse than any death, even from the rot, be sure of that." He smiled and gave Joron a gentle push into the cell. "I will listen for you, as you give up your secrets. I will dance to the song of your pain, Black Pirate." He shut the door, then spat through the bars into Joron's face. The spittle was warm on his cheek, stung where it hit the sores, but he did not wipe it away. Only stood, staring at the man, unblinking as it rolled down his face, warm as tears.

"I will not forget your kindness," said Joron. The man laughed, turned to his friend.

"You hear that, Franir, I think the rot-cursed pirate threatens me, ey? From inside his cell."

"Look to what pride gets you in this place, pirate," said Franir from the shadows, then they left, taking the torch with them and leaving only the faint glow of one wanelight behind.

Joron wiped the spittle from his face with his sleeve. "Wherever I go, it seems I make friends," he said to himself. Then laughed. A bit of forced and stupid levity but the laughter within wanted more, it wanted to grow and consume him. Leave him capable of nothing else and while it was bubbling up he realised there was no joy in it, no mirth. This was cold laughter, like an ice island within, and trapped within the ice were hundreds of bodies – no, more; a thousand, and bits of ship and broken gallowbows and ropes from which men and women hung, faces distended and purple, tongues swollen as they were starved of air and the laughter still wanted to come, to fight up and out of his body as strong and clear as the song of the keyshan. But it was warped and impure in a way the songs never were.

A moan.

A noise.

A shifting of material.

He turned to find he had a companion in the cell. A small figure, curled up into a ball in the corner. In the dim light he could barely make out anything about them. Only that they were hurt and frightened and when he stepped closer to them they tried to make themselves smaller. Tried to push themselves even further into the corner of the cell.

"I will not hurt you," he said. "We are in the same boat, if anything, so you need not fear me." At the sound of his voice the figure in the corner froze, then turned toward him. He could make little out of them. A pale face, a ragged bandage over one eye. Filthy clothes and hair. He wondered how long they had been here.

"Joron?" The word a croak. They knew him? How did they know him? Had they been warned of who was to share the cell, had they . . . no. The plains of the face, the voice. Such faint markers in the gloom and his confusion, but markers nonetheless. "Is it really you, Joron? Or are you another dream come to increase my torment?"

"Hag's breath," he said, and he was down on his knees before her. Gathering her up so he could look into her face, only one eye showing, the other covered by a filthy bandage. "Meas? It is you, Meas."

"You should not have come, Joron."

A moment of silence, such pain in her one eye.

"I promised," he said. She let out a breath, lifted a hand, the nails strangely gnarled, and touched his face.

"I have wished for nothing but to see you." She coughed, almost doubled over by it. Then lifted her head again. "I was wrong to." She brought up her other hand, cupped his face, not bothered by the sores that so many others turned away from. "I was wrong," she said, "you should not have come. My mother knows no pity, she will . . ."

"Meas," he said gently. "It is not your mother who holds us here. It is not your mother who has held you for so long. It is Indyl Karrad."

"Did she tell you that?" her words a scar on the air. "You cannot trust her, look what she has done to me and . . ."

"No," he said, though he knew his words must hurt her as much as any torture, "she did not tell me that. She thought you dead. Karrad himself told me. He has overthrown your mother and moved to take over the island. His people shot Narza down before my eyes." She stared at him, and he waited for some emotion. Some fury at this betrayal by a man she had once loved. Some mark of the woman he had known, who had made him. Who was strong and who was hard. But there was no emotion at all in the one eye looking at him. No expression on her face.

"Indyl has done all this?" she said. He nodded. The hands left his face, cold where there had been warmth, and she wrapped her arms about herself, drew her legs up into a ball once more and when she spoke it was no longer to him. "And I thought they had wracked all the pain they could from me."

"Meas, I—"

"Let me alone, Joron." That sharpness back, hard, shipwife as ever, before softening. "Just for a while, please, let me be alone."

So he did. Left her to her corner and wondered what must be going through her head, long months of pain and all the time sure she knew who was to blame, no doubt living off the hate. Now he came and he had changed everything with only a few words. Turned her world on its head the way his had been turned barely half an hour ago. But for him it was no great shock, he had trusted neither Meas's mother nor Karrad, which of them betrayed him made little difference in the end. For her though?

"We were happy once." The words were so quiet he could

barely hear them. Meas did not turn toward him, did not speak to him as much as to the wall. "Young once, everything is simpler when you are young." She turned, one eye glittering, the other hidden behind the dirty bandage. "I should have known, really, Joron, should have guessed. My life here has been a circle; pain, sleep, heal, repeat. Again and again and again until I had become fully convinced I lived in some terrible dream. Everything is circles, Joron," she said. Then she closed her eye and turned from him, he thought he heard weeping but said nothing. Tried not to listen. Tried to close his ears and when that did not work he tried to listen for other sounds in the darkness, hints to where he was, to who else might be kept in the cells around them. The Thirteenbern must be somewhere. Eventually the sobbing died away and she spoke again. "We were chosen, Indyl and I." That quiet voice once more, as if she felt the need to force the story out. "For each other. He had been one of my mother's favourites. I already had my first command, a small thing, not much more than flukeboat with a skeleton of bone, called *Hagswrath*, and how I loved him. But I was not meant for the decks, never meant for it . . ." Her voice tailed off. "Win a little respect, command a boneship for a little, then children, and climb the ladder of the Bern. That was my future. That was my plan." She let out a small laugh. "That was my route to vengeance on my mother. I lived to spite her." This spat out, more of the Meas he knew in those words than he had heard before.

"Maybe that was her plan?" She laughed then, full throated and real, his shipwife back for a moment, inhabiting this ghostly figure curled up in the corner. Then the laughter died away.

"Oh Joron," she said. "Oh Joron you should not have come."

"How could I not?" he said. And he was holding her, did not think about propriety or what was right, he just held her. Became a place of human contact and warmth for a woman denied it for so long. "You are the shipwife, Meas Gilbryn, the greatest who ever lived. You are Lucky Meas, the witch of

Keelhulme Sounding. You are my shipwife. And if you wish to change the world then the world will change. And for the better."

"But we have not made it better, Joron. We have brought only pain. I should have died. It would be better if I had . . ."

"No!" he hissed it. "The deckkeeper serves the shipwife — without you, I do not know what to do."

"Of course you do," she said, looked up at him. "I betrayed you, Joron. I told them about you. I do not deserve your loyalty. Karrad will seek to use what—"

"It does not matter," he said. "We will escape, return to our fleet, they should be parading up and down just outside the Hundred Isles defence ring by now. He will not keep us."

"You have a plan?"

He shook his head. "Truthfully, I never expected to get this far."

She coughed, bent over by it, all the pain and hurt flowing back, and when she spoke the shipwife was gone once again, the shattered woman below remaining. "But Cwell is here, Karrad thinks she has gone over to him but she has not. I have got this far, Meas. I will get us out."

"You trust her?" she said.

"I have no other choice."

A noise from outside the cell. He let go of her and stood.

The cell door opened as he turned to see the Thirteenbern stood there. Behind her was an officer Joron recognised. Gueste, and seeing her nearly broke him, nearly made him stumble. Sudden memories of darkness and the box and the pain in his throat. The terror the woman had put him through, the place she had intended Joron to end up. Fed into a cauldron of blood and bone in the depths of Sleighthulme.

"Joron Twiner," said Gueste, breezy and bright as ever. "Kept Karrad wishes to speak with you." She pushed Thirteenbern Gilbryn into the cell. "I am sure Meas and her mother have plenty to talk about. Family reunions can be messy affairs, you are better out of it."

"You and I," said Joron, "we have unfinished business."

"We do?" she said, a finely formed eyebrow raised in surprise. "I can understand how you may feel that way, but I have only ever done my duty, as an officer." She stepped to one side and motioned him through. Joron saw Cwell behind her. Gueste paused a moment as she saw his unmasked face.

"A strange sense of duty you have, Gueste," he said, "to betray your ruler." Gueste smiled at him and Cwell's face remained stone. Was he wrong to trust her?

"You try to rile me," said Gueste, "I would expect little else. I, however, hold no animosity toward you, it would be unprofessional." As Joron passed her she grabbed his arm and whispered, "That is the difference between you and I. One of us was born to this, the other is a usurper. Weak blood has no place on the rump of a boneship. You show the sores of the weak. You sicken me."

She let go and, for a moment, Joron considered striking her, but waiting further down the corridor stood two seaguard and he knew it would be fruitless; if anything, it would give them an excuse to beat him and he was sure Gueste would enjoy that. Joron gave her a small bow.

"And yet," said Joron with a smile, "it is me your master wishes to see. Despite he hates me, which must mean he sees some use in me." Gueste's smile faltered.

"Or he simply wishes to see your face when he tells you that you are to die," she said. Joron smiled. "Vile as that face is." He stood taller.

"I am crew of *Tide Child*, a black ship, a ship of the dead, Gueste. I have been dead for many years so it will take more than the threat of death to scare me." He saw it, a moment of confusion on Gueste's face, then it was gone. And was he imagining it or did Cwell also stand a little straighter?

"Talk is easy, Twiner," she said. "Follow the seaguard."

"Gladly," said Joron.

From there they went, and up and up. At first, Joron thought they may be heading to the throne room, and he expected to find Indyl Karrad sat upon the throne, the first man to ever sit there. But when they entered the ground floor of the Grand Bothy the seaguard led him to a side door and away from the main dome. From there down vaulting corridors into a smaller bothy, one Joron had never been in before. The echo of his feet and those around him on the polished stone floor was the only sound in this place. They stopped before a door, taller than Joron, made of cured varisk.

"Go in," said Gueste. Joron did, the door opening easily despite its size, and as he passed through he imagined the pulleys and counterweights that made the opening so smooth, all part of the mechanics of the sea, the lifting and moving and tying-on that had become so much part of him. Inside Karrad sat at a desk, full of papers, his quill working as he wrote something. Then he sat back, scattered sand over the ink to dry it before looking up.

"Gueste," he said quietly, "you can leave."

"But—"

"I said you can leave." The woman next to Joron stiffened, then gave a small bow.

"Of course, Kept Karrad," she said, backing away and closing the door behind her. When the door was closed Karrad motioned toward the chair in front of his desk. Behind him wanelights glowed, the eyeholes looking like strange spirits in the darkness, guarding the man. Joron stepped forward, foot and spur tapping on the floor. Sat in the chair, comfortably upholstered in birdleather, and looked at the man opposite him. Almost impossibly handsome, no scars, hair still thick despite the grey of advancing years. He was staring at Joron, eyes locked on to him, slight movements as they took him in. Then he took a deep breath. Let it out.

"I hate you," he said. "I want that out in the open, first, before we talk any further. I want you to know it."

"I know it. I killed your son after all. I can expect little else but hate from you." Karrad sat back.

"Oh, it is so much more than that, Twiner. I see the mark

of keyshan's rot upon your face and should not be surprised, the Mother writes your moral failings upon your skin. And yes, everything that has happened up to this moment. It is your fault. All of it."

"All of it?" He should have been shocked – a younger Joron would have been but not this one, not the man who had become the Black Pirate. "I think you give me more credit than I deserve." Karrad still stared at him. Something missing from him, something empty.

"Sometimes, Joron Twiner, the smallest ripple becomes the greatest wave. So it is with you. My son was my future, my chance of retirement. His mother was well placed, she died in a shipwreck. But his blood was good, he would find himself a Bern and father children. Relatives to ensure my safety in later life, that none would steal any money I had hidden away to survive on. That was all I wished for, Twiner, to survive. I did not want to join an insurrection."

"You were in touch with Meas before your son died."

"To watch her," he said. "I had no wish to do anything more." He leaned forward. "I never expected her to be so successful. Then when she was, her talk of a fairer world wormed its way within me." He looked almost disgusted. "And I saw an unfairness she did not. As time passed the Thirteenbern became less trusting of me. The more successful Meas was, the less well it reflected on me. So I had to safeguard my position and that meant finishing her. You were never meant to survive that first journey, escorting a keyshan into the north. None of you. And yet you did. Still, I kept you away, bided my time for when you could easily be destroyed."

"But?"

"But someone raised a keyshan. And with that everything changed."

Silence in the room.

"You tortured her," said Joron.

Karrad stared back, showed no temper, or anger.

"Yes," he said.

"You could have just asked her to join you."

"To accept a man taking over? She never would."

"You may have been surprised."

Karrad smiled. "Says the man who is still a deckkeeper."

"I chose that."

Did Karrad waver, did he question himself for just a moment? If so it was not for long.

"Then she has trained you well, I suppose." Karrad leaned forward. "Still, I only ever wanted leverage. Then you presented me with a once in a lifetime opportunity. A third of the Bern's shipwives in dock when they brought that monstrosity in. They had to empty the harbour of most of the ships, but her officers lined the dock to salute our victory."

"Not you," said Joron.

"I was not invited, I was not in favour. I was kept up here giving reports on your actions to the Bern while the whole town celebrated." He looked away; to hide a smile, Joron suspected. "And later died."

"And all this was my fault."

"Little ripples, Joron Twiner."

"You tortured half to death a woman you once loved." Karrad stared at him, tapped his finger on the desk.

"It is not really love, if you are both ordered to do it, is it?" And Joron had no answer to that. Karrad sat back. "I brought in those loyal to me to replace the dead. I am in charge now and will ask you one thing, Twiner," he said. "One thing and I ask you to answer me truly." Joron stared, said nothing. "Is what she said true, Twiner? Is it you that raises the keyshans?" Joron stared at him. Wondering how much he should say and then realising it did not matter. Meas would have told her torturer everything, there was little point in lying. But also little point in saying too much.

"The wakewyrm, I did not bring it. And most of the others risen since, where they came from I do not know."

"But you brought the wakewyrm to your aid? And you woke the keyshan that lived within McLean's Rock?"

"Yes," he said. 'I broke McLean's Rock."

"Can you teach me?" he said. Joron shook his head.

"No."

"Why not?"

"I need our gullaime, and it is aboard *Tide Child*."

"We have plenty of gullaime here."

"Not like ours." Karrad nodded.

"The keyshans within the island, will they awake anyway?"

"No," said Joron, and he sounded so very sure when he was anything but. Karrad stared at him.

"So you are exactly the weapon I surmised," he said, as much to himself as to Joron, "on your say-so whole islands can be destroyed."

"Yes," said Joron. Quiet filled the room. The only noise the *tap*, *tap*, *tap* of Karrad's finger on his desk. "But without the gullaime on *Tide Child* I can do nothing."

"Why should I believe you?"

Joron leaned forward, picked up Karrad's pen and looked at it.

"Because if I could raise the keyshan that lives within Shipshulme now, Indyl Karrad," he said, "when all looks rather bleak for me and mine, why wouldn't I?"

Karrad smiled, laughed. Clapped his hands slowly.

"Well done, Twiner. I was going to have you put under the hands of my hagpriest, she is good at getting at the truth. But you do not lie, do you? If you thought bringing the island down around our ears may give you and Meas a chance of escape you would take it, I can tell." He smiled. "A man who tells the truth is a rare thing. So, you are the Caller and your gullaime is the Windseer," he said.

"You know about that?"

"It is gullaime talk, that is all. A windseer is always rising among them. We let them. But this is the first I have heard of a caller rising too." He leaned across. "Is there a priest?" he said.

"Priest?"

"One who controls the Windseer, a fanatic." Joron nodded. "They generally kill them quickly enough," Karrad added.

"The priests?"

"No, the windseers. If they will not do what the priest wants, the priest kills them so the Windseer will reincarnate." He sat back. "We generally leave them to it, they are little more than animals really." He rubbed his hands together slowly. "I never thought there was anything in it."

"They say this power, whatever the Windseer has, will destroy the world."

"Well, Joron Twiner, they are an excitable species and are given to flights of fancy, that is why they must be controlled. By us, women and men. For their own safety. So I will make you an offer. I will make it once, and give you the night to think it over. I will put aside my hatred, Joron Twiner. The Hundred Isles are sadly depleted, and if the Gaunt Islanders push us hard enough we will collapse. We need a weapon, Joron Twiner, we need you. Join me."

"You are doomed. The hagpriests will never let a man—"

"They blame the Thirteenbern for keeping Meas alive as a child, to them this is all her fault. Her family's fault. A new Bern will sit on the throne, but I will control the fleet and with that comes the real power. This new Bern will be my puppet." Joron opened his mouth but before he spoke Karrad raised a hand. "Do not answer me now," he said. "Spend the night in the cells, with your shipwife and her mother. Look over your shipwife well, and ask yourself if you prefer the chair you sit in now, or the one she has been spending her time in since we took her. You were prepared to risk death to save her; all I am asking is that you live, but in my service."

34

The Choice

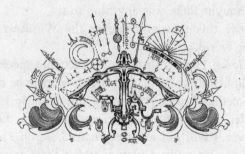

He entered the cell and Meas and her mother broke apart, both turning to look at him at as he stepped through the door, and it struck him again how similar they looked. The pain had aged Meas, her mother was wrapped in a simple variskweave cloak, their shared blood could not have been more apparent. They looked more like sisters than mother and daughter.

"He asked you to join him," said Meas. No question there. Joron nodded.

"I will not." She smiled, nodded.

"You should," said the Thirteenbern.

"Joron has honour." Meas snapped the words out, almost choking with emotion, then the words came fast, tumbling out of her. "And he knows Indyl cannot be trusted, he—"

"He was an excellent spymaster but has never been trustworthy, Daughter. Few of the Kept are."

"A little late for you to say that," said Joron. The Thirteenbern shook her head.

"I misjudged him, yes. Circumstances moved in ways I could never have predicted, he gathered more power more quickly than I had expected when my garrison shipwives died." She stood, took a step toward Joron. "I have people close to him. People I trust." Laughter, from Meas, a slow, cruel, mocking noise.

"You think you can return to power still, Mother? You think he would move without being entirely sure of his position?"

"Meas is right," said Joron. "He owns the fleet here. He has made sure all the ships are his people. Anyone who isn't has probably been sent away to your defensive ring. The hagpriests support him also." Gilbryn blew air through her nose, a half smile on her face.

"Clever," she said. "We kept my best away to defend us, kept those I need least nearest. He fed me my own prejudices and I gorged on them." She shook her head. "And to lose the hagpriests also? What a fool I have been."

"You cannot walk out of here and take your throne back," said Meas. Her mother stared at her. Then she let out a sigh, a great breath of air.

"No," said Gilbryn, but she stayed focused on Joron. "It appears not." She took a step closer to him. Lifted her arm. Placed a hand on his shoulder and looked up into his eyes. "Black Pirate, here is my command to you. Do what you came to do, save your shipwife. Do whatever you need for that to happen and know you have my blessing." She placed her other hand on his shoulder, looked directly into his eyes, holding him with the power of her gaze. "Save my daughter, Joron Twiner. Please." Behind her, Meas stood, hissing with pain.

"You left it a little late to care," she said, the words vicious, aimed to wound. "I never so much as once doubted you would have me tortured." Gilbryn rounded on her. Shouting like a shipwife in a gale.

"I have always cared for you, Meas," and did he see a tear in the Thirteenbern's eye? "How many times do you think I kept you alive when hagpriests wanted you bled over a ship? Or saved your position when a shipmother wanted you stripped of command for ignoring orders? And how long do you think I wept at the end when I condemned you for—"

"No!" Meas shouted. "Do not say it." Then she bowed her head, unable to look at her mother, her broken body seeming smaller, meeker than Joron had ever known her.

"He does not know?" said Gilbryn. "Your own deckkeeper and he does not know? Well, some things are for you to share with those closest to you. Not I." The Thirteenbern turned away from her daughter and looked to Joron. "But you should know this, Joron Twiner, if you escape Karrad will come after you with all he has. Not for vengeance, but because he cannot allow you to live. Meas has told me what you are, what you can do. He will think you will come back for him, for vengeance."

"We would not. We want peace. We only want the fighting to stop."

"He cannot understand that," she said. "And even if he could understand it he still would not let you go; if I was in power, I would not either. You know why."

"The Windseer," he said. She nodded.

"Gullaime have spoken of it for ever."

"Madorra, their priest, says it will bring them peace through the destruction of everything."

"A little extreme," said Gilbryn. "The birds are given to drama."

"Can you blame them?" he said. "We blind them at birth, force them to bring wind even though we know the price they pay is terrible. Though we are lucky – it does not matter what Madorra wants, our gullaime has no appetite for destruction."

"Often the way with the windseers, but it has never mattered before because there has been no caller, Twiner, so they have not had to make the decision. Now there is."

"How do you know what they believe?" said Meas from the back of the room.

"I am the Thirteenbern of the Hundred Isles, I know everything that happens in my realm."

"Plainly not true," said Meas, looking around the cell with a snort. The elder Gilbryn ignored her.

"The priest, what do you call it, Madorra? It will be pushing your gullaime hard to burn, to pull all the power of the winds to it."

"The Gullaime will not," said Joron. "Karrad said Madorra would kill it eventually."

"It may, they do. But if it feels it is genuinely close to their prophecy coming true? Then it will not be as quick to act as they have been in the past."

"The Gullaime will not do what Madorra wants." The Thirteenbern shrugged.

"You underestimate the power Madorra holds over it."

"What power?" said Joron, anger suddenly rising. "It so often seems to me I am in the middle of conversations where everyone has all the facts but none share them with me." Gilbryn cocked her head, smiled.

"You really don't know?"

"Know what?" Joron found himself shouting, took a deep breath, regained control.

"Do you ever wonder why men are given so little power, Joron?"

"Because the Maiden, Mother and Hag . . ."

"That is what we say, and maybe it is even true. But more than that, it is because we have seen what happens when you give males power."

"I don't understand," said Joron.

"The gullaime," she said, "the windtalkers are female, always."

"The Gullaime is a she?" he said, and now he knew it seemed right. Correct. Maybe inside he had always known, or maybe he had simply never thought of it. But he was not surprised.

"Yes, and the windshorn are male. When they need to control the windtalkers in their society they steal their eggs." Joron opened his mouth but had no words, no speech. Nothing would come. He cleared his throat.

"She has a child," he said, and it filled him with wonder. With an odd joy.

"An egg," said Gilbryn.

"So that is Madorra's control over our gullaime." He spoke more to himself than to the women in the cell. "She is protecting her child and I have not known and I have not done anything to help."

"Your gullaime will give in, eventually, Twiner. It will do what this Madorra wants. What mother would not?"

"But if the prophecy is true," he said, "the Gullaime will die, and its egg along with it." Gilbryn shook her head.

"Gullaime eggs are resilient, can be left for decades in all conditions and still hatch when the right warmth is applied. But the egg is more than a child to them. It is how they believe they live again, Twiner. All will be destroyed but their eggs will live through the fire, they will still hatch." He found he was sitting, suddenly overcome by her words.

"I have been so foolish, I never even thought to ask what . . ."

"And how do you have that conversation?"

"I could have asked its . . ." he caught himself, "*her* name. All this time, and I never even asked her name." Then he looked up. "She will not do it," he said. "Egg or not. She will not do it."

"Then you have another reason you need to get out, Joron Twiner," she said. "The gullaime believe in reincarnation, and they are patient but Karrad was right. If this Madorra becomes sure your gullaime will never do what it wants," she shrugged, "then Madorra will kill it."

He turned to Meas.

"Shipwife?"

"If my mother is right, we need to get back to our ship. We need a plan."

"A plan needs resources," said Gilbryn, "and what do we have? An old woman, a broken woman and a one-legged man, it is not much of an army." Meas stood, he saw her wince with pain, her hand came up to touch the bandage over her eye, making sure that it had not moved.

"And me," said another voice. They turned. Cwell stood in

the doorway. Had entered so quietly none had heard her. She stood closer to the barred door.

"Cwell," said Joron.

"You doubted me?" she said.

"No," he said. "I did not."

"I cannot stay long, they will realise I have gone."

"Why have you come?" said Meas.

"I have been asking around. Your position is stronger than you know," she said, glanced over her shoulder. "Karrad holds on to power by his fingertips, D'keeper. That he moved so quick surprised many who would have seen him gone the moment the Thirteenbern was snatched up. He keeps those most loyal to him nearest but knows if he missteps, they will move on him. He needs you, Deckkeeper."

"Then we must use that," said Meas. She limped over, put a hand on Joron's arm and leaned in close. "Forget about me. He will never let me free, get yourself away. Do whatever you need to do. Tell him whatever he needs to hear." He shook his head.

"I have not come this far, and through so much, to walk away now, Meas," he said. "Both of us or neither of us." She stared up at him. Smiled a little, looked over at her mother.

"That's the trouble when you raise someone up from being lowborn," Meas said to her, "no respect for the chain of command." She patted his arm and turned to Cwell. "Does Karrad trust you?"

"Not really, but he needs me. Already I have four of my uncle's lieutenants on my side."

"Good, we may need that trust."

"Now I must go," said Cwell. "I should not be down here and they will notice I am missing soon." She slipped out of the cell.

"You have a plan, daughter?" said Gilbryn. Meas nodded.

"Ey, you want to catch a fish? You offer it the bait it likes best," she said. "Karrad wants the power to raise keyshans? Well, Joron will offer it to him in exchange for our freedom."

She glanced at her mother. "Freedom for all." And Meas began to talk, haltingly, voice hoarse, body slow to obey and nicked with new scars. "You said we do not have an army, Mother," said Meas, "but we do, the gullaime, none think about them, but they can fight like devils when aroused."

"You think gullaime will fight for you?" said the Thirteenbern.

"No," said Meas, "they will not fight for me, nor for Joron. But they will fight for their windseer." Then she unfurled her plan, delicate, full of risk and dependant on more than a fair amount of luck. And as she did a small joy rose within Joron. *They have not broken you*, he thought, *they have done nothing to diminish your brilliance*.

That night, while Meas slept, he could not. He lay there, listening to the regular in and out of Meas's breathing and wishing for sleep, wishing for the morning when the plan could be put into action. And when he tried to banish those thoughts, others intruded, of the way Meas was hurt, of the scars on her body, of what it must have taken to make the indomitable women he knew give him up. Of the bandage over her eye. He felt a tug on his sleeve, and found the Thirteenbern looking at him. She beckoned him over to a corner of the cell, away from Meas.

"I would not wake her," she said quietly.

"What do you wish her not to hear?

"It is about her plan," said Gilbryn.

"Ah, criticism." She shook her head.

"No, it is risky but it is a good plan. All of it, but one part."

"So it is criticism?"

"Ey, but gentle," she said. "Take her with you, as you both want. He would expect that, but do not ask to take me."

"Meas was—"

"Insistent, ey, and I see that confused you. Hate and love live closer together than most know, boy. But if you ask to take me from this place," she whispered, "Karrad will be suspicious, more suspicious."

"She asked, she is my shipwife."

"If rank matters so much to you," she said, her voice harsh with restrained anger, "I am Thirteenbern of the Hundred Isles." Her hand tightened around his bicep. Then he felt it loose. Saw her breathe in, regain control. "Sorry, Twiner, for my anger. I am not used to being questioned. I want her to live, you understand?" He nodded.

"If you both . . ."

"Karrad cannot let me leave this place, my loyal shipwives will come straight to me the moment I am free. No, for him to be successful, I must die. There is no other way, and if that is the price of her life, I will pay it." He nodded. "Promise me," she said, and her hand once more tightened on his arm. "Promise me you will do whatever it takes to get her out." Her eyes so intent it felt like she pierced his chest, looked right into him.

"I promise," he said.

"Whatever it takes," she said again, her hand closing even tighter around his wrist.

"Yes."

"Good." She let go of him. "And thank you."

"Wait," he said. She stopped. "My face, the rot, you have not even mentioned it."

"Anyone can get sick, Twiner." She moved away, pausing only to add quietly, "She chose well in you. Now try and sleep, you will need your wits about you to deal with Karrad."

He lay awake long into the night, all too aware of how fragile their plan was, how easily it could go wrong. He did sleep, eventually, but it was not a comforting or good sleep, it was a fitful slumber full of half-remembered nightmares and strange and mournful keyshan songs that felt like being entombed in walls of sound.

35

A Test

They woke him by shaking the bars of the cell, calling out his name. Two well-dressed Kept, chests gleaming beneath leather straps, the embroidery around their groin freshly done, the thread still shiny with new metal woven into it.

"Twiner," said the taller of the two. "You have had your thinking time, the Bernholder wants you." He looked up, stood. Turned to look at the two women lying on the pallets behind him and straightened his jacket.

"Go," said the Thirteenbern, "prove yourself as weak as we know men are," and even though he knew she play-acted a part, he still felt the sting of her words. The two Kept only smiled at him.

"She says weak, but it is not men who lie in a cell with no power, aye, Twiner?" said one of them, and then opened the door, letting Joron out and locking it again behind him. "Put this on and come with us," said the smaller of the two, handing him a scarf. "No one wants to look at what remains of your face." Joron wrapped the scarf around his mouth and nose and followed, up and into the building. Once more through and into Kept Karrad's room where he sat once again at the desk, writing in a ledger. He did not look up as the two Kept brought

Joron. Or as they left. He did not invite Joron to sit, so rather than stand and wait and feel as if Karrad was in control Joron walked forward and sat down in the seat opposite the desk. For a moment he was sure Karrad's writing slowed a little, but not for long. Finishing whatever it was he was involved in, sanding the page to dry the ink. Blowing the sand from the page before closing the ledger. Then he looked up. Stared at Joron. Said nothing, barely moved, only considered him.

"Well?" he said.

"Well?" asked Joron.

"Do not play games. You were asked a question, now I desire an answer. Do you waste your life, or do you join me?" He sat back in his chair. In better light Joron saw that his muscle tone, so defined once, was no longer really so. He had applied sparkling make-up around his eyes but it could not hide the lines wrought by stress and worry.

"You call yourself Bernholder now, I hear?"

"People like titles," he said, "and this one provides some continuity. Now, give me your answer." Was there desperation there?

"I will join you," said Joron, and he tried to understand the look on Karrad's face. It was not disappointment, not exactly. Neither was it relief and it was there and gone so quickly that he was not even sure he had seen it.

"Good," said Karrad, though he hardly sounded filled with joy, barely met Joron's eye. "You had little choice, of course."

"There is always a choice," said Joron. "And I also have conditions." Karrad tapped his hand on the desk, smiled.

"Conditions?" He grinned at Joron. "I hardly think that you are in a position to have conditions. You must prove yourself first. Maybe in a few months, when I trust you a little more, then we will talk of conditions." Joron shook his head.

"I think not. You no longer deal with the frightened boy I was when Meas first brought me here, Kept Karrad. I am Joron Twiner, the Black Pirate. I have wrought my vengeance upon the Hundred Isles from east to west, north to south. I have commanded fleets, and sent women and men to die on my word." He leaned forward. "I am not someone who will simply bow down."

"You do not fear death?"

"I have walked hand in hand with the Hag since you had me sent to the black ships, I am inured to death." Karrad stared at him, then nodded.

"Well," he said, "I had forgotten you were so fearsome." He could not keep the mockery from his voice. He let out a short laugh, then was serious once more. "Tell me of your conditions and I will consider them." He looked away and Joron felt like he had won a small victory, and if he could win one then he could win more. What had felt to him like a desperate plan – a last-ditch effort, hatched with no surety in the dead of night in a cell – suddenly became more possible. Because now he knew that Cwell had been right, he was not the only one in this room on a knife edge, not the only one whose survival was precarious. Karrad was just as vulnerable as Joron; oh, he ruled Bernshulme right now, but there were still ships out there loyal to the Thirteenbern, and should they turn against him he would not last. The people would not accept a man in charge in all but name unless his power was absolute. Thirteenbern Gilbryn had been right, Karrad would never release her, but as for the other things Joron wished for? Well, he suddenly thought them far more likely than they had felt in the dead of night after this plan was hatched.

"I want Meas," he said. Karrad laughed and shook his head.

"The daughter of the Thirteenbern? I think not."

"The traitorous daughter of the Thirteenbern," said Joron. "And you have broken her." As he said it his own voice almost cracked at what felt like a betrayal of her.

"Then she is of no use to you."

"All I have done has been in her name. All my crews have suffered has been to bring her back." Karrad stared at him. "All she wants," said Joron, "all she has ever wanted, is peace. You have said you wanted that, and you need it, do you not? There will be enough strife here without the Gaunt Islander fleet arriving on your borders." Karrad stared at him. "Give her to me, give us permission for a colony." He leaned forward. "If I go back to my people without her, I will lose all their support. All I have put them through and then I walk away from the shipwife? They will throw me to the longthresh and you will not get what it is you want most."

"What about," said Karrad slowly, "if I give you her body. None but you and I will know." He nodded, just a small nod, as if that could influence Joron's decision.

"No," said Joron. "She walks on the slate of *Tide Child* again, or you may as well put us both to death."

"And if she walks the slate? In return I get you?"

"I am not done yet," he said, and Karrad laughed again.

"I think you overreach yourself, Twiner."

"No." Joron shook his head, with a growing confidence. "You want to raise keyshans? You want that power because you think it will ensure your rule?" Karrad did not reply, only stared at Joron, and he could almost feel the worry coming off the man. Chose to press Karrad a little. "Have you even told the people you rule yet?" Karrad sat back, made a slight noise, a "*hmph*."

"Not yet," he said at last. "When the time comes I will rule through a female proxy, I think it is for the best. While people get used to the title of Bernholder."

"If the Bern you choose does not have you killed first." Joron saw he had scored a point there, hit on a very real fear.

"Twiner, tell me what it is you want." Karrad sounded tired. As if this was all more than he could bear.

"It is not what I want, it is what you need, and what you are prepared to offer for it."

"Explain."

"You understand I need the gullaime aboard *Tide Child* to raise the keyshans for you?" He nodded.

"Meas's explanations were quite full, in the end," he said. Joron made a fist out of sight beneath the table. Dug his nails into his flesh.

"So you want me to bring the Gullaime to you?"

"I expect you to."

"You have clearly not met it, or really listened to any description of it that Meas may have given to you. The Gullaime will not come simply because I ask, and it will not come to you simply to save human lives. It—" he caught himself, still getting used to how to refer to the Gullaime correctly. "*She* does not care about me, or Meas."

"It is a gullaime," said Karrad, as if talking to a child, "you order them, you do not ask."

"She is a gullaime unlike any other, and you ask her, you do not order. You must offer our gullaime something she wants if you wish her to help you. It is what I did, it is what Meas did." Karrad did not speak, not immediately. He blinked, twice. Letting this thought filter through his mind, no doubt comparing it to what Meas had said under the unkind attentions of his torturer.

"And what do I have, that it wants?"

"Her people, Indyl Karrad. You have her people."

Karrad burst out laughing. It was true, and real and immediate laughter. As if Joron had said something ridiculous.

"The first man to rule the Hundred Isles is also the one that frees all his gullaime? Leaves the fleets without the power to manoeuvre in battle? Do you think me an idiot, Twiner? I had thought you serious, realistic in what you asked for. I had thought us men who may have disagreements, but could find a common ground in not being under the boot of the Bern—"

"You misunderstand," said Joron, and was there an edge of panic in his voice? Fear he was losing Karrad. The Kept sat back, spreading his arms mockingly.

"Make me understand then, or find yourself back in the cells and awaiting the attention of my pet hagpriest."

"I know you cannot give up all the gullaime, only a fool would." He tried to stay calm, for without gullaime all was lost. "But some? You can spare some. Send me your weakest. Make them mostly windshorn if you must. A hundred, can you spare that from the lamyards? You have fewer ships now, I saw to that, ey?" Karrad stared at him. Weighing up what he said. "And do not forget," continued Joron, "that when I bring my fleet across to you, as it comes with me, you will get these gullaime back."

"If Meas does not steal them away to this 'colony' you speak of," he said.

"What are a hundred gullaime, to the power to raise keyshans? Destroy islands? Bring your enemy to their knees by calling a sea dragon? You will not even need a fleet." Silence, sand passing slowly through a glass. "But you will only get that if you can bring the Gullaime onto your side. It wants its people free, offer it that and she will come gladly."

"And you," said Karrad, "you will come gladly too? You do not act like it." Joron stared at him. More silence. Time tipping by. Joron leaned forward.

"I have no love for you, Karrad," he said. "No wish to serve you or to help your cause." He found he was hissing, his words full of very real venom. Karrad sat back a little. "But I owe all I am to the shipwife, and I have a people. Women and men I care about and I will do whatever is needed to keep them safe. I will be your weapon, knowing all the while Meas and our colony will be your hostage. So no, I do not come gladly. I come because I must, and because duty demands it of me. I make myself your slave for those I love."

"So, how do we proceed with this exchange, Twiner?"

Time was ticking slowly by. Two men, gazes locked until Karrad let out a breath, a sigh.

"I take it my black fleet patrols the waters to the east of Sankrey Island by now?" Karrad nodded.

"An attempt to lure my ships out, but I am no fool." Joron nodded.

"In Hundred Isles waters there is an place called Kluff Island, not much more than a rock really." Joron scratched the side of his head. "Take me there; we have someone ready to receive messages. They will take notice to the black fleet of what I wish. That we intend to exchange Meas for the Gullaime, and where to meet us to do it. You may choose where, but it must be out of water you control or my ships will not come."

"I could just send a fast ship to this island, take your messenger," said Karrad.

"Why risk it? You do not know the codes they will require, and you have Meas as a hostage to my good behaviour. I am not about to leave her behind."

Karrad watched him as he sat back. The Kept licked his lips.

"Gueste!" he shouted. The door opened and Gueste came in, together with Cwell. "Did you hear all of that?" She nodded. "And what do you think?" Gueste walked around the desk, leaving Cwell in the doorway.

"In his shoes, I would say anything," she said, "for a chance at escape." Joron stared at her – Hag, how he hated this woman. "But him," she pointed at Joron, "all he has done was for her. He came here expecting to die, for her. For their people." She managed to make the word "people" sound like a curse. Brought a finger to her mouth and bit on her nail. "I think he tells the truth about this island."

"You believe he will join us then, to save her?" said Karrad.

"There is no real way of knowing how far he is prepared to go for her until he is tested." Then she smiled. Leaned over and whispered something into Karrad's ear. The Kept glanced at Joron, back to Gueste. Was he worried?

"Very well," said Karrad, turning back to Joron. "I will do as you ask, but in turn I have my own conditions, you will be kept under guard." Joron nodded. "And I know song is part of the raising of these beasts. So when we bring you this gullaime, if you so much as hum without my permission I will have you killed. And then I will have your colony scorched and every woman and man in it I will use in experiments to perfect hiyl poison." Joron nodded again. "You agree to this?" Another nod. "Good," he turned from Joron. "Gueste," he said, "take him away." Joron stood and Gueste headed for the door.

"Follow me," she said and he did. They walked through the

bothy, Gueste by his side, Cwell behind them. "I have been talking with your friend, Cwell," she said as they wove through the building. "My, you must be regretting your treatment of her now, ey?" she laughed. "To make Mulvan Cahanny's niece your slave and think it would never come back to haunt you." She stopped by a door guarded by two seaguard, turned to him. "I thought you were cleverer than that, Twiner."

"It seemed a good idea at the time," he said, and he was aware of Cwell behind him. Aware how Gueste's words could be seen as true. Could he really trust Cwell? What if she simply played her own game? The opportunity to take over her uncle's organisation must be tempting.

"Karrad," said Gueste, "is a clever one, but surprisingly weak sometimes, Joron Twiner."

"Do you mean to kill me?" said Joron, and it felt likely. He was glad his voice did not waver. That he showed no fear. She shook her head.

"No, I see the use in you just as he does. But I meant what I said to Karrad back there. We cannot know how far you will go in service to us until you are truly tested." She put her hand on the door handle. "And I mean to test you." She pushed open the door and ushered him in to a small white room and there, bound and kneeling in the centre, was Mevans. "Your man here," she pointed at him, "he took some subduing." Mevans looked up, his face bruised with all the colours of a storm-wracked sky at sunset, purple and red and blue. He managed a smile, showing he was missing teeth from his upper and lower jaw.

"D'keeper," he said. "Good to see you. I'm afraid I let you down. Karrad escaped. Load of seaguard came from nowhere."

"It was not your fault, Mevans," he said. "Narza betrayed us, probably left her guard conscious outside. They promised her the shipwife in exchange for us."

"How did that go for her?" he said.

"They killed her." Mevans nodded, as if this was a foregone conclusion. "Cwell turned on me also." Mevans looked at him, glanced behind him and past Gueste to where Cwell stood, between the two seaguard.

"Did she so," he said, and Joron fought down a smile, for he knew from the tone of his voice that the man before him did not believe it for a second and Joron felt bad he had doubted her only a moment ago.

"Touching as this reunion is," said Gueste, and he turned to her, "we are here for a reason, Twiner." She drew her blade and he felt his muscles freeze, waited for the burn of the cut. It did not come. "This man," she gestured at Mevans, "is a criminal, sentenced to death." Turning back to Joron, she stared into his eyes. "On the floor before him is your sword. It is precious to you, I understand, and Karrad wanted you to have it back. Now, you can pick up your blade and make some heroic attempt at escape if you wish, Twiner. I will not lie, part of me hopes you do. Or you can prove how far you will go for your shipwife, and put this man, who you have served with for years, to death." She smiled. "For me."

"In cold blood?" he said, for it felt like Gueste had trapped him once more within a nightmare.

"It's not like you are a stranger to that, Black Pirate. I have seen the gallows lined up along the shores of the towns you raided."

Joron had no answer. He turned, bent down oh-so slowly and picked up the straightsword. Drew the blade, saw the engraving along it. Felt the familiar shape of the hilt in his hand. He swallowed, it felt like too much weight to carry. Took a deep breath. Looked down at Mevans, who lifted his head. Stared straight into his eyes. Joron shifted his grip on the blade. He could take Gueste, he was sure of it. Spin on the spot, take her by surprise. Then there would be the two seaguard.

As if reading his thoughts, Mevans gave a small, almost imperceptible shake of his head, eyes flicking from Joron to somewhere behind him. Joron turned, just in time to see Cwell, her eyes locked on Mevans, move her hand away from the bone knife she carried.

"He is my hatkeep," said Joron. "I trust him. I need him."

"Why else would I choose him?" said Gueste quietly, amusement in her voice. "What use a test if it is not . . . testing?"

In the back of his mind he heard Meas, and heard her mother, saying: *Promise me you will do whatever it takes to get her out.* But he could not do this. He could not. Not Mevans.

Whatever it takes.

Joron lifted the sword. Put the tip in the hollow of Mevans neck, holding the blade vertically. Held the hilt in both hands so he could thrust it down in a swift and kind killing blow through heart and lungs.

Mevans's breath rasping in his lungs.

Whatever it takes.

Joron could not do it. He could not do this thing.

Mevans's bruised eye opened and he looked Joron in the face. Those eyes. As friendly as always. Breath rasping. Mevans forcing words from his cracked and bloodied lips.

"Only the day is undecided, D'keeper," he said. Then gave him the smallest smile and the briefest nod of his head. "Do it."

Whatever it takes.

And, with a scream that felt like it ripped out his heart, Joron forced the blade down.

36

The Exchange

They took away Mevans's body and left Joron in the room, a streak of blood across the floor that he could not take his eyes from. They did not take his sword from him and once he was alone he let it drop from his hand. There it lay in a pool of Mevans's blood while he crouched in a corner of the room, fighting back the pain and grief that washed over him in waves.

He felt like he was drowning.

The door opened. Meas was pushed through, ragged and small, limping. She looked down, her feet were bare and she stood in the pool of Mevans's blood. When she looked up at him the question was plain on her face but he could not look at her, only bowed his head and stared at the floor.

"Mevans," the name said so quietly it barely escaped his lips. "It was the price Gueste asked of me, to prove I would do as they say." She looked down at the blood. Walked forward and he heard her feet lifting on stone sticky with blood. The pause as she stopped to scoop up his sword. Then she walked toward him and in the edge of his vision he saw her bloody red footprints. He felt her stand by him. Felt her hand on his shoulder, a short squeeze.

"We leave a trail of blood wherever we go," she said quietly. "Sometimes it is our own, more often that of others. It is what duty demands of us. Mevans knew that." He nodded; he knew it also. Not that it made it any easier. Not that it dulled the throbbing pain within him.

"How could he think I could ever forgive . . ."

"Karrad had Gueste to do it for a reason, Joron. No doubt later he will apologise, tell you she acted on her own initiative. He was always manipulative." He looked up at her. "People like Karrad and my mother, Joron, they are capable of terrible things because they see those they consider below them as pieces to move about in pursuit of their own agenda."

"I have also done terrible things," he said.

"I know."

"You do not." He could feel it, guilt, choking him. Not just for Mevans. For so many more. For Dinyl, Coughlin, Jennil and every deckchilder who had fallen to blade or shot or simple accident. For all those whose necks he had stretched for being in nothing more than the wrong place at the wrong time. For the hundreds, maybe thousands of innocents in Bernshulme who had fallen to the keyshan's poison.

"I do," she said, "of course I do. My mother told me all you did. All you wrought."

"Not done for duty," he said, "not done for honour. Done from rage, done from fear and because I did not know what else to do." He found himself looking up at her through a diamond haze of tears. "I just wanted you back, to tell me what to do."

"Well, I am here now," she said, squeezed his shoulder once more.

"You would not have done the things I did," he said. "You would have had a plan." She smiled then.

"How long have you commanded my fleet, Joron? And yet you still think I always knew what I was doing?"

"But you . . ."

"Ran on hope and improvisation, Joron. On making the

most of what I had at any one point." He stood, looked at her, the eye bandage, the scars, the stooped and pained posture. When she spoke he heard the way her voice had changed, the damage done from screaming while they tortured her. He wondered what damage he could not see.

"You are Lucky Meas," he said, "you are the witch of Keelhulme Sounding, the greatest shipwife who ever lived." She looked back at him, that one eye watery, and he wondered whether she was near to tears also.

"You have never once asked, Joron Twiner, why they sent me to the black ships." He moved over to the side, let her sit beside him for it was plain to him that standing was causing her pain. She sighed as she sat. "And I was glad of that. At the start I would never have told you, later I did not want to." She laughed. "But you, Joron, you hold yourself to a standard too high."

"I killed those who did not deserve it," he said, and the words broke from him, threatening to flood him in tears and when she replied it was his shipwife who spoke, not the woman. Harsh, not to be questioned.

"You did what you believed was necessary. I will not say I agree with all of it. And you are right to feel guilt for many things, Joron, for a shipwife who does not wear as much guilt as they do trinkets is one who has not learned." He wanted to interrupt, to tell her she was wrong but dared not. The steel was back in her, even if only for a moment. "And if you do not believe we all do things that we regret then know this. They sent me to the black ships, Joron," she said, "because I ran away."

Silence.

"Ran?" He did not understand. She nodded.

"I ran. I turned my ship around and headed in the opposite direction to the enemy."

"No," he said.

"Denying it, Joron, does not make it less true." She looked at him, but she was very far away. In another time, another place. "Three Gaunt Island two-ribbers coming back off a raid. Day as clear as you could wish for. We were fresh out of port and had ridden the Eaststorm for a week, all my gullaime fresh and unused. Day couldn't have been better for us, the positioning neither. They couldn't escape and I commanded the *Hag's Hunter*, the most feared ship in the entire archipelago after the *Arakeesian Dread*. We had all the advantages." She licked her lips. Looked away. "I think of that day a lot. I tell myself I looked at my crew, thought of the carnage to come and wanted to save them from it. I tell myself I thought that, even were our action successful, most of the stolen children aboard those Gaunt Island ships would die during it. I have thought, and I have wondered, and I have made a lot of excuses." Then she looked back, her one eye meeting his two. "But the truth is, Joron, I was scared for myself. Of the pain that I may suffer, of death. I felt that day as if my luck had run out and the Hag sat at my steering oar. So I turned my ship, that great and powerful ship, and I ran away."

"Meas . . ." he said, and she held up a hand.

"I do not want pity, or understanding." She stood. "I want you to know that no one is perfect, we are all flawed. I have raided for children, killed more innocents than I can count because they lived on the wrong side of Skearith's Spine." She stopped, gathered herself as if she were on the rump of a ship about to take a broadside. "And I have been a coward." She reached over, put a hand on his shoulder. "I feel shame for it, every day. But not as much shame as I feel for . . ." Her voice died away. She gathered herself, took a deep breath. "For what I did to you, for telling them about you."

"Meas . . ."

"No," she said, "do not try and give me succour. Joron, we cannot change what we have done. Do you understand? We can only try and do what is right as we go forward into the future."

"And what is right?" he said. She shrugged.

"I am not sure I know. But I have had a long time to think.

I see what Karrad does, what my mother did, some of what you have done. What I did." She raised a hand, touched the bandage where they had taken her eye. "And I think on what we do to the gullaime and I know it is wrong. So, Joron Twiner, maybe rather than trying to always do right, we should concentrate on trying not to do what is wrong, for now anyway. Ey?" He nodded.

"Ey, Shipwife," he said.

"Ey indeed." She leaned back against the wall and Joron moved from his crouch to sitting by her. "I hate waiting. I wish they would hurry up and take us to our ship or do whatever it is they plan. Better to be underway and suffering what is, than worrying about what may be."

They waited a long time, sat in silence, waiting for someone to come and get them.

"He would not let my mother leave?" she said eventually. Part statement, part question.

"No," said Joron.

"Did you ask?" she said.

"No." He knew he could have lied, told her half a truth but she was his shipwife and he would not do that. "Your mother asked me not to, said he would never let her go. Karrad told me as much himself." Meas seemed to deflate a little. The silence hanging over them. "I am sorry, if I have let you down."

"No," she said with a gentle shake of her head, "you have not. I should not have insisted on it. I realised that the moment you had left." She shrugged. "My imprisonment here, it has left me confused at times."

"No," said Joron, "she is your mother. No matter what she has done, there is always that." He smiled. "Never a day goes by without me thinking of my father." She stared at the floor and nodded.

"I am jealous of what you had there, you know."

"Jealous that I am haunted by his death?" She shook her head.

"No, jealous of what you had before," she said. "Of the days you spent flying the water with him on your fisher's boat. I have rarely heard anyone speak about a time in life that brought them such pure happiness."

"It was often hard," he said.

"Ey," she said, "but time wears away at memory, it leaves behind what was important, and you were happy. That is what remains." She looked at him. "I have few such times to look back on."

"You once told me, people like you do not have friends." She nodded.

"Ey," she said, "we do not. It is a lonely life, to rule the rump of a boneship," and she was about to say more but the door opened. Karrad entered, together with his shipwife Gueste. Both Joron and Meas stood, took two paces forward. Standing in the blood of Mevans as Karrad and Gueste stopped opposite them. For a moment Karrad stood there, looking at them, and Joron saw the shock on his face when he saw Meas, what had been done to her in his name.

"Meas . . ." he began.

"Don't," she said, sharp and bitter, "there is nothing you can say." He stood there a moment longer, nodded.

"My plan has long been in place, I could let nothing get in the way of it. Not even you." As he spoke Joron watched Gueste, the woman smirked back at him. "But for what it is worth I am genuinely sorry." He sounded so contrite, real. As if her torture had been forced upon him. Meas looked up at him.

"What do you want, Indyl?" she said. "I doubt it is me, not after what your pet hagpriest has done. If you ever really wanted me at all." He stared at her. Considering, thinking.

"I did," he said, more softly than Joron had ever heard him speak before, and his mask fell away. "At one point, I thought we could rule together, I thought that would be the eventual outcome. Equals," he said. "Your star was rising. Even though you could not see it, you were the natural successor to your mother."

"Not without children," she spat.

"You were only a few years away from control of the fleet. You think children cannot be procured for the powerful, Meas? You think every Bern actually has all the children they claim? There are more young girls come up to the Grand Bothy than ever make it to Bern, have you never noticed that? You think we really let the children of Berncast in to rule?" She stared at him, something like shock on her face though Joron felt no such thing. Why should another layer of corruption surprise him?

"I was never at the bothies to see that, Indyl, I was always at sea." She stared at him, all challenge, and his concern melted away and Joron wondered whether it was iron control on his part, or if he was simply a good actor. Wearing the face he thought each situation needed.

"Well," he said, "if you had been a little more attentive maybe you would not be here now, not in this state anyway," and all handsomeness fled from his face, replaced by a sneer.

"You are angry because I chose the sea over you?" she said. He clearly was, and his anger overcame him, swift and loud and as surprising as a sea squall, shouting loud enough to surprise Gueste, who took a step back.

"I am angry because you ruined everything!" he shouted. "Everything! We could have taken the whole machinery of this place apart if you had succeeded your mother." He stepped closer. "But you had to run away from a fight you could easily have won. You had to be a coward." He saw how that cut her. How she flinched at those words and he was willing to bet they hurt her more than any torture. "You ruined everything," he said. "Then, if that was not enough, there was him." He pointed at Joron and he found himself, unwillingly, taking a step back just like Gueste had. "The damage he has caused to my fleets. He has brought back ancient magics and creatures that we all know are best left in the sea where they belong. You and he have forced me to become all I ever hated to protect the islands I love."

Silence after his outburst. Joron felt guilt creeping up on him, for Karrad was right. What he could do, it was better left in the sea. What he had wrought in his desperation to have Meas back had been terrible, as heedless to what he destroyed as the keyshan had been to his ship when it had fought the toothreaches. But not her, not Meas. She had fought hard, for change, for peace. Were they wrong? Was Meas in the wrong? Had they simply made everything worse, only guaranteed another cycle of war and death?

"I ruined your peace?" said Meas, the words sounding bitter on her tongue. "We," she nodded to Joron, "ruined your peace?"

"Ey," said Karrad. "And I am glad that is out in the open now. Glad you know what you have done. That you, Meas, and your protégé, lie at the base of all I have had to do." She bowed her head, spoke.

"I am sorry, Indyl," she said. Then raised her head. "So allow me to put right what I have wrought." She smiled, a small smile but one he knew, an echo of her old confidence. "Joron is in touch with the Gaunt Islanders."

"As am I, you have forced that on me," said Karrad.

"Well," she said, "that makes things even easier. Join them. Be the one who joins the Hundred Isles and the Gaunt Islands in peace. Rule as regent, become part of their Bern family. Whatever you must do, do it. You have enough of a fleet left to exact promises from them." She glanced at Joron. "And you have him. Indyl, you need not even send us off on your ship and pick up our gullaime. You can make real and lasting peace. You could save thousands of lives and be the one who changes the archipelago for ever." In that moment, all doubt fled from Joron. For here was Meas, putting aside the terrible things the man had done to her, months and months of agony and pain. Charting a clear path, a better course to what could be a real and lasting peace.

For a moment, Indyl saw it too. Joron could tell from the look on his face, he saw a way forward that would change everything. He saw a pathway toward the peace that Meas definitely dreamed of, and maybe he once had.

Then he shook his head.

"You would have me beholden to a woman once more? Give up everything I have fought for? The work of years, and pass it over to a Gaunt Islander?" He looked down on her, then turned to Gueste. "Get them to the ship," he said, and as he left he added, "And have the floor of this room cleaned."

37

Toward the End

Gueste led them, with Cwell and a contingent of seaguard, through the gion forest and over the island.

"What is she doing here?" said Joron, staring at Cwell. "I would have thought you would leave her in Bernshulme."

"That was the plan," said Gueste. "But then it occurred to me, we will need to make contact with your people. I cannot send you, obviously. So it would be useful to have a friendly face for them." Joron nodded, as it had been part of their plan for Cwell to seek help once they were gone. But he and Meas had thought Cwell would be taking a fast ship, and an explanation, out to where the black fleet taunted the Hundred Isles ships. Now their plans must change. He turned to Cwell.

"Traitor," he said. She only stared in return and Gueste laughed.

The great gion plants were at their height and the huge leaves caught any moisture in the air, most of it funnelling back into the plants but a fair amount of it falling through the canopy. It did not have the rhythmic consistency of rain, not persistent enough to let you get used to it. Just an arrhythmic dripping of water with a talent for finding its way down the backs of necks or through gaps in clothing. Some quality of the contact with the plant caused the water to leave behind an unpleasant, greasy feel upon the skin; and should it get into your mouth a faint and rank taste that never quite went away.

It was an annoyance to Joron, but nothing more, he had weathered storms and ice and gallowbow shots, so an unpleasant walk was little to him, even one-legged and tired as he was. But as they made their way up the hill, it was plain to Joron that every step Meas took pained her, that her strength, once so bountiful, had fled. That her time in the cell and under the care of her torturer had stolen it from her.

"We should get you a litter," he said quietly.

"No," she said.

"You have been sore treated, and by them – they cannot expect you to carry on as if it was not the case."

"No," she said, her voice hoarse. "I'll not show weakness, and especially not in front of Gueste." She wiped a spot of liquid from her face and it left a silvery smear. "She would enjoy it too much. There is something very wrong with that woman."

"I will not disagree on that. But lean on me if you need it."

"Get help from a crippled man? She would enjoy that even more." The words stung despite her forcing a smile as she said it, despite knowing she meant it in jest.

"Do you trust Cwell?" she said.

"We have little choice," he replied. Meas stared at him, put a hand on his arm. "But yes, I do."

"Good," she said, "so do I."

It took them most of the day to wind their way to the top of the hill, and on their way they stopped at the lamyard. Joron had never seen Shipshulme Lamyard before. It was named for the island not the town, for the town wanted as little to do with it and its inhabitants as possible.

He heard it before he saw it.

He felt it before he heard it.

The song of the island growing in intensity. The long and

mournful howl of something trapped and sleeping, deep within the rock. That song amplified by the presence of so many gullaime. After the song within came the song without. A mixture of the gullaimes' musical chirping, whistling, clicking, fluting language and the more guttural squawks and caws and sounds of surprise and annoyance and insult that Joron was well used to from his friend on the ship. But these gullaime were nothing like his friend. They filled the lamyard cages, which were huge things, built as squares, the insides spiked to stop gullaime climbing. Between the cages were aisles where human guards walked, and often they were accompanied by what Joron now knew must be windshorn. Within the cages Joron could barely see the ground for gullaime. This was not like the previous lamyards he had seen, and far from the places they had set up for their own gullaime, where design had come from the gullaime themselves, and space and air and vegetation were the key. This was a place of intensive breeding, not dissimilar to the battery cages Joron was used to seeing on the farms where they bred kively for food, too many creatures in too small a space. The air stinking, the nearness of it unpleasant and claustrophobic with unthinking cruelty.

"Can't even think why you like these filthy things," said Gueste.

"They're not filthy if you let them clean themselves," said Joron. Gueste looked at him.

"Filth," she said, "takes more than a wash to get rid of. I can still smell the streets on you." If Gueste had thought the insult would wound Joron she was disappointed. Instead he smiled at the shipwife.

"Had you ever had to work for a thing, Gueste, rather than just be handed it because of who you are, maybe you would recognise the sweet smell of honest sweat." Her hand went to her blade but Cwell stopped her, holding Gueste's hand on the hilt.

"We need him, remember," said Cwell. "Kill Karrad's hopes of using the keyshans as a weapon and I imagine it'll go badly for you." Gueste nodded, breathed in through her nose and made a pained face, though whether it was because of the smell or because of Joron, he did not know.

"Let the seaguard deal with them, then," said Gueste, and stalked away from the lamyard to wait at the forest edge. Cwell watched her go and turned to Joron. Gave him the smallest nod of acknowledgement and walked away as the seaguard officer approached. Joron found the man who approached familiar, though it took a moment to place him. Tassar, one of the Kept who had been close to the Thirteenbern. When Meas had first brought him to the bothies Tasser tried to goad him into a fight he would undoubtedly have lost.

"I had hoped never to meet you again," said Joron.

"And I you." He stood closer, words coming in a whisper. "I'd love to see you hanging from a scaffold for what you have done to Bernshulme, but I am loyal to the Thirteenbern. She said you matter and I must help you if I can."

"How was she?"

"Fine, then." He straightened up, his body gleaming with oil, and his face struggling to contain emotion. "Shortly afterwards they hung her, as a traitor to the Hundred Isles. Said she knew what the keyshan was, that she brought the plague in deliberately."

"My mother?" said Meas.

"I walked her to the scaffold myself," said Tassar, and he looked genuinely pained. "She went bravely, Shipwife, despite that the people she had spent her life protecting mocked and laughed at her." Meas stared at him, taking in what he said. Then she walked away. Tassar turned back to Joron. "I made the Bern a promise. She asked me to get you safely to the ship and that I will do, as it was her wish. But when that task is done expect nothing more from me. I blame you for all this, Twiner, and given the chance for revenge I plan to take it."

"Then I will just have to ensure I stay unthreatening for as long as we are together, ey?" Joron said. "Shall we pick up our gullaime? That is why we are here, is it not?" Tassar nodded.

"I will go see the yard master," he said, "hopefully she will be ready and we will not have to stay here too long." Tassar turned and Joron watched him walk into the lamyard. As he walked down the muddy lane between towering cages his passage was followed by flapping and crowing and fury as the gullaime registered the presence of a human. Though when Tassar stopped and turned his gaze toward the cages the gullaime there, even in their blindness, must have sensed it as they quickly quietened, lowering themselves to the ground in subservience. And a wave of bowing white figures marked his passage as if he were a rock and they the surf breaking around him.

"It is not right." He turned and found Meas.

"What?"

"That," she pointed at the bowing gullaime. "Once I would not have thought twice about it. Now I think if any saw humans doing the same they would name the one all bowed to as a tyrant." She touched the bandage that covered her empty eye socket.

"We have been their tyrants for many years."

She watched, her eyes very far away. "No wonder Madorra wants us all dead," she said.

"You do not blame it?" he asked. She shook her head.

"No, but neither can I allow it." Meas stood a little nearer to him, and he could hear her breathing, ragged, hurting. "And I will not allow Madorra to murder our gullaime either."

"Because our plan hinges on it?" She looked up at him, the briefest of smiles and Joron wondered how he would get the Gullaime's egg away from the windshorn.

"Ey, that, and more. It is part of our crew, it is one of us." Her one eye scanned his face. "Too many have died." He nodded.

"I am sorry about your mother, Shipwife," he said. She bit her bottom lip, holding it between her teeth for a moment before letting go.

"There will be a time for grief, Joron, but it is not now."

Before she could say any more they were interrupted by a squawking and a row like he had never heard before. Above it the high crack of the whip followed by the pitiable sounds of gullaime, frightened and in pain. He turned, saw a gaggle of gullaime approaching, a small crowd of windtalkers, all chained together, and around them a larger number of windshorn. Walking in front was Tassar and to the side a hagpriest, it was she who held the whip and she who wielded it. And it was she who Meas was now heading toward as fast as she could walk. Joron swiftly followed. The hagpriest raised her whip again and the crowd of gullaime tried to flow away from her, but were hemmed in by angrily screeching windshorn.

The whip never fell.

The hagpriest's hand was held firm in Meas's grip, maybe not as iron as it once was, but iron enough. The hagpriest turned on Meas. A woman of a similar age, though not as scarred, not as tried by life.

"Who are you to dare lay hand on me?"

"No more whips," said Meas.

"Pain is all they understand." Almost before she had finished speaking Meas's other hand came up, a bunched fist to the face of the hagpriest and she fell like a rotten gion. The whip left in Meas's hand.

"No more whips," said Meas.

"How dare you," said the woman, hand coming up to her bloodied nose. "It is forbidden to lay hands upon us."

"No more whips," said Meas again. "Do not make me teach you this lesson again, for in my experience pain is all you understand." The priest stared at her, until Gueste, Cwell and Tassar ran up. Meas backed away. "Just laying down some rules," she said, and dropped the whip in the mud before walking away.

Cwell and the Kept helped the hagpriest up as Gueste watched. Joron was pleased to see the whip left where Meas had dropped it in the mud.

The gullaime were taken by Tassar and their handlers a

longer way around, expected to walk through the night. The humans made their way up through the forest, winding through brightly coloured trunks and cutting through writhing varisk vines as thick as an arm, until they found the porter's campsite where Joron had stopped on his way to Bernshulme.

"We stop here," said Gueste. "No doubt the shipwife needs a rest."

"I can carry on if you wish," said Meas, though it was plain to Joron she could not.

"Well I am glad of the rest," said Joron. "It is hard for a one-legged man to walk up such steep hills." Meas glanced over at him, and was there thanks there, in her one good eye? Suddenly he could not bear it, could not stand to see her this way, could not cope with the fact that when he looked upon her his first emotion was pity. He turned and walked to the edge of the hill so he could look down on Bernshulme. In the dying of the day lamplighters were working their way through the town, a stark circle of darkness showing where the dead keyshan's poison had made Bernshulme uninhabitable. He could just make out the massive corpse lying in the harbour, stretching out into the deeper sea. The once great keyshan slain by one of its sither, brought here by humans, by him in part, slowly rotting away, darkness seeping from it to kill anything that came too close. He felt Meas come to stand by him. Heard her steps, not as confident as they once were. Not as strong as she once was.

"What horrors we wreak, eh Joron?" she said quietly.

"I have tried not to think about it, but ey, what I did fills me with loathing. I see it, and do not know how I can ever put it right."

"You cannot, Joron. You made a decision in the heat of the moment. Right, wrong, we never know."

"I knew."

"But you did not bring it here." She stared down at the harbour. "They could have left the corpse. When they realised their deckchilder were dying, they could have taken it to the flensing yards on the other side of Shipshulme." She let out a long breath. "You put events in motion, right enough. But you did not control them, and the fact this haunts you? Well, that is a good thing in itself."

"I am no better than your mother, or Karrad, happy to ship the dying to feed into vats in the hope of power."

"No." A sudden seriousness in her voice. She turned him so he looked at her. "That is wrong, Joron. Do not let them make you believe otherwise. You made a decision in battle, in war, in the moment. A cruel one, a hard one right enough. What was done by my mother, and Karrad, that was cold, and that was calculated." She held up a hand, showed him how twisted her fingers were, how not all the nails had grown back. "Crush my hand in battle, I will curse you, but understand. Even torture me for answers needed in the moment, I may even understand that too. The doing of this though?" She rotated her hand, so she was looking at her palm and twisted fingers. "This was cold, Joron, done well past when it could help. They had taken all they could from me and still they did not stop." She let her hand fall. "What is done in desperation can be terrible; what is done from cold calculation, well, that is evil. Or so I count it."

"I am not sure those I took to the gallows would agree," he said.

"Or those I raided for my mother, and whose children I stole," she said quietly. "But we must make our case with the Hag for them, and hope for forgiveness by the fire from those we wronged. Terrible acts, Joron, they are often unthinking. We learn, and we get better. It is those who do not learn, or simply embrace and become inured to the terrible things we do that must be feared, and must be stopped." She glanced over her shoulder. "I think Karrad is one of those people now, and he surrounds himself with those like him." She looked at Joron. "I cannot change what I was, what I did cannot be made less wrong. But I can give all I have to stop those things happening again, and the world can ask no more of me."

"Your mother . . ." he began.

"It hurts, Joron. I feel like I had only just begun to see the truth of her." She bowed her head. Took a deep breath. Then looked up. "But make no mistake, Joron, for what she did? For the deaths of all those people who could not help themselves? If I had taken Bernshulme I would have led her to the gallows myself." She turned and walked away before he could say any more.

In the morning they headed down the hill, fighting their way through the forest once more until they reached the bustling makeshift port they had originally arrived at. They were met by a phalanx of seaguard, all armoured and armed, who escorted them roughly through the crowds coming on shore and down to the beach where flukeboats waited. Gueste ushered them aboard one.

"I travel in consort with Karrad, escorting his flagship in my own command, *Painful Loss*. He has no wish to see you every day so I may see you another time, Twiner," she said. "But do not worry, the shipwife you will travel with is an old friend of yours." She smiled and turned away.

"Where are the gullaime?" said Joron, a sudden sense of panic rising, for any hope they had of escape rested on them. Gueste turned back.

"Do not worry, they are already loaded and you will travel amid their stink as you seem to like it so much." Then she nodded to the flukeboat's crew who pushed it up to the water and Joron and Meas were taken across to a waiting boneship, a two-ribber, named *Wyrm Sither*. As they climbed on board the shipwife was there to meet them, along with Tasser. It took a moment for Joron to place the man stood before him. When he did it was with a sinking feeling.

"Barnt," he said.

"I am gratified you remember me," he said, then he drew the straightsword he wore so Joron could see it. Something inside him tightened. That was his sword, the one he had been forced to kill Mevans with. Cwell had given it to Barnt a long time ago, to spite Joron. Then taken it back for him while an island disintegrated around them, to prove herself. "Kept Karrad had your belongings sent over, and in among them I found this. I must say, I am glad to have it back, it is far too good a weapon for someone who was dragged up from the docks to have."

"I must admit," said Joron, "I am surprised you survived the destruction of McLean's Rock, Shipwife Barnt."

"I am very much a survivor," he said.

"Well," said Joron, "I intend to have my sword back."

"Over my corpse you will," said Barnt, "and I doubt you are capable of besting me in an honourable fight." He smiled and Joron thought there was something unbearably smug about the man. "But maybe if you prove yourself to Karrad you will earn your own weapon." Joron, for just a second, considered launching himself at the man, but it was clear that was what Barnt wanted. Tassar too, so Joron took a deep breath instead. Let it out. Barnt looked at Meas, small and bent and hurt, dismissed her with sneer and then he saw Cwell. "You," he said, and he pointed the tip of the sword at her. "You gave me this on McLean's Rock." He touched the scar on his face. Cwell nodded. "You and I have unfinished business."

"Ey," she said, "it is true. Should have killed you back on McLean's Rock, but I were pressed for time. But that is the past now, I work with Karrad and our business will have to wait."

"Take them below," said Barnt, and Joron could not help being amused at the shipwife's face when the seaguard took hold of him and Meas, but left Cwell on the deck.

38

A Deal Struck

Wyrm Sither left the makeshift port for Kluff Island, his hold full of squabbling gullaime and his slate decks full of deckchilder and seaguard. In the deckkeeper's cabin sat Joron and Meas, both lost in their own worlds, both planning a terrible future for those above them. Occasionally he heard the voice of the shipwife giving orders. Often he thought of Gueste, and what he would do if he were ever alone with her and had a blade in his hand. During the march down the hill to the waiting flukeboats of *Wyrm Sither* Joron had only grown to hate her more. She was casually cruel to those under her command, just as when they had begun their journey she had been casually cruel to those in the makeshift market outside Bernshulme: her hard boots kicking out at soft bodies to make way, those beggars either too deformed or hurt to move quickly suffering the worst of it, the harshest words, the hardest blows.

For Meas, he was sure it was different. Sometimes he watched her, staring at her ruined hands, touching the bandages over her eye, and though he could never truly know what was going through her mind, he was sure he could guess. Thoughts of betrayal, all that time in a cell, time being tortured and she had thought it was her mother, only to find that she had been betrayed by one of the few people she had trusted. No doubt her mind now drifted through the tides of memory, considering every pain, every insult done to her, physical. And mental. And how she could lay them at the feet of a man she had once loved. No doubt she also thought of her mother, a woman more complex and committed to her than either of them had known. A woman she would never get to know.

He stood. Walked across to the bowpeek and pushed it open. Leaned out, the wind catching his braids and twisting them around behind his head. For'ard he saw the wide sea, an island rising to seaward of them that was thick with wild pinks and purples. Behind him the island of Shipshulme, gradually receding, and a line of ships, all heeled over as they caught the same wind *Wyrm Sither* rode. Six ships at the moment, in the middle of them the massive *Arakeesian Dread*. Four decks of gallowbows and power, eighteen corpselights dancing above him. Joron wondered if Karrad was truly aboard that ship, then was certain he must be. Karrad was not the type of man to trust his underlings, he would be here. But he was also not the kind of man to get too close to the sharp end of the wyrm-pike so a place on the largest and safest ship made sense.

"They follow us, Shipwife," he said. When there was no reply, he turned, found her sat and staring at her hands. Her mouth moving silently. "Shipwife!" He said it sharp, like a command when the deckchilder were slacking. She sat up straight, eye focused on him.

"Deckkeeper?"

"I said Karrad's ships are following us, we draw them after us like longthresh following blood." She stood, walked over and leaned out of the bowpeek with him, her hair blowing into his face, smelling of grease and dirt.

"I count six," she said, "one of them the *Dread*. My bet is he's bringing everything he has to spare for when we meet with our fleet." She leaned out further, staring and blinking at the ships silhouetted by Skearith's Eye, the glare turning them into a line of black squares reflected in the ocean, a funeral procession of ships. On the highest mast of the *Dread* something red flared. "They have sent up a signal flare, Joron." Something cold within him. "How many ships do you think he can bring and still leave some to defend the home isles?" she said.

"Twenty decent ships," said Joron, "maybe thirty." She nodded.

"And our fleet?"

"Twelve fighting ships." She nodded to herself. "And two brownbones, but they hold all of our people."

"Who leads it?" He pulled his head back in from the bowpeek, the air in the cabin feeling peculiarly still, and full of the smell of bodies now he was out of the fresh winds. Meas followed him, shutting the bowpeek and turning to him. "I asked a question, Deckkeeper."

"Brekir," he said.

"I am glad she still lives," said Meas quietly. "She will know to keep the brownbones back when she is signalled for parlay." She was utterly still for a moment. "How is he to find them?" She swore gently under her breath. "All these things I should know, should have discussed with you." She turned away from him, he heard her breathing, a shudder of her shoulders. A fight within her. When she turned back there was the gleam of moisture beneath her eye. "But I will ask them now, no point in hiding from my mistakes."

"I made arrangements with Brekir to leave someone on Kluff Island."

"Will they stay if they see a white boneship coming?"

"Ey," said Joron. "For 'tis just a fisher's camp and nothing else to the unknowing." Meas smiled at him. "From there we can get a message to Brekir."

"It's a fair bet that Karrad plans a trap, he is calling his fleet, he will try something." Joron nodded.

"I do not doubt it. I will make sure the message I send . . ." He tailed off. "I act the shipwife, not the deckkeeper," he said, and smiled. "Sorry, I forget I am in the presence of my ship-wife." He gave a bow of his head. She smiled in return, lifted her bandage and rubbed at the raw hollow beneath.

"It aches," she said, "always feels like I have grit in it."

"My missing leg aches constantly, it seems our minds refuse to believe what our bodies know." She stared at him.

"Ey," she said, her voice sounding very far away. "That is often the way."

"What would you tell our fisher, Shipwife?"

"You know, Joron, you have been doing this for long on long without me."

"But you are my shipwife," he said, "and I follow your orders." Rewarded with a smile. She pushed thick grey hair from her face.

"Very well. I would have Brekir hold back the brownbones, well over the horizon. And position our fleet near to the meeting in such a way they can use the prevailing winds. Send one ship only to the actual meeting, a fast one with plenty of gullaime aboard." Joron nodded. Then Meas put her finger to her mouth, sucked on the knuckle. "You have been in contact with the Gaunt Islanders?" He nodded. "Trust them?"

"Not really," he said.

"Trust them more than Karrad?"

"Their Bern is just as hungry for power as your mother ever was." Meas looked up at the white overbones of the cabin.

"We should also send a ship to them," she said, "tell them Karrad has the secret of raising keyshans. Tell them they'll need every ship they have to stop him." Joron nodded and Meas smiled. "You have thought of all this." Joron shrugged, smiled back.

"There is another thing," said Joron. "I am worried for the Gullaime. Madorra will kill it," again, he caught himself, "will kill *her*, if he realises the Gullaime will never give him what he wants." Meas nodded.

"I know. But that is a problem for when we are stood on *Tide Child*'s deck." She held up a hand before Joron could speak. "The creature is dear to me as well. But we can do little from here. We must trust her to the Mother's protection." Joron nodded though he knew that the worry, that constant nagging awareness in the back of his mind, would not leave.

And so they flew on, all the time gathering more ships and hearing more feet on the slate deck above.

While they journeyed Meas's health improved, if slowly. Some days he had his shipwife back, strong, sure and indomitable. Other days she was gone entirely. Would not look or speak to him, simply stared into the middle distance and her darkness was infectious. Joron felt it like a battering ram at the doors of his subconscious, pulling him down into the same dark maelstrom that subsumed Meas. On those days he let himself drift into the song of the sea. Where there had once been one song, now there were many. Those first songs had been quiet and slow, long, drawn-out notes that he had barely been aware of. But every day the songs became louder and, he was sure, faster. The notes not quite as long, not quite as drawn-out and there was a growing surety within him that the songs were running counterpoint to each other. That in these slow voices was a call and response. A grammar of music that he did not understand. He was also sure that there were many singers, far more than he could account for in the fifteen or so keyshans that had been reported so far. Hundreds of voices, and when he thought of what that meant then he felt a similar darkness within to that which must be consuming his shipwife. Because if the keyshans were waking, then they brought the destruction of the islands, fire and death, just like the prophecy of the Windseer had said.

"We're slowing."

"What?" he said, shaken from his reverie. The singing fading to the back of his mind taking all associated thoughts with it. He wondered if the Gullaime was still alive. A moment later a knock on the cabin door and Cwell walked in.

"Shipwife, Deckkeeper," she whispered.

"I had thought you had forgotten about us," said Joron.

"Ey, well, Barnt is hardly trusting of me, and does not know I am here now. But he is busy with the ship. Quickly, you must tell me what message you wish delivered to the island."

"Why?" said Meas.

"I had planned to take it," said Joron.

"They will not let you out of their sight, Deckkeeper," said Cwell. "Barnt wants to send your message with his own people, but we may be able to convince him it is wiser to send me." He looked to Meas. She looked to him. "We do not have much time, Deckkeeper, tell me now what you really wish said for they will be listening to anything said on deck when we approach the island," said Cwell. He was about to ask why he should trust her, then stopped. He trusted her, she was his crew.

"Very well," he said. "I will tell you our plan, what we have of one, in full." She stooped to listen and, when it was done, the instructions committed to Cwell's memory, she left, vanishing into the underdecks and he felt the ship coming to a full stop. When that action was finished, seastay dropped, wings furled, Tassar and two seaguard opened the door.

"You are wanted on deck," he said. Joron and Meas stood. "Not her," said Tassar.

"She needs air," said Joron. "We have been stuck in this cabin far too long. There can be no exchange if she sickens and dies." Tassar stated at him, then looked to Meas. "Where is she likely to run to?"

"Very well," said Tassar, "but I will be watching."

It was a relief to be out of the cabin, to stand on the slate and feel the salt breeze in his hair and against his face, where the mask did not cover it. To hear the crack of rope and the splash of sea against the hull.

"We are at your island," said Barnt; he wore a full dress uniform, his jacket strung with feathers and crossbows.

"Then I will go," said Joron.

"I think not," said Barnt. "Give me your message. Tassar and I will deliver it." Joron shook his head.

"A Hundred Isles ship will have our contact on the island nervous already. If they see you going ashore they are likely to flee and all you will find is a deserted campsite." Barnt looked him over, his gaze travelling to Joron's missing foot.

"You are pitiable, Twiner," he said, staring at the bone spur. "Truly pitiable. Do you think I cannot see through your transparent attempt to pass on messages that will aid your fellows? Very well, you go, and we will accompany you."

"It will not work," said Meas. "They will not trust whatever message is delivered with you there."

"We are only delivering notice of a meeting place," said Barnt, plainly frustrated.

"Our fleet will scatter if some attempt is not made to plan more than that," said Meas.

"We have spent a year flying rings around you," said Joron. "They will see it for a trap if some attempt is not made to deliver a secret message." Barnt stared at him. Then Cwell stepped forward.

"I will take the message," said Cwell.

"Betrayer," hissed Meas. Barnt smiled at that.

"Is nothing personal," said Cwell to her, "is just I have found I live longer if I try to stay on the winning side is all."

"And what trick will you try and sell them?" said Barnt.

"I will tell them not to bring their fleet, and barely crew what ship they do send. To rob you of the trap you plan."

"But we do not plan a trap," said Barnt. "We do not need to, we hold all the cards."

"Exactly," said Cwell. Barnt thought about this for a moment, glanced at Tassar, who nodded.

"Very well," he said. He took a packet from his jacket. "This is a map with where to meet on it. We will wait here until you return." Cwell nodded and with that she went over the side and into a waiting flukeboat, and Joron and Meas were taken back to their cabin to wait.

39

The Meeting

Message delivered and they flew on to the rendezvous, and each day they flew the Hundred Isles fleet grew as more ships joined them. Meas continued to alternate between the woman he knew and a woman trapped in a deep darkness that he did not. At those times she seemed insensible to him and he could not break through to her.

"I do hear you, Joron," she said one day.

"Sorry, Shipwife?"

"When you speak to me, and I seem lost." She was looking at him, but also looking past him. The way you unfocused your eyes in mist, to try and catch movement out on the water within the thick clouds. "But it is as if my mind is becalmed and I cannot get enough wind in my wings to reply; it is worse when there is nothing to do, this mental becalming." He nodded.

"I will ask one of the deckchilder who brings our food for some dice," he said. She nodded, but he did not think dice would be enough to distract her and, in any case, even when he asked none were brought.

And they flew on, Joron always listening to the action on the deck above him, the ringing of bells, shouting of orders, hoping for some clue as to their position and how much further to the meeting with his ships. Talking of what he had heard with Meas when she was with him, thinking of how to reach her when she was lost in her darkness. Talking to her of Mevans, of Coughlin and of Coxward and the many others lost along the way – of the crew who remained and how they had fared without their shipwife. His own darkness threatened to overwhelm him, worry about the Gullaime, worry about their plan, worry about the growing sores on his back and face, worry about the madness the rot brought. He understood why Meas was so lost in inaction. Felt despair lapping against his consciousness.

"Joron!" The voice calling to him from the surface, while he dreamed of drifting beneath the waves. "Joron!" Rising and rising to answer the echoes of a voice suspended in the sea, a memory held in water. "Joron?" Eyes open. Meas's face above him in the dark.

"Ey, Shipwife?" The words automatic, even though he was barely awake.

"Shh," she said, "listen." He did, sitting up as she leaned back. Heard the knock of varisk on bone, heard soft feet moving across slate, heard hushed voices and movement at the side of the ship.

"Taking on cargo? More crew?" She shrugged then moved over to the bowpeek.

"I am sure it is on the other side," she said, "but curiosity demands I look." She pushed the hatch out a little and Joron went to join her. No flukeboat there, or clue to what was happening. Only the ghostly glow of the bone hull, stretching out behind them, and the luminescent trail of night-time creatures, alarmed and shining to show the warship's passage. In the distance he saw the glow of corpselights from the rest of the fleet.

"Must be thirty ships or more out there now." He put his head back in and Meas let the bowpeek shut.

"Ey," she said. "Brekir would be wise to stay away when

she sees how many ships are here. I do not think Karrad means her, or I, to escape."

"He promised," said Joron, "he needs my cooperation." Meas shrugged.

"Were I in his position, and of his temperament, I would let our fleet go, take you away from here. Then hunt them down once you were over the horizon, and how would you know any different?"

"Deckchilder talk," said Joron, "I would find out eventually." Meas nodded.

"Ey, which makes me suspect that, even were we to do as he wanted, you would not live long. He only really needs the threat of you to make the Gaunt Islanders back off. His eye is on Bernshulme and his power there." She looked at him. "He cares for little else and does not forgive a slight; among the Kept grudges are a matter of honour and it is a hard habit to break, I reckon. They have not learned the reward of forgiveness." She sat down and he realised he was losing her. "It is hard thing to do," she said, voice fading, "to forgive."

When he woke the next morning, to the same breakfast of porridge they had been served every day, he found Meas pacing the small cabin. She did not pace out of boredom though, not pacing like a caged animal. She smiled to herself as she walked, one hand holding her bowl, the other a spoon. Back and forth, back and forth.

"You feel it, Joron?" she said.

"Feel what?"

"Try it," she said, "stand on the deck, and take your boot off." He did, sliding the boot off his good leg, feeling self-conscious as he had tried to keep his boots on until it was dark. He had taken to sleeping in them so she did not see the sores on his leg. But she paid no attention to the sores, nor his hisses of pain as the boots pulled away scabs. Then he stood. Felt the cold of the deck on his foot. Felt the ship around him, its movements transferred to his body through his leg and his bone spur.

"Choppy," he said, waited a moment, listened, "but the wind doesn't seem to be getting up."

"Ey," Meas grinned at him, "and listen more, wait for it, wait." He listened, as the ship bucked and twisted in subtle ways most would not notice, just enough to let him know it did not run as smoothly as it once had. He heard deckchilder shouting, heard the ever-present chatter of the gullaime they had brought from Bernshulme below, heard the shipwife shouting. But was there an edge there now, something brittle, as though he were stretched, angry – no, not angry. Frustrated. "You hear it?" she asked.

"I do," he said, "and I feel the ship too, something is not right here."

"I think we are near our destination," Meas said.

"What makes you think so, Shipwife?" She grinned, and he would never have believed that lost soul he saw just the other evening could live within her. This was his shipwife, full of energy, full of hope and knowledge and sure in herself.

"Ship does not run well, as you say. His Shipwife is all on edge and I reckon I know why."

"And why is that, Shipwife?" He could not keep the grin from his face. This was his Meas, all thought and knowledge of the sea and the ships that flew it.

"I cannot be sure, you understand." She raised a hand to his face, pointing at him. Her one eye full of life and light.

"Of course." She nodded back, the grin still on her face.

"Last night, what we heard?" He nodded. "They were changing crew, taking off deckchilder, bringing on seaguard."

"That is why the ship runs badly," he said.

"And why Barnt is so out of sorts," she smiled.

"Why risk the running of the ship?"

"Because they have a big fleet to call on, and they do not think the risk is from our fleet. But they still expect some sort of trick. Maybe that we will try and storm this ship, though I doubt they will allow more than an honour guard aboard. Definitely not enough to take a ship."

"But they are being careful."

"Ey," said Meas. "They are."

A knock on the cabin door.

"One moment," said Joron, "I am not yet fully dressed." He pulled on his boot, wrapped the scarf around his face to hide the shame of his disease before nodding to Meas. She opened the door. Behind it stood the ship's deckholder, a smartly dressed woman called Vertis.

"The shipwife wishes to see you both on deck," she said. Meas said nothing, only stared at the woman. "Are you deaf?" said the deckholder.

"I have a rank," said Meas without moving, iron in her voice, "and so does Joron. And we outrank you, D'older, so I would ask you to address us correctly." Vertis looked them over.

"You both look Berncast to me, and the imperfect hold no rank in the Hundred Isles, so do as I say."

"I will not," said Meas. "Now decide if you wish to inconvenience your shipwife with unneeded delay, or if you will act as an officer should and show the courtesy required to your superiors." Vertis stood there a moment, anger radiating off her, and then she stepped back and gave a mocking bow.

"Please, make your way to the deck, Shipwife," she said, but there was little respect in her tone. Meas ignored it, her point having been made.

"Come, Deckkeeper," she said. "I fancy a walk, it has done my mood no good to be stuck in that little cabin for so long." She gave Vertis a smile and swept past, followed by Joron, who did not even give the woman a glance. Up through the ship, the dark underdeck, into the bright light of the maindeck. Meas glanced around, smiling to herself as she saw the crew was mainly men, mainly seaguard just as she had surmised. Barnt stood on the rump of the ship with his deckkeeper, Tassar and Cwell. Tassar stared at Joron, and there was clear hatred there.

Meas did not immediately make her way to the rump and

the waiting shipwife. Instead she paused. Glanced to landward where the rest of Karrad's fleet could be seen, holding station on the horizon. As she counted the masts Joron came to stand beside her, he looked out to seaward, joy rising within in him at what he saw there, but he did not speak, did not comment. Only waited for his shipwife to turn, for her to see the huge dark shape that sat at its seastay on the still water of the ocean, her *Tide Child*.

When she turned she did not react, not immediately, it was more as if she simply stopped, took in a sharp breath. "Oh," she said. Became utterly still, as if by not moving or breathing she could make this moment last longer. This golden moment, the crests of the wavelets and the tops of the black ship gilded by the light of Skearith's Eye. The only noise the chink of rigging and the lonely cry of skeers. Then she spoke, not to Joron, not to the seaguard around her, or to any of those stood around on the slate. Words said only to herself as she stared at the black ship.

"I never thought to see you again," she said, a half smile on her thin lips.

It looked to Joron as if Meas stood a little straighter, put on another set of armour at the sight of her command, grew just a little taller at the proximity of her ship. She nodded toward it, then laughed to herself. "I like to think they can see me, Joron," she said. "A foolishness." But Joron did not think so, he had no doubt that every eye on that ship was locked upon *Wyrm Sither*, hoping for a glimpse of their shipwife. Joron in turn stared over the water, hoping for sight of the Gullaime and his watching was rewarded with a flash of bright robes, a movement not quite human that he felt sure was his strange friend. Now his turn to smile, though he had little time for enjoyment. Meas was striding up the ship, invigorated. Barnt met her with a nod. Joron and Meas had whispered of this moment, rehearsed their positions, decided what they could and couldn't live with and the best way to get the things they absolutely must have.

"Signal for my flukeboat, Barnt," said Meas immediately, "and I will go over to my ship then send back the Gullaime." Barnt seemed taken aback for a moment. Did not speak, only stared at Meas.

"I am not used to being ordered about on my own ship," he said. Meas dropped her gaze to the deck.

"Forgive me, Shipwife Barnt, I forget my place as prisoner. Old habits die hard, ey?"

"Indeed." Barnt looked at her. "And I am not so foolish as to simply send you across so you can raise your ship's wings and fly away." Meas looked up.

"It insults me," said Meas, "that you believe I would run away and leave behind a member of my crew who has done so much for me."

"My apologies," said Barnt, "I thought it common knowledge that you ran away." He let the insult hang in the air for a moment. "I will send Cwell across." And Joron felt cold, would they trust Cwell aboard *Tide Child*? He was not sure.

"Will not work," said Cwell. "Some deckchild on an island may take my word, but whoever commands *Tide Child* will want to speak to another officer." She spat on the deck. "Right stuck-up lot they are, pretending they be fleet and all." Barnt stared at her, touched the scar on his face as he considered this, then turned back to Joron and Meas.

"Very well," he said. "My flukeboat will take Twiner across, he will return with the gullaime and then we will let you go back to your ship." Meas nodded, as if considering this.

"What if he runs?" said Cwell. Barnt grinned at her.

"After all that work he has done to get Meas back? No, and we also know how much that gullaime cares for its kin." He looked down the deck. "Deckmother! Bring up those gullaime we have stored below so it can see what we offer." The deck-mother nodded and called a group of seaguard to her before heading down to the hold.

"If I may make a suggestion before I leave?" said Joron.

"You may make one," said Barnt, smiling at Joron, so confident in his position on the ship. "I do not guarantee I will listen." The first of the gullaime was brought on deck, part of a long line, chained at the foot to the next one. Around them came windshorn, and what struck Joron as odd, so odd he did not speak for a moment, was their silence. He had very rarely seen gullaime be truly silent.

"I have two suggestions," he said. "You are obviously familiar with gullaime?"

"Only as much as I have to be to work my ship, but yes, I know their ways."

"Well, you will know how foolish and skittish they can be."

Barnt nodded, "Were we not here to look after them, I am sure they would throw themselves into the sea."

"Exactly," said Joron. "Well, *Tide Child*'s gullaime is the very shipwife of such foolishness. It is stubborn, resentful, capricious and most of all, suspicious."

"I do not doubt it," said Barnt, and Joron smiled, for in many ways what he had told the man was true.

"Well, firstly, if you send your boat I doubt it will get into it. It prizes familiarity above all things. It will be far quicker for you to allow *Tide Child* to send a boat across for me, then I will go back and bring the Gullaime."

"Can it not just bring the Gullaime straight to us?"

"It will need convincing," said Joron. "And for that you must send either Meas or myself." Barnt let out a small laugh.

"You wish to get some of your deckchilder on my ship," said Barnt. "I am no fool." Joron looked about him.

"You think my flukeboat's crew of ten are capable of taking on all these seaguard? I am flattered," said Joron and Meas chimed in.

"I am surprised you have such little faith in your own people, Shipwife." If Barnt realised he was being manipulated he did not show it, remained aloof.

"There is no fear of your rabble on my ship," he said.

"What he says is true," said Cwell, "the creature is ungovernable and will answer only to him or the woman." It seemed that the world paused for a moment while Barnt considered this. It would not destroy their plan if they did not have their own people in the boat, the gullaime were what counted, but Joron would feel a whole lot more comfortable with some of those he knew backing him up. Then Barnt sighed.

"If it will speed up the transfer then by all means, I will signal for your boat." Joron nodded.

"Thank you," he said. "There is one other thing."

"Yes?"

"The Gullaime is more likely to come across if its people are not chained."

"How would it know? It cannot see."

"I ask you to send some across with me, as a goodwill gesture. Let them tell it." He leaned in closer. "I know you have no love for me, but anything that will placate the creature on my ship is worthwhile. That is if you do not want to have to explain to Karrad why this exchange fell apart." Barnt stared at Joron, plainly frustrated.

"Very well," he said, "Deckkeeper, have the gullaime unchained and sort out a windtalker to go with Twiner to his ship." He lowered his voice. "But know this, Twiner. I will have your shipwife stood by me, and at the first hint you plan some sort of treachery, I will put a crossbow bolt in her head, you understand?"

"I do, Shipwife," he said with small bow.

"Good," he said. "Then I will have the signal made to bring your flukeboat across."

40

The Boarding of *Wyrm Sither*

Joron left the deck of *Wyrm Sither*, needing help from Solemn Muffaz to find his place in the flukeboat that bobbed alongside, bringing condescending grins from those aboard the bigger ship, but Joron did not care. He only knew that the touch of Solemn Muffaz's great sturdy hand on his arm as he was helped toward the beak felt like coming home, and caused something that had been wound tight within him to loosen, just a little. The big man did not meet his eye and Joron realised he must get used to command again. Without speaking Joron stood in the beak of the small boat and he did not look back at the white ship behind him, or at Cwell and his shipwife on its rump as the windtalker was brought aboard. He focused on the black ship before him, and the crew that lined its rails, silently watching as the flukeboat rowed across the sea between them, causing panic to the tiny fish and creatures scudding below.

There was a strange tension on that flukeboat, and he reckoned that every deckchild at the oar was expecting to hear the echo of commands from behind as one of *Wyrm Sither*'s gallowbows was spun up, the unmistakeable order of betrayal. But Joron had no worry of such a thing. What they believed he had was worth too much for them to simply betray him, no matter how much Barnt and the Kept, Tassar, may like to see him floundering in the water as food for longthresh. Stroke by stroke they approached *Tide Child* and Joron was gladdened to see many faces he knew among them, and saddened by thoughts of Mevans, who he would not see until he sat at the Hag's bonefire to beg his forgiveness.

Solemn Muffaz preceded him onto the ship, then eager hands helped him up and he was brought aboard with the confused windtalker from *Wyrm Sither*. Once more Joron stood in his rightful place on the deck of *Tide Child*. He looked the ship up and down, saw new gallowbows well and smartly trussed, the slate clean enough to eat from, the wings furled and well kept, rigging chinking and chattering and swaying in the growing breeze. On the rump stood Brekir and the Gullaime in her colourful robes, which made his heart sing. Madorra skulked behind, a haunt of misfortune. With them was Farys, dressed in the hat and blue jacket of a deckholder and it pleased Joron mightily that Brekir had seen fit to clothe her so. To recognise her officially, a thing he, as only deckkeeper, had never been able to do. He saw Gavith, one-armed now, but still busy at a task by the bonerail. He wanted to greet him, say how happy he was that he had recovered well enough to be back on deck but he did not manage to catch his eye. It was ever natural that, for a deckchilder to avoid an officer's gaze. Even so Joron felt a stab of pain as he had thought Gavith more familiar with him, had half pegged him as a prospective hatkeep and for him to take such a position he would need to be less shy of officers, just as Mevans had been.

Ah, Mevans. The name almost a physical pain in his chest. He was so distracted that he failed to notice how the deckchilder were gathering, lining his path as he walked up the deck. When he did notice, he did not know how to react. Could not speak, found himself suddenly without words as his crew, this crew, the strongest, fiercest women and men he had ever known, removed their headwear and bowed their heads in respect. The click of his spur on the deck, the soft fall of his foot and no other sound, save the constant sounds of a ship at rest.

"Deckkeeper," said Brekir with a nod.

"Shipwife," he said, and nodded back.

"We received Cwell's message. I've explained what is required to your flukeboat crew, and as much as I can to the Gullaime."

"Thank you, Brekir." Then he turned to Farys, about to speak but his words died in his mouth, for Farys's belly had the unmistakeable swell of late pregnancy. Now the tension on the flukeboat, and Solemn Muffaz and Gavith's unwillingness to meet his eye, made sense. Opposite sex relationships were against the Bernlaw, the rules of the sea. For a moment he stumbled, he had asked Solemn Muffaz to deal with Farys and Gavith. Anger at Muffaz swelled within him but he put it aside. This was not the time. Though he knew this was not something a commander could allow to pass, he needed his crew on side, for him, for Meas. Besides, he was no longer in charge of this ship, and such discipline was no longer his to mete out. It would be for the shipwife when she returned to deal with Farys and it cut Joron deep within that he knew that the only penalty available was death.

Farys's scarred face twisted, glad that he had returned undoubtably, but misery was there too, for she knew she had done wrong by the ship. They exchanged a glance, an acknowledgement, but before the moment could be soured both Brekir and Farys were rudely pushed out of the way by a joyful riotously noisy creature of colour and feather.

"Joron Twiner! Joron Twiner!" The Gullaime croaked his name out, twirling and spinning around him. "Joron Twiner!" she said again as she came to a stop before him. Then she stood, with that utterly alien stillness her species were capable of. Behind her Madorra watched, his brown eye blinking. Joron felt a surge of sudden and irrational hate. Remembered he had his own plan to put into action before he left this place, even if he could not do anything about Madorra at this moment. "Where ship woman? Where? Where?" the Gullaime shrieked.

"She is on the other ship, Gullaime," he said. The windtalker cocked her head to one side.

"Where bad woman?" she said more quietly.

"Cwell is on the other ship too." The Gullaime let out a loud yark, whether in joy or disapproval he did not know. "We found Narza, and lost her also." An intake of breath at that, he felt it. Knew it was a blow as the whole ship had believed her immortal, unkillable. A strange and almost magical being. Worse, he knew the confusion of Narza's passing would be nothing to what he must say next. "And Mevans. We lost Mevans."

There was nothing said then. No one spoke, for the crew had loved their hatkeep, depended on him. Joron knew the entire personality of *Tide Child* would change without him. He felt a warmth against his side as the Gullaime pushed herself against him.

"Sad," she said, "all sad."

"Yes, Gullaime," he said. But no more as they were interrupted by a shout from above.

"Ship rising!" Joron's misery fell away, and the same for the crew as that shout was one of action, and no thought was ever greater in the mind of a crew than to mind the ship. Brekir stood forward.

"What do you, see, Topboy?" she shouted.

"Flukeboat," was shouted back, Joron recognised that voice – Alvit? He thought so. "He's rigged for speed, looks like a messenger ship from the Hundred Isles fleet, headed for *Wyrm Sither.*"

"Well," said Brekir, her face as mournful as ever, "that sounds like nothing good. I take it you and Meas are ready to act, Joron?"

"Ey," said Joron, and he felt all sadness and pity and fear finally fall away, for it was inaction that was his enemy as much as it was those aboard Karrad's fleet. "Ey, I need the deckchilder that are our best fighters. I need you, Gullaime," he took a breath, "and I also need you, Madorra."

"And *Tide Child*," said Brekir, "do we ready him for war?"

"No," said Joron, "simply be ready to leave, and in a hurry. Where is our fleet?"

"Over the horizon to the north-east," she said.

"Good." Then he grinned. "Have some crew ready to transfer across to *Wyrm Sither*."

"You mean to take it?" said Brekir. "I see Meas has not changed."

Joron did not know how to answer that, but was saved by a shout from the topboy above: "Messenger ship's coming in fast, Shipwife!"

"I do not like that," said Joron. "If Karrad sends a messenger I fear it can bring only ill news for us. Brekir, we need to be back on *Wyrm Sither* before that flukeboat." Brekir nodded, grinned the grin of a predator.

"Then let us make sure that happens." She raised her voice, "Ready the flukeboat!"

As they readied the boat, he looked about for Gavith, called him over and, though he would not meet Joron's gaze, he came. *Well you might look ashamed*, he thought, but now was not the time for discipline.

"Gavith," he whispered, "while Madorra is away, I have an important job for you," and he barely had time to give him his task before the flukeboat was ready and he was back on board, the crew rowing hard as they could for *Wyrm Sither*, the Gullaime and Madorra crouched in the well of the boat. The two bigger ships had drifted a little at their seastays, allowing Joron to look past the white hull of *Wyrm Sither* and see the messenger flukeboat. It was under full wing, heeled over and catching all the wind it could. He saw the form of a gullaime crouched before the central mast.

"That boat is in a true hurry, Solemn Muffaz," said Joron "Have them row harder, but I don't want them to look too urgent about it. When we dock, be ready to board on my order, and show no quarter to those that stand against you."

"Ey, Shipwife," he said, and not a woman or man in the small boat seemed bothered in the least that they may end up facing the entire crew of a boneship. He felt the flukeboat pick up speed as the crew rowed harder. Then Joron spoke to Madorra and the Gullaime, making sure they knew what he needed from them when they boarded *Wyrm Sither*. That done he took his place in the beak of the boat and stared at the messenger flukeboat under wing, cursed a little as he knew enough of the sea and of ships to know it would be first to dock with *Wyrm Sither*. He looked back at *Tide Child*, watched it growing smaller. Then he turned away from the black ship, all he should concentrate on now was survival, that of him and those with him and his shipwife. He touched his jacket, felt the bone knife hidden within. Smiled at that, at the thought of putting it to the throat of Barnt as he took his sword back. Well, maybe that would come to pass and maybe it would not.

"Incoming boat is showing message flags, D'keeper," said Solemn Muffaz. "Important message," he added. "Priority boarding."

"Carry on as normal, Solemn Muffaz," he said.

"And if they try and stop us boarding?" he said.

"We've come this far, and our shipwife is waiting for us on their deck," he said, nodding at *Wyrm Sither*. "We've lost too much to simply bob about on the surface waiting. We'll force our way aboard if we have to."

"I like the sound of that," said Solemn Muffaz. "Like it right proper." From the looks exchanged between the rowers they did too. Joron watched the messenger flukeboat glide up to the boneship until it was lost from view, even its spines hidden as Joron's own flukeboat came up against the other side of *Wyrm Sither*.

"Well," he said. "They have not stopped us." A rope ladder was thrown over the side and Joron grabbed hold, steadied it. Looked around his boat. "Are you ready?" he said. Every human nodded while the two gullaime remained low in the well of the boat. "Gullaime, are you ready, you know the part you must play?" They did not reply, but Joron had to presume they heard him, that all were prepared and he put both hands on the ladder. Took a deep breath, pulled himself up. Hand over hand, most of the weight taken by his arms as his bone spur could be treacherous on a rope ladder. He did not look down, did not stare at what was ahead only pulled himself up and over the bonerail. Stood on the deck.

Saw an entire crew, ready and prepared for him. Most with blades out, ready for an attack, officers with crossbows. Barnt, flanked by Cwell, Tassar and two seaguard. The shipwife held Meas by her arm and pointed a crossbow at her head. She looked weak, beaten, hanging like a ragdoll in his grip. Toward the beak of the ship the flock of gullaime milled about, sensing the nearness of violence. They made short, mournful chirping sounds. Barnt was smiling at Joron, a full, bloody, piratical smile.

"It amazes me, Twiner," he said. "The strength of some people."

"What do you mean?" he said. Took a step forward and Barnt let go of Meas. Joron watched as Tassar took hold of her arm. Barnt took a note from his jacket pocket. Joron stepped forward and crossbows were pointed at him. He stopped.

"I mean that she," Barnt pointed at Meas, "went through so much pain, and still managed to lie to us."

"I told no lies," said Meas.

"No," said Joron. "She spoke the truth; only the Gullaime and I together can raise the keyshans in the islands." Barnt let out a laugh.

"Indeed? I am sure that is what you wish us to believe, what you even had Karrad believing, and he has shown himself a fool at the last, ey?" He turned to Meas. "What is it the bern say, ey? Never trust a man to do a woman's job, Shipwife, right?"

"I do not understand," said Joron.

"Four islands gone!" shouted Barnt, lifting the message parchment into the air. "Four islands and every woman and man and ship on them gone." The look of confusion on Joron's face was so honest, so real, that he thought it probably saved his life. That if he had not looked so confused Barnt would have had him shot down there and then. "You really do not know?" he said. Joron shook his head. "Well, Joron Twiner, if you do not know the keyshans are rising of their own accord, then I do not think it can be you that controls them, can it?" He laughed again, more to himself than anything else. "So, what use are you to us?"

"That cannot be," said Joron, and as he did the Gullaime crawled over the rail to landward of him, grand in her fine robes and decorated mask. To seaward Madorra came, and as the windshorn crowned the rail he called out something harsh and hard in the gullaime language.

"All this travelling, running around for you," said Barnt, "and it seems we need none of you." He raised his crossbow and pointed it at Joron. "Karrad writes he still believes you have power." Barnt stared at him. "He requests you and that gullaime of yours are taken alive." He sighted along the weapon. "I think, power or not, we are all better off if you are dead."

Tassar stayed Barnt's hand. "He's mine," he said. "I want to hurt him for what he brought upon my Thirteenbern." He pushed Meas over to Barnt, drew his curnow and walked toward Joron, leaving Meas in the company of his seaguard, Barnt and Cwell. Again, Madorra let out his scream – a shout, a song, a call.

"What is that racket?" shouted Barnt. Joron knew, but could not say. Knew that Madorra called out in its own language, telling the gathered gullaime that here was the Windseer, the windtalkers' saviour, the creature that would free them from bondage. But what had been hoped for, that the gaggle of now unchained gullaime down the ship would react and fight for them, did not happen. They only milled around the deck, confused. Tassar approached, smiling at Joron, promising nothing but pain to come.

"This is the Windseer!" shouted Joron, pointing at his

gullaime, and she stood on the rail, beautiful in robe and feather. "Your Windseer is here!" he shouted.

And all that came in reply was laughter. From Barnt. From Tassar making his way down the ship with his bared blade. The crew of the ship, nudging one another, grinning.

"Was this your plan?" said Barnt, laughing. "Was this it?" he shouted. "You hoped to stoke a flock of windtalkers to revolution?" He stared down the deck at Joron. "You are fools, both of you." Then he raised his crossbow and pointed it at the Gullaime. "This all ends here. Tassar, kill Twiner, get it over with."

The Gullaime, in answer, screamed. She opened her mouth and let out a roar the like of which Joron had never heard. At the same time, she ripped off her mask, showing those eyes, those bright and shining eyes with their spiral pupils and her call filled the air around them. Battering and buffeting ears like the fiercest gale, and with the sound came heat and following the heat came the wind. A great wall of it, a shock of it. It smashed *Wyrm Sither* backwards and into the messenger boat moored alongside, spars and spines breaking, the brittle hull no doubt holed and cracked by the weight of bone. The sudden movement throwing all those aboard *Wyrm Sither* to the slate deck. Joron heard shouts, heard fear, heard confusion and he pushed himself up and forward, toward the nearest of the seaguard masquerading as deckchilder and took up his dropped spear. Found his voice. Knew there was only one order, only one possibility as the wind howled around him, heeling over the warship.

"Into them!" he shouted. "Into them!" He ran forward, driving his spear into the side of a man trying to find his feet. He heard his boatcrew shouting as they came over the rail behind him with nothing but bone knives and fury. Madorra launched itself at the nearest seaguard and the Gullaime remained on the rail, still screaming up a ferocious wind. Up the deck he saw Meas wrestling with Barnt over his sword, behind her Cwell took on two seaguard and he knew he was needed there. But there were too many between him and his shipwife. Meas, poor, misused Meas, had not the strength she once had and was fighting a battle she was bound to lose. He glanced around the deck and saw that, despite the howling wind, the ship's crew were coming together. Tassar, curse his name, pushing them into a line of sword and spear and small shield. Not a wonderful line, not one that Coughlin would have been proud of, it was ragged and poor, but enough to hold back Joron and his ten, despite the wind.

"I'll end you, Twiner!" shouted Tassar.

And Joron knew he would, his seaguard would push Joron and his people back into the sea. Meas would fall to Barnt and even if he escaped with his people on the flukeboat, before they could get far enough away the bigger ship would have its bows untrussed and shoot them from the water.

Then the flock of gullaime woke.

Joron had been so distracted by the forming battle line he had taken his eyes from the gullaime further down the deck. Not seen the reaction of the windshorn when they saw the Gullaime's eyes. Not seen the reaction of the windtalkers when the windshorn called out, telling the windtalkers what they saw in chirps and caws and creaks. Not been prepared for the utter fury that was unleashed. Beaks snapping, claws slashing, gullaime calling to one another to coordinate attacks. The windshorn leading, the windtalkers following, guided by the calls of those who had been their jailers. A volcano that had been waiting for generations to explode crashed into *Wyrm Sither*'s seaguard. Gullaime bit and slashed long past when those they attacked were dead, had to be bodily moved on by the windshorn who directed their fury.

"Meas," shouted Joron, but she could not hear him, was still in a life-or-death struggle with Barnt, one she was losing. He tried to push forward but there, bloody sword held firmly in his hand, stood Tassar.

"Time to die, Twiner." He lunged forward, pushing Joron back and Joron cursed. He could not beat the man, knew it.

He was no great swordsman, never had been. Tassar had trained with a blade since he had been old enough to hold one. "Never liked you. I'll make it slow, Twiner," said Tassar with a grin. From behind he heard a cry he recognised, the shout of his Gullaime. He turned his head, hoping against hope not to see her hurt and there she stood, proud upon the bonerail, still calling. Joron knew himself for a fool as he turned back, for only a fool turns their head from a swordsman like Tassar. The man was in mid-lunge, sword reaching for Joron's stomach. A cruel killing blow that would end his life in slow agony.

A moment where time slowed.

He saw the mayhem around him.

The blood and the feathers and the noise. It all faded away. The end. Here it was. His spirit would be freed to find the Hag's fire, to join his father there. To find peace beside the flames.

Tassar vanished.

Hit by three or four or more gullaime, all biting and clawing and furious as they dragged him to the deck. Joron saw his face, bent into agony, crying out "No! No!" and then all Joron saw was white feather and pink skin. And a path up the ship, as if it had been opened just for him.

Running up the ship. Dodging past fights. Cwell killed one of the seaguard, was fighting the other. Barnt pushed Meas to the floor. Raised his sword, Joron's sword. And with no other option Joron roared, "No!" Distracted Barnt briefly, for just long enough. Meas rolled away and then Joron was near enough to be a threat. Barnt came at him, unleashing a flurry of sword strokes that he barely managed to block with the spear. He stepped back, and Barnt laughed at him. Behind him, Meas lay on the deck, struggling to catch her breath.

"I'll kill you with your own blade," said Barnt, and began to advance.

"No," said Cwell, stepping between Joron and Brandt. Blood ran freely from a cut on her temple and a slash on her arm. She held a curnow in one hand and a bone knife on the other.

She pointed her dagger at Barnt. "That sword," she said, "is not yours and I will not leave my job undone this time."

"Treacherous lowborn scum," said Barnt, and he slashed at her. She caught the blade on her curnow and drove her bone knife into his chest. Then stepped back, bringing her curnow round in an arc and striking him on the side of the head with the flat of it, felling him.

"Cease!" shouted Meas, struggling to her feet. "The shipwife is beaten! The ship is mine! Cease!" All down the deck the gullaime carried on their attacks. Joron's ten rowers, down to seven now, had been forced to stand behind Madorra and *Tide Child*'s Gullaime, who protected them. "Gullaime," shouted Meas. "Stop this now!" But no matter how much the Gullaime shouted and squawked, or how much Madorra joined in, their people's fury could not be contained and it continued until only Meas, Joron and his seven remained standing.

A quiet fell.

The gullaime stood around as if confused, their white robes and feathers spattered with blood. Meas stared out over the rail toward the rest of the Hundred Isles fleet.

"We need to get out of here," she said.

"Ey," said Joron.

"We'll take this ship, I think," she said.

"With only nine of us?" he asked. She grinned, and again he saw the woman he knew so well, the shipwife he had missed so much.

"Nine from *Tide Child*," she said, then pointed at the flock of gullaime on the deck and grinned more broadly, "but now we have nearly a hundred new crewmembers. It should not be too much of a challenge."

41

The Escape

As he pulled on a rope and tied it off Joron thought of how far he had come. Once, he would not have believed that nine women and men and a gaggle of gullaime with no training could get something as massive as a boneship moving, would have thought such a feat needed a full crew, a hundred or more pulling on ropes and furling wings.

Of course, now he knew different, had known it even when he had been surprised that Meas intended to take the ship rather than simply row back to Brekir in the flukeboat. Joron was not even sure they had enough people in their fleet to crew another fighting ship, but there was ever the pirate within the soul of Meas and besides, he found a strange joy in her rapaciousness. The problem they had with *Wyrm Sither* was not in getting the ship moving – getting a boneship moving was the easy part, especially with a fresh breeze and nearly a hundred willing gullaime. No, the crew were needed for the subtleties of the ship, for steering, and tacking and, most importantly, for stopping. As the tiny crew worked to get the ship ready Meas stood upon the rump, staring at the far horizon, watching the Hundred Isles fleet.

"Do they give chase?" asked Joron. She shook her head.

"No, we have enough distance that they cannot see what happens here. When we move away, well, then we may see some action from them." She grinned, rubbed the bandage that covered her missing eye. "Though they are too far away to catch us, this ship is ours now."

"Are we sure taking the ship is a good idea, Meas?" he said. She stiffened a little, then relaxed.

"Why, Deckkeeper?"

"I fear we do not have enough deckchilder spare in our fleet to crew him." He touched the rearspine. "Magnificent as he is." Meas looked up at the corpselights bobbing above the ship.

"When I first came onto the black ships, Joron," she said, "I thought of them as relics, dead things." She took a breath, squinted up into the wings. "But now, I see those lights, and see the real relics, the real dead things that we should have left behind as a people so long ago. We kill our children and for what, pretty lights?" She stared down the deck at the gaggle of gullaime, picking their way through the bodies of the slain, occasionally pecking curiously at them. "We blind and enslave those who should be our allies. I have had plenty of time to think about this, Joron." She tapped her bandaged eye. "About what we do, what we think is right." She stepped forward and took up an axe from where it had fallen on the deck. Blood still marked the blade and the haft. She walked to the rear of the ship, where the rope of the seastay moved gently in the groove worn in the rail. "I see more clearly than ever, it all has to change, Joron; what we value must change if we are to survive." She lifted the axe and brought it down on the rope holding the ship at his seastay, half severing it.

"We will need the seastay, shipwife, to bring over at least some crew if you want this ship." She shook her head. Brought the axe down again with a grunt. Still not cut through.

"I don't want this ship for our fleet," she said. The axe fell again. "I want it to send a signal." She looked up at the unfurled wings, white as sweet cloud. "Take the steering oar, Joron," she said and grinned at him. "I think us ready to fly." Then she brought the axe down for a final time and the entire ship shuddered as it was freed from the seastay and began to move forward. "Solemn Muffaz!" shouted Meas. "Raise a flag so Brekir does not think we come to attack her." She stood on the rump, nodding to herself, then turned to Joron. "They'll see we are leaving soon enough," she said, more to herself than to him.

"Should we bring the cargo and stores up?" said Joron.

"Why?" said Meas.

"We are sore pressed, Shipwife," he said. "Our fleet will need whatever it can get." She stared into the distance. Then slowly shook her head.

"I want nothing of theirs," she said quietly. "Nothing, do you hear me?" Then she raised her voice. "What are all these bodies doing lying about my deck?" she said. "Get them over the side." Her crew sprang to action, gathering the dead and throwing them over. Meas watched, as if hungry, as hungry as the long-thresh the corpses were sure to bring. She reminded him of the Mother then, full of grace and love for those who did her bidding, implacable in her judgement on those who stood against her will. As her deckchilder worked their way up the deck Joron stared at the gullaime gathered at the beak of the ship, gathered around his gullaime.

Though she was dressed in her finery, her colourful robes adorned with trinkets and feathers, she looked small, beaten. Like Meas had looked when he first found her in the cell, and he wanted to go to his friend, but for the first time, after seeing them in action, he felt afraid of the gullaime. Maybe he would not have, but for the fact that Madorra stood to one side of the group, his one eye unerringly locked on Joron and he knew, more than ever before, that for reasons beyond both of them the two were set against each other. *I will deal with you*, he thought, though there was no comfort in that, for without question the one-eyed windshorn thought the same of him.

"Shipwife." Joron turned at the call – it was Zafir speaking, one of the crew who had never known Meas and she was shy of the woman on the rump, seeing her only through the lens of stories that made her more than human.

"Ey, deckchilder?" said Meas.

"This one still lives," said Zafir. Meas stared at the officer she pointed at. Joron did too. It was Barnt.

"There is one here too that lives," said Leman from further down the deck and Joron saw he had Tassar. Truly, the Maiden still played tricks on them. "One here," said another voice, they at least had a simple seaguard.

"Bind them and bring any of those who still live up to me," said Meas. They were brought, and none too gently, to the rump of the ship to join Barnt. They were few, and they were sorely wounded, but not with wounds that Joron recognised, not spear thrusts, not curnow slashes, not knife slices. These unfamiliar wounds were equally terrible: wounds from hooked beaks, from curved and razor-sharp claws, from needle teeth. Two died as they were dragged up the ship, and joined the trail of bodies that *Wyrm Sither* left behind, it dissolving into a slick of dark water as the longthresh ripped them apart. Barnt woke as he was lain against the spine of the ship and Tassar awoke when Meas unceremoniously tipped a bucket of water over him. Both fought their bonds, but only for a moment. Barnt looked up at Meas, who stood over him, squinting when the shipwife moved to let the light of Skearith's Eye fall on the man.

"Well played, Meas," said Barnt weakly. He looked down the deck, then looked away as another body went over. "Seems everything they said about you was true." He glanced at Tassar, who let out a groan, blood from hundreds of cuts tainted the pool of water around the man. "I am luckier than Tassar, by the sight of it."

"His gut has been opened," said Meas.

"Well, he is finished then. A pity, he was a good-looking man." He spat on the deck. "So many fell to gullaime," he said. "Never thought they were worth anything," he tried to smile through his pain. "Regret how many we put over the side now I know they can fight. Could have used them."

"May be wise to mind what you say about the gullaime, with so many on the ship," said Meas. Barnt moved, trying to find a comfortable place against the spine. He used his feet to push against the deck so he sat more upright.

"We know how this works now, Meas," he said, "my family are rich. Choose yourself an envoy and send it to the fleet. Name your price, they will pay it."

"Did I ever ask a price, for those I took?" said Joron, his words full of ire, his body fizzing with anger, but Meas cooled him with a glance.

"You did not," said Barnt, though he did not look at him. "You simply murdered them. But you are a pirate, a Berncast man promoted to a position beyond your place. No one would have paid you. If they had, those taken by you would have died of shame if they had returned." Joron took a step toward him but Meas held up a hand, stopped him before he got close enough to Barnt to hurt him.

"We are alike, that is what you say, Barnt?" said Meas. The Hundred Isles shipwife nodded, his hair tangling in the pitch around the spine.

"We are fleet, are we not? We would stop to take those of the enemy we can from the water. We have a code of honour, we follow a higher path that it is difficult for the lowborn to understand." Meas squatted down, rubbing her bandaged eye and grunting with pain as her joints complained.

"I do not know exactly how long I was away. Do you, Joron?"

"Over a year and a half, Shipwife," he said.

"So long," she repeated quietly. "I have been afraid to ask, if I am truthful, Barnt." Her voice rose a little. "At least once every week I met with Karrad's hagpriest. I was ministered to by her. Sometimes she healed what harm she had caused. Sometimes she undid her healing." Meas's voice was wavering, as if she barely held in check what was within her. "Where was this code then, Barnt? Where was this honour then? Where were your fleet ways then?" Joron had never heard Meas speak with such venom. "They were not there, because they are a fiction, only brought up when they are useful to those such as you. Well, I intend to bring about a change, a resounding change." She stood, turned away from the man.

"And what of me?" shouted Barnt. "Am I to remain your prisoner?" Meas shook her head.

"No, you are dead to me, Barnt. You hear me? You are dead." She turned away, walked to the rear rail of the ship so none could see her face. "And you have seen what I do with the dead on this ship, they go over the side."

"No!" shouted Barnt. "No! You cannot—"

"Cwell!" shouted Meas. "I gave an order." Joron's shadow walked up to Barnt and looked down on him.

"Said I'd make sure of you this time." She picked him up, throwing his bound body over her shoulder. Then strode to the side of the ship and threw him over, quickly coming back for Tassar, who barely even moved, and repeating the action. Meas remained at the rail, watching the trail of bodies behind the ship and Joron wondered if she found pleasure in the screams of Barnt as the longthresh found him, for he did not. When the screams had finished he joined her at the rail.

"Shipwife," he said.

"If you have come to tell me that was badly done, then I know it," she said.

"I have flown that course, the one of vengeance," he said. "Found my destination is always on the horizon, the journey never to be over." Meas nodded. He reached into his coat. "I picked up my jacket on *Tide Child*," he said, "this was in it. I have been looking after it." He handed over her nearglass. She did not say anything. Just took it, ran a hand over the bone casement and then brought it to her good eye to look at the horizon.

"Our course may be over sooner than you think," she said.

"I count over forty ships now. That must be almost the entire Hundred Isles fleet."

"I do not think we are finished, no matter how many ships they bring against us."

"And why is that, Deckkeeper?" she said.

"Because you are Lucky Meas," he said. "The witch of Keelhulme Sounding, and the greatest shipwife who ever lived."

She did not look at him. She was staring at the slick of blood and body parts that trailed *Wyrm Sither*.

"Am I?" She closed the nearglass. "In truth, I am not so sure." She tried to smile and failed, then glanced behind him. "I think Cwell has something for you," she said. He turned to find his shadow behind him, holding out his sword.

"Try not to lose it again," she said. "It's the Hag's arse to get back."

"Thank you, Cwell," he said, and when he turned back to where Meas had been she was gone. Walking down the deck of the ship, her every step a testament to the pain she had been put through, and her unwillingness to give in to it.

42

The Desperate

It took three days for *Wyrm Sither* and *Tide Child* to catch up with their fleet, and Joron and Meas stayed on the Hundred Isles ship for that time. Meas did not want to slow even for as long as it took to change ships, knowing a fleet could never keep up with two ships. Now *Wyrm Sither* burned and, somewhere, back over the horizon Joron knew a fleet of white ships would be making all the speed they could for the pillar of smoke.

Meas stood on the rump of *Tide Child* with four of her shipwives. There was Coult of the *Sharp Sither*, fearsome, looking older than Joron remembered, more tired. Adrantchi of the *Beakwyrm's Glee*, looking more worn than ever; a scar marred his face and his uniform, so colourful once, was worn, faded and much mended. The loss of his deckkeeper, Black Ani, sat like a weight upon him. Turrimore of the *Bloodskeer*, tall and dark and fierce, but missing teeth in her top jaw now, as well as all those from the bottom, and there was something of the hunted in her eyes. Her skin, that had been as dark and smooth as a calm sea in the middle of the night, was now nicked and rutted with scar tissue. Lastly there was Brekir of the *Snarltooth*, mournful as ever, unchanging and steadfast.

They stood and watched the burning ship and did they seem a little disappointed in the woman he had brought back, this ragged, pained figure?

"We should have taken its stores," said Coult to Joron, his voice gruff, barely more than a growl. Then he glanced toward Meas, her eye bandaged, her damaged hands bent into claws, her posture slightly stooped, "But I understand why she may want nothing to do with it." Joron said nothing, despite that Coult echoed his own thoughts. "Animals," said Coult. "We deal enough death without dirtying our hands with torture." Joron tried not to show his surprise – of all the shipwives he had thought Coult the most likely to use torture, his nature was one of viciousness.

"My cabin," said Meas. "Let me tell you what I have planned." She turned and headed down the hatch to her great cabin, followed by Joron and the shipwives. Once there, they sat around her desk, pulled out into its table form. No food. The entire fleet was short on provisions but Joron was sure, if Mevans had been here, there would have been food. Farys probably would have provided it but Meas had taken one look at her, at the swell of her belly, and coldly said, "I will deal with you later," before confining her to her quarters.

So they sat without food or drink and waited for Meas to speak.

"First," she said, "I thank you all for keeping my fleet together while I was . . ." Her voice faded a little. She coughed. Spoke once more, strong and loud: "Away."

"Thank the deckkeeper for bringing you back," said Adrantchi, little good cheer or jollity in the voice of a man once famed for it. "He planned, he kept us going. Never let us give up hope."

"We have had little rest or respite and times have been hard," said Turrimore, "but we knew that when we signed on."

"Well," said Meas, "I thank you all, and I apologise that I have not fed or watered you upon visiting my ship. But time is of the essence." She looked around at those gathered. "You all know by now that Karrad has betrayed us. More, he has taken the Hundred Isles for himself."

"Will he not take us back, then? It was the Thirteenbern we fought, we have served his cause," said Adrantchi.

"Karrad's cause," said Meas quietly, "is Karrad. I have had plenty of time to learn that. He used us."

"We should give him a bloody nose," said Coult.

"I would like nothing more," said Meas, "that and to give him a bloody stump for a neck, but he outnumbers us. He has drawn the whole of the remaining fleet to him. Near forty ships to our fourteen. And they are not held back by brown-bones full of stonebound to protect, we cannot outrun them without leaving our people behind."

"Ey," said Adrantchi, "that is true, but now you are back the deckkeeper no longer has to keep himself in check. We can call the keyshans to our aid."

"Oh to be on Karrad's flagship when he sees them coming for him," said Turrimore. "I would laugh, even as I went into the jaws of the beast."

"If the deckkeeper's powers were so accurate I would do it in a moment," said Meas, looking around the table, "but they are not. Those who were at McLean's Rock know what happened. The keyshan woke, ey, but it cared not a jot for us. If we had gone down with the island then I doubt it would have noticed."

"Do they not want to be woken from their slumber? Are they not thankful?" said Brekir.

"Those that sleep beneath the islands are waking anyway," said Meas. "That was what almost got us killed on Barnt's ship."

"Maybe he lied," said Coult.

"He did not." This voice from the door. Garriya stood there, old and ragged and huffing and blowing as if she had run through the ship.

"This is a place for shipwives, old woman," said Meas, her voice low and cold. "Your place is in the hagbower."

"Shipwives," she said, and walked forward, her steps halting through age but no less determined for it, "talking strategy, aye?" Her gaze wandering across them. "The Calling has begun, oh grand and mighty shipwives, and once begun it cannot be stopped. The keyshans return. The world turns and all that was begins again."

"We do not want your mystical talk," said Meas. "Can it help us plan?" Garriya shrugged.

"All knowledge is worthwhile, is it not? Maybe it will not help you fight, but it will help you stay alive."

"Why is she allowed in here?" said Adrantchi. "Stop at any island and you can find the deranged calling out of doom. Is she any different?"

"Who knows," said Meas.

"Listen to her," said Joron. "She has not steered me wrong, her advice has always been true, though oft as not confusing."

"Run," Garriya said, her gaze passing across those gathered. "That is what you must do, run." Then she turned to Meas. "You know who you are, you walk upon the bones of your truth." And as the old woman spoke the song within Joron increased in volume, became a thousand voices and he had to fight to keep his footing. Garriya turned to Joron. "And you waste your time here with chitter-chatter when the one you are blood-tied to is in real danger. Think on what matters, boy."

"Leave here," said Meas quietly. "Go to your place and stay away, old woman." Garriya did not move.

"You do not want to hear, mighty Shipwife, what you have always known."

"Get out!" shouted Meas. "Now!"

"You know the truth, ship woman," said Garriya, backing away. "You know."

"Out!" shouted Meas, and the old woman left.

"What did she talk of, Meas?" said Coult.

"Who knows? She has always been strange, half mad."

"And you do not cast her off?" said Turrimore.

"She is a good healer," said Meas, but Joron was hardly listening. Since he had come back to *Tide Child* he had not had a moment, a second to check on the Gullaime. She had been rushed off by Madorra as soon as he had come aboard, as had been the case for long on long. But Garriya's words brought back a memory, one of feeding the windsick gullaime by hand long ago when Joron had been new to his place at Meas's side. A drop of his own blood that dripped into the windtalker's beak. Could it really be that simple, could the tie that bound them be one caused by that single accidental sharing?

It did not shock him, nor did it surprise him. For the Hundred Isles was born of blood.

He was filled with the need to leave, to go to the Gullaime, but could not. To do so would give credence to Garriya's words and it was plain that Meas wanted none of it. So he sat, the urge to leave and his worry for the Gullaime growing as the shipwives argued and planned what they must do. It seemed to take an age. Every moment that passed feeling twice, three, four times the length of any other before it. Eventually a course of action was agreed, plans made.

"So, we are decided then," said Meas.

"I do not like this," said Brekir, "it puts you at needless risk."

"We are all here to die, Brekir," said Meas, "only the day is undecided." She gave the other shipwife a smile. "I will take *Tide Child*, fly a flag of truce and talk with Karrad."

"You think he still fears Joron's ability to raise the keyshans?" asked Coult.

"Yes, he only has the . . ." She coughed. Sat very still. Took a moment. Composed herself. "He only has the information taken from me on how Joron's powers work," said Meas quietly. "So he is unsure of just what Joron can do."

"So you will try and bluff." She nodded.

"I hope he will see sense," she said, "he may stop all this. Peace can still be made." Coult let out a snort of disbelief. "He nearly did before, Coult, you did not see him. But it does not matter, that is not why I go. We will hold him in talks as long as we can, his fleet is large and slow, we outpaced it easily."

"Slower than a couple of boneships maybe," said Brekir, "but we have those brownbones with us."

"You must use the delay we create to get the brownbones with our people and the rest of the gullaime aboard as far from here as you can. With any luck you will make the Gaunt Islands. They have promised to attack the Hundred Isles fleet, if we can bring it out of the defensive ring far enough. The nearer we get to the Gaunt Islands the more likely that becomes. Brekir will fly ahead of you and warn them of our coming."

"And if Karrad decides not to talk, or to double-cross you?"

"Then our job is made harder, right enough," she said, "but we are of the sea, we are used to hard, ey?"

"Ey," said Coult, "that is not a thing we can gainsay."

"Back to your ships then," said Meas, "we set off immediately." Then the meeting was done, the shipwives breaking up and the small fleet of black ships and huge brownbones let down their wings, caught the wind. On Tide Child all was action as the ship was readied. Meas commanded the Gullaime be brought up on deck and Joron felt his breathing ease a little as she slinked up, followed by Madorra and the gaggle of white-robed acolytes. Meas watched them.

"Feel a little easier now, Deckkeeper?" she said.

"Ey," he said.

Tide Child heeled over, catching the wind and turning while Meas raised her nearglass and stared at the far horizon.

"Do you see them?" asked Joron, as he watched his Gullaime, hopping sadly around the beak of the ship while the deckchilder worked. Meas shook her head.

"Not yet," she said. "And I do not expect to see them for a day at least." She put away the nearglass. "I wish to be over the horizon and out of the sight of the rest of our fleet before I meet Karrad. And I must deal with some disciplinary matters." He knew she meant Farys. A coldness within Joron. "You have let your hand slip," she said. A deckchilder walked by and she stopped her. "You," a space where usually there would be a name, "why are you on the rump?" The deckchild did not look at her.

"Taking water to Barlay on the oar, Shipwife," she said. Meas nodded, turned back to Joron.

"Those disciplinary matters," he said quietly, "you have told me many times how your ship is run differently and . . ."

"I will see her in my cabin in two bells time, Joron, and you as well." She did not look at him, only walked past, her head down. "Come," she said quietly. "I know you care for Farys. But boneships run on discipline, it has always been my way." He wanted to argue, to tell her she was wrong, but in the end it was her ship, he had risked everything to bring her back and how would it look if he defied her? Her ship had always run because all knew their place. All knew her discipline may be harsh, but it was fair and she showed no favouritism. "You understand, do you not?" she said.

"Ey," he said, then something further down the ship caught his attention. A sudden squawk of outrage. When he looked the Gullaime was cowering on the deck before Madorra while the windshorn pecked and bit at her. "Excuse me," said Joron, "I must deal with that." Meas nodded and Joron strode down the deck, boot and bone spur clacking on the slate. "What is this!" he shouted. "What is this about, Madorra?" The windshorn hissed at Joron, leaping back and spreading the wings under his robe to make himself bigger. Behind him the acolytes chattered and chirped.

"Bad gullaime!" he spat. "Lazy gullaime!"

"That is no excuse for attacking her, Madorra," said Joron. The windshorn sidled forward, making himself low and small.

"Not do duty, ship man," he said. "Gullaime not do duty. Duty matter, yes yes?"

"The Gullaime's duty is the same as mine, or yours or any other's on this ship." Joron barked the words out, full of anger.

"Our duty is to do what the shipwife tells us, and it is never to attack another member of the crew."

"Oh," said Madorra, making the word sound like a coo. "Not attack, no. Play. Ship man not understand gullaime ways. Is only play."

"It did not look like play," said Joron. "Gullaime, is this true? Was it play?" His heart went out to the windtalker, she was pressed low to the deck. Looked beaten, worn down. Like he felt, like *Tide Child* himself.

"Not attack," said the Gullaime, her voice low and dull. "Was not attack. Only play. Yes, play." Joron stood there, unsure what to do, knowing he could do little in that moment.

"Very well," he said. "But know this, Madorra, I watch you." The windshorn's single eye sparkled and he hopped forward so he was near enough that he could speak and no other could hear.

"Sea sither rising now, man," Madorra hissed. "Not need you. Watch you." Then he hopped away as if nothing had happened. Joron wanted to act, felt no doubt that the windshorn was a threat to not only him, but the Gullaime. Then the Gullaime approached him.

"No trouble, Joron Twiner. No trouble," she said, and Joron had never heard her sound so sad.

"I can stop it," said Joron. "I can imprison Madorra."

"Must not. Must not." Her eyes, uncovered since she had revealed herself on *Wyrm Sither*, became wide with panic.

"Very well," said Joron. "I will not." The bell rang and Solemn Muffaz passed him. Joron knew that soon the deckmother was ordered to collect Farys and take her to the shipwife's cabin to face her discipline. Joron watched the Gullaime slip away, it looked broken and forlorn and he felt they shared a stronger kinship than ever.

43

Only the Day is Undecided

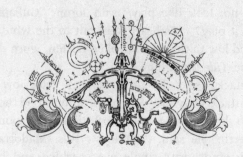

Early evening and he stood behind Meas in her cabin, the both of them splendid in all the feathers and trinkets of their best uniforms. Behind them *Tide Child*'s wake stretched out across a grey and choppy sea, one that was always changing and always the same, uninterested in the small dramas of women and men aboard the ship crossing its surface. Meas sat so straight it made him uncomfortable to see it. Outside the room he knew Solemn Muffaz waited, no doubt dreading the order to bring Farys, Joron's second and a favourite, up. For just like Joron, Solemn Muffaz knew what was to come.

On her desk Meas had set her two-tail hat to one side and in front of her sat one of her books, open at the Bernlaw: the set of decrees by which the crew of a boneship lived their lives. Harsh, most would think them. But life aboard these ships was harsh, and discipline was what held them together, as much a part of the ship's life as the bone of the hull, the variskcloth of the wings or the great bows upon the deck.

The words of the Bernlaw were writ large on the page before Meas, illuminated in expensive coloured inks, large enough for him to read though he knew them by heart, having read them to the crew so many times each Menday of their long voyages.

"Shall keep themselves in good health. To go against this is punishable by death."

And it did not matter to him.

"Shall obey those the Bern put above them. To go against this is punishable by death."

And he found himself questioning.

"Shall pay true honour to the Maiden, Mother and Hag. To go against this is punishable by death."

And he found an anger rising.

"And woman may lay with woman and man may lay with man but woman may not lay with man and risk a child aboard ship. To go against this is punishable by death."

And he felt like his heart was being ripped out through his throat.

As if knowing he had read the words before her, Meas shut the book, the heavy pages making a sound like a fist impacting on skin. Felt like a punch to his gut. She took a deep breath, and as she did it was as if she drew all the power and seriousness of a shipwife to her, even though he could not see her face he could sense it hardening.

"It gives me no pleasure, Joron," she said. "Farys knew the Bernlaw when she chose to disobey it."

"Were I in command—"

"You are not," she said, her words as short and cutting as the icy rain of the far south.

"But I was," he said softly. "When this happened, I was." It was all he could do not to beg and he wished she would turn so he could see her face, know what she was thinking. "I saw what was between them and should have stepped in personally instead of asking Solemn Muffaz. This is my failing, not that of Farys and Gavith." She put her hands on the desk, stretched her arms out to either side of her along the dark surface.

"So you know who the father is." He did not speak then, not for a moment. He knew Meas believed in the rules in the book before her, had lived most of her life by them. She turned and looked at him, he saw her wince as some pain coursed through her from the sudden movement. Her one eye blinked. "You are sure it is him?"

"I suspect," he said, "but I did not witness anything, and suspicion is not enough to condemn someone to death. Can we not just put aside—"

"Is it the law of the sea!" She shouted it, smashing her hand down on her desk. Made him jump, like he would have done the first time she ever brought him in here, when he had been nothing but a frightened boy. But he was that no longer.

"No," he said it calmly, but with surety. "It is the law of the Bern. And we are not—"

"Quiet, Joron!" She stood, her chair falling backward as she span on the spot to face him, all the fierceness in her rising. "I command *Tide Child*! Not you." She stabbed him with her finger. "Not you!" Her breathing coming hard, her lips pursed into a thin line. It was like some battle went on within her, some storm raged and it took all she had to hold it in check. When she spoke again it was more quietly, but no less intently. "If you cannot abide by my decisions when they are hard, Deckkeeper, then you should resign your place." He stared at her. Two people, broken by the sea and their duty upon it. Bodies and minds wracked by events beyond their control.

"I only say," and he spoke no less intently than she had, "that maybe there is another way."

"It is the Bernlaw, Joron," she said, and there was no joy in her words, only a cold and stark devotion to the life and duty that had defined her. A duty he knew she must have clung to through long months of torture. That must have been her everything when she had not even hope left.

"We have fought," he said, fighting for control of his voice as hard as he had fought any action on the slate of the ship, "storm to storm, on your say-so. We have fought against the cruelty of the Bern. And yet you would condemn those who have never wavered in your name, in the name of those we stood against."

Her eye on him, her breathing coming slowly, her body wilting as if weighed down by the crushing pressure of command.

"Joron, there are near forty ships over the horizon and they will not let up on us. What is to come will press us sorely if we are to survive and I cannot afford to be seen as weak. I cannot risk the crew thinking Karrad and his torturer broke me." She took a breath, fought to swallow air and for a moment he thought she may break down. Meas bowed her head and it felt like something within him cracked as she whispered to him. "I barely know the names of half this crew, Joron. I have been away for so long and they have heard so much about me, but I have returned to my ship much diminished."

"No, Meas," he said, "not diminished at all, not in their eyes or mine." She raised her head and stared at him, and he knew she wanted more than anything for him to understand why she must do what she believed she must do.

"I have to be strong, Joron."

"Then I beg you," he said, "use your strength for change, do not simply fall back on what you know. You said, Meas, that you saw we must change." She took a deep breath, blinked.

"Yes," she said. "But the Bernlaw is the spine of the fleet. I cannot simply break it." Then she turned away and sat once more at her desk. "Solemn Muffaz!" The door opened and the deckmother stood there waiting for her order. When it came it was said without inflection or emotion. "Bring Farys to me."

They waited in silence and Joron used every moment to curse himself. He had seen the growing affection between Farys and Gavith. Seen it and put the responsibility of it onto Solemn Muffaz. Partly because she was a favourite, and so was the boy. They had both been with him so long, and maybe somewhere within he had felt he could not begrudge them a little pleasure. For life was short and hard and they had known little else. What happened here was on him and he must face that. Then Solemn Muffaz brought Farys in, stood her before Meas's desk and left the room without a word. *You suffer also, Solemn Muffaz*, thought Joron, *for you love her like a daughter*.

And that suffering fell on Joron's shoulders too. Maybe Meas was right, if this was where a little kindness led it may be better to put such gentleness aside on the deck of a boneship.

Farys stood before them, making no attempt to hide her swelling belly, and his heart broke a little. *This is on me*, he thought. *This is my failing.*

Meas took her hat from her desk, placed it on her grey hair. Sat straighter.

"Farys," she said and the word barely disturbed the thick air of the cabin.

"Shipwife," she came to attention. Stared straight ahead, her eyes bright though she did not look at either of them.

"You know why you are here?"

"Yes, Shipwife." Before Meas could say any more she continued. "I know the Bernlaw, I knew it when I broke it. I knew the penalty and I know any judgement here is not put upon me out of malice or cruelty. I accept what must be." She looked at Joron. "And do not blame Solemn Muffaz for this, D'keeper; he spoke to me as you asked, and in most serious and firm terms. Mevans too, Hag bless his memory." She touched her swollen belly, only briefly, as if for some reassurance. "But it was too late by then, the life within me was already kindled." She stood straighter, stared ahead. "I know what verdict you must pronounce, Shipwife," she spoke formally, "but would ask one thing."

"One thing?" said Meas, by her tone Joron thought Farys's words had surprised her.

"Ey, and only one. I am not far from when the child is due, weeks at most," she said. "And some of the deckchilder have told me that, in times past, a deckchild who took a babe upon her could choose death by the blade when the babe came. Cut their child out of them so the babe would live and not suffer death for the mother's crime." Still she stared straight ahead, as calm and as sure as if she spoke about the weather. "I ask that to be my punishment."

"Meas," said Joron, and he felt his voice crack, "please . . ."

"Deckkeeper," Farys said, used the same voice she would have used on deck to get his attention. "I broke the Bernlaw, knowing a price may have to be paid." She took a breath. Did not waver and he marvelled at her iron will. "This is a ship of the dead, sentence was passed on me long ago. Only the day was undecided." Then she looked at him, met his gaze with her own. "I am thankful for everything you have given me," she said, "but this must be. It is for the good of the ship."

Then silence.

Only silence, and he knew that, though he may wish to defend her, she did not want it. Just like Meas, she was raised in the Bernlaw and on the rules of the sea, it was part of her.

"The good of the ship," said Meas and paused, as if to let the words hang in the air. "And yet," she took a deep breath, "is it?" She sat back a little in her chair. "Is it really for the good of the ship?"

"I want no favouritism," said Farys.

"We have fought the Bern," said Meas, and she opened her book at the Bernlaw. "But, as Joron told me, we unthinkingly continue their rule, follow their laws." She looked up. "They did this to me," she pointed at the ragged bandage over her missing eye. "What honour do they deserve?" Then she put her damaged and twisted hand on the first page of the Bernlaw, pressed down, pulling her fingers in and slowly ripping it from the book. "You have knowingly broken the rules of the ship," said Meas, "and that cannot go without punishment for there must be discipline. The ship will not run without it. But not death, I am not the Hag and will not take a life simply because you brought one into being." She let out a long breath. "Both you and the father will be broken to the lowest rank, stonebound, and you will also be confined to the brig until the child is born. That is your punishment." She turned to Joron and he gave her a small nod, trying not to smile, trying to hide this sudden elation that washed over him. "Now, Farys, name the father and all this can be over with."

"No," said Farys.

"Farys," said Joron, "you must."

"I will not name him," said Farys.

"Farys," said Meas, "please."

"I know what you are trying to do," she said, and now Farys's careful composure was starting to come apart. "I know you see this as a kindness. But the crew will not accept this, Shipwife." She rubbed a tear from her eye. "I will be outcast. I will be hated. This is not the way of the sea, they will consider me forever unlucky and I could not bear that."

"We all know it was Gavith," said Meas. "Confirm his name, Farys, and this is over."

"No," said Farys and stood straighter. "I will not."

"If you disobey a direct order," said Joron, "you leave the Shipwife little choice in her sentence. There must still be discipline."

"I know," said Farys and hung her head. "I know. She must condemn me. She must."

No one moved.

No one spoke.

They were trapped in a web spun by generations of expectations, traditions and superstitions. He wondered if he and Meas were fools. Did they fly the sea in service to dreams of a better world no one wanted? His thoughts were interrupted by the sounds of commotion on deck. Shouting and braying, and the drumming of feet on the slate. A moment later there was a hammering on the door.

"Shipwife!" Aelerin's voice. "You must come on deck now, Shipwife!" And all Joron's thoughts – of the world they lived in and the one Meas hoped to create, and whether that was even possible – were washed away by the call to action and the way it filled his body with energy, with a need to strike out.. Then he was following Meas out the cabin through the underdeck and up into the light on *Tide Child*'s slate. And there he found tragedy, not action. The commotion and call was not from ships on the horizon, or ships attacking, it was for the deckmother, Solemn Muffaz. The man who should have been stood outside Meas's great cabin while sentence was imposed on Farys, indeed, had been.

But was no longer.

Solemn Muffaz stood upon the rump of *Tide Child* shouting at the top of his voice, "Listen all! Listen to me!"

"What is the meaning of this, Solemn Muffaz?" shouted Meas, striding up the deck, the crowd of deckchilder parting around her.

"I stand up here, Shipwife," he shouted, "so that all know what I did to Deckholder Farys!"

"You?" said Meas, the confusion on her face as apparent to Joron as the confusion he felt within. "You are her lover?" Solemn Muffaz shook his great head.

"No," he said. "I was never her lover, but it is my child!" Joron saw Gavith before him in the crowd. Staring up at the big man. "All know why I am on this ship, ey?" He looked from woman to man, man to woman, his eyes wild. "I murdered my wife. Committed a crime against the Hag. And I did not learn my lesson and have committed another crime just as foul. I forced myself on the girl." As he said that, Joron looked about for Farys. Found her standing at the back of the crowd, the word "no" forming on her mouth, tears in her eyes. "There is only one crime, here, Shipwife," shouted Solemn Muffaz, "and it is mine."

Meas stared at him, wrong-footed for just a moment.

"Is there a witness to this?" she said. Turned, scanned the crowd. "Farys, is this true?" And all on the deck knew it was not. As Farys opened her mouth to say so, Solemn Muffaz raised his own voice. No longer wild, but sure, and slow and dangerous.

"If any here," he said, "wish to call me a liar, then they may draw their blade and I will meet them on the slate and the Hag can sort this out." For a moment Joron could not speak. He was overcome, for he knew Solemn Muffaz, giant, silent, Solemn Muffaz must have heard what went on in Meas's cabin. Realised the situation, and seen a way out for the woman he had taken under his wing.

Joron cursed, as before him he saw Gavith take a step forward, as if to call out the deckmother, but the deckchilder around him were quick to act. One grabbed his shoulder, another grabbed his one arm and they held him, all the while whispering intently to him.

Solemn Muffaz stared down at the gathered crew.

"This crime is mine," he shouted. "And I will be punished for it. Farys should live for she did naught wrong." Meas stepped up to the rump, followed by Joron, and they stood before the deckmother. Meas spoke so quietly only Joron heard the exchange of words.

"Solemn Muffaz," she said, "you tried to help her. This is not your fault and will not win you forgiveness for your crimes at the Hag's fire. She cares nothing for bravery or sacrifice. She does not forgive." Solemn Muffaz smiled sadly.

"Ey," he said, "I know that. I have lived a life, Shipwife, and taken one I should never have." He glanced at Farys. "I do this for our future. Look after her." Meas locked gazes with him. Nodded.

"Very well," she said. Stepped back. Raised her voice. "Deckholder Farys, you have committed no crime. Deckmother Muffaz. Your crime is unpardonable. The sentence is death," and she added, but only Joron heard, "but you knew that." Muffaz nodded.

"I need no accompaniment, Shipwife," he said. "And you can save your shackles. I go to this willingly." Meas let out a breath.

"Ey," she said. As she spoke Farys pushed through the crowd, ran up to the Deckmother.

"Muffaz . . ." she said, and the small woman reached out a hand to the huge deckmother. He took her hand in his, patted it, then gently pushed it back down to her side.

"It is for the good of the ship, lass, you know that," he said to her. Then smiled. "The good of the ship is what matters."

He raised his head, looked at the assembled crew but said nothing. Had nothing to say, the deckmother was there for discipline and never a popular figure. He just gave them a simple nod and, in return, those who wore hats removed them, those who did not bowed their heads and Joron thought he saw a smile cross Solemn Muffaz's face at that. "Shipwife, Deckkeeper," he said. "Sentence was passed. The day is decided." He turned to the side of the ship and without looking about him or back at the crew he climbed the rail. Paused a moment, looking out over the scintillating sea, and stepped out into the air.

A splash.

A strangled sob from Farys.

Meas stared at the spot where Muffaz had gone over the side, then without another word made her way back through the crew, down into the underdecks.

Joron made to go to Farys but she turned away from him, went to the rear of the ship to stare out at the sparkling wake and Joron left her with her grief. As the crew started to disperse he could not help thinking this was a poor start for Meas's return, and a bad omen for their future. As he stood there he felt a presence at his shoulder, turned to find Cwell.

"He was a brave man," she said.

"Yes," said Joron.

"Sounds like you are not so sure."

"Oh I am," he replied. "It is only that I always expected him to fall in battle."

"What makes you think he didn't?" she replied. Then turned and walked up the ship, stopping to stand by Farys. Gently placing a hand on her shoulder and that small gesture almost crippled Joron, almost had him break down upon the deck.

He spent the afternoon on the slate, charting the course of *Tide Child* with Aelerin, all the while aware of the way the crew moved around him. Not as quick as usual, not as whip-smart as usual. On another day he would have called them on it, had words, had the deckmother threaten to cord a few but this was not another day, and the deckmother was gone. He watched a deckchild grease the for'ard seaward gallowbow, his actions oddly languorous, then made his way back up the ship to the courser.

"The mood on the ship, Deckkeeper," they said as he came to stand with them by the bell, "it is not good."

"No," said Joron, "it is not. Hold this course, Aelerin, I will go and see the shipwife." The courser nodded and Joron, with a call of "The courser has the deck," left to go below. Down through the dim underdeck, the atmosphere somehow more oppressive than ever. He stopped outside the door to his cabin. No, not his, not any more. Hers now, hers once more and just as it should be. He took a deep breath, and as he was about to knock she called out.

"Come in, Deckkeeper." He let out the breath he had been holding and opened the door. Going from the dark of the underdeck to the light of her cabin. The sea stretching away behind them. Skearith's Eye just low enough that he had to squint and Meas and her desk turned into a silhouette, a dark, flat shadow in front of the large windows, writing in her journal.

"Shipwife," he said. Unsure whether to sit or not. She put down her quill and looked at the book. Let out a sigh as she scattered sand on it to dry the ink.

"I will never be a scribe now." She raised a damaged hand. He did not know what to say, she had always had beautiful handwriting. Meas stood. Closed the book. Turned around to look out to sea. "Solemn Muffaz," she said, "he should not have died."

"Farys should?" he said, sharper than he meant to. Not as sharply as he would have liked.

"By the Bernlaw, and her own want, yes," said Meas quietly, "she should have." She put a hand on the window. "I have been in here, wondering if made a mistake in listening to you. In trying to put aside what the crew of this ship have always known," she said. He was about to speak but she held up a hand, fingers curled and gnarled. "I did not. We need discipline, that needs to be enforced and I will not apologise for that. But to do it the way it has been done . . ." She let her words tail off, the way *Tide Child*'s wake faded from white to grey until it was once more part of the ever-shifting sea. "I have been away too long, maybe I was too eager to put my stamp back on the ship. And you were right when you said we are not the Hundred Isles, not the Bern; our ways are different. I should have handled it better."

"It is your ship, Shipwife," he said. Stiff. Formal. "To be commanded how you see fit." She turned, walked over to him. Looked him up and down and he felt as if the keyshan's rot that ran wild over his body had all started to itch at once.

"It is one of the great skills of a good deckkeeper, you know," she smiled sadly at him, "to express great disapproval through only the tone of voice." Once he would have jumped in there, to tell her she was wrong. But she was not, and he did not. "For what it is worth, I am immeasurably sad to have lost Solemn Muffaz, though it is tempered a little by the fact we did not lose Farys. I think if my . . ." She stopped. "If my miscalculation had cost her life, then it may have caused damage between us that could never be fixed." She was staring at him, hard. "I am hoping that is not the case."

He was angry with her. And yet, as that anger burned he could also hear a voice, his own voice, wrapped in the songs of the windspires and the great sea dragons. *Can you not see she takes off her mask?* And the anger was tamped down as her misery washed over him. He had stood where she was. He had commanded a vessel and made hard decisions. He had made wrong decisions and had got people killed, good people.

"It is the fleet way, Shipwife," he said. "Even when the damage seems beyond repair, we will make do, somehow." She walked around the desk to him. Put a hand on his arm and squeezed gently.

"Thank you," she said. The ship creaked alarmingly. He saw another worry register on her face. She may have been away from *Tide Child* for long upon long but she knew her ship. Knew that noise for the sort that was not healthy. "This ship has been through a lot while I was away," she said, and walked back to the window, placing her hand on the bone frame. Patted the substance of the ship as if to reassure the bone hull, or maybe to seek reassurance from it. "We all have. I look upon the deck and there is barely a face I know. They do not speak to me like I am a shipwife, half of them seem terrified of me."

"You are not a shipwife to them," he said, "you are a legend."

"A legend," she spoke more to herself than him. She turned. "Joron, we need something before we meet Indyl Karrad. I need to give the crew something to make up for the loss of Solemn Muffaz. But I do not know what . . ." She sounded desperate, almost lost.

"I may do, Shipwife," he said. "Leave it with me." She nodded, a brief look of relief washing over her.

He left the great cabin and went up on deck. Looking about for the deckchild he needed.

He found Gavith near the beak of the ship, tying knots with his one good arm.

"You are very dextrous," said Joron.

"Ey," he said, not looking up. "What Solemn Muffaz did . . ."

"Speak no more of it, he made a decision for the good of the ship. Do not make it a wasted life, Gavith."

"It was my fault. If I had—"

"It was not that simple. Learn from it. Solemn Muffaz wanted you and Farys to live. So live, and do not spend your life looking back at what could have been."

"As you say, D'keeper," he said. He wiped at his face with his arm. Joron leaned in closer.

"That other business I set you to, how are you doing with it?"

"I think I have found the thing you seek," he said, still not looking at him. "But the windshorn keeps moving it."

"A different place each time?" asked Joron. Gavith shook

his head, used one hand to tie a complicated knot and Joron found that oddly pleasing. In the midst of the tension and the pain there was pleasure in watching someone do a simple task well.

"The bird has certain places it likes, the same ones." He sat back from his knot. "Mostly, anyway."

"Mostly?"

"Occasionally it finds a new place, and that can take me a while to discover." Joron leaned in closer.

"Find it, Gavith," he said. "Then bring it onto the deck when we gather there, you will know when."

"The bird will try and stop us," he said.

"The bird will be otherwise occupied," said Joron.

44

The Court of Birds

Early next norning, he knocked on Meas's cabin door. She opened it in her full dress uniform, best coat, adorned with feathers and trinkets, black lines around her eyes, metallic colours across her cheek and dye in her grey hair. He was sure she had been waiting, dressed just so, since he had told her what he intended. She was probably as unsure as he was whether this would work, though she would never show it. Just as he had come to realise he did not show it either, though the mask covering half his face made it easier.

"Are we ready?" she said.

"As we can be."

At the steps to the deck she turned and he saw her catch herself before she shouted out a command. Usually she would have relayed any request through Solemn Muffaz, but no longer, and he saw the habit break on her face like waves on a rock. "You," she said to a passing deckchild, "Benlir?" The woman smiled at being recognised. "Ask the Gullaime to come up on deck if you would. Please tell it that the deckkeeper wants a word."

"Ey, Shipwife," she said, and vanished into the gloom.

"Come then, Joron," said Meas, "let us act. I will be on the rump."

As he followed her he could only hope that Gavith would come through. Only hope the crew would react how he believed they would. Only hope that events would turn out as he wished. And all he knew was that there were no guarantees. He would wish for success and if it did not come then *Tide Child* would fly on under a cloud of misfortune and, Joron thought, it may also carry on without its deckkeeper, for he was under no doubt of the danger in what he was intending to do. Today he would challenge Madorra and, as he knew, the windshorn's reaction was likely to be a violent one. He had been careful to avoid coming in between the two gullaime before, knowing that the windshorn had some hold over his friend. But he could stand it no longer. He touched the sword at his hip as he came onto the deck. Skearith's Eye was bright, the wind brisk and the crew hard at work. He could feel how they did not sit right, how Solemn Muffaz's death had affected them, and despite the brightness he felt as though a squall were about to break aboard the ship. That some important piece had been taken from the board – not so much the loss of Solemn Muffaz himself, though Joron had liked the man and would miss him keenly, more the way it was done. That all the crew knew he had sacrificed himself for Farys, and though there was no doubt the crew's mood would have been the same if Farys had gone, that would have been, in that odd way of the fleet, correct.

It did not sit well with anyone that a man had died for a crime he was innocent of. But at the same time they respected bravery and his decision, but whether they accepted it, or rejected it and with that, rejected Farys? Well, that could all depend on what happened here. On his success.

Joron left Meas on the rump, and went to walk the deck, passing Black Orris, sat on the bone handles of the great capstan in the centre of the deck. The bird watched him with beady black eyes.

"Hag's arse!" it said, and Joron wondered if that was a good or a bad omen, though in the end it did not matter. He had set a course and now he must fly it. At the beak of the ship he found Fogle, the seakeep, with the topboy Bearna. They had untrussed the for'ard seaward gallowbow and were working on it with carving tools. When he approached they tried to hide what they were doing, looking shamefaced as they hid their tools behind their backs.

"What are you about there, Fogle?" said Joron to the much older woman, surprised she felt the need to hide anything from him. He wondered if Fogle was drunk, if so this would be the last time he cut them some slack.

"Don't punish Bearna for this, D'keeper," she said. "It were all my idea, swear it by the Mother, I do." Joron stepped forward. The old bows – now abandoned at the bottom of the sea – had been covered in an elaborate filigree of scrimshaw and kept in exquisite condition by their proud bowcrews. These new ones were kept in the same condition but had not yet been covered in carvings. The name of this one, "Keyshan's Jaw", had been removed. Now, along the barrel of the bow, below where the great bolts would sit and where the bow's names were traditionally carved, an area in the elaborate scrimshaw had been cleared by careful sanding down. The bow had a new name and it was plain for all to see, freshly carved there in the clear space: "Solemn Muffaz". And around the name were already the markings for a new set of the most fine and elaborate carvings Joron had ever seen. He knew that Bearna had talent but she must have pushed herself harder than ever, though now the woman stood, shamefaced and unable to look at Joron, keeping her eyes on the deck.

"It is beautiful work, and fitting," said Joron. "Carry on." He left them to the bow and went to stand in the very point of the beak, looking out at the unceasing sea over the bowsprit. He wondered if Solemn Muffaz was out there now, denied a place by the Hag's bonefire because of his crimes. Wandering the cold darkness at the bottom of the sea, forever alone. He hoped not, he hoped there was no such thing as the Hag, the Maiden and the Mother. He hoped they were simply the inventions of women and men, and when you died – what? You ceased to be? His mind rejected such an idea.

How could one simply cease to be? How was that possible?

Maybe the gullaime had it right, and women and men were part of some eternal cycle, born and reborn and never learning. Was it likely there were no gods? Was it likely that Skearith never flew? That it was not the godbird's eye that warmed his skin?

He had heard some talk that way. He doubted Indyl Karrad believed in such things, how could he do what he did if he believed the Hag would one day come to judge him? *Tide Child* juddered as he hit a crosswave, a creak coming from the hull, and Joron had to reach out to steady himself on the bonerail. No, he could not discount the Hag, or the Maiden or the Mother. How could he when he had seen gullaime change the wind with only a thought? When he heard the song of the windspires and saw the majesty of the arakeesians as they woke from slumber? He felt like he was the plaything of the archipelago's spirits sometimes, that he was dragged hither and thither into peril so often he must be part of some bigger plan. For if not, then what was it all for?

"Jo-ron Twi-ner." He turned at the soft articulation of his name. Found the Gullaime, and for all her finery she looked beaten, her head low, the shining eyes only half open. By her stood Madorra, the windshorn in contrast looking proud. Further back on the deck the gaggle of acolytes. Madorra had fed well on the decks of *Tide Child* and filled out. Though physically smaller than the Gullaime he was stockier, stronger-looking and more aggressive. His one good eye twinkled in the light.

"Twiner," said Madorra, and even in the saying of his name there was a challenge, as if Madorra was aware that Joron would always do his best to stand between him and the Gullaime. "What want, Twiner. Busy. We busy. Do gullaime things. Why interfere?" Why why?" Joron pushed himself away from the bonerail. Behind the two gullaime Bearna and

Fogle were still working on the bow while trying to listen in on what they spoke of. He stared down the ship. The crew hard at work. The six great gallowbows, all but Solemn Muffaz, well trussed up. The three thick spines. The great capstan, the central square that could be opened to allow access to the hold. Past that the stairs that led down into the underdeck, the covering hatches open to let in a breeze. Behind that the rump. Where Meas stood with Aelerin and Farys. Farys pointed at the sandglass and said something, Meas nodded. He was proud of the girl, doing her duty though only the day before Meas had been ready to send her to her death.

But death was the destination of them all. Why would Farys be upset when she had lived the majority of her life on this ship, under threat of death every day? He brought his attention back to Madorra, noticed that the ship's gullaime was limping. The slate deck below her spotted with blood dripping from a wound somewhere and Joron was filled with anger. An anger he had to fight back, lest he lash out prematurely. Was the anger his? Or was the rot working, and as if in confirmation every sore and lesion on his body started to itch and if he had been alone he would have been set to dancing, trying to scratch at his body. But he was not. He focused on the Gullaime's dripping blood. Banished thoughts of itching. He had a duty. He had a ship to protect. A friend that needed looking after.

"Madorra, is the Gullaime bleeding? I would have Garriya look it her wounds if so."

"Her wounds, ship man?" said Madorra, and he wondered if he had slipped up in saying that, giving away he knew which gullaime were "he" and which "her". But no matter, not now. "Gullaime fine. Have accident is all. Madorra fix."

The Gullaime nodded her head sadly. "Madorra fix," she breathed into the air.

"Madorra, it is my responsibility to make sure that the members of my crew are well cared for. Garriya saw to the Gullaime before you came on board and is well versed in wounds of all kinds. Kindly go back to the cabin and I will take the—"

"No," said Madorra, and he put himself between the Gullaime and Joron. His feet clicking on the slate deck, and though he had not spread his wings in a threat posture, Joron noticed the long fighting claws on his feet had extended. "Man not interfere," he hissed.

As if a breeze blew through *Tide Child*, filling the air with word of confrontation, Joron noticed that the crew's attention was drawn toward them. Heads were turned, put together and whispers were exchanged. Like the deckchilder could sense impending violence the way they could sense a coming storm.

"It is my duty," began Joron and then the Gullaime pushed Madorra out the way; still keeping low she stepped forward, slowly, carefully, as if afraid Joron may attack her.

"No, Joron Twiner, no," she said. "No trouble. All good. All fine. Gullaime foolish, hurt self. All good now."

"Gullaime . . ." he began.

"No no. All good. Please, please," she said, And Joron felt the situation slipping away from him. He needed Gavith to show up with the Gullaime's egg, to free her from Madorra's influence. Until then he felt almost paralysed by how clearly terrified of the windshorn the Gullaime was. He had lost Solemn Muffaz, and it was plain that Madorra was not afraid to use violence against the Gullaime, he would not lose her. She stepped slightly nearer, whispered only for him. "Not bring fire," she said. "Not be Windseer for Madorra. Die first. Be safe. Joron stay back. Be safe." Then she stepped away. Turned and began to make for the rear of the ship and back to the underdeck. For a moment Joron was paralysed, his friend's fear had left him unsure how to act. What if he made things worse? What if he made Madorra push harder for the Gullaime to act as Windseer, and begin whatever the windshorn believed needed to happen to burn the world, to bring about the terrible prophecy Madorra believed in? What if the windshorn killed the Gullaime because it would not do as it wished? Joron watched them walking away. The Gullaime stumbled, almost fell – and what decided Joron was not that it happened. It was that Madorra paid no mind to it. Made no attempt to help her. Only walked on. When the Gullaime righted herself and continued to limp down the deck one of the deckchilder tried to help and Madorra bit out at him, hissed at him.

No, thought Joron. He walked forward.

"Madorra!" shouted from the rump, by the shipwife. Making their confrontation inevitable. The windshorn turned. The Gullaime paused and it turned also. "What are you at there?" Meas shouted.

"Please. Joron Twiner. Please not. Stop ship woman," the Gullaime said, and Joron knew he could not look on any more. He had looked on for too long while Madorra controlled his friend. Today he would act and it would not be because of any prophecy, it would not even be to improve the mood of the ship. It would be because it was right.

"I did not give you leave to walk away, Madorra." Joron made his voice as harsh as Meas's, spoke in the most officerly fashion and now he had the attention of every woman and man on the crew. "Kindly stay on deck, as I believe the ship-wife wishes to speak to all," he said, and on the rump his shipwife watched him and the crew began to gather.

"Listen to me," shouted Meas. "For I have been away and many of you do not know me, so I would address you, and introduce myself. Bring up those who sleep and work below to hear me!" She stood before the rearspine, hands behind her back, straight and unapologetic as more crew appeared on deck. "I am Lucky Meas, the witch of Keelhulme Sounding. Some of you know me, and some of you only know of me, and all of you, I know, are proud to serve on this ship." She looked over the assembled crew. "My ship!" Some nodding, a few quiet "ey"s. She began to pace, landward to seaward and back again, and Joron saw she held something tightly in her hands. "Well, you may be proud of that," she said more quietly. "But not as proud as I am of you! Every one of you!" she shouted, coming to a stop in the centre of the deck. "More proud than you can believe, proud of your deckkeeper for finding me when I thought all hope gone, proud of the way you have kept this ship while he and I were away." She stared down the deck. "Though the ship has suffered a little, I see. But that is the nature of a warship." Some laughs. Women and men looking to one another. Some tentative smiles. Meas tried to smile, but did not quite manage it and he wondered whether this was some physical damage she had suffered, or some other damage, the type that could not be seen. If he had not known her better he would have said she was nervous. "I commend you all, each and every one of you. I cheer you, and call you the best of the sea." She raised her head and spoke quietly, so they had to strain to listen. "*Tide Child* has suffered many wounds. As have I, as has Joron, as have you all. And with the loss of Solemn Muffaz we are wounded again." She let time slip by, meeting the gazes of the gathered crew, some puzzled, some approving, some unsure of this woman they only knew through stories. She lifted her seaward arm, and in it she held Solemn Muffaz's cord, the tool used by deckmothers to whip those who transgressed as long as there had been a fleet. "We come into this world expecting pain, and yet, I think we should not. Solemn Muffaz knew that. He saw an injustice in the way our lives are lived. And he gave his life to make *us see*." She shouted the last two words, used the cord to point at the crew then let her hand fall back to her side. "He died to make me see." Meas took a deep breath, raised her voice. "And I see!" She lifted the cord. "Today I draw a line!" she shouted. "I want an end to a world that crushes us underfoot! And I would rather die than give up on that dream!" She let her words settle, watched the crew. "There will be pain," she said, and she spoke into a silence that felt so profound even the wind dare not disturb it. "But that pain . . ." Her voice almost broke. She took a moment, gathered herself. "That pain will not come from me!" And with that she threw the cord overboard. Stood there, breathing as heavy as she would after fighting an action, staring out full of defiance and energy. "So," she said, her voice only just loud enough for them to hear, "what say you, my girls and my boys?" She looked at the crew, gaze flicking from one to another of them. "Do you commit to my dream? Do you commit to me?"

There was nothing at first. Just a shifting of feet on the slate. Joron watched, knowing he could not be the one to lead here. Meas needed her crew, and it was them that must make the decision. Farys was the first to step forward.

"I commit," she said.

Then Fogle.

"I commit."

And Bearna.

"I commit!"

And then a raucous, shouting mob erupted, so many voices calling out their belief in their shipwife. At some point someone shouted, "For Lucky Meas!" and that was taken up, then, "An end to pain!" was shouted. Meas stood on the rump and he watched her. The smile on her face real. Her muscles taut, the better to hold in her emotions. She held up her hands for quiet. *Now it comes*, thought Joron watching from the back of the crowd. *Now it comes*.

"And what of you, Madorra," said Meas, pointing down the deck. "Do you commit?"

Joron turned. Looked at the two gullaime. "Well," he said, "you heard the shipwife. Do you commit, Madorra? No more pain?"

The Gullaime stood stock-still, then started rocking back and forth, like a flightless bird caught between a predator and the edge of a cliff, unable to choose which death was preferable. Madorra did no such thing. He walked back up the deck, now his wings were out, his head slightly to one side so he could use his open good eye to study Joron. When he was nearer, not near enough for Joron to lash out with his sword, but near enough for Madorra to leap on him with his vicious fighting claws, it stopped.

Madorra hissed at him, beak wide open.

"What ship man want? What ship woman want?" it said. "Madorra not part of your rules. Madorra not of the ship. Not do as ship man say." It yarked twice, the sound angry, and threatening. "You obey ship woman rules. Gullaime obey gullaime rules. Gullaime obey me."

"Maybe that is true," said Joron. "Maybe it is not. I believe you struck her, fiercely enough to cause her to bleed."

"What if," hissed Madorra, "what if? what if? Gullaime lazy. Gullaime mad. Must know place."

"So you do not even deny it?" said Joron. "That you struck the Gullaime?"

"Not part of your rules," it hissed again. "Not crew. Not fleet."

"So you will not commit," said Joron, and as he spoke he continued to move back down the deck toward Meas. Drawing the two gullaime with him. "I had planned to separate you and the Gullaime, as I believe you are bad for my friend. But no longer," said Joron. The Gullaime relaxed a little, its shuddering lessened, its crest of feathers opened, just a little, to show the bright red within. Madorra nodded its head, beak moving up and down as if it had always known this would happen. A gleam of triumph in its one brown eye. "But fleet or not, part of this ship or not," said Joron, "this crew and its officers, we have committed to ending the pain." He looked about, saw the entire crew were watching, many holding makeshift weapons.

"Not officer," said the windshorn. "Not crew. Just windtalker."

"Now, Madorra," said Meas from the rump, "surely you must be aware that some time ago I made the Gullaime an officer on this ship." The Gullaime froze. Madorra froze. "Barlay," said Meas, noticing the big woman near the front rank of those assembled, "kindly arrest Madorra and place him in the brig until he can be put off the ship." The crew surged forward. With a screech Madorra spun on the spot, vicious claw lashing out and it was only by luck that none were caught on it. The Gullaime let out a tormented screech and Madorra moved, swift as wind. Launching himself at Joron. He heard Meas shout, "Move!" The crew split and she stood, small crossbow extended, and loosed a bolt at Madorra. The windshorn dodged without breaking stride and before Joron could draw his blade it was on him, smashing into his upper body. Maybe if he still had both his legs he would have kept his balance, but he did not and he did not. He fell backwards and hit the slate deck, the air knocked from his body. Felt Madorra's claw at his neck. The windshorn keeping low, his wings out to cover Joron.

"Come near, I kill!" he screamed. "Come near, I kill!" Further back on the deck the crew stood paralysed and the Gullaime ran backwards and forwards, screeching and yarking in panic.

"Quiet yourself, Gullaime!" shouted Meas. She did. The shipwife strode down the deck, and if she had ever been worried about losing her authority Joron could not see it. She stopped near enough that Joron was sure Madorra could reach her if he wished and stared at the windshorn. Madorra blinked once. "Well," Meas said, "we appear to have ourselves a situation." The Gullaime appeared from behind her, just its head peering around her and it was almost comical. Joron had to fight not to laugh, to dissolve into a fit of giggles, and only the sudden fear that it was caused by the insidious tentacles of keyshan's rot reaching into his mind stopped him.

"Not do," said the Gullaime, and she hopped in front of Meas. It touched Joron, as he realised she was putting her body between Meas and Madorra. Protecting the shipwife, even when Joron knew the Gullaime must be frantic for her egg, hidden away on the ship by Madorra. Joron wished he could have told the Gullaime what he planned, that he understood her fear. But when could he have?"

"Away go," said Madorra. The claw pushed against Joron's neck.

"This is my ship," said Meas, "I cannot leave it." Madorra blinked at her. Looked down at Joron.

"Bring boat," he said. "Put man in boat. Put Madorra in boat. Put gullaime in boat. Away go." His voice changed, became wheedling. "Let man off at island. Not hurt." Joron felt the claw dig further into his neck, a thin line of blood ran down his skin and he knew that Madorra would never let him live. Meas nodded to herself.

"I would like you off my deck, that is true," she said, staring at the man and the bird. Madorra put his head down so he could whisper to Joron.

"Kill you," he said. "Kill you on water. Leave for big fish. Enjoy."

"You can't though, can you?" Joron whispered back.

"Can do what want," said Madorra.

"No you can't. I know about the egg. You can't leave here without it. Because without it, you can't control the Gullaime." Madorra hissed into his face.

"Kill you now," he said, and he reared back so he had room to move. As he did Joron saw a commotion on the deck and Gavith appeared.

"Look!" he shouted. Madorra froze. Saw Gavith, saw the large bright purple egg he held in his one hand. Saw the Gullaime turn.

"No!" shouted the windshorn. Joron readied himself for the pain. For the end, but it did not come.

"Give boat," Madorra said again. "Give egg. Take man. Take Gullaime. Go." Meas stared at the windshorn.

"I believe," she said, "that if you will not commit to our cause, Madorra, then you are the enemy. And this is a ship of war, we know what to do with the enemy."

And the Gullaime hit Madorra, a ball of feather and fury knocking the windshorn backwards. Madorra managed to land on his feet. Spread his wings for balance, one foot coming up, claw extended. But the Gullaime would not be stopped, it flew at the windshorn once more. Smaller claws scratching, beak pecking. The windshorn was forced back and back until with a final furious attack the Gullaime's clawed feet made contact with Madorra's neck.

The force of the blow cut straight through the wiry sinew, decapitating the creature, and its head fell overboard. The body stood for a moment, blood fountaining onto the deck, then it collapsed. The Gullaime backed away slowly. Then she let out a call, a huge shout of triumph. The feathers on her neck stuck out, and the red crest on her head raised and the air around *Tide Child* shivered and the masts shook and the wind came. A gale that was as sudden and as quick and as shocking as it was short.

When the blast of air passed, Joron stood, looking about at the crew, who seemed as shocked as he felt. Barlay began to clap. She shouted out, "Well done the Gullaime!" And the cry went around the crew until they were all clapping and shouting and Joron felt the warmth of the Gullaime by him. She looked up at him.

"Egg safe," she said softly. "Thanking." Then she rested her head against his side. "Thanking friend," she said. "Friend." And for a brief moment, his damaged body felt no pain.

45

A Meeting of Lovers

"Ship rising!"

They sighted the Hundred Isles fleet later in the morning. Thirty-six ships of it in sight now and at their head the greatest ship of the fleet, the *Arakeesian Dread*, the mighty five-ribber a billowing mass of white wings.

"Topboy!" shouted Meas. "We'll turn toward them, then when we are nearer signal the enemy fleet for parlay. Tell them to send a two-ribber only." She came to stand by Joron and straightened her jacket, checked the small crossbows hanging from it and ran her hand across the feathers sewn into the shoulder pieces, straightening them. She paid particular attention to the two bright red feathers given to her that morning by the Gullaime, which squatted on the deck before the rump-spine. Her missing eye was covered by a patch made by one of the youngest wingwrights, and passed up the chain of command until it was in her hand.

"You think they will talk, and not simply attack?" asked Joron.

"Yes," replied Meas. "Indyl will be aboard the *Dread*, it is too big and slow to bring in easily for rendezvous anyway."

"They could turn the whole fleet on us," said Farys.

"A fleet moves too slowly to catch one ship, he could send some smaller ships after us but he won't."

"Why?" said Farys.

"Because we are just one ship," said Joron, standing straighter, "and he will want our whole fleet. Much easier to follow us back to it than comb the seas looking for it."

"He is right, in a way," said Meas, and she stared out at the fleet of ships. "But more than that, Karrad has always been behind the scenes, never in the thick of the action. He knows the dangers of ship-to-ship fighting, the randomness of it. How no one is ever really safe. He will want to avoid it if at all possible."

"He is a coward then," said Joron. Meas looked to him, and he did not know how to read her face. Not a confirmation of what he said, that he was sure of.

"Not a coward, no," she said. "Only a fool seeks action if it can be avoided."

"I have never seen you avoid it, or send another in your place." She let out a short laugh.

"Ey, and what does that say of me?"

"You are no fool, Shipwife," said Farys. Meas stared at her, and was it relief that Joron saw on her face, or some other emotion washing across her jagged features that the burned girl held no malice toward her?

"Thank you for that, Deckholder," she said, "but sometimes I am not so sure." Then the day consisted of waiting, flying *Tide Child* toward the enemy fleet. Occasionally Joron would catch deckchilder about something, needles and thread out, but when they saw him they hid whatever they did and he let them have their secrets.

"Signals, Shipwife!" shouted down from above. "A boat is leaving the *Dread*, flying flags for parlay! Making for one of their two-ribbers."

"Hold station!" shouted Meas. Then she turned to Joron and spoke more quietly. "We'll make him come to us in that two-ribber. Farys, have the bowsells ready their teams and stand by their bows. Drip some paint on the spines, I want us ready to loose if we need it."

"You think their shipwife will try something under a flag of parlay?"

"A shipwife would not. But Karrad is no shipwife, Joron. I want the crews ready to load our gallowbows with rocks so we can sweep their decks clean of life if they try something. Let us hope Solemn Muffaz and his friends do not need to speak today."

Joron lifted his nearglass and stared across the sea at the Hundred Isles fleet, saw ropes thrown from the two-ribber and caught by the crew of the flukeboat, the smaller craft pulled toward the larger and three people transferred across. Then the flukeboat was let loose and the two-ribber's wings filled with wind, it turned in a tight circle, throwing up a wave of water.

"They're on their way, using their gullaime hard by the look of it." He put away the nearglass. "Needlessly cruel, we are going nowhere."

"Sithers," said the Gullaime and hopped over to stand on the bonerail.

"He was ever cruel," said Meas, and she shut up her near-glass, struggling a little with her damaged hands. "It just took me a long while to realise it, is all." They watched the two-ribber drawing nearer. "It is the *Painful Loss*," said Meas.

"Gueste's ship," said Joron quietly.

"He thinks to unbalance you by sending her, Joron. Do not let him."

"But he does not try to unbalance you by bringing himself?"

"Of course he does," she said, and smiled at Joron, "and I will not let him." She took a step forward and stood with her hands behind her back, watching the ship come in. "Untruss our gallowbows," she shouted.

"Is that wise?" asked Joron. "We meet under a flag of truce and it is not the fleet thing to do."

"No," she said, looking over her shoulder at him. "But

neither Karrad nor Gueste consider us fleet, do they? So let us do some unsettling of our own, and besides," she held her nearglass out to her side, "look at that ship." He stepped forward and took her nearglass, the one he had used for so long. Looked it over, the fine etching on the metal and bone of the hollow tubes, the smooth way they slid, so much better than his own more ragged instrument. He stared at the ship, saw Gueste on the rump, Indyl Karrad by her.

"They have not untrussed their bows," he said.

"Look to the rear, past Gueste," said Meas. He moved the view along, the ship bowing and twisting within the imperfections of the lens.

"Something at the rear, covered in wingcloth."

"Ey, said Meas, coming to stand by him. "Gallowbows is my bet, Deckkeeper. He comes, talks to us and when he doesn't get what he wants then he turns his ship around and looses on us from the rump as he flies away. My bet is those bows are untrussed and ready to send hagspit at us, leave us burning."

"Is that a fleet way to act, Shipwife?" said Farys.

"No, Deckholder, it is not. But I think Karrad only cares about winning and staying as safe as he can."

"We should kill him the moment he comes aside," said Barlay from the steering oar.

"No, Oarturner," said Meas. "Much as it appeals to me, we will try not to become our enemy. We have wrought enough damage already." Joron felt a stab at that, felt a weight upon him as heavy as the corpse of a keyshan, lying in the bay of a town he had once loved.

Painful Loss cut through the water toward them, spry and spruce as can be.

"Joron," said Meas, "there were more ships than those we can currently see, so send up another topboy to scan the horizon before us and to seaward. I'll not be trapped between two fleets." Joron nodded and continued watching the approaching ship.

"Do you trust them?" he asked.

"No," she said, "not at all." She walked over to the rail.

"But we must do this." *Painful Loss* came closer, matching speed with *Tide Child*.

"Will we go to them, or make them come to us?"

"We will go to them," said Meas. "Karrad will not expect it, he will expect to have to persuade us, and that he does not need to will worry him."

"You are not concerned he will simply try to take us?"

"Of course I am."

"He may just kill us."

"He will probably try." She turned, looked at the Gullaime idly pecking at a piece of rope hanging from a spar, watched by the white-robed acolytes. "But we have a powerful weapon on our side." She nodded, then raised her voice, "Gullaime! Come to me if you will." The windtalker ceased pecking at the rope, took two steps toward them then span around in a blur of brightly coloured robes and made a leap, catching the rope in her beak and swinging wildly backwards and forwards until Meas called out. "Gullaime! Attend your shipwife!" The windtalker let go, blinked twice, snapped once more at the rope and then waddled over.

"Won," she said. "Gullaime won."

"Concentrate, Gullaime," said Meas.

"Me-as Gil-bryn," she croaked out.

"Your egg, it is . . ." She let the sentence die away, unsure of how to phrase it and then, like a ship at full speed, realised it was too late to stop. "Your egg is well?"

"Is well. Is well," the Gullaime trilled out then shuffled in a circle. "Egg is well. Safe in nest."

"Good, I am pleased. Now, concentrate, Gullaime."

"Yes yes."

"You see that ship coming towards us?"

"Blow ship away," she said, and stretched up.

"No, Gullaime. Joron and I must go aboard that ship. And it may be they will try to play some trick, or steal us away." The Gullaime stared at her, beak slightly open, eyes burning. She blinked once more.

"Not steal," it said.

"No," said Meas. "So when we go aboard I require your concentration; should Farys tell you it is needed. We may require wind."

"Big wind."

"If that is what it takes," said Meas, "then yes."

"Gullaime can do."

"Good, and you will wait and watch, not be distracted." The windtalker shook her head.

"Watch watch," she said. Then squawked loudly and turned on the spot. Leaping into the air and fluttering the wings beneath her robe, beak snapping out to grab the rope once more, swinging wildly about.

"I am not sure, Joron," said Meas softly, "your friend can be trusted not to get distracted."

"Farys can be trusted though, Shipwife," he said. "And she will mind the Gullaime."

"Ey," said Meas, "She can, though I am not sure I have earned her trust." Meas looked away, at the fast approaching two-ribber. "Barlay," she shouted, "prepare my flukeboat." She nodded as Barlay put the order out and the boat crew assembled.

"I do not understand," said Joron, watching the ships, "why he talks to us. He has all the advantages, the fleet, places to refit. We have nothing."

"Because he still wants you, Joron, and the Gullaime and what you can do." She rubbed the skin above her eyepatch.

"But the message he sent Barnt," said Joron, "he knows the keyshans rise without my help."

"He wants to avoid a fight as well, if he can." Joron watched her, as she stared into the white caps of the wavelets running along the hull of *Tide Child*.

"No," he said, and looked up at *Painful Loss*. "I think he wants forgiveness," said Joron. "From you."

"Well, let us hope so," said Meas, "as our purpose here is to buy time for our fleet to get as near the Gaunt Islands as they can, and he will have to wait until the oceans dry up before he receives my absolution." He laughed at that, and she looked at him with a scowl on her face before the humour of her words caught up with her and she laughed also. "Come, Joron," she said, "if we go to him before he asks for parlay it makes it appear to be our decision, not his. I will undermine him at every opportunity I can."

The boat was prepared and weapons and shields loaded onto it, efficiently as on any fleet ship. As *Painful Loss* made its approach the flukeboat was casting off. Meas stood in the beak, Joron at the steering oar and the wing went up, catching the wind, bellying out and pulling the little ship across the water. Joron watched the sides of *Painful Loss* grow, white and sharp, covered with spikes and hooks. It occurred to him that his adventure could finish here. All *Painful Loss* would need to do was untruss a gallowbow and aim it well and that would be it. Once, he would have had to fight that thought down, been filled with fear almost to the point of breaking. But now that fear crashed upon something within, something hard and cold and accepting. He would not survive all of this, he was sure. His time upon the face of this world was drawing to a close, the danger growing too deep and black and cold to survive. He was a drowning man in a freezing sea, the longthresh gathering, circling, the odds shortening with each turn. And, just as with the sea, if those that wanted him actively dead did not get him, the rot would drown him anyway.

He had feared death once, feared pain, but now he felt that all it brought would be respite. He thought of Solemn Muffaz and the moment he had stepped off the deck of *Tide Child*, how what he had seen on the deckmother's face had puzzled him at the time. He understood it well enough now though. Solemn Muffaz had looked at peace. The pain of the world left behind.

"Are you with us, Deckkeeper?" Hauled back into the world. The rocking ship, the salt spray, the hiss of wings being furled, the knock and swoosh of the oars.

"Ey, Shipwife," he said, though they both knew he had not been. He stooped to pick up the rope by his feet and, as they approached *Painful Loss*, threw it to a waiting deckchild who pulled the rope tight, the same happened at the beak, bringing the flukeboat up against the side of the boneship. A moment later a rope ladder came over the side and before it had even stilled Meas was making her way up, though not as quick and spry as she would have once. Grunting with effort as she ascended. Joron passed the steering oar to Barlay, glanced at where the ropes were tied on to the flukeboat. "Have our ends of those ropes tied slack," he said, "we may need to make a quick getaway." Barlay nodded. Cwell made to follow him and he shook his head.

"Stay until you are needed," he said. She nodded.

Then it was Joron's turn to climb the ladder. Not fast, but steady. When he came over the rail he saw deckchilder lined up along the deck, a whistle played to welcome him and Meas aboard as if they were true officers of the fleet. On the rump stood Gueste, in a fine coat the same blue as Meas's. By her stood her deckkeeper and to the other side was Indyl Karrad, no longer in the leather straps and embroidered trousers of the Kept – now he wore a shipwife's coat and a two-tail hat. He watched Meas as she looked back at him, a brief look of contempt crossing her face.

"Let us go speak to the shipwives," said Meas. A flash of amusement on her face, one meant only for him and then she was walking down the length of the ship. Karrad watching her all the way. Never taking his eyes from her and Joron wondered at the man, for despite all he had said and done, he clearly felt something for her.

"Meas," said Karrad as she came to a stop before him.

"Shipwife," she replied, any respect drowned by her smirk.

"I thought I would have to work hard to win enough trust for you to come aboard."

"There is not enough work to be found in the entire archipelago for you to have my trust, Indyl," she said. Did he crack a little, look a little crestfallen at her lack of respect? How could he expect anything else?

"I did not want this to work out like it has, Meas," he said.

"The time for that decision, Indyl, was before you put me into the hands of your torturers. You could simply have asked me what you wished to know." He stared at her, and Joron wondered what answer he would give to that.

"It was a mistake," he said.

"Some mistakes cannot be forgiven," she said. A flush of anger across Karrad's face.

"Like poisoning half a town with a rotting keyshan?" and he spat the words out.

"We all have to draw our own lines, Karrad," said Meas. Joron wondered at her. Marvelled at her. Here she was, on someone else's ship, outnumbered and in front of a man who had been involved in torturing her half to death. But she did not waver, there was no question about who set the agenda here. "So, Indyl, what do you want from me?"

"You asked for this parlay," he said, and straightened a little, as if realising he had lost control of the talk. He took a step closer, as did Gueste, staring at Joron as she did. "I thought it was you who wanted something from me."

"Ey, I do," said Meas. "Your surrender. You betrayed your people, betrayed my mother, the rightful ruler. Surrender and I will let you live."

"Let me live, aye?" said Karrad, a smile on his face. He and Gueste stepped a little closer. Joron's hand fell to his side, hand on the hilt of his straightsword.

"Ey, let you live, otherwise I will have Joron raise every keyshan in the Hundred Isles against you."

Karrad nodded to himself. "That is all you have?" he said quietly. "I thought you may have some hidden fleet, some reinforcements to call on. But you do not, or you would not go straight to the threat of arakeesians."

"You are weak," she said, then she raised her voice, spoke so the entire ship could hear, "you need Joron's power to survive."

"His power?" said Karrad. "We lost four islands and all who lived on them. I thought it a betrayal, at first. But when our coursers worked out the timing, Joron Twiner was not with his Gullaime."

"The Hundred Isles needs Joron Twiner's power to survive," she said again more loudly.

"If he has any," said Gueste.

"He does," said Meas. Karrad stared at her. A skeer called. He nodded.

"I suspect he does, no one could hold out under torture as long as you did and continue to lie. But, Meas, if you are such a patriot, and care about our islands so much . . ." Gueste stepped a little closer as he spoke. ". . . then give him to me." Meas shook her head.

"I think we both know that cannot happen." Karrad smiled, nodded, looked at the deck. His hand almost within reach of Meas's hand. She stepped forward, Joron too. Spoke in a whisper, a kinder voice. "I speak as the woman not the ship-wife, Indyl," she said, "for what we once had, just let us go. We will leave, set up on our own. We have no wish for war. We will let it be known we align with the Hundred Isles and the threat of us raising keyshans will keep you safe. Just let us and my ships go." He stared at her and once more Joron felt a terrible sadness from the man, trapped between two things he clearly loved, Meas and power.

"I want to do that, Meas," he said softly, "but it seems the keyshans are rising whether he calls them or not. And they will be hunted. By us or by the Gaunt Islanders, and to hunt them requires hiyl, you know that. And you know what is required in the making of hiyl – bodies. Human and gullaime. Would you really step away and leave me to it? Or the Gaunt Islanders?"

"So many deaths already on your conscience, Indyl, you would really add more?"

"I am already far down that path, Meas. It is too late to leave it." The two were staring at each other, gazes locked, as intent as any lovers. Indyl's hand strayed to his sword, released the leather strap that kept it in its scabbard. "Would you do it? Walk away, and let me sacrifice the lives needed to make hiyl, Meas?"

"No," she said, the word barely heard. "You know I would not." He nodded. Turned to Joron.

"And what of you, Twiner? You are a man, just like I. Destined to be crushed under the foot of the Bern." Joron stared at him, and for a moment he felt sorry for the man. Karrad believed what he said, at least in part. "Will you continue to serve with her?" He nodded at Meas. "I plan a better world for our sex. Free of the Bern's unfair rule. Will you continue to serve the daughter of a tyrant?"

"One of the Bern stands by your side, Kept Karrad." Joron pointed at Gueste.

"She has earned my trust."

"And Meas mine," said Joron. Karrad pursed his lips, stared at the deck for a moment, then turned back to Meas.

"We are done here, I think," said Meas before he could speak. Wind whistled through the rigging.

"I dreamed such a future for us, Meas," Karrad said.

"Dreams fade when we awake to reality, Indyl," she said softly.

"Aye," said Karrad, "so what is left?" With that he drew his sword, slowly. Stared at the blade. "As you say, we are done." Then he lunged. Joron did not cry out. He trusted his shipwife, and before Karrad's lunge was complete her own sword was there. Batting his aside, lunging back and he heard her hiss with pain at the impact on her blade. Worried for a moment her twisted hands may drop the sword. Then a great cry went up from the crew, weapons were drawn. He had no time to think as Gueste lunged at him. But she was not battle-trained the way Joron was. Not forged in the heat of combat the way he had been. Not had every nerve stretched until they sang. She had lived a life of indolence. Her lunge was sloppy, lazy. Not quick enough to get the drop on even a sick man with one leg. He danced around her, let her come forward. Moved behind her. As she tried to recover from her lunge he was on her. Bringing down the hilt of his blade on the back of her neck. She staggered under the blow and he wrapped an arm around her throat, the other bringing up his sword so he held the edge against the skin of her neck.

"Stop!" he shouted. "I have your shipwife! Stop!"

Everything froze. Meas and Karrad both in first position, about to cross swords. The crew, some with raised weapons, some with only their fists. The seaguard, in a line, crossbows at the ready.

Meas took it all in, just that bit quicker to react than anyone else and she dived across the deck so she was behind Joron and Gueste. He heard the twang of loosing crossbows. Bolts bouncing off the slate where she had stood.

"Hold or I kill her!" shouted Joron. He felt Meas come in to stand close behind him.

"Well done, Deckkeeper," she said.

"You will not get away with this," said Gueste.

"For your sake," said Meas, "you should hope he does." She moved so she had her back to his. Then they edged down the deck toward where the flukeboat was moored, the space between full of threatening faces. Women and men full of anger, heavy brows above glowering eyes, scarred cheeks, missing eyes and fingers, a constant undertow of angry voices eager to drag them to their deaths.

"You think I won't kill her, to get to you?" shouted Karrad. He felt Gueste stiffen in his arms. Saw some of those baleful stares move from him and Meas to Karrad. Only a fool threatened a shipwife on their own ship.

"Try giving that order, Karrad," shouted Meas, "see how it goes down when you tell a crew to murder their own shipwife."

Karrad stepped forward.

"She treats them badly, whips them constantly," he said, half a smile on his face. He was so confident, so sure of himself. "They would probably welcome it." Joron again felt Gueste stiffen in his embrace. He felt the mood of the crew change and Karrad felt it also, but he did not understand that he had insulted them.

"You do not understand ships," said Meas. "Nor the ways they work." Karrad's confidence faltered, and in that moment Joron knew he would never give the order to shoot them down. Meas had called his bluff and he did not have it in him to risk the crew disobeying. Joron moved more confidently, the crew of *Painful Loss* parting as he moved down the ship, a bubble of clear deck among the crowding deckchilder until they reached the rope ladder.

"You go over first, Meas," said Joron.

"Ey," she said.

"Be ready for me," he said, "I will be coming down quick."

"We will be," she replied. He heard Meas go over, the side, down the hull of *Painful Loss*. Heard her welcomed by familiar voices.

"You'll never make it back to your ship," said Gueste to him. "We'll have our bows untrussed and shoot you out of the water before you're even a third of the way back."

"You won't," he said.

"Why," she laughed. "Do you plan to kill me? Avenge yourself because I stuck you in a box?"

"No," said Joron, and he grabbed her forehead, pulled back her head to bare her throat. "This is for Mevans," he said and pulled the straightsword across her neck. Pushed her body forward into her crew, her hands coming up in a vain attempt to stem the flow of blood. Her crew roared. He heard Karrad shouting, "Shoot him down! Shoot him down!" Too late, he was gone, throwing himself over the rail, bracing for the impact as he hit the flukeboat, but he was cushioned by the waiting arms of his crew, lifted and ready to catch him. Like the petals of a flower closing at night, they enfolded him, pulled him down to the bottom of the boat and he gently descended, his heart beating madly with adrenaline, hearing shouted orders.

"Cast off!" The bump and scratch of gaffs against the hull

of *Painful Loss*. The feel of the sea beneath them as the little boat moved away. "Shields!" Darkness as shields blocked out Skearith's light. The rattle of crossbow bolts on hardened varisk. "Row, Hag curse your weak arms," shouted Meas, "row as if your lives depend on it for they surely do." Joron tried to stand, found his way blocked from above by the elbows of those pulling on the oars. Then Meas was there, pushing her way through and offering her twisted hand to pull him up to stand, bent over, beneath the roof of shields. Another rattle of bolts.

"You killed Gueste?" she said.

"Ey."

"I do not remember, Deckkeeper," she said, "giving you the order to do away with her." But she was grinning, her fierce and predatory pirate's grin. "I hope it made you feel better?"

"It was for Mevans, not for me," he said. She nodded.

"Ey, well, maybe not the best time for it, but it was definitely deserved." She stood, pushing up a shield so she could see the boneship. Quickly pulling the shield down again as more bolts rattled off the varisk. "Mevans would have appreciated it," she said, her grin falling away, "he always liked a bit of drama." She lifted the shield again. "We're out of range of the crossbows, which means they'll be crewing the gallowbows," she said. "Shields down!" A flood of light, the smells of the enclosed, sweating bodies whipped away to be replaced by the freshness of the sea. Meas turned to look at *Tide Child*, shielding her eyes. "Now we must hope our Gullaime is paying attention."

46

The Last Escape

They rowed away from *Painful Loss* with all the speed their muscles could give them as the boneship made ready to loose. And at every stroke Joron wondered where the Gullaime was.

"No sign of the Hag-cursed thing on *Tide Child*'s deck," said Meas.

"She will come," said Joron, and he was sure she would. But all of his attention was now on *Painful Loss*. His execution, for that is how he thought of it, of Gueste was not entirely done from a need for vengeance. Not entirely an act of payback for a lost comrade. A boneship was run by its shipwife, and from them came command and from them came order.

A good ship could lose its shipwife, the deckkeeper would step up and none would notice, and maybe *Painful Loss* did have a good deckkeeper – in fact, Joron felt sure it would. But it also had Indyl Karrad, a man who had never been shipwife but now wore the uniform of one. Joron had bet his life, and the lives of all those around him, that Karrad was not the sort of man to easily hand over power. That he would not stand back and let Gueste's deckkeeper take over. He would need to feel in command, to be seen to be doing something. And as such, would muddy the waters and interfere, and from the way *Painful Loss* was currently drifting, Joron was sure he would have won his bet.

"This will not last, Joron," said Meas, as the wing of their small boat was hoisted. As if they heard her, order began to be restored to *Painful Loss*. The crew along the sides moved to give room for the gallowbow crews to work. Already the bows were untrussed and the crews were working on stringing them. "Come on, Gullaime," said Meas, looking forward to *Tide Child*. Then the black ship's wings fell, great swathes of dark wingcloth shrouding the spines. Joron heard the cries of the gullaime aboard *Painful Loss* as they brought their wind, pushing the two-ribber round so it was easier for the bows to be brought to bear on the flukeboat. *Tide Child* began to move, slowly at first, then more and more quickly as its wings filled with wind. Joron glanced back at the two-ribber, but its gullaime were not as powerful, its movement slower. *Tide Child* came on more quickly, heeling him over as he began his turn.

"Farys is bringing him round," said Meas.

"I had expected our gullaime's intervention to be more direct," said Joron.

"Yes," said Meas, and glanced back at the white ship, "me too, but there will be reasons. And *Painful Loss* cannot take on *Tide Child* bow to bow, it will have to break off soon if it is to escape a fight."

"Does Karrad know that?" He watched *Painful Loss* as it came closer and closer to where its bows would be in the best position to loose directly at their flukeboat.

"Karrad will have an eye on his own skin." She glanced at *Tide Child*, gathering more speed, then back to *Painful Loss*. "Hag curse it," she spat, "he'll have time to loose on us at least once before he needs to make a break and escape."

"Hard to miss at this range," said Joron.

"Such things happen though," said Meas. She stood taller in the beak, straightened her jacket. Joron found himself doing the same.

"Spin!"

The word echoed over the water and Joron saw the winders go to work on the bows of *Painful Loss*. He took a breath. Enjoyed the day, the way Skearith's Eye caught the waves and light and danced over the water. The low song of the warmoan as the bows came to tension. The beauty of *Painful Loss*, so bright and so white.

"Steady, my girls and boys," said Meas quietly.

"Load!"

A bird called out and a fish broke the surface of the water with a gentle splash.

"Aim."

He realised that, in this moment, his hearing had become exceedingly selective. He heard the breathing of those around him, the crack of wind in the wing, the creak of the ropes.

"Loose!"

They stood, those around him. He wondered why, for it would make no difference. At the same time he understood the need to face your death as it came toward you, standing on your own feet, dying on your own terms.

He heard the call of a skeer, such a lonely sound.

They were hit. A massive, juddering shock. The whole boat knocked to one side. The crew thrown over each other, tumbling into the bottom of the boat in a tangle of arms and legs, unable to keep their balance against the sudden, violent motion. Joron was only saved from being thrown into the water by the rigging he clung on to. He swung around, fighting to find his footing, seeing, as if in slow motion, the great bolts from *Painful Loss* passing through the air around them, splashing into the sea an arms-length away. Hitting where the flukeboat had been, but where it was no longer. The impact they had felt was from a huge gust of wind. The flukeboat had been punched to land-ward, out of the path of the bolts, and amid the groans and shock and surprise of their little crew he heard laughter. Meas's laughter. Coming from the bottom of the boat where she lay amid a tangle of deckchilder arms and legs.

"She was watching, Joron!" she shouted. "Our gullaime, she was watching all the time!" More laughter, then she was lashing out around her, cursing those still lying in the bottom of the boat, demanding they get up and set about getting them moving. Joron, now laughing himself, full of the lightness of being that is brought by finding out you are alive after facing certain death, struggled to get his feet under himself. Saw that Meas, and Farys, had called the situation right. After letting off its broadside *Painful Loss* was moving off, not willing to risk the wrath of *Tide Child*'s great bows.

When they were back aboard the familiar cracked slate of *Tide Child*, Meas ordered Farys to set course, with all possible speed, away from the Hundred Isles fleet and toward their rendezvous with Brekir and the rest of the black fleet. Then she returned to her place on the rump. Joron tarried a little, lingering in thought, as it was only after being on the finely kept decks of the *Painful Loss* that he realised just how weathered his beloved *Tide Child* had become. Always he had been a tired ship, though when the work was put in still a fine one, one of the finest, as Meas had often said. But even the greatest of the boneships required constant care and attention to keep it in fleet condition, and a fighting boneship required even more attention, needing resources that Joron and his fleet had been sorely lacking. So now, with the *Painful Loss* still fresh in his head, he felt for *Tide Child* as he walked up the deck, so proud once, now so tattered. His paintwork chipped and showing the off-white bone beneath, wings ragged, rigging much knotted and frayed and retied, and his hull repeatedly patched and stuffed with a mixture of bone fragments, old cloth and bone glue.

Joron knew that in the hold the stores were sadly depleted; *Tide Child* had spent the last few years in a constant state of having only just enough, always afraid the next run may not yield enough supplies to allow them to carry on. He knew that beneath the water the hull was once more growing a tapering beard of weed that slowed them down, and that recently the familiar creaks and groans of the ship underway had become more strained, more worrying and less familiar. He made his way up the deck, to join Meas by the rearspine.

"Do not compare, Joron," said Meas gently as she joined him. "*Tide Child* is what he is, and we do what we can. I tell you this, Joron, no ship on these seas has a greater heart. None, and I have served aboard many. Not one can match ours." She rubbed her hand against the rearspine. "Of all the ships I have served on, *Tide Child* is my most beloved, the swiftest for his size and the fastest to answer to the oar." It seemed to him that she was lost for a moment, her twisted hand on the spine, connecting her to every movement and complaint of the ship as he sped over the waves. "So many times, Joron, I dreamed myself back here, away from the pain. And after the first month, well, I never once believed it would happen." She left her hand on the spine a moment longer, then turned away, her moment of contemplation passed. "Now we return to the black fleet, and plan our next move."

"Will they catch us, shipwife?" said Farys. Meas turned to her and Black Orris fluttered down to sit upon her shoulder.

"As a fleet? No. They only move as quickly as their slowest ship and the *Arakeesian Dread* is mighty but slow. They may send smaller ships out to harass us, but we have enough gullaime aboard to outpace or outmanoeuvre anything they send, I am confident of that." She paused, and looked about. "Talking of the windtalkers, where is our Hag-cursed bird?"

"Hag's arse!" shouted Black Orris, and flapped his wings.

"In its cabin, Shipwife," said Farys, "with its egg. It spends every spare moment with it. That is why we were not as quick as I would have liked when you needed us."

"But you came, Deckholder," she said to Farys, "and that is what matters. Was it your idea to bring in *Tide Child* and use the Gullaime to move our flukeboat?"

"Ey Shipwife," she said quietly, as if sure she had made an error.

"Well, it was a good one." She raised her voice so all of

those on deck could hear. "You should all know that Joron killed Shipwife Gueste on board *Painful Loss*. It was her," and on that last word she looked at Joron, as if she could will acceptance onto him with her one good eye, "who was responsible for the death of Mevans. Your hatkeep is avenged."

"And a good thing that," said Barlay from the oar.

"Ey," another voice from the deck, "and I hope the Hag turns her away."

"Now, Joron," said Meas, "go and see why that bird is skulking about belowdeck rather than being a nuisance above it. I would hate for something to be bothering her and us not helping if we can."

"It has been acting right odd," said Farys.

"She," said Meas.

"Ey, Shipwife," said Farys, "I am still getting used to that."

"Well, do so," she said, and turned from her. "Joron, go attend to your friend."

"Ey, Shipwife," he said. As he walked the deck he noticed that every deckchild made sure they met his gaze, and each returned a nod or a smile or some little acknowledgement that he had done a thing they all approved of in avenging Mevans. He went down the steps into the underdeck grasping the hilt of his straightsword but he did not feel the memory of it slicing into Gueste's neck, no, his hand still held on to that terrible moment when he had plunged the sword into the body of his hatkeep, and Joron felt that he would never be free of that, no matter what vengeance he took or how far he travelled. It was a sore on his soul the same way the keyshan's rot left sores on his body.

Worse, he worried he would be turned away by the Hag for his actions as the Black Pirate. That she would see the wounds his spirit bore, the many lives he had taken that he could have spared, all the deaths in Bernshulme she would lay at his feet. He may have avenged Mevans in this life, but if there was another life then would he ever get to tell Mevans how sorry he was for that moment on that day when he had sacrificed himself for Joron? Or would he, like Solemn Muffaz, end up wandering the cold and dark sea floor? Alone, for ever?

He felt a stab within, stumbled, his bone spur momentarily betraying him and he fell against the wall of *Tide Child*.

"Hag curse it," he said. Near him, Bonin, an old hand, was just waking, pulling himself from the meagre comfort of his hammock.

"Reckon the *Child* took an off wave there, so I do, D'keeper," he said softly, then shuffled past him and out onto the deck.

"Ey," said Joron, thankful for the small comfort offered, "I reckon something hit an off wave."

He knocked gently on the door of the Gullaime's nest cabin.

"Come, Joron Twiner," she said, and he entered into the riotous explosion of colour and objects that was her space. Without Madorra to rein her in the Gullaime had added even more to her nest and sent away the acolytes to another part of the ship. Joron had to bob and weave between strings of objects, some mundane – broken washers, bits of ragged wing-cloth, old clothes and broken pans from the galley – and some strange, salvaged by the Gullaime from islands they had visited, odd shells and rocks, bits of weed and old bones. The Gullaime sat upon her nest, blinking her burning white eyes at him. "Sad Joron Twiner," she said softly. "Not be sad."

"I only think, Gullaime, of all the damage I have done. All the deaths that lie at my feet."

"Friends?" she said.

"Ey, friends, and not friends too. All those I sent to the Hag who did not deserve it." The Gullaime blinked at him.

"Humans bad," she said.

"All of us?"

The Gullaime made a chirping sound, her beak half open. Then she yarked twice, loudly. "Not all. Most."

"They don't know any better, Gullaime, just like I did not know when I first met you. They see only what is, not what could be."

"Not help Gullaime." She snapped at something in the air

he could not see. "Joron Twiner, Ship woman. They help Gullaime." Then she shuffled to one side. "Come, look. Come come." He went to her, moving aside a string of shells to get closer and he saw that she had uncovered the egg in its nest. "Good thing, yes? Good?"

"I think so, I hope so but . . ."

"No but. No but. Listen," she said, drawing the word out in a most un-gullaime way. "Listen Joron Twiner. Listen." He did, letting the many and various sounds of the ship settle over him, sorting them in his mind into what should and should not be. There, in among the sounds he knew he found one he did not, a ticking and a scratching that was unfamiliar to him. He moved his head from side to side, identifying the direction of the sound, realising it came from the egg – no, not from it, but from what lay within it. He stretched out a hand, freezing when the Gullaime almost bit him, her whole body darting forward, sharp beak open, a hiss coming from her mouth. But she stopped moving when he did. The Gullaime's head, now below his, twisted on her neck, one glowing eye looking up at him. She slowly withdrew. Made a high-pitched chirp of song, clacked her beak together. "Do, do," she said.

"Are you sure? It looked like you were going to bite me."

"Women, men. In lamyards. Only take egg. Only hurt egg."

"Then I will not tou—"

"Do," she said, "do. Trust Joron Twiner. Touch." Once more he reached out his hand, watching the Gullaime, but this time she did not move, though her eyes remained fixed on him. He laid his fingers on the smooth, colourful surface of the egg, watched all the time by the Gullaime, her head now twitching back and forth between his hand and his face. The egg, where he touched it, was warm, from the heat of the Gullaime's body, he presumed. Then, he heard the ticking noise again, felt it too. Felt something in the egg moving.

"A chick?" he said, and he was filled with wonder. "It will hatch?" The Gullaime nodded, fidgeted and Joron took his hand back, let the Gullaime shuffle back over the egg. "When?"

"Soon, soon. This day, that day, next day. Not know. Call Joron Twiner when."

"New life, in the middle of such death, it is like a miracle, Gullaime, truly. Thank you for showing me."

"First free gullaime. First not fear blinding. First not clipped. Not starved." She lifted a wingclaw and touched his face. "Good thing, Joron Twiner. Make a good thing." Now he nodded, suddenly aware that a single crystal-clear tear was running down his cheek.

"I do not know, Gullaime, how long it will stay free."

"We escape," she said.

"We did," he said softly. "But they will pursue us, and they have more ships than we do."

"We keep free," she said. "Caller, Windseer. We keep free."

He wondered what she meant by that, because she had fought so hard against the idea of the Windseer before, saying it brought only fire and death.

"I thought the Windseer was bad, Gullaime?"

"We do what is needed," she said, but he was not sure it was the Gullaime's voice he heard. It was more like that other voice, the one he was only half sure existed, that lived between them, and which he sometimes heard in the back of his mind. And he was never sure if it was helping him, or driving him on toward madness.

47

For Those Who Fly: Fly Fast, Fly Far

*T*ide Child caught the wind. Alone on the sea, running from the enemy fleet and toward his own. And if he creaked and groaned in ways a boneship should not then Joron, Meas and the crew choose not to hear it, and only to celebrate the way he flew fast and true through the waves. No sign of their inevitable pursuers on the horizon stretching far behind them as Skearith's Eye fell beneath the water, the black and jagged jaw of Skearith's Spine to one side, and a thousand islands to the other, some twinkling with the lights of humanity, most dark and lonely. Joron could not shake the feeling that those islands only waited for the moment the song called them to break open and reveal what lived within, eager to escape centuries of confinement.

Through the night they flew, winds kind, crew working under the glowering eye of Barlay and the capable hands of Fogle, who had put aside her drink on the return of Meas and stood bright and alert under the stars. In the great cabin, Joron joined Aelerin and Meas, standing over the map table.

"We are here," said Aelerin, pointing at a wide blue space on their map. "Heading north toward Skearith's Spine." They moved their finger up the map. "Our destination is here, further north." They tapped a gap in the black line of the spine. "Namwen's Pass. It is the only way into the Gaunt Islands this far north and is well defended. Our fleet should be somewhere here." Aelerin used their finger to draw a circle in the wide blue area between Namwen's Pass and where they had placed the small model of *Tide Child*. "They are about a day and a half away from us at this speed, if they have travelled at a decent speed themselves."

"They will be slowed by the brownbones," said Joron. Meas looked at him, rubbed her mouth in thought then turned back to the map.

"Where is Karrad and his fleet?"

"By my reckoning, and from when you logged losing sight of them, about here," said Aelerin, tapping the map behind the model of *Tide Child*.

"Can we make the pass into the Gaunt Islands without being caught?" she said, her face drawn and worried as Joron suspected she already knew the answer.

"Not unless we leave the brownbones behind," said the courser, "but if all goes well, and if the winds favour us then we may make sight of Namwen's Pass." Meas nodded, looking grim.

"If we do then our boneships should be able to hold off Karrad's fleet for long enough to get the brownbones and our people to safety in the pass," said Joron. Meas nodded, staring at the chart as if the truths of geography, current and wind were an insult of the most personal sort.

"They should, but we will pay a high price." Meas pointed at a scattering of paint and some crudely modelled lumps and bumps on the map. "What is here, to the north-west of the pass?"

"Islands," said Aelerin. "Mostly small and uncharted but marked with plenty of windspires if the gullaime need them." Meas stared at them, slowly nodding. "And past that," added Aelerin, "there is only the Northstorm, it has come down much further than usual. That generally promises a hard year coming."

"Mevans said as much to me," Joron smiled at that memory, the hatkeep commenting on the uncommon speed of the gion's growth. "Hag bless him."

"How many gullaime do we have in our fleet, Joron?" said Meas.

"Just under one hundred fifty windtalkers," he said, "and almost one hundred and fifty windshorn with us as well."

"A good number," said Aelerin. "They could bring us the wind we need."

"You do not dream good winds, Aelerin?" said Meas.

"I do not understand my dreams, Shipwife," said the courser, "they are full of storms, and the winds spin in circles and it all makes so little sense that I can only tell the weather by reading the clouds and the winds. I am of no more use than any other deckchild."

"Nonsense," said Meas, and Aelerin took comfort – not from her tone, which was brusque and dismissive, but from the plain way Meas put aside the notion the courser was anything but useful. "You had such dreams of storms before the keyshan ripped itself from McLean's Rock, did you not?"

"Ey," said the courser, "it is true."

"Well, it is plain the keyshans are rising, and if you are having such troubles I am sure that lesser coursers are having worse. What do the clouds and the currents tell you?"

"Fine winds but not strong ones, and unlikely to be of great benefit to us."

"Then also unlikely to be of much use to our pursuers either. The problem is in gullaime," she said softly. "They will have more, and be more willing to use them harshly."

"All of our gullaime would come to the slate for you," said Joron, "you know that." She nodded but did not look at him.

"I will ask them, do not worry, Joron. But not simply for us to run, for if we have to fight we will need them then, and I will be forced to ask them to give their power, knowing most will sicken and many will die." She looked bereft. Then said, in hushed voice, words meant only for her and the two stood with her, "I swear, the more desperate our situation becomes the more I value every life we have." She placed a hand on her desk to still a sudden shaking that both Joron and Aelerin pretended they did not see.

"I may have some good news to share, Shipwife," said Joron.

"We sore need it." She looked at him. "Well, man? Out with it."

"The Gullaime's egg, it is close to hatching." Meas's face lit up.

"Well, there is joy in that, and I believe Farys's time comes close as well." Meas's face darkened a little. "I hope with all my heart that the Hag spares her and she makes it through childbirth," she said. "I would not have Solemn Muffaz's sacrifice be for naught."

"She is strong," said Joron.

"Ey, but the Hag cares naught for strength when you are on the sea. I will hold off sharing knowledge of the Gullaime's child a little, maybe until we know it lives. It will give the crew a lift. Hard as it sounds, if Farys and her child are lost in the birthing it will be a blow, but they are used to women dying that way. To lose the Gullaime's child as well? That may be the thing that pushes them over the edge and makes them lose all hope."

"Odd how they have come to love the Gullaime, is it not?" said Aelerin.

"Often," said Meas, "I find we lose our fear of a thing when we realise we are more alike than not, despite how we look." She stood fully, rubbed her back where it ached from leaning over the map. "There is little we can do now but make the best speed we can. Joron, get some sleep. Aelerin, you have the deck, I will be here if you need me."

When Joron woke, the sound of bell fresh in his ear, it was to the familiar rhythm of a ship moving well over the sea. A feeling of peace in a moment that all was as it should be. He did not think of what had passed, or of what was to come and he felt no pain from the scar on his back, the stump of his leg or sores on his body and face. It would not last, with movement came pain. He anointed his sores with the salve made by Garriya before putting on his clothes and wrapping his face. As he did he heard a scratching on his door, soft and subtle.

"Hello?" he said, "who is that?"

"Gavith, D'keeper," came the reply.

"Come in," said Joron. As Gavith entered he struggled a little with the door, having lost his arm in the battle with the toothreaches. "How can I help?" said Joron.

"The shipwife sent me, D'keeper, to tell you Farys has started with the birth pangs," he said and bowed his head, unable to look at Joron.

"And Garriya watches over her, I take it?" Gavith nodded. "Then there are no better hands she could be in." He nodded again and Joron pushed himself from his hammock. "You are worried for her, ey?" Again Gavith nodded, and then he spoke so very quietly that Joron knew he forced the words past a ball of pain and misery in his throat.

"It should have been me," he said.

"What should?"

"Solemn Muffaz," he said. "It should have been me, not him that went over the side." Then he looked up, straight into Joron's face, tears running down his cheeks. "You took me on, and I have let you down. It should have been me." Joron thought for a moment, on his words, on what to say. That Gavith was the father of Farys's child he had been sure of, and that knowledge had soured their relationship.

"You have not let me down, Gavith. We have all made mistakes. And Solemn Muffaz made a choice. He decided that Farys's life, and your life, was worth his."

"I am not worth him," said Gavith. "Look at me, a one-armed man. What use am I to the ship? Takes me twice as long as any other to do the simplest task. I should end my misery, D'keeper, for I am sure I bring bad luck now. That is why the tide has turned against the ship." Joron realised that, though

Gavith was wracked with guilt for Solemn Muffaz and worry for the woman he loved, it was not the only reason he was here. He brought a warning, a rumble from belowdecks, whether he wanted it or not. Joron's words would go to the heart of the ship. They would be carried by Gavith, and Gavith's reaction, his demeanour, could affect the whole crew for he had always been popular as one of the shipwife's chosen.

"Is that what is being said belowdeck, Gavith? That the Hag has turned on Meas?" Gavith did not speak at first, only nodded.

"Not by all," he said, and sniffed, wiped at his nose. "Not even by most. But by some it is whispered. I think some of 'em that did not know her expected more than what they got, see."

"Well let me tell you this. First, respect Solemn Muffaz's choice, he knew this ship as well as any, and decided you were worthy. And I – look at me boy," he said harshly, as Gavith tried once more to commune with the floor in his shame. His eyes snapped back to Joron. "I consider you worthy, for no woman or man on this deck can aim a gallowbow with your skill. If you had stepped forward, rather than Solemn Muffaz, we would have not only lost you, but also Farys and the child within her, do not doubt that for we were trapped within law and tradition. And lastly, you listen to me. The shipwife went through torture every moment she was away, and yet she did not break. For she knew the truth, our ship is called *Tide Child*, for the prophecy of one who will bring the Hundred and Gaunt Islands together in peace, and with all my heart I believe that to be Meas Gilbryn, your shipwife. Do you understand?" Gavith stared at him, blinking as he took it in and Joron, having already put one step on the ladder of prophecy decided he had nothing to lose by ascending it fully. "The gullaime have a prophecy also. In it they name me Caller, and I bring the keyshans. And if our shipwife asks me, I will bring every keyshan in the sea to our aid, and life is coming to this ship. New life, not only Farys's babe, but more than that, you mark my words. I feel it as sure as I feel the keyshans deep below us, do you understand, Gavith? Something wonderful is coming." He nodded, and Joron could feel a change in him. "Be off then," he said, "I am sure you have duties." Gavith turned and opened the door, having to push past Garriya who stood outside it. She watched him go. Then humphed to herself.

"Told him just enough but not too much. That was well done, Caller," she said.

"That or madness, to make solid lower-deck rumours of prophecy," he replied. "So do your job, old woman, and bring that girl through her birthing." She grinned at him, further wrinkling up her wrinkled old face.

"Heh, what has it come to when some deckchild thinks he can tell old Garriya her job, aye, for you are all fools on the sea," she cackled and began to shuffle off, "and all would die without me. You just keep this heap of old bone floating, Caller, I will do the rest. Yes, old Garriya will do the rest." She vanished into the gloom of the underdeck.

The mood on deck was taut; news of Farys's birth pains starting had passed quickly through the crew and they feared for her, even as they knew such things were beyond the control of women and men. All knew women who had fallen to childbirth, and their thoughts, unbidden, turned to those of the ship they had lost. As Joron climbed the stair to the slate he heard a strangled scream of pain from the hagbower far below, and as if in answer a twinge of pain shot up from the stump of his leg. On deck he found Meas stood on the rump, staring out with her nearglass. When she put it down she looked white as sea ice, too pale for good news though she hid it quickly.

"Our fleet is on the horizon, Joron," she said. And he felt a sliver of cold ice down his back.

"No," he said, "it cannot be. It is too soon to catch sight of them, far too soon. We should not see them until much later. Karrad will catch us with ease if they are so slow." Meas nodded as he took his nearglass from his coat and lifted it to his eye. Scanning the horizon through the dirty circle of vision. At first he saw nothing, only the jagged spires of Skearith's Spine, then as he worked along from the mountain range he found the last thing he wanted to see, the spines of ships. Only two, but he knew they must be the outriders of their fleet and his heart sunk. As if in mockery, the confirmation came from above.

"Ship rising to for'ard!"

"Ey," he said, "and Hag curse that for being true."

The Song of Lucky Meas

She flew across the sea
Black ship upon the wa-ter
And Joron Twiner stood
As always right beside her
But the hagpriest tret her cruel
Said "We should take her eye."

Thirteenbern called out
"Give the child to the ships!"
And the sea came to her rescue
As word left the Bern's lips.

PART III
THE WAKE OF SHIPS

48
Departures and Arrivals

On their approach there had been a frenzied exchange of signals between *Tide Child* and the vessels of the black fleet, Meas letting her shipwives know their presence was needed on her ship. As *Tide Child* caught up with the fleet she vanished to her cabin and left Joron to watch the fluke-boats of the shipwives coming to them. Then to stare worriedly through his nearglass behind them, expecting to see the spines of their pursuers at any moment. He was glad of the distraction when the shipwives started to board, of having to arrange all the due ceremony *Tide Child* could muster. Fogle took them to the underdeck, rather than Meas's cabin, and gave them what food and drink could be spared while they stood between the small gallowbows. Of Meas there was no sign, and Joron walked among them, aware of some odd feeling in the room, as it was not long since he had commanded them, been above them, and now he was once more a deckkeeper, not even their equal. In fact he, like them, was unsure of his position for he held a strange place now – deckkeeper, ey, but also the one who had gone in and against all odds brought Meas back to them. Maybe once such things would have worried him but he was long used to command and the awkwardness it carried with it. He had found that to simply carry on, acting as normal as possible, was nearly always best. Soon he was talking with them, collecting news, small news only, talk of how ships flew, of how their crews were — a worrying outbreak of disease on the *Waveturner*, that *Spinebreaker* was low on stores — and Joron, much practised in the ways of a shipwife now, hid his dismay on finding that, though there was plenty of news, there was nothing good in it and that the thing in shortest supply was hope. But still he walked among them, greeting every shipwife by name. And knowing what each of them waited to hear and what each of them dreaded hearing also.

"Ship rising!" came from above, shouted so loud all could hear it and the tension in the room broke, for it is always better to know than to wait. Some there nodded, some bowed their heads, some clicked their tongues and others let out a breath, as if they had been holding it until that inevitable moment when the first outrider of the Hundred Isles fleet pursuing them was spotted by the topboys.

"Well," said Adrantchi, his black brows furrowed, "there it is."

"Ey," said Coult. "There it is indeed."

That was when Meas chose to appear. She wore her dress uniform, her best, deep blue, festooned with feathers and crossbows and shining trinkets. Her gifted eyepatch had been embroidered with small pearls sewn into a stylised eye. Her two-tail now sported a fine red feather that Joron would swear was from their gullaime. Among the gathered shipwives there was an intake of breath. For here was Meas. Those who had seen her before saw the shipwife now, not the tortured survivor. And those who had not yet seen her took in a breath for even though they had been told she had returned, it was a hard thing to believe. That even Meas could escape from Bernshulme after a year of imprisonment. But here she was, the shipwife, the witch of Keelhulme Sounding in all her glory. Did they all stand a little straighter? Joron thought they did, except for Brekir, who Joron saw smile and nod to herself at the reaction of her comrades. As if a thing she had always known had simply been proven true.

An unearthly wail from belowdecks broke the moment. One that caused alarm even among the gathered and much-bloodied shipwives of the black fleet. Meas smiled.

"Worry not," she said. "You only hear a new world coming into being. You hear the pain of birthing a child, just as we experience the pain of birthing new ways."

"Have you put aside the Bernlaw on this ship?" said Turrimore, and Joron could not read her – was she pleased, or was she furious?

"I have put aside its needless cruelties," said Meas, "just as I would put aside the Bern and theirs." She looked around the shipwives. "A well-run ship should have no need of the cord, and all the ships of my fleet are well run, are they not?" And Joron had to hide a smile at the way she trapped them; either admit she was right or admit to a poorly run ship, which none would do.

"I applaud these new ways," said Brekir, "but they may not last long, Meas, unless you bring us happy news from your meeting with Karrad?"

"Indeed I do," she said, striding through the shipwives so she stood below the open loading hatch to the underdeck, bathed in light. "Gueste, who tried to murder Joron, and did murder Mevans, is dead at my deckkeeper's hand."

Another smothered scream from below.

"Well," said fierce Coult, his metal tooth shining, "I'll raise a cup to the death of any of my enemies. Well done, Twiner."

"I take it," said Tussan of *Skearith's Beak*, with an odd giggle, "that the rest of the meeting did not go well."

A scream again, one of long and sustained agony. He caught Meas wincing, felt a twinge of answering pain in his leg.

"It went as well as expected," said Meas. "I bought us time and that was all I ever intended, though I had hoped you would travel further."

"Well," said Bakin, a small man who commanded one of the

two brownbones that carried their people, "that is my fault, Shipmother," he said. "I do what I can but my brownbone, *Waveholder*, is not fast, and lost a spar which slowed everyone. I told them to leave us behind, but they would not." Meas smiled, and went forward to the man, who looked as truly miserable as any Joron had ever seen. She took him by the arm.

"We leave no one behind, Bakin, and we blame none for the misfortunes of the sea. We are in this together."

"Thank you, Shipmother," he said.

"What happens now?" said Coult.

"Hard decisions," said Meas. "That is what happens now." She gave a small smile, a baring of teeth. "Brekir, you are to take *Snarltooth*, he flies faster than any other, and make for Namwen's Pass. Tell Tenbern Aileen we have done as she asks and bring her the Hundred Isles fleet, so she can bring the Gaunt Islands fleet out and crush them. We will do what we can to stay ahead of Karrad's fleet in the meantime." Brekir nodded, made no argument, understood the sense of the order as her two-ribber was well known as the quickest.

"And how do we last long enough to meet them, Shipmother?" asked Turrimore. "It is plain to anyone who understands a chart that they will catch us. We are outnumbered, and will be forced to stay close and protect the brownbones. They will pick us off from a distance."

"Then we must stop them getting close."

Another scream from below.

"And how do we do that?" said Turrimore, and as always there was aggression in her voice. It was in her nature to challenge those in authority. Joron had once been worried by that but had come to value her forthrightness, and from the smile on Meas's face she did the same.

"With sacrifice, if need be, Turrimore, that is how." The tall shipwife nodded at Meas, as if this was to be expected, was desired even. "When they get near, we must send some of our fighting ships out to harry them."

"They will not survive such an encounter long," said Chiver.

Another scream from below.

"No, they will not," said Meas quietly. "So *Tide Child* will be first to attack, I'll not ask any of you to—"

"No, Meas," said Coult, "*Tide Child* will not lead any attack. Like it or not you are shipmother of this fleet." She stared at him, a hard stare.

"So as shipmother, I should lead it, and you should follow my orders."

"Ey, I will not disagree. That is how it us usually done." He looked about himself, at the gathered shipwives. "But we have new ways now, as you say. And whoever goes back, goes back to die. You do not realise what you and this ship have become among the other crews. Most of them have never met you, or served under you. They know you only through stories: the witch of Keelhulme Sounding, the greatest shipwife who ever lived, the one who went away. The Tide Child. That is how they think of you now, you are more than human to most of them. Ey, and to those of us who know you well, maybe we think it a little too." He grinned, looked around the under-deck once more. His words met with nods, and quiet "ey"s. "Joron there, Meas, he led us on a crusade for no other reason than to bring you back, even though it seemed hopeless. And yet, here you are. Back from the dead as far as many of 'em are concerned."

"No one comes back from the dead," she said.

"Ey, and we all know it," said Coult. "We fight for a dream, and we're ready to die for it, Meas, it's what we signed up for. But if you go out and die on the first day, it all dies — their belief in you, the dream." He stepped forward, this hard warrior's voice now soft. "They don't see you as a woman, any more, Meas, you are more than that now, so you must live if you expect your fleet to."

"I am only a shipwife," she said softly.

"No," said Brekir, "you are not. Coult is right, Meas, I know you hate it but it is true. You must live, that is more important than anything else."

As if giving voice to Meas's frustration at finding herself trapped within her own legend, another scream came from below. This one slow, this one lingering, and it sent a shiver down Joron's spine.

"Let us go to my cabin," said Meas, and led them to the great cabin at the rear.

"We will attack first," said Adrantchi when all were settled, "they took Black Ani from me, and I will not be sad to go down to the Hag and join her at the fire. But I'll take as many of them as I can with me first."

"No," said Turrimore, "I should go. *Bloodskeer* is faster and more manoeuvrable. But he is low on stores, has problems with his hull. We are running the pumps day and night to stay afloat and if we do not fight soon my crew will be too tired to fight at all."

"No," said Adrantchi, "it should be me, I made the offer first."

"And I made the case for *Bloodskeer*," said Turrimore. "I am willing to decide this by blade if that is your wish?" Adrantchi's hand went to his weapon and Meas stepped forward.

"Save your blades for the enemy," she said. "And do not be eager to die. We do not know what is coming and we may make better time than expected." She looked from Turrimore to Adrantchi. "You two have never been great friends, but I would rather see you both live to argue in old age than throw you away."

Adrantchi nodded, stood down. Turrimore did the same.

"Eager to prove ourselves is all," she said.

"Ey," said Adrantchi. "It is true."

Meas stared at them, and Joron wondered she did not break down. For he felt it, felt the fierce loyalty of these women and men. He knew, without asking, or checking, that every single one of them, even the shipwife of the brownbone, would fly to their death in defence of Meas and her dream of peace.

"We only need to reach the Gaunt Islands fleet. Brekir will bring them to us," said Meas quietly. "There is safety there. If they make good time we will join with them. Once Tenbern

Aileen has broken Karrad's fleet there will a real chance for peace. Land will be our price for giving her this gift."

Another scream from below, this one even longer, more pained, a wail of hurt and tired despair. Then it shut off.

Silence in the cabin, as if that scream spoke of their future, the pain and sacrifice that all knew was coming. The sudden silence of death. None spoke. They only waited until there was a soft knock on the door.

"Open it," said Meas and Joron did.

There stood Garriya, her hands still wet with blood.

"Shipwife," she said quietly, her face hidden by shadow. Joron's mouth became dry.

"Come forth, old woman," said Meas. The hagshand shuffled forward.

"Old, aye," she said, "but have you looked in the glass recently?" She laughed to herself but before anyone could speak or reprimand her for her words Joron interrupted.

"Farys," he said, "how is she?" It felt, in that moment, as if so much rested on that question. Meas had said the screams were the sound of their future, and now Garriya, unknowingly, brought that news, held the omens of what was to come at her bosom.

"Tired, Caller," she said, "but the girl lives, she is strong."

"And the babe?" said Meas, the softness of her voice barely hiding the urgency of her request. "What of the babe?"

"Lives too, has all the strength of a keyshan." At that Meas smiled. The omens were good, the child lived. Then, as they listened they heard it, the squalling of a babe from below.

"A daughter," said Meas quietly. Then she raised her voice. "She is a daughter of the sea!"

"Ey!" came the reply from the gathered shipwives, a sudden rush of good cheer.

"Well," said Coult, "while the omens are good we should return to our ships."

"There will be grumbling about this when we do," said Brekir, "childer are not to be bern on boneships."

"No," said Meas, raising her voice, "do not allow such words on your decks." She pointed behind her, towards the pursuing fleet. "That was their way. But it is no longer *the* way. You go to your ships, and you will tell your crews that we are no longer ships of the dead. We are now ships of life, and Mother look down on me as I say this . . ." She raised her face to the sky, hidden by the overbones of the cabin. "I intend us to live."

They saw the shipwives off, again with all the ceremony that could be mustered. Brekir was last to leave and as the dour woman stood at the rail Meas did something Joron had never seen her do. Rather than simply saluting her, Meas clasped Brekir to her. For a moment *Snarltooth*'s shipwife looked confused, her face almost comical, and then she closed her eyes and clasped Meas also. Then the two split apart.

"We have served together a long time," said Brekir.

"Ey," said Meas, "and I trust no other with a job as important as bringing the Gaunt Island fleet."

"Thank you," said Brekir. "What if they will not come? What if Tenbern Aileen has no wish to—"

"They will," said Meas. Then she stepped a little closer. Spoke so softly only Brekir and Joron could hear. "And if they will not, then for the Maiden's sake, Brekir, do not come back. And I do not say that in reprimand, you understand. Only that we are the longest serving shipwives of this fleet, we believe in the same future, and I would have at least one of us survive." Brekir nodded.

"Needless advice," she said, a rare smile on her face. "I will bring the Tenbern to you if I have to carry her on my shoulders. You need not worry." Then she leaned in close. "Let the others take the strain, Meas, you have been through much, more than any other 'cept perhaps your deckkeeper. Wait a while before you throw yourself into another battle where you are wildly outnumbered and must work your miracles." Meas snorted a laugh, quickly regained her control.

"I will heed your advice, good Brekir. Now, away, the sooner you are back the sooner I can cease worrying about that fleet that follows in our wake."

"I will fly with all speed. *Snarltooth* has two good gullaime, we call them Clack and Crark for the noises they make. The windtalkers seem well pleased with those names and willing to aid us however they can." She put one leg over the rail then paused. "And I should add, as none said it, something that has become normal to us while Joron was away finding you: use the windshorn!"

"For what?" said Meas, and did Joron hear some cloud in that, some worry that Brekir would lay a new problem at her door?

"They make excellent crew," she laughed, "who would have thought it? A good head for heights, good at intricate work like knots too. Many of them serve now and they serve well."

"They get on with the deckchilder?" Meas asked, and Brekir smiled, a rare thing.

"Shipmother, they *are* deckchilder." With that she was over the rail and her flukeboat was casting off to take her back to her ship and the desperate journey she must make. Joron could already see her ship preparing to make way, as Brekir was a sly one and probably knew Meas's wishes before she had spoken them. Meas stayed at the rail, looking out at the assembled fleet of black ships, all in station around the two brownbones that contained their people.

"Did you know about these gullaime deckchilder, Joron?" she said.

"I did not, Shipwife."

"Well, you can make up for that oversight by bringing some aboard, it does not do that the shipmother of a fleet is lacking something all others have."

"No, Shipwife," he said. She remained at the rail.

"Do you know, Joron," she said, staring out at the forest of spines as her fleet beat through the waves, "from the moment I first set foot on a boneship I dreamed of being a shipmother, of commanding fleets and sending them to battle."

"And now you are that," he said.

"Ey," she replied, barely louder than the breeze, "now I am. If you had told me that my fleet would be black ships I would have hated you for it. But I have never been prouder." She let out a breath, the cloud hanging in the air for just a moment and he made a mental note to get out the cold weather clothes. She turned to him. "There has never been a group of people I have less wanted to put in harm's way than the crew of those ships out there. Only now, I realise that it is a poor shipmother who wants to send her people out, or one who has lost touch with them, at least." For a moment, he thought she would cry, but she gritted her teeth. "Nonetheless, it must be done. Those shipwives I saw today, it will be the last time I see many of them before I sit at the Hag's fire. All our conversations now will be by message flags or messenger flukeboats." She sighed. "We must decide, you and I, which of those great souls out there is first to die for us. What a task," she said, "to make a list, and decide on the value of each life on it."

"Give me a ship," he said, "and I will—"

"No," she put her hand on his arm, gripped it tightly. "Not you," she said, her voice thick with emotion. "I need you. There is barely a face on this deck left from when we started our journey, and if I stumble, I trust you to catch me." She looked up at him, one good eye, skin wrinkled beneath the black lines and shining colours. He wondered when she had become old. Could he really be surprised she had aged considering what she had been through? "Who would ever have guessed it, ey, Deckkeeper," she said, "all that time ago on the beach, that we would still be here." She let go and walked past him. "I will be in my cabin making hard decisions. Call me if you need me."

"Ey, Shipwife, if I need you," he said. She stopped, turned to him and the look she gave him was rueful, at once proud and sad.

"Though," she said, "you will not." Then she was gone below, into the darkness of the ship and he was left upon the rump. The cold air biting into him as they journeyed north, towards the darkest and most dangerous of the storms that ringed their world, and islands of ice that could destroy an unwary ship. He watched the sea, the ships before him and watched *Snarltooth* setting off, signal flags flying. He took out his nearglass and read them. Hearing the message as it was shouted down to him from above.

"Message from Snarltooth, D'keeper," came the topboy's voice. "Reads: 'Leaving formation. Fly well and fly safe.'" He smiled. Raised his voice.

"Send back, 'Message received,' and give Shipwife Brekir our best wishes for a safe journey and swift return."

"Ey, D'keeper," came the reply. And he returned to watching the sea slowly changing from blue to icy grey, and the ships as they moved through it toward the greatest storm in the Scattered Archipelago.

49
Last Sight/First Sight

They flew on, running ahead of an enemy fleet that remained, a few outriders apart, mostly over the horizon. On each day it became noticeably colder, the winds rising until the whistling of air through the rigging of the ships was a constant. Stinker coats were brought out. The windshorn who Meas brought aboard did not notice the cold and, just as had been promised, acquitted themselves admirably as deckchilder. Quick to follow orders, if anything Joron found them a little too subservient and unwilling to think for themselves, but he supposed that was to be expected from a people who had been little more than slaves. They were used to a life where to do anything but exactly what they were told had put them in danger of their lives, and such habits were hard to change. So he practised patience as best he could when they did not show initiative, or when they were too literal with commands, sure they would come around eventually. In those rare moments when *Tide Child*'s Gullaime came on deck they were even more subservient, creeping round as though terrified, bowing before her which served to do nothing but annoy the Gullaime. Twice Meas had to severely reprimand her for biting the windshorn, once so badly the unfortunate creature had to be sent to Garriya for the wound to be stitched up.

He discovered the windshorn were useless when it came to crewing the gallowbows, but good with knots and rigging, and they made quite wonderful topboys, their eyesight being far superior to a human's, though their understanding of flags and signals was somewhat wanting.

On the morning of the third day, with Skearith's Spine growing to seaward of them, black and forbidding, they finally lost contact with *Snarltooth*. And as if the Maiden thought that a ship out of view needed a replacement, the call came from above:

"Ship riser! Ship riser!" And though there was a tightening of all on deck at that call, and what it meant, that another ship of the pursuing fleet could now be seen, there was also humour and smiles exchanged, because no matter how many times they were told, the windshorn could not get the calls quite right.

Despite the danger, and the worry and the fear, those days were strangely light. Maybe it was news of Farys's babe – she had named the girl Muffaz and all aboard thought that a good and right name. A steady stream of deckchilder made their way down into the ship, quiet as could be, to talk to her and coo at the child.

By the fifth day the Hundred Isles fleet was plain for all to see, three fighting ships to every one that Meas's black fleet could muster, but the deckchilder of *Tide Child* gave them no thought. As Joron passed through the ship he heard their talk – "For sure, do we not have Lucky Meas in charge, and that Hag-cursed Karrad couldn't kill her when he 'ad 'er in his dungeon, can't think he will manage now," and, "A babe, what more luck could there be than that, what more of a new beginning?" He noticed some of the deckchilder about some task they hid from him, but he let them have their secrets as they seemed in good spirits. Joron did his best to share their good cheer but he struggled. Only he saw the other side of Meas, sunk into a darkness so deep he could not reach her. Struggling with the pain in her body, or – and this was worst for him

– on the point of despair, unable to see where they would go should the Gaunt Islands fleet not come to their aid.

Too often, he found her sat at her desk, pouring over charts, making plans with Aelerin, or calling him to make plans of the most desperate kind, choosing who first to send against the pursuing fleet. She made lists of the fastest ships, the ones most likely to escape. Imagined ways to turn the brownbones into fireships, send their people off on other vessels. Thought up decoys and feints, worried over the best ways to use their stores of bolts. Each day a different plan, and each night she sunk further and further into a dark place, as dangerous and cold as the sea floor where those denied the Hag's fire walked. Each day he walked the deck, wishing she would show her face because he knew the crew's good spirits could not last. The fleet behind them held a weight, a knowledge that would wear away at good spirits, and Meas being seen on deck would alleviate that, put off that moment when the crew began to feel it.

But she stayed below.

On the evening of the sixth day, when the sky was slowly pinking, and the clouds were gathering around the tops of Skearith's Spine, he went below again. Found her in the great cabin, back turned to the ships on the darkening horizon, wanelights burning as she sorted through the charts on her desk. There was a franticness to her that he did not much like.

"You have not been on deck for a long time, Shipwife," he said.

"It is likely Karrad will catch and overrun us. Aelerin says those ships are gaining, even if only slowly. I have too much to do." No shrift given, his presence barely acknowledged.

"Always much to do aboard a boneship," he said.

"Ey, so leave me to it."

"It would mean a lot to the crew," he said softly, "to see you on the rump."

"They have done fine without me so far," her words sharp.

"They have longed for your return."

"Then they will not mind waiting." She snapped the words at him and he was ready to bite back. He held his tongue, knowing it would not help.

"I will leave you to your charts then," he said with a bow of his head and turned. As his hand touched the door handle she spoke again.

"Wait!" and that one word was an entreaty, not an order. So he let go of the door, turned back to his shipwife.

"Always," he said. She stood, hunched over the charts. Looked up, her one eye sparkling. Then let herself fall back into her chair.

"I do not deserve you, Joron," she said. "It would be better for this ship to put me in a flukeboat and send me back to Karrad. Maybe he would be happy with that. Maybe he would let the rest of you go."

"He would not." She stared at him, only the sounds of the ship accompanying them in the great cabin, the groan of strained bone, the rush of water past the hull, the whistle of the wind in the rigging. "I think we have rather upset him," said Joron, "and as you said, he cannot risk me being free." She blinked once.

"Did they break me, Joron?" she spoke in barely a whisper, and lifted her twisted hands to show him. "I can hardly hold a pen some days, never mind pull on a rope or dash up the rigging. I make a good show of holding my sword, but I could not hold it tight enough to fight with, no matter how desperate the action."

"You managed on Gueste's ship."

"Barely," she said. "I am expected to work miracles when I am not sure I work at all." She stared at him. "When I close my eyes, I see that hagpriest coming at me, Joron, with all her tools at the ready." She rubbed her eyepatch. "I cannot sleep at all."

"After I was put in the box," he said, "and Gueste took my voice, I was plagued with bad dreams. Garriya gave me tinctures that helped me sleep, and in that sleep I did not dream."

"I cannot show weakness."

"It is not weakness to confront a problem. Maybe if you saw Farys," he said, "saw her babe, rather than locked yourself in here, it may lift your spirits a little?"

"The babe that would most likely be dead had Solemn Muffaz not interfered? I got it wrong and do not need reminding of it. Now, when it matters, I do not know what is wrong and what is right. I plan, replan, second-guess." She stared at the desk. "Truthfully, do you believe the Gaunt Islanders will come?"

"I do not know," he said. "I would hope so. Tenbern Aileen said that if I could get Karrad's fleet out far enough she would move on it." Meas nodded. "She has no love for the Hundred Isles."

"I hear the deckchilder, and they talk of me as if I am as powerful as the Maiden, Mother or Hag," she said quietly. "They think me unbeatable, but I am just a woman like any other." She looked up, her face drawn, thin and angular. Pained. "It is too much for me."

He stared at her, at this woman who had been through so much, who meant so much to him, and the naked pain on her face was almost more than he could bear. She always had the words, when they were needed, or the action, when it was needed. Now she needed those words, now she needed an action, and there was only him to speak or do. He started to talk, got as far as 'I . . .' Stopped. Regrouped. Considered. Spoke.

"Nothing has changed, Meas." He stood a little straighter. "From the moment you stepped on the slate of *Tide Child* there have been those who would gladly die for you. Not many at first, and I did not count myself among them. Indeed, I would have gladly seen you die." He laughed, "I was a fool then. The more you have led, the more we have believed. The deckchilder talk of you as legend, and they are right to do so, for you are. But you need not feel like it weighs upon you, Meas, for it is simply who you are, may as well ask you to stop breathing as to stop being that. It is your nature, and even if none of us survive – and I believe we will, but even if we all die, we die for what we believe is right. There is not one of us who will see our death as your failure. Better to die attempting something grand, than live in the world the Bern gave us." She stared at him, as if she needed more. "Do you know," and he could not keep the smile from his face, "that they think I am your son? And I have, not once, ever, tried to disabuse them of that fact. Sometimes, the fact that they could even think that – well, it was all that kept me going."

"If the Gaunt Islanders do not come," she said softly, "can you bring the keyshans to help us?" He shook his head.

"I do not believe that is how it works. Even the wakewyrm, when it saved us. If it had not been there, by us at the time, I doubt we could have called it. I am still not sure I did." She nodded.

"I knew as much. I am sure Karrad thinks you control them, he does not understand that you may as well try and control a storm." She wet her lips with the tip of her tongue. "We have few options; in truth, it looks like we will all die, Joron, or worse, be taken by Karrad and sacrificed in an attempt to make hiyl so he can hunt the keyshans and the whole vile business of war can start again."

"No," said Joron, and he was surprised by the strength in his voice. He stepped forward, pulled out a chart of the north from the mess of charts on her deck. "If they do not come, we go north-west before Namwen's Pass, steer into those small islands."

"I have thought of that. He will still catch us within them, send his two-ribbers in after us. His big ships will go around to hem us in at the far side. Maybe a few ships will escape but . . ."

"You misunderstand. It is his ships that will not escape – granted we may not either but it is worth the risk. Those islands are mostly uninhabited, but Aelerin said many had windspires," Joron said, his mouth drawn into a thin line, his voice like waves breaking on rocks. "I will sing every keyshan there up, and I will bring them out of those islands in our wake." You saw what it was like at McLean's Rock, the chaos will be terrible. She stared at him. Then gave a nod and pulled the chart over to her.

"From there," she said, "what ships escape can skirt the Northstorm, also a risk, and we may lose some, but so will they. Karrad may baulk at such a risk, especially after any losses he suffers in the islands. But I trust my shipwives."

"Ey, Shipwife," he said. She stood.

"North then," she said, "if all goes wrong. But it is a desperate plan, Joron, so let us hope it does not."

"Let us hope that," he said. Meas straightened her jacket and ran her fingers through her hair.

"Farys is still with Garriya?" He nodded. She screwed her eye shut, ran a hand down her face. He had never seen her look so tired. "Then I will go see her, and young Muffaz. And you were right, I should show my face on deck."

"And ask Garriya for something to help you sleep," he said.

"Do not fuss, Joron." She stood and walked toward the door, making him move out of the way.

"But you will ask," he said. "Or I will tell her you are having trouble sleeping, and then you will have to answer to her." A trace of a smile on Meas's face as she turned to consider him.

"Very well," she said. "I will ask or you will have her chasing me round the deck with bottles and pills."

She left him standing in the great cabin and he went to the desk, tidied up her charts and under them he found her journal, laying open beneath them. He remembered seeing this book many times, wondering what was in it. At first, because he wanted to use those things against her, then, from curiosity. He knew it was written in code, and he knew how to decipher that code as she had supplied him with the cipher, long ago in Sleighthulme when she thought she went to her death and he would need to read her orders. Day after day he had looked at her journal in its place within the desk, and it had become a talisman to him. He had believed that if he opened it, read it, then it was as good as admitting she was gone so there had been little temptation to do so. It was a thing put away and forgotten about. But now he was worried about her. He knew her most private thoughts would be in that journal. Maybe that violation of her space was the right thing to do; it was his job, after all, to ensure the shipwife was making good decisions.

He shut the book.

If she worried, she would tell him. If she doubted, she would share those doubts. Eventually.

He left the great cabin, only to be intercepted by the Gullaime as soon as he entered the gloomy underdeck. She let out a loud squawk, span on the spot and chanted his name over and over again.

"Joron Twiner! Joron Twiner!" Interspersing the chants and fluttering and dancing with yarks and calls and whistles.

"Calm down, Gullaime," he said, "what has happened? What is the problem?"

"Time, Joron Twiner!" she squawked. "Come! Come!" Then she hopped away from him toward her nest cabin while Joron stood, bemused for a moment. "Come!" she said again, then evidently finding his lack of movement displeasing she hopped back, grabbed his sleeve with her beak and pulled him forward.

"Your egg!" he said, realising what the windtalker must mean. "I am coming. Gullaime, let go or you will ruin my jacket, by the Hag." But he was filled with excitement and the Gullaime was the same, no fear here, not like with Farys. The windtalker seemed not to be at all worried. Though worry fell on Joron enough for both of them, like clouds over Skearith's Eye. He wanted, as he walked to the nest-cabin, to tell the Gullaime she must stay quiet, that if the chick did not survive the crew must not know. For as much as Farys the Gullaime was loved, and the death of her chick would ripple through the crew. And where Farys would have borne up if she lost the child, would have held her misery and pain in, the Gullaime was not a creature that could dissemble. Everything she felt was immediately passed through her body and either came from her beak or was shown in her actions. He dreaded to think of the effect the Gullaime, sloping around the decks in abject misery of grief, would have on the crew.

"Come! Come!" shouted the Gullaime, and he did. Put aside his thoughts and went into the nest cabin. Watched as the windtalker scuttled in between the threads of rope and string and myriad jingling, jangling, glinting and shining trinkets to the nest. There to sit before the egg, shining eyes focused on it. Her head flicked to Joron. Then back to the egg. And back to Joron and again and again and again. "Listen listen," she said.

Joron did. At first he heard nothing, then, behind the normal noises of the ship he heard a very faint, very high-pitched chirping.

"That is it?" he said softly. The Gullaime nodded its head, two quick nods.

"Windtalker," she said. Joron approached, coming as close as he could.

"Should we help it get out?" He reached out his hand and the Gullaime snapped at him.

"No," she said. "Make own way. You listen. Listen."

"Very well," he said, and he did. But not only with his ears, he listened to the song within him, the twisting, looping curling song of the isles. He could make out the song of the keyshans, all very far away but slowly growing in volume, and his song and the Gullaime's song and something else. Something new. So quiet and soft to be barely there but so very bright. A new song, full of yearning, but also full of hope and excitement. It was similar to the melodies he heard from the Gullaime when she chirped and sang to herself, but very definitely different. A melody that had never been heard before in the whole archipelago, and it filled him with wonder.

He heard a second noise, overlooked at first. The same gentle tapping he had heard before, but louder and quicker and more insistent. The Gullaime focused on the egg and Joron saw lines appear on the purple surface, one, then two, then more and a tiny bit of the shell fell away, the chirping from within rising in volume and the Gullaime, without moving at all, appeared to double her focus on the egg. Joron found he was holding his breath.

Tap

Tap

Tap

As constant and rhythmic as sand falling through a glass, and with every tap a little more of the shell fell away until, eventually, the top of the egg collapsed and something within squeaked in outrage, shook itself, sending bits of eggshell flying, and raised its head.

So small.

So incredibly ugly.

And yet so wonderful.

Huge eyes, not yet open, but glowing beneath the closed lids. The sharp beak, like the Gullaime's in miniature, but tipped with a small horn for breaking the egg. Her skin pink, covered with thin, yet-to-be feathers that were black, soaked through with the liquid of the egg. Then one eye opened, bright and glowing just like her mother's, then the other. She looked about the cabin, taking it all in, tiny wings flapping uselessly. Her gaze found the Gullaime, recognised something in her and made a soft sound. A high-pitched "ah-rarr?" The Gullaime answered with the same noise and the chick tried to climb out of the egg using her wingclaws, fell backwards, small clawed feet beating uselessly at the air while she squeaked and chirped to herself until she was righted. Then once more she set to climbing, this time making it out of the egg, out of the nest, falling over again, struggling to right herself. When she finally did she squatted before the Gullaime, managing to look oddly bad tempered. The Guilliame fished about within her robes, finding a morsel of food which she dropped into the chick's mouth.

"She is wonderful," said Joron. Wondering at this creature, no bigger than Farys's babe but already far more able.

"Yes yes," said the Gullaime gently, "wonderful." She picked the chick up, placing it within her robe. A moment later the chick's tiny, ugly head stuck out of the feathers at the Gullaime's shoulder, studying Joron.

"What will you call her?" he asked.

The Gullaime let out a short song. Then yarked to herself, scaring the chick which vanished into its mother's feathers and the Gullaime had to coo and coax it to come out. When it finally did, the gullaime turned to Joron. "That gullaime name," she said, calling out the short song again. "Give human name too." The Gullaime used her beak to pluck the chick from her shoulder, then passed it over. Joron quickly put out his hands and the chick was dropped into them. She was warm, so very warm. He held her close, cradling it against him and was filled with such joy as he had rarely known.

"And what name will that be?" said Joron softly, looking down at it.

"Shorn," said the Gullaime. "Will call Shorn. After father."

50

The Turn

Though the horizon to their rear was full of ships, their pursuers impossible to forget, the mood aboard *Tide Child* was buoyant. Farys's child, and then the Gullaime's chick, had raised the mood of those aboard. Meas being back on the rump helped, Joron was sure of that. She had slept, looked less worn, and if she was worried about the ships behind them then she gave no sign of it. Three times a day she would bring Aelerin up and they would take measurements – of Skearith's Eye, of the wind – mark their place against the vast and rising towers of Skearith's Spine, and lastly, always lastly, mark the places of the pursuing fleet. Then the courser would scuttle down to the main cabin to place their measurements on their charts. Among the crew there were jokes and mocking of the Hundred Isles fleet as, though it pursued them, it did not seem to gain. This they blamed on poor skills and worse ships – "Not a one can touch *Tide Child*, ey D'keeper?" was a thing he heard from every other mouth. Though Joron was not so sure it was a simple as the crew believed.

He kept busy running the ship. Farys was not ready to take her place by him yet, and though she protested otherwise neither Meas nor Garriya would let her back on deck in an official capacity. Still, she regularly came up on deck with the tiny scrap of life that was Muffaz strapped to her and walked round with Joron. The crew took great delight in seeing her and these violent women and men became as gentle as the softest breeze when faced with her child.

And the same with Shorn, though the gullaime chick was as different to the human babe as could be. Where Muffaz was helpless, Shorn was learning at a rate that Joron could barely believe. Only a couple of days old and barely up to his knee but she could already say a few words – though she displayed a worrying affinity for Black Orris and the words she had picked up were, maybe, not the ones Joron would have chosen for a child. She could walk too, and was just as curious as the Gullaime, though much smaller. Joron found himself either shouting at the Gullaime to keep her offspring under control or in a constant sense of heightened alertness as deckchilder moved around her, their bare feet which could easily break her delicate bones hammering on the deck. Though truthfully, the gullaime chick was in little danger, few people were as aware of their surroundings as deckchilder, and those that were maybe not as careful as they should be around Shorn quickly learned that though young, she could give a painful bite if she felt threatened. Once that bite was delivered she would scurry back to her mother and hide in her feathers, her small head peeking out of the Gullaime's feathery shoulders, turning the windtalker into a strange, and quite foul-mouthed, two-headed creature.

Though Shorn's presence was joy for the deckchilder, Joron had eventually banned the young gullaime from all but the quieter rump of the deck for his own sanity.

On the evening of the ninth day Meas requested Joron to her cabin, he handed control of the ship to Barlay and went below.

He found her standing before the window watching the Hundred Isles fleet. Her body stiff, as if she held every muscle in tension. Aelerin, to one side of her, gave Joron a nod and a smile but they looked every bit as tense as Meas.

"That fleet out there," said Meas, "they do not catch us, and that bothers me."

"It has played upon my mind as well, Shipwife," he said.

"Is it not good," said Aelerin softly, "that they cannot overtake us?"

"The *Arakeesian Dread* is not a fast ship," said Meas, "but needless to say, even with that in mind, it is faster than the brownbones we fly with. They should be catching us."

"But they do not," said Joron.

"No," said Meas. "Which begs the question, why?"

"You have said before, Shipwife," said Joron, "that you believe he is a coward, afraid to bring us to the bow. Could it be that simple?"

"I think not," she said. "He may indeed be a coward but he intends on being the first man to rule the Hundred Isles." She turned away from the window to look at him. "He cannot afford to look weak in front of his shipwives, they would throw him overboard."

"Maybe he just wishes us gone," said Aelerin quietly. "Maybe he simply follows us to make sure we leave his waters and that will be that, we will never have to throw our ships into battle against him."

"It seems unlikely," said Meas. "The keyshans are rising, and if he believes, even for a second, that Joron may have any control over them, then he cannot risk him getting to the Gaunt Islanders."

"Yes," said Aelerin. "So in that case why not catch us, and force us to battle? It makes no sense. He has all the advantages."

"Does he fear I will bring the keyshans down on him?" said Joron.

"He may," said Meas.

"Surely then," said Aelerin, "he should hasten to battle. Time passes, more keyshans will rise or we will be near islands with windspires." Meas sat. Tapped her finger on her desk and as she did Joron remembered something said by Karrad back in Bernshulme. Something that sent a coldness through his body. A terrible feeling. A fear like few he had known.

"Karrad," said Joron, "when we spoke in his rooms, said he was in touch with the Gaunt Islanders." Meas stared at him, tapping her finger on the dark surface of the desk.

"You think he has some form of agreement with them?" she said. "He did not seem open to an alliance when we suggested it."

"He need not be their ally," said Joron. "It could be that they have decided among themselves that I am simply too dangerous. And as the keyshans are rising anyway, they do not need me."

"You think they will move against us?" said Aelerin.

"That is an overt action," said Meas, "with risks, if they believe Joron can bring keyshans to his call. Remember none really know what he can do." She looked at the charts before her, "But it would not shock me if they simply closed Namwen's Pass to us."

"Then Karrad would have no need to hurry," said Aelerin, coming to the same slow, horrible realisation that had crept down Joron's spine moments ago. "He follows until it is too late for us to escape, and we find ourselves stuck between Skearith's Spine and his fleet. Then he can destroy us at his leisure." Meas nodded.

"He herds us like kively to the slaughter," said Aelerin.

"It is possible," said Meas.

"Even if he herds us," said Joron. "It does not mean we are definitely lost." All eyes turned to him. "Tenbern Aileen is canny, and if she wants my power, what better way to ensure it gets to her than to have Indyl Karrad safely escort us all the way to her territory?"

"That does sound like the sort of thing Aileen would do," said Meas. "Woman has plans within plans." Meas stood, turned back to stand before her great windows, not speaking as the wake of *Tide Child* stretched out behind her. "We will know if this pass is closed, because Brekir will tell us," she said.

"If her ship is not destroyed," said Joron.

"Many have tried to end Brekir," said Meas, "and none have

succeeded. If anyone can outthink the Tenbern it is her."
Silence, then Aelerin added:

"Or you, Shipwife, of course." He heard Meas give an amused grunt.

"Of course," she replied. "First, though, we must know if we are being herded, or if it is just that Karrad is a very poor commander. I will signal Coult to take *Last Light* and *Waveturner* and steer as if they are making a break from our fleet. We will see how they react."

"And if it turns out we are being herded to Namwen's Pass?" said Aelerin.

"Then we must head that way still," said Meas. "If we do not meet Brekir coming the other way then we know for sure this is a trap. Until then we must presume that the lure of Joron's power is enough to bring Tenbern Aileen to our aid and hope we see Brekir making all speed for us with the Gaunt Islands fleet on our side."

"If we do not," said Aelerin, "what then?"

"We fly north, and Joron will raise every keyshan he can."

"We fly the sea in hope then?" said Joron.

"Ey," said Meas, "but has that not ever been our way?"

51

The Tying of the Knot

The next morning they watched Coult in his *Sharp Sither* with *Last Light* and *Waveturner* split from the fleet, heading westward to see if Karrad sent ships to head them off. Meas stood, statue-still on the rising and falling deck of *Tide Child*, staring forward through her nearglass. The air was another couple of degrees colder, the seas rose and fell a little further, the waves were a little sharper crested. In the north, between squalls of freezing rain, Joron could see the Northstorm, the greatest and most furious of the walls of cloud that ringed the Scattered Archipelago. Only a line, a faraway line, the cloud so black it looked as if ink had been spilled across the sea, and below that a lighter line of long low islands.

Joron wrapped his stinker coat around himself, the sores on his arms, legs and face stung as saltwater found its way through his clothes and mask. He tried not to think, for since the meeting with Meas and Aelerin he only had one thought: if the Gaunt Islands had turned against them, where would they run to? The plan of heading further north was all well and good but what would happen if they did escape? What then? He hoped Meas had something, some idea she kept close to her chest – he knew it was often her way. Maybe she knew an island that was defensible and could supply enough crops to feed their people, they could not number over a thousand now. And if they escaped Karrad's fleet, rising keyshans and the skirts of the Northstorm, he suspected they would number much less.

He racked his mind, trying to think of some place they could go, failing.

"I will do my rounds," he shouted into the growing wind and Meas nodded. Still staring ahead. Then she pivoted on her foot to look behind at the pursuing fleet. It remained on station. Not falling behind, not catching up. Those ships were beginning to weigh on him. It was not the fight that was hard, as he had heard more than one old hand say, it was the waiting. The moments while you stood there under shot, the enemy raining destruction down on you and you not able to answer. This was like that, though the shot they rained down was not a physical threat, it was a draining, a shadow in the mind. He wondered if he should bring the Gullaime and Shorn up on deck, or ask Farys to bring up Muffaz, or maybe both would lighten his mood. He looked around, the flukeboat, neatly tied down over the central hatch. The great bone windlass was newly oiled. The shot was well stacked and secure. All was as it should be and he itched for some indiscretion or fault he could point out, something for him to do to make himself feel useful.

Some of the older hands, the most experienced deckchilder, were watching Coult's ships break away and he knew that if Karrad's ships moved to intercept, it would not be long before the crew realised what he and Meas had.

"It is hard, is it not, Joron?" He turned to find Aelerin wrapped in a stinker. "That fleet hanging over us like skeers above a corpse."

"Ey," he said. "I only wish they would act. It would give me something to do."

"I would have thought," said Aelerin, "that a deckkeeper always has something to do." He smiled at the courser, aware they could not see it under his mask, but would pick it up from his eyes.

"We have trained our crew too well, it seems," he said and Aelerin laughed. "Are you not busy with our charts?" The courser shrugged.

"The further north we go," they said, "the less choices our course gives us. I have planned all possible routes."

"So you, also, have been too efficient?" he asked. Aelerin grinned at him.

"Ey, though I did not work for long before exhausting our opportunities." Joron leaned in closer to them.

"Do you know where she plans to take us? After . . ."

"The charts are not complete up here," said Aelerin quickly. "A shipwife would know the waters better than any chart."

"That is a very complimentary-to-Meas way of saying 'no', Aelerin."

"It is true though," said the courser. "Mostly I have charted us escape routes, ways into the those islands to the north-west that will be difficult for Karrad's bigger ships to traverse. It is hard to find a channel deep enough for us, but not also for their bigger ships."

"To go into the islands was my idea, I am sorry if it has caused you problems."

"Come with me," said Aelerin and he followed them, down into the bowels of the ship and into the courser's cabin, the walls elaborately decorated with drawings of winds and current. Aelerin took a chart from a rack by their bed and rolled it out on a drop-down table. "At this time in the cycle of years, the Northstorm is far down the archipelago, most of the real ice is consumed by it."

"How far is the storm's edge from Namwen's Pass?"

"Two weeks at most."

"That does not give us much room." Aelerin shook their head.

"If we are denied the pass and left with no other choice, we take this channel here, Barcles Bight." They pointed to a place between two of the bigger north-western islands on the map. "In open sea we will be caught. This channel between islands is deep enough for *Tide Child* but too shallow for the *Arakeesian Dread* to follow, as well as being too narrow for ship to ship fighting. Further in it is a mess of small islands."

"That is good," said Joron. "They will go around though."

"Ey, but it will free us of them for a while, I think Meas fears the *Dread*'s broadside more than the rest of that fleet combined."

"With good reason," said Joron. "And what of these islands, Aelerin? When I mentioned it to Meas I was speaking the first thought into my head. You dissembled before, but do you think there is somewhere big enough for us to defend? Live on, even, among them?"

"Not here, no," they said, "but the shipwife will have a plan." He nodded, but suspected she did not. Fought back a sudden feeling of helplessness, sure that if the Gaunt Islanders had turned against them they were lost.

"Only the day is undecided," he said under his breath.

"Sorry, Deckkeeper?" said Aelerin.

"Nothing," he said. "Just that Meas has not shared anything with me." He looked away. "Has she told you something?" The courser shrugged. "Aelerin, I will not let her know you shared her confidences, but it would be good to be forewarned."

"She has told me nothing," Aelerin added quietly.

"But you have gleaned something from her?" The courser shook their head.

"Nothing more than we already knew, that Meas plans to run the fleet through the edges of the Northstorm."

"A wrecker's course," said Joron.

"Ey," said the courser, "I think her hope is that they will lose far more ships than we will."

"It is good to know she rates our seacraft so highly," said Joron, as he leaned over the table, looking at the chart.

"But storms care naught for skill," said Aelerin. "And the Northstorm cares less than any other. It is a great risk she takes."

"Desperate times," said Joron quietly, "call for desperate

measures." He turned, some sixth sense telling him they were watched, and there in the doorway stood the Gullaime, considering them with her bright eyes. Shorn's head pushed its way out of her shoulder feathers. The Gullaime blinked twice then turned away, shuffling back to her nest cabin.

"How long do you think she was there for?" asked Aelerin.

"I do not know," said Joron, "but I wish the Gullaime had not heard that I consider us desperate, she will worry, and I would not have her worry. She tends to pull out her feathers."

He left Aelerin in their cabin, and as he walked along the underdeck Farys approached with Barlay.

"D'keeper," she said, "the oarturner would like to show you something."

"Very well," said Joron.

"It is in the hold, D'Keeper," she said and he had to fight not to look crestfallen, not to look worried about whatever new problem they had discovered that was important enough to need his attention.

He left Farys and followed Barlay into the hold, there he found two deckchilder, Stark and Ashton, standing and looking uncomfortable while they waited for him.

"Well," he said, "what is it?"

"It is only . . ." began Stark.

"That we have made a thing," said Ashton, but neither looked at him, instead finding the floor intensely interesting.

"Show him," said Barlay, "if you cannot bring yourselves to speak to him." Stark nodded and Joron saw she held a roll of black material. Ashton took one end and they began to unroll it until he saw they had made a pennant. A long, thin triangle of black material. Embroidered upon it was the winding body of a keyshan, tail at the thin end of the flag and head at the thick end. Over one of the keyshan's many eyes there was a patch and on the patch an eye was picked out in tiny pearls, just like on Meas's own patch. At first, Joron could not speak, he only stared. Then he knelt to run his hand along the material.

"We made one for each spine," said Stark. "On the other ships too, childer 'ave been doing the same."

Joron leaned back on his heels. "How many know about this?"

"Only those involved in the making of 'em," said Barlay. "Will you ask the shipwife if we can put 'em up?" Joron stared at the flag, thinking.

"No," he said. The two deckchilder looked crestfallen.

"Have we done wrong?" said Barlay.

"Not at all," said Joron. "Take them to the tops, and be ready for my order. I will send word to the other ships on the next messenger boat." He smiled beneath his mask and then laughed to himself. "Even the greatest shipwife who ever lived can enjoy a surprise on occasion, ey?"

Back on the deck, he wandered to the rear where Meas stood, staring out over a grey and choppy sea at the three ships which had broken away from her fleet. As he stood by her she gave no sign that she had noticed him, though of course she had. A moment later she passed him her nearglass.

"Three points to seaward off the rump," she said quietly. He lifted the nearglass to his eye, a circle of sea. He steadied himself, got used to the rise and fall of the ship before scanning along the horizon. Finding the main body of Karrad's fleet, trying not to think about how many ships he saw there. No sign of the *Dread*. Then he moved the circle again, altering focus to keep the horizon a clear line and found three ships – the mighty *Arakeesian Dread*, a tower of billowing white wings, and a pair of two-ribbers.

"He moves to stop their escape," said Joron.

"Ey," she said, staring across the water. "So, they do wish us to remain on this course."

"It could simply be he wants us out of Hundred Isles waters," he said, though with little commitment.

"Is that what you really think?" she said.

He shook his head.

"No."

"Exactly. I feel more and more sure every day that Karrad expects us to turn up and find Namwen's Pass closed to us."

"Do we steer away?" She shook her head.

"No, as we said, who knows which of us Tenbern Aileen will decide to cross." She stared at him. "A man who can raise keyshans is a formidable enemy, Joron. We should not presume that just because Karrad thinks a thing, then that thing will be. Maybe Aileen is drawing him further out, not us." She turned so she was looking toward the beak of *Tide Child*. "No sign of Brekir yet."

"No," said Joron, and he felt something within him wilt like gion in the dying season.

"Still, it is early to expect her, it'll be tomorrow morning before I ask the topboys to keep an eye out for *Snarltooth*."

"And if the pass is closed?" he said.

"Well, then it becomes about desperate choices, Deckkeeper," she squinted into the distance, "and we will make those desperate choices." He nodded and passed her the nearglass back. "Signal Coult, tell him to return to his station. We know what we need to know now. Remain on a course to the northeast along the spine."

"At least the weather is relatively fine," he said. She turned to him, grinned.

"For a day trip, ey, Deckkeeper. A fog, or a howling gale with poor visibility would suit us better." Meas touched the rim of her hat with a bent finger. She looked tired. "I will be in my cabin."

For the next four days the weather stayed fine and *Tide Child*, together with the black fleet, made good progress, though there was no sign of Brekir and *Snarltooth*. Little changed on board ship apart from a growing feeling of dread as even the most intractably minded deckchild began to realise this was not normal, that the enemy fleet shadowing their movements signalled something, and not something good. That they should have sighted Brekir and they had not. The *Arakeesian Dread* and his consorts chose not to return to the main fleet, instead they held station further out from Skearith's Spine; in sight, but apart from their fellows.

"Fallen out, do you think?" said Joron one evening. Meas shook her head and took out her nearglass, raising it to her eye.

"No, they are putting themselves in a good position, tactically, in case we try and break out that way when we get to Namwen's Pass."

"Three ships cannot hold us all," he said.

"You have never seen the *Dread* loose his entire weight of shot," said Meas quietly.

"No," he said, and he was glad of that. Twenty gallowbows a side on the *Dread*'s maindeck, and he did not want to ask how many below, though he knew it had three decks of bowpeeks. *Tide Child*, he felt sure, could weather at least one broadside, the smaller ships he was not sure about, and the brownbones, well, they were not designed for fighting. "I imagine it is terrible," he said eventually.

"Nothing we have can stand against it, Joron," she lowered the nearglass. "One broadside will leave even *Tide Child* a smoking wreck in the water. It will rip every wing from our spars. I have seen it," she glanced at him, "I have even commanded it done, when I was deckkeeper aboard him."

"There will be a way, Meas," he said. "There is always a way."

"Is there," she said, and straightened up. "Maybe there is, ey?" She put her nearglass away and set her two-tail a little harder on her head. "I have a job that requires a little delicacy, Joron," she said. "I would have you talk with Farys. I want her to leave *Tide Child*, and for her and the babe to go aboard one of our brownbones."

"She is our deckholder," he said, affronted that Meas should send away his own picked officer. "The child has not made her any less quick-witted or fierce or—"

"I want them to survive, Joron," said Meas, and she sounded so tired, so worn down. "That is all. I want them to survive.

With all the death visited on Bernshulme, Karrad would be a fool to throw every civilian with us into his vats for hiyl, and he is not a fool. If we lose he will take the brownbones unscathed I am sure. Farys is a capable deckchild, she will find a way for her and young Muffaz to survive."

"She will think this punishment," he said.

"And that is why I cannot tell her," said Meas. "You must." She leaned in close. "And more than this, those brownbone shipwives are still only that, they are not fleet. She *is* fleet; I will send a letter with her that, when it comes to it, puts the brownbones under her command."

"She will still not like it," he said.

"When has what we like mattered?" Meas shrugged. "That is not the way, Deckkeeper, we work for the good of all." He nodded and stepped back. "Joron," she said. He turned. "The Gullaime as well. A warship is no place for children."

"Without her, I cannot . . ."

"I will send you to her, if that is what is needed." He nodded.

"Shipwife," he said with a smile, "I can order Farys to do as you say. But the Gullaime will do what she wishes, as we both know." Meas gave him a nod.

"Ey, well, do your best. I grew up without a mother. I would not wish it on anyone else."

Later, once he had finished his duties, he went down into the underdeck. First to visit the Gullaime who sat upon her nest, imperious as any Bern.

"What want?" she croaked as he entered.

"The shipwife," he said, "is worried for your safety and that of Shorn. She has given orders that you leave—"

"Not leave!" squawked the Gullaime, and she shuffled upon her nest, raised her beak toward the overbones. "Too important," she said haughtily. "Too important."

"Then maybe Shorn should go over to—" And the Gullaime let out such a screech so loud and piercing that Joron had to cover his ears. "There are people on the other ships who would—"

"People?" she squawked, standing up from her nest, eyes open wide, body angled for outrage.

"Not people," said Joron quickly, "other gullaime and—"

"Other!" screeched the Gullaime and this gave rise to such a squawking and hissing and snapping and biting and throwing of things that Joron was left with no option but to retreat from the nest cabin, glad he had escaped without being bloodied. Even once he had left the noise from within continued.

He decided it best to leave the Gullaime and to find Farys. It had been days since he had seen her in anything but passing on the deck. She and little Muffaz were in the d'older's cabin, the smallest of all. He had offered her his own but she would not take it. Joron knocked before entering. Found Farys nursing the child and felt he should not be there, for to feed a child was sacred to the Maiden and men had no part in it.

"Come in, Deckkeeper," she said. Then, as he slipped in through the door, she removed little Muffaz, who was fast asleep, from her breast and laid the child in her bed. "She feeds so much," said Farys, "I believe she will become the size of her namesake."

"A strong body never held anyone back in the Hundred Isles," he said.

"No," said Farys. "When this is all over, when we follow Meas's new ways, she will be a shipwife one day."

"She will," said Joron. He sat by her as she watched the child sleep.

"You can touch her," said Farys, "I am not worried she will catch the rot from you."

"I am," he said. "And I come with hard news."

"Meas is sending me away," said Farys.

"Not as punishment," he said, hurrying the words out, surprised she had pre-empted what he had come to say. Though he should not have been. She had always been a clever one.

"No," said Farys, "I understand what the babe means to those aboard. If they think us safe they will fight harder."

"Meas will give you command of the brownbones, if it comes

to battle. But if we lose, she feels sure Karrad will want as many people as he can get, since Bernshulme is sorely lacking in them now. She wants you and the child to be safe." Farys looked up at him, the scarred skin of her face twisting her mouth.

"Without Meas, we will never be safe," said Farys quietly. "And I cannot shake the feeling, D'keeper, that the shipwife is getting ready to die." She could not look at him, instead turning to the child. "She is perfect, my little Muffaz, not a blemish or spot upon her." Then she turned back to him. "We must not lose. For you know what they do to the first perfect child of a woman. They will take her for the ships. They will pretend I, a rough deckchilder, am somehow welcome among the Bern, and quietly vanish me. Though I will not care; if they take my little Muffaz away I will not want to live."

"We will not allow that to happen," said Joron as he stared down at the gently breathing babe. "I will give my last breath if I have to, Farys, but I will not allow it." She stood. Put her hand on his arm.

"I know," she said. "You are a good man. You have always been good to me. And you must make sure that the shipwife never loses hope." He nodded, unable to speak. "Thank you," said Farys. "Now, I must pack." He nodded and left, wondering if he would ever see her again. Wondering if you could grieve for the loss of someone who still lived.

52

The Tightening of the Noose

They spent the rest of the morning watching Coult's *Sharp Sither*, *Last Light* and *Waveturner* bringing themselves back into formation.

"The *Dread* still isn't moving back," said Meas, peering through her nearglass.

"If there was any doubt they were herding us it is gone now," said Joron.

"Ey," said Meas, then she turned to Barlay. "Send a signal, to Coult, Turrimore and Adrantchi. I wish to speak with them." The signals were sent, and *Tide Child* slowed his speed through the water to pick up the flukeboats of the other shipwives. There was no meal prepared, no hurrying of the shipwives down to her cabin; Meas met them on deck with all her crew at their jobs and *Tide Child* cutting smartly through the water.

"You wanted us and we come, Shipmother." Coult's metal tooth glinted in the light.

"Ey," said Meas, "though I bring no joy to this meeting."

"It is about the *Dread*," said Turrimore.

"Ey," said Meas, "it is about the *Dread*. It sits out there to cut off our escape should we be barred from the Gaunt Islands.

I hope we are not, but if that is the case then we will have to pass him."

"You need ships to take him on," said Coult. "We have nothing big enough to . . ."

"It is suicide to take even *Tide Child* against him," said Turrimore, "madness."

"And yet," said Meas, "it must be done. I hope it does not come to it. But if it does the *Dread*'s broadside must be kept from our brownbones, so our people stand a chance of getting in among the islands and what shelter can be found there."

"And what then?" said Adrantchi quietly. "They will not stop hunting us."

"Hit-and-run attacks from the boneships when we are among the islands," said Meas, "and Joron will raise the keyshans; hopefully in the confusion the brownbones can escape."

"From what has been said," said Turrimore, "the keyshans are like as much to be a danger to us as to Karrad's fleet."

"True," she said. "But so is a storm, and every deckchild knows a shipwife has been thankful for a storm on occasion."

"And if we escape, where do we go?" said Turrimore. Meas ignored her.

"I would lead the attack on *Arakeesian Dread*," said Adrantchi, and he rubbed his furrowed brow. There were bags under his eyes and he was sallow and ill-looking. "*Beakwyrm's Glee* is second only to *Tide Child* in size, Meas," he said, "it is no choice really, it cannot be you, so we should go up against the *Dread*."

"I am not sure," said Meas quietly, "that size will matter much when compared to the *Dread*'s weight of shot, Adrantchi." He shrugged.

"It will help, we may last a little longer than a smaller ship."

"I will go with him," said Turrimore, and even Meas could not hide her surprise; the two shipwives had never seemed to get on and yet, here they were, choosing to go together against an enemy they had little hope of prevailing against. Turrimore must have sensed the confusion and she shrugged. "I cannot have a man grasping all the glory, it would not do." Meas bowed her head, to hide a smile, to hide her pain that these shipwives and their crews were prepared to go to almost certain death for her.

"No, of course not," said Meas, and raised her head. "It would not do at all. But I do not plan for us to attack the *Dread*," she said.

"Oh?"

"No, he is best used as a fighting platform." She unrolled a sheet of parchment on which Aelerin had drawn a rough map. "Joron, if you would," she said, and he held it down on the bone rail so all could see it. "This is Barcles Bight," she said, pointing at a place between two islands. "The only place deep enough for *Tide Child* and *Beakwyrm's Glee*. They will know that, and were I in charge of the *Dread* I would place him where he has sight across the entrance, then loose at us as we enter." Coult stared at the map, nodded.

"Makes sense," said Adrantchi.

"Without Brekir, we have fighting ships. We will make a screen of them, nine ships the side nearest the *Dread*, arranged in two lines, inner one of four, outer of five. *Tide Child* and Adrantchi's *Glee* will head the lines. Turrimore, stay at the back and keep everyone in place. And though I would rather not be, I know you will insist I am on the inner line where there is more protection, so that is how it will be. We will soak up the shot for the brownbones."

"That'll be hard," said Turrimore. "He'll have range on us, but not us on him."

"It will indeed be hard," said Meas.

"We should just attack," said Adrantchi. Turrimore nodded.

"We have nothing that can puncture his hull," said Meas, "and we will not last any time at all up close against his broadside," she looked at the gathered shipwives, "but we may last long enough at range to get into the Bight, and besides, it is the brownbones we are here to protect. They contain our people. They are the priority."

"What of the other two ships?" said Coult.

"You on *Sharp Sither* and Chiver on the *Last Light*," she said, "will guard the other side of our formation from those two-ribbers. One-on-one I have no doubt you will come off best." Coult nodded. "But remember, Coult, the aim is to get the brownbones away, not to get into a protracted fight." He nodded again.

"I do not like it, I am a fighting shipwife," said Turrimore. "But I suppose it is the way it must be."

"It is," said Meas. And all nodded except Adrantchi, who continued to stare at the map. Before Meas could ask him what he was thinking, they were interrupted.

"Ship rising!" The call was magnetic, heads raised in direction of the topboy.

"Where is it, topboy?" shouted Meas, and Joron rolled up the map.

"Ahead, five points to seaward." As if attracted by these words the shipwives and Joron all made their way to the beak of *Tide Child*. Nearglasses came out and they stared at the horizon, seeing nothing yet. Time passed, then another call.

"Ships rising!"

"Say again, topboy?" said Meas.

"Ships rising, shipwife! A whole fleet of them, they are following the first ship."

"The Gaunt Islanders," said Meas, and she could not keep the relief from her voice. "I did not believe it would happen, but they have come." She turned from Joron, staring over the rump at the Hundred Isles fleet pursuing them. "They have come, Joron. I should have known Brekir would not let us down." Then she raised her voice, "They have come!" she shouted. "The Gaunt Islands fleet has come!" A ragged cheer greeted her voice. More cheers, from the ships around them as they also saw the fleet. The gathered shipwives grinning at one another. "Make best speed! Drop all the wings, catch all the wind there is!" Black wings were unfurled and *Tide Child* leapt forward, all around them the fleet was doing the same.

"Signal the rest of the fleet to keep pace with the brownbones," shouted Meas, "we will go ahead to greet Brekir." She turned, "Coult, Turrimore, Adrantchi, return to your ships."

"Ey, Shipmother," came the reply, and there was a giddiness, a joy in all of them, except Adrantchi, who looked as grey and sad as ever. Meas saw them over the side, watching her shipwives leave. As Adrantchi made to go over the rail Turrimore walked over to him, leaned in close, and said something into his ear, though what it was Joron and Meas were too far away to hear. Adrantchi said something back, also whispered, and more words were exchanged until Turrimore drew away. The two shipwives stared hard at one another and, for a moment, Joron thought they may come to blows. Then Adrantchi put out his arm and they grasped one another, hands around wrists, and Adrantchi gave the taller, darker shipwife a nod.

Well, thought Joron, *you may never be friends, but it seems at least you have found some accord.*

With that they were over the side and into their flukeboats, then Meas gave her ship full reign, eking every rock of speed out of him until Brekir's *Snarltooth* could be made out without a nearglass. Still, Joron and Meas raised theirs, to get a better look at this bringer of good fortune. Joron stared through his nearglass, hope, which had been hard to find in the last few days, burning within him.

Bless you Brekir, he thought as he stared at her ship. He was fitted for all speed, spines raked back and all his wings out. He let his nearglass drop and turned to Meas. "She can barely wait to see us," he said.

"Ey," said Meas, something thoughtful there, "a waste of her gullaime's strength though, as we are coming to her . . ." As she spoke her words tailed off. "No," she said.

"What?" A coldness ran through Joron, as if he were dipped into the icy sea. He raised his nearglass to look at *Snarltooth* again but could see nothing wrong. Just the black ship leading the Gaunt Islands fleet toward them. But, were those wings a little ragged? Were there wisps of smoke coming up from the ship? That made no sense, unless she had a fire on deck but why would that be? Why would Brekir have fires ready for hagspit bolts? And were her bows rigged? She was too far from Karrad's fleet, and too canny a shipwife to have bows strung and fire on deck for any longer than needed.

As if in answer, *Snarltooth* slewed around, bringing himself side-on to the Gaunt Islands fleet and Joron saw him loose. A full broadside of wingbolts bright with hagspit that cut into the ship leading the Gaunt Islands fleet. Smashing into the hull in small explosions of fiery liquid, one of which must have hit a wing as the cloth lit up, flame shooting up into the sky.

"No," said Meas again.

The burning ship launched at *Snarltooth*, but the black ship had better positioning, the bolts either passed through its rigging or bounced off the hull. Then Brekir loosed again, this time a devastating salvo that brought down the Gaunt Islander's mainspine. *Snarltooth* started to turn again, but not towards Meas, toward the Gaunt Island fleet which had split in two behind the stricken ship. One half steering for Meas and her fleet, the other coming line-on to *Snarltooth*.

"No," said Joron.

The first ship loosed and Joron knew that these bolts were better aimed. Fancied he heard the screaming as they passed across the decks of Brekir's ship, killing and maiming. *Snarltooth* loosed again. Not as many bolts flew this time. Then the second ship in the line was loosing and now Meas was running down her deck.

"North," she shouted, "steer us north! We are betrayed! Steer for the islands! Make signals to the fleet to follow!"

"I don't understand," said Joron, his mind frozen, mired in shock. "Why did she attack them? Why would Brekir, of all people, betray us?" He was numb, not thinking straight. *Tide Child* started to turn, a hard turn, throwing up a wave. Joron stumbled, unprepared for the manoeuvre, almost dropping his nearglass. He raised it again, saw another broadside hit

Snarltooth, this one almost certainly fatal as the rumpspine came down in a sheet of flame and the ship appeared to have lost steerage, was slowing, drifting away from the line of ships attacking. But their attack was relentless, the ships at the start of the line had come about, and were loosing directly down *Snarltooth*'s deck as they passed. The most devastating way to loose on a ship, bolts passing the whole length of it, the carnage aboard would be terrible, total. "I don't understand," he said again. "Why would Brekir betray us?" He lowered the near-glass.

"She would not," said Meas, once more by his side and she looked close to tears. He saw her swallow her grief, bite down on it and force the mask of shipwife back on. "The Gaunt Islanders have."

"Then why did she not simply run?"

"Because she had to warn us, Joron," said Meas. "She waited until she knew we could see her, and then she sacrificed herself to give us enough warning that we may have a chance for escape."

"I had thought—" began Joron.

"We go north," said Meas, forcefully. "And we must face the *Arakeesian Dread*'s broadside." He could not speak. Only a moment ago it had felt like this was all over. They were saved. "Get a grip, Deckkeeper," hissed Meas, "the crew are watching." And that was enough. He nodded, lifted his nearglass once more and found *Snarltooth*, the ship alight, his spine broken and the rump slowly sinking beneath the waves while his enemies, remorselessly, continued to loose upon him.

"Hag accept you, Brekir," he said, "and all yours." He turned, saw the *Arakeesian Dread* where it had come to a stop, ready to protect Barcles Bight with its terrifying weight of shot. "Though we may see each other again soon enough."

53

A Day of Dread

She stood on the deck of *Tide Child* before her gathered crew, women and men on deck, gullaime perched in the rigging. Joron on one side, Aelerin on the other, two fleets closing on them.

"I give us hours," she said, "before we must fight for our lives. And make no mistake, it is a fight for our lives. Nothing more and nothing less. I have sent written orders to the other ships, but you are my crew, and you deserve to hear this from me." There was general mutter and agreement among the deckchilder that this was a most officerly thing to do. "We head due north, to Barcles Bight. The pursuing fleets cannot catch us before we are there, and once through the bight there are many islands, small and big. The channels are too shallow for their biggest ships, so the odds will suit us better."

"Hit-and-run attacks, we know 'em well from our Black Pirate days," said Barlay.

"Ey," said Meas. She looked over the gathered crew. "And what you have been told, what you think may be? Well, it is true, the deckkeeper and the Gullaime can call the keyshans. And this they will do."

"We cannot lose with the sea dragons on our side!" was shouted from the crowd but Meas raised her hands.

"I warn you, my deckchilder, not to make the mistake of thinking the keyshans are on our side. They are huge and fearsome and we are as nothing to them. They will sow confusion among our enemies, but they will not fight for us. Do not expect it. Our advantage lies in that we know they will be coming."

"What of the *Arakeesian Dread*?" shouted another.

"We have a plan for him, don't you worry."

"Good," shouted Cwell. "I've not liked all this running, could do with a fight." To this was a chorus of "ey"s and laughter. Meas stepped forward.

"Many of you," she said, "do not really know me." She braced her hands on the rail of the rump, looked over the deckchilder, human, windshorn and windtalker alike. "And I do not know many of you as well as I should. But Joron picked you. And I trust him to have picked the best. And I have seen how you run this ship, so I know you are the best." She smiled, met as many of their gazes as she could and Joron knew that with that simple sentence, she had every single one of them on her side. "What is coming is hard," she shouted. "What we must weather will be hard. But we will weather it. And there is no finer and greater crew afloat, no group of woman and men," she looked into the rigging, "and gullaime, I would rather weather it with, ey?"

"Ey!" came the reply. Loud enough to hurt Joron's ears. Then a lone voice shouted out.

"For the Maiden!"

"Ey!" the crew returned.

"For the Mother!"

"Ey!" the crew returned.

"For the Hag!"

"Ey!" the crew returned.

"For the Shipwife!"

"For the Shipwife!" the crew returned. With that they broke

ranks, running to their stations aboard ship, and they left Meas standing next to Joron, speechless.

"They barely know me," she said quietly. "And yet they rise whenever asked."

"They know enough," said Joron. She nodded. Swallowed.

"To your station, Deckkeeper," she said, "I would be alone a moment." He nodded, almost as overcome with emotion as she so clearly was.

Tide Child cut through the sea. The islands bracketing Barcles Bight growing, a low and hazy rough line across the horizon. Before the islands the tower of white wing that was the *Arakeesian Dread* at his seastay and the smaller towers of its consorts by him. *Beakwyrm's Glee* came alongside, behind them a line of black ships, behind *Tide Child* the same. Meas came to join Joron. Looked up into the tops. Looked down the ship at her crew, busy in the running of him.

"Are you ready, Deckkeeper?" she said.

"Almost, Shipwife," he replied and he stared up into their tower of black wings. "Topboy!" he shouted. "Flags!" And from the spinepoints of *Tide Child* long thin flags of black material were loosed, and upon them writhed the sinuous stylised form of a keyshan with an eyepatch. Then a call came from the tops.

"Keyshan flying!"

A moment later he heard the same from *Beakwyrm's Glee* as his flags were loosed. And all up and down the line, on warship and brownbone alike, they let loose their pennants and the cry of "keyshan flying!" echoed back and forth across the water

Meas stood, watching; he heard her sigh, a smile upon her face.

"This is your doing, Joron?"

"Not mine, Shipwife, this was your crew. It was all of the crews." She wiped at her good eye, some fluke of the wind or bit of dust causing it to water no doubt. Then she stepped forward.

"We fly the keyshan flag!" she shouted, then raised her voice further. "Look to our flag, my girls and boys! And let us be as keyshans among our enemies. Let us reave and let us destroy like the force of nature we are, for you are the fleet of Lucky Meas, you fly with the Black Pirate and the witch of Keelhulme Sounding! Now, prepare to untruss your bows and get ready to serenade me with the warmoan. And you show no quarter and you show no mercy, for they will show us none. We fly for hope!" she shouted. And it was shouted back to her, the words full of energy, the women and men too. And that cry – "For hope!" – echoed across the water from every ship that streamed a keyshan as its pennant. Meas stood watching, imperious on the rump of her *Tide Child*. Then she looked over the seaward side of the ship at the Gaunt Islands fleet. Glanced over her shoulder, at the Hundred Isles fleet. Looked to landward where the *Arakeesian Dread* waited before Barcles Bight with his consorts. As Meas looked, Joron saw, and only because he knew her so well and had known her for so long, how much the last days had taken from her. Saw a barely noticeable change in her posture and her face. But she did not give in, she stood, letting the wind blow her hair and tangle it with the tails of her hat, watching her crew.

"Shipwife?" he said.

"I will be in my cabin." Walked past him, just too quickly, just too fast. Down the stair. He stood, glanced behind at Barlay on the steering oar. Turned to Aelerin, knowing something was wrong but not what.

"Go to her," said the courser. He nodded. Made his way down the ship, having to stop and talk to members of the crew. Feeling that beneath their bravado there was worry, for they were not fools. So he was glad-handing, reassuring, complimenting and making a slow way through the ship, down into the underdeck. Then he knocked on her door. Waited until he heard her voice from inside.

"One moment," she said. He waited. "Come in." He did. Found her at her desk, comfortable in its place, worn into the ruts on the floor. Her two-tail on the desk before her, her head bowed over it. "I am not fit to wear this, I should have said something better to the crew," she said without looking up.

"It was a good speech," said Joron. "Better than any I could do."

"All I did was prepare them to die," she said. "There is nowhere for us to go, Joron. I have led us to nothing but death. Flown us straight into the jaws of a trap. Such is the price for dreaming in the Hundred Isles. Our crews are good women and men, the best of them. They deserve more."

"I do not regret a moment, and neither do they," he said and she looked up at him.

"Well you should," she said. "Do not believe in the foolishness of heroic sacrifice, what use all the pain and suffering and death if it is for naught, ey?" She looked away. "I have led us on a fool's errand, and only when it is too late do I see it."

"That is not true," said Joron, shaken by her vehemence, how defeated she seemed.

"The truth is we are beaten, Joron. The *Arakeesian Dread* will—"

"You are not beaten." They turned at this voice, found the hagshand, Garriya, standing in the doorway.

"This is not your place, old woman," said Meas, the shipwife's mask back on her face.

"Right enough," she chuckled to herself and shuffled forward. "Would much rather be on land, warming these old bones in the sun. But this is where Garriya is, this is where Garriya is needed. So I tell you, Tide Child, you are not beaten."

"Do not call me that," said Meas.

"Why not? It is what you are. You are where you need to be, just as I am. Just as he is," she nodded her head at Joron, "just as the bird is as well. The people will be joined."

"I have joined Hundred and Gaunt Island fleets in the wish for my death, maybe," said Meas, "that is hardly the peace that I dreamed of." The old woman chuckled again, shuffled further forward.

"Speak to the bird," she said, "it is time for you to speak to the bird."

Meas stared at her, and before she could speak a shout went up from above: "Call the shipwife!"

"No, old woman," said Meas, and took her hat from the desk, placed it firmly on her head and it was as if she forced herself to shed all the worry and doubt as she stood. "The time for talk is over. It is time for me to go to war." She walked past the old woman and Joron to the door, calling for her deckkeeper to follow but before he could the old woman grabbed his arm.

"The Gullaime. The keyshans, you all have a part to play, Caller," she whispered urgently. "When the time comes, you must make sure she listens."

"Joron!" he heard Meas shout. "I am in need of your company!"

"Listen to what?" he said.

"When you hear the song. You will know," said Garriya, "now go, she needs you. And we need her."

54

The Last Battle

He stood next to Meas on the beak of *Tide Child*, staring out to sea. Barcles Bight, in the centre of their vision, flanked by two low islands thick with the grey weed that grew this far north. Past the bight the shadows of more islands, and Joron knew that past them was the ice, although the black and rising clouds of the Northstorm were so near this year that Joron thought the ice islands probably engulfed. Even from this distance he could make out the strobing flashes of lightning within the whirling clouds. Meas planned to skirt that monstrous storm if she had to, to use its violence to escape.

But there were other obstacles to pass first. Chief of them, the ships before Barcles Bight. The two-ribbers, *Mother's Frown* and *Tunir's Claw*, sat in the entrance to the bight, he was not overly worried about them. Coult in *Sharp Sither* and Chiver in *Last Light* should easily be their equal. It was the *Arakeesian Dread* that worried him, worried them all. The massive ship had come to a full halt, confident in its power, and waited for them to come to it. The shipwife had positioned it just as Meas had said they would, so its full broadside reached right across the bight and any ships wishing to pass must weather its weight of shot. Even *Tide Child* would be lucky to survive. At close range it would destroy them utterly. At the range they would pass – well, the damage taken by their ships would still be terrible. He looked to their own fleet and it gladdened his heart to see Meas's ships flying in such good order, nine ships in two neat lines forming a screen between the *Dread* and the brownbones. *Sharp Sither* and *Last Light* on the opposite side. All the fleet's gullaime had volunteered their services but Meas had divided them into two groups – half stayed safer on the brownbones, half on the ships with both windtalkers and windshorn scattered throughout the fleet.

"This will be hard," said Meas. She looked over her shoulder at the pursuing fleets behind, both Hundred and Gaunt Islander. "And we have no time for clever tactics, the *Dread* only needs to delay us, it need not destroy us."

"So we must not be delayed," said Joron.

"Ey," she said. The way she looked forward, he knew she was measuring distance, in her mind running through the time it would take her ships to carry out manoeuvres. "I think we can untruss the bows, Deckkeeper, it may make our crews feel a little better." She said it so calmly. Then added, "And have the signal flags put up. Maintain speed, do not tarry, and keep formation." He nodded and gave the order knowing it was their best chance, and at the same time hating that these proud fighting ships would essentially become a soak for the *Dread*'s shot, and every one of those shipwives must know they would be lucky to escape this still afloat. He did not want to think about the state those boneships would be in that did escape, no doubt some would have to be abandoned and their crews spread among what remained.

Adrantchi and the *Beakwyrm's Glee* came alongside *Tide Child*, distracting Joron. The *Glee* was the biggest of the boneships after *Tide Child*. Behind Adrantchi's ship came Turrimore in *Bloodskeer*, behind them three more black ships, each valued, important, full of people who had fought for Meas, just like the three ships that followed *Tide Child*, just like the two guarding the other side, just like the brownbones – and Joron thought them all doomed. He knew Meas hated such passivity, felt that *Tide Child* should be on the outside line, ready to take the punishment and protect his fleet, but also knew that it could not be allowed.

Now others would die in her place, and Meas would weather it, the same way she weathered being under shot, or a storm or any other situation, and he would stand by her like a deck-keeper should, ready whenever he was needed.

"How long until we are in range of the *Dread*?" he asked. Meas turned away from the huge ship.

"As the next bell rings, we will be coming into range." Joron glanced back at the boneship, three decks of bows, all the bowpeeks open. It was a magnificent thing, so white it hurt to look at him.

"He can loose a long way then."

"Ey," she said, "we'll be under shot from him for at least a quarter of a turn."

"And no way to loose back."

"No," she said, and she straightened a little, "but we will weather it."

"Do you think Karrad is aboard?"

"Undoubtedly. Come, we should be on the rump," she said, and started to stride away from him. "Hurry, Joron, when the loosing starts it would not do for *Tide Child*'s officers to die anywhere but in their proper place." She walked down the deck, inspecting the action around her as the ropes were placed across the deck, sand strewn to catch the blood, the nets put up to catch falling spars and rigging. Black Orris fluttered down to land on Meas's shoulder.

"Big arse," said the bird.

"A fine tactical summation, Orris," said Meas, and handed the bird some titbit from her pocket to which he set up a happy, noisy racket.

"Shipwife!" She turned, found Mellin, one of her newest crewmembers, pointing to landward. Turrimore's *Bloodskeer* had dropped all his wings and was moving away toward the *Arakeesian Dread*.

"What is she doing?" said Meas. Then Adrantchi's ship, *Beakwyrm's Glee*, did the same and Meas stood there, watching, and he heard her saying under her breath, "The fools, the absolute fools." Then she raised her voice. "They go to distract the *Dread*, so let us make of that what we can. Signal the other ships, be ready to drop all the wings they can and make best speed when Adrantchi and Turrimore engage." Meas could not take her eyes from the two ships, even as she gave the orders. They had come into line, heading straight for the *Arakeesian Dread*, *Bloodskeer* in front, *Beakwyrm's Glee* directly behind.

"Shipwife," said Joron, pointing for'ard, "the enemy two-ribbers have dropped their wings and are moving to engage." She tore her gaze from her own ships and turned to seaward, raised her nearglass.

"They are indeed, left it later than I would have. Sloppy."

"Coult and Chiver are moving to intercept."

"Well," said Meas, "if they consider our flank to be weak then savage old Coult and Chiver will give them a nasty shock." She scanned her nearglass along the ships. "The furthest of them is *Mother's Frown*, he has got enough of a start to make it around the front of our formation." She took a moment, making all the calculations of wind and speed and weather in her head. "The nearer, *Tunir's Claw*, may not. If we can put our fleet in between those two ships it may stop the *Dread* loosing on us for fear of hitting their own."

"May?" said Joron. Meas bit her lip and leaned in close to him.

"I think that Karrad will sacrifice anything to stop us now, even his own ships. We made him look weak when we killed Gueste and he cannot afford us to escape," she said, then raised her voice. "Make all speed we can without outpacing the brownbones! Two points to seaward if you will!" More wings fell and Joron heard the familiar crack as they filled with wind, the creak of ropes as they took the strain, and *Tide Child* groaned as his speed increased. He saw Meas reach out a hand and touch the bones of the ship. Heard her whisper, "Me too, old friend, me too." Then she turned to landward and raised her nearglass, staring intently as *Beakwyrm's Glee* and *Bloodskeer* cut through the water.

"When will they be in his range?" said Joron, watching the two ships under a sky that was clear, light blue and beautiful, touched by only a few lines of cloud that hurried northward as if eager to join the ominous black wall of the Northstorm.

The bell rang.

"They already are," said Meas, "we all are."

"But he does not loose."

"No," she brought the nearglass down, "I think he wants to make sure of them."

"What are they thinking," said Joron, "to disobey your orders?"

"Turrimore has no wish to be told what to do, never has had, and Adrantchi . . ." she let out a sigh, "I think he died the day he lost Black Ani."

"And now he throws away our second biggest ship for nothing," said Joron.

"Well, let us hope it is not for nothing." She raised the nearglass. "Let us hope they have some plan." The ships flew on, nearer and nearer, and Meas's fleet put space between them and the *Arakeesian Dread*, coming closer to the enemy two-ribbers. Joron could not take his eyes from the flight of *Bloodskeer* and *Beakwyrm's Glee*. Still, the five-ribber did not loose on them. He began to wonder if the *Dread* had some problem, if it could not loose its gallowbows, then to hope that its shipwife was undecided on the rightness of their action. Maybe they would change sides, and would not loose at all.

Then they did.

Joron had seen many ships loose. Seen the weight of shot leave the bows, heard the warmoan just before the whistle of shot cutting through the air, but he had never seen anything like the moment *Arakeesian Dread* let loose its weapons. Three decks worth of gallowbows, the top deck's bows even larger than *Tide Child*'s. The massive ship punched back in the water and a cloud of dust rose from it as the violence of its action shook the immense hull. A moment later the sound, the deep *thrumm* of the warbows and the heavy thud of over a hundred cords launching their projectiles reached them. Meas shouting.

"Down! Everyone down!" From instinct, from the long years of unthinkingly obeying the voice from the rump, everyone hit the deck. Though to Joron it seemed impossible that they should worry. They were so far from the enemy ship. Then he heard the crash of shot hitting bone echo across the water as the *Dread*'s broadside hit *Bloodskeer*. Moments later the whistling of incoming wingshot, and though he could barely believe it, something cut through the air over above him, shot splashed down in the sea around them, throwing water over *Tide Child* and his crew. Almost immediately Joron was standing again, looking around the deck for the wounded, finding none. Looking up into the wings to find a hole ripped in the mainwing.

"Such power," and he could not keep the awe from his voice. Meas did not answer, she was staring out over the side of *Tide Child*. Joron followed her gaze. Turrimore's *Bloodskeer* was a wreck – what had once been a black ship, a powerhouse of wing and weapon, was now a sad and broken thing. A cloud of bonedust surrounded the ship and his spines had been entirely ripped away. *Bloodskeer* still carried a little headway but without wings its speed was falling off and the ship was slewing to seaward. His decks were entirely clear of any life. Only the hull remained of the ship, and that was burning, alight and spewing black smoke into the air. "Hag's breath," said Joron, "they never stood a chance."

"No," said Meas, but the action was not yet over. *Beakwyrm's Glee* had taken damage, lost some of his topspines but was still carrying plenty of speed. Joron raised his nearglass, saw on the *Glee*'s deck seven gullaime crouched before the mainspine. He could make out Adrantchi on the rump, sword held aloft as he shouted orders. His crew working feverishly around him. The *Glee* swerved around the wreck of *Bloodskeer*, metal-clad beak punching through smoke and bone dust. "She sacrificed herself to get the bigger ship near, in hope Adrantchi could to do some damage," said Meas, and he noticed she was tapping a finger against her leg as she spoke, mentally counting out the passing of time so she knew how long it took the *Dread* to reload and loose again.

"Will he get near enough?" said Joron. Meas stared at the ship as it cut through the water.

"I doubt it," she said, "he may get off one broadside, but . . ." she bunched her fists in frustration. "He is a fool, Joron, he should be steering for the rudder. On a ship that size little else is vulnerable, any other damage he can cause is unlikely to be more than cosmetic."

"Unless he takes down a spine; without wings the *Dread* will be even slower," said Joron.

"He will not."

"But—"

"Watch," she said, pointing at the ship, "and be ready to hit the deck."

Beakwyrm's Glee sped onwards, cutting through the water and sending up a bright bow wave as he smashed through heaving grey sea. Then the *Arakeesian Dread* shuddered once more as he loosed his bows. Joron heard it, but this time he did not hit the floor when Meas shouted, and neither did she. Instead they remained standing, watching as the full violence of the five-ribber was unleashed upon Adrantchi's ship. They saw the wings and spines torn away, bodies flying from the deck, bone dust coming up in clouds. Saw filthy blossoms of flame and smoke as wingshot treated with hagspit smashed into the hull. Then more shot whistled overhead, none hitting *Tide Child* this time, but *Beakwyrm's Glee* was finished, little more than a floating wreck.

"The fool," said Meas.

"But brave," said Joron.

"No, they achieved nothing," said Meas, "fools."

Beakwyrm's Glee drifted on even though he was dead, his speed carrying him until the ship was almost against the hull of the *Arakeesian Dread*. Joron could hear the big ship's crew shouting and jeering.

"Do you think Adrantchi meant to ram them?"

"If so it would have smashed his ships to pieces, and—"

Her words were torn from her mouth by a roar so loud it drowned all noise out, filled the air, shook the sea and the wings of *Tide Child*, forced Joron and Meas to grab on to the bonerail to maintain balance. Over the sea *Beakwyrm's Glee* was no more, instead a huge tower of black smoke rose into the air, obscuring the *Arakeesian Dread*. "Hag's tits," said Meas, "he blew himself up!"

"Is it gone?" said Joron. He found he was fighting for breath, his body flooded with the energy that fear brought. Before Meas spoke his question was answered. The wind grabbed the smoke and blew it from the site of the explosion – *Beakwyrm's Glee* was gone, nothing of it remained but a slow rain of bone shards and drifting smoke. The *Dread* was blackened, its whole side no longer white. All its wings had been ripped away by the explosion. Meas raised her nearglass and stared at the bigger ship.

"He's wounded but not dead," she said, "lost most of his bows on this side, plenty of his spars down and many dead. I can see fires but they're already working on putting them out." Then she lowered the nearglass. "Joron, I take back what I said of Adrantchi and Turrimore. They gave their lives and have bought us what we need most, time." Then she raised her voice.

"Get me the Gullaime up here!" she shouted. "Message flags up. We need all the speed we can muster on every ship, and Hag take all worry of us damaging them." The Gullaime swiftly appeared, their gullaime, in all her finery, and with five of those who had been Madorra's acolytes following in their simple white robes. Immediately their Gullaime yarked and called and sounded and the wind came, hurting Joron's ears, and once she had brought the wind she relaxed and her fellows maintained what she had brought. While they did the Gullaime danced up and down the deck, flinging her wings up into the air and letting the wind whip her robes around her.

"Jor-on Twi-ner, Jor-on Twi-ner," she called, and as she danced, Black Orris flew around her head, crowing and swearing and swearing and crowing.

"String the bows!" shouted Meas, pointing forward at the second of the two enemy ships before them. "While the *Dread* licks his wounds we will deal with *Tunir's Claw* and Coult and Chiver will do for *Mother's Frown*. Then we are away into the bight and safe!" And the bows were strung and Meas stood on the rear of the ship, staring down her deck at her crew and the rapidly approaching two-ribbers. "Wait," shouted Meas, "we've no time for pretty manoeuvres and fighting, but I want *Tunir's Claw* out of the way of my fleet. Change of plan! Truss the bows. All my deckchilder, get out of the spines, and get below. I only want those on deck who must be here!" Then she turned to Joron and grinned. "Gullaime," she shouted, "bring me a gale! Give me ramming speed!"

"Shipwife," said Joron, "if we ram that ship we may end up tangled up with it, it will save us no time."

"I am fully aware of the downside of such a tactic, Deckkeeper," she said, standing taller on the rump. "Barlay, aim for the rear of *Tunir's Claw*. Let's try and take his rudder off, if we can rip the entire rump off him then all the better. Seaguard, get crossbows and wait below in case they board us. Bearna!" she shouted as the topboy jumped from the bottom of the mainspine. "I want a crew ready with boarding axes in case we need to cut ourselves free. You will lead them."

"Ey, shipwife," shouted Bearna and ran grinning, to arm herself and pick a crew.

Meas grinned at Joron, and it was a something fierce to see. With her one eye and her scarred face and her sparkling cloak of feathers she had never looked more the pirate. "He'll be loosing right down our decks as we approach, my girls and boys," she shouted, "so it'll be rough for us, but you mark my words, we'll bite back far harder than he ever could, so be ready. Gullaime!" she added. "Come to me, Gullaime!" The windtalker came, still dancing and pirouetting around the deck.

"What ship woman want?"

"That ship," she pointed forward, "it'll be loosing something fierce at us as we approach, take you and yours below." The Gullaime yarked and danced.

"Yes yes yes," she said and danced away. As she did, Meas raised her voice.

"Gullaime!" she said.

"Yes yes?"

"Your child, she is safe?" The Gullaime cried out and danced in a circle.

"Safe safe. With hag in hagbower. Safe."

"Good," said Meas, "and Gullaime?"

"What what? Busy busy."

"Thank you for staying." The windtalker nodded, then seemed to deflate a little.

"Must be here," she said, and then danced away, but this time the dance was slower and more stately, somehow sad. Meas stared after her, as if confused, then looked to Joron.

"I will never understand that bird," she said, "but now we must concentrate on the job at hand." She raised her voice. "Out of the rigging anyone left in it, my girls and my boys, get below if you have no place on deck. We'll take some punishment before this is over!"

"Are you sure about this, Shipwife?" said Joron as they stood on the rump. "*Tide Child* has been through much, can he survive ramming another ship?" She stared at him, then turned to look behind them at the gathered fleets of two nations bearing down on them.

"I am touched, Joron," she said in a brittle whisper, "that you think it matters." He did not know how to reply, did not understand for a moment what she was saying and then he grabbed her in anger, his face near hers, his hands on her upper arms in a way that a deckkeeper should never touch their shipwife. The words came into his mouth, at a volume only for her.

"You have given up?" and he hissed the words, his fury and his fear coming through gritted teeth. She stared back, and in that one good eye he saw desolation, tiredness, disappointment, pain – a world of loss. Then it was gone, back was the shipwife, the hardness.

"Take your hands off me, Deckkeeper," she said. "Or I'll forget all I said and have you corded in front of the whole crew like a common deckchild." He kept her gaze a moment longer, simply to ensure that she was back, his shipwife.

"Of course," he said, and let go, stepped back.

"Now," she straightened her jacket, "eyes on the prize, my girls and boys. Eyes on the prize." She stared forward, at the rapidly approaching ship. "Barlay," shouted Meas, "keep us on course," and she was full of life once more, grinning at the world. "Brace yourself, Joron!"

55

The Bight

A moment of extreme violence.

Joron had seen *Tide Child*'s ram used before, but only on much smaller ships such as flukeboats, he had never thought to use it against another boneship. Never considered the risk to his own ship worth it. But here, now, in this second, Meas did and he followed her orders. To seaward of them, *Sharp Sither* and *Last Light* engaged *Mother's Frown*, shot flying back and forth as the gallowbows worked and a quick glance told Joron it would be a short battle; the black ships had surrounded the Hundred Isles one, and were loosing almost twice as fast. Blood already streaked its hull.

He turned back to their quarry, *Tunir's Claw*. He was big for a two-ribber, not as big as Adrantchi's *Beakwyrm's Glee* had been, but big enough that Joron knew he was an older ship, and the blinking corpselights above told of one not in the greatest condition. He hated this moment, this final speeding into battle, only moments from when the first shots would be loosed by *Tunir's Claw*, and *Tide Child*, coming head-on at him, would be unable to answer. They would have to weather the storm. Then would come the collision and he could barely imagine what that would be like, barely think why Meas chose this course of action. He knew what she would say, that she feared losing time, or feared that *Tunir's Claw* would ignore any attack with gallowbows and get through to the brownbones. They were valid concerns, but they did not ring true, not that it mattered. She had set the course and her word was law.

And something in him relished the idea too. The violence of it, the immense physicality of the attack, their ship against the enemy, the might of *Tide Child*'s ram against the hard hull of *Tunir's Claw*. He glanced at Meas, watched, all her concentration on the approaching ship. Knowing that timing was all.

"A touch to landward, Barlay," she said, "then tie the steering oar off." The big woman followed her shipwife's order, leaned into the oar and set it with knot. Meas raised her nearglass, watched the other ship. Time ticked by until she shouted "Down! Everyone flat on the deck!" Joron threw himself to the slate, knowing how close Meas liked to cut it. A moment later the whistle of shot, the crash of bolts hitting the hull, the rip of wingcloth being torn and a scream from somewhere on the ship. When the shot had passed Joron jumped up, not as fast as Meas, never as fast as Meas, and though he could blame his missing leg he knew it was not so.

"Someone get that man to Garriya," she shouted, pointing at a deckchild writhing on the deck, a shard of bone sticking out of his leg. "The heart is pumping now, ey, Joron?" she said, pushing the two-tail harder onto her head. "They'll hit us twice more before we hit them." Joron stared at the rapidly growing ship, saw it was slowing. "They think we will slow to turn and deliver a broadside," said Meas. "So they slow to loose better down our body, thinking to hit us hard. Well," she took a step forward, "we will see who is hardest hit."

"We'll make them regret every shot," said Joron.

"Ey, that we will. Barlay, cut that knot, another point to landward and tie it off again," said Meas and he felt *Tide Child* turn a little. Watched as the figures on the deck of *Tunir's Claw* crowded around the gallowbows, stepped back to avoid the loosing arms.

"Down!" shouted Meas and again, the repetition: the whistle of shot, the crash of bolts hitting the hull, the rip of wingcloth being torn and a scream from somewhere further down the deck. When the shot had passed Joron jumped up, not as fast as Meas, never as fast as Meas.

"Not long," said Meas. And Joron saw the moment the shipwife of *Tunir's Claw* realised they had made an error, that they had misjudged their enemy's tactics. The shipwife was shouting, pointing at the wings, telling the crew to get up and loose more cloth. A mistake, Joron thought, the collision was inevitable now, the ship could not move far enough or quickly enough, the man should have concentrated on putting bolts into *Tide Child*. Instead he simply muddied his message, divided his women and men, and the third round of shot never came. *Tide Child* sped on, if anything increasing in speed in the final moments. Skidding over the waves, smashing through the water. "Brace!" shouted Meas. "Brace!" and they wrapped their arms around the rumpspine. In every place above and below-deck crew were finding something to hang on to.

Then the impact.

A moment of extreme violence.

The ship under stress, making a noise like some massive, wounded animal, like nothing he'd heard from *Tide Child* before. The air full of the sound of rending bone. Joron's arms almost torn from their sockets by the sudden cessation of movement. The crashing of rigging coming down. The screaming of the hurt below and above deck. Dust, grey-white bone dust everywhere, great rising clouds of it. Choking him, making him cough. Meas coughing too, he saw her spit. Wipe at the dust that made her face pale as any boneship.

"Seaguard for'ard!" she shouted, then she was doubled over by another fit of coughing.

"Seaguard to for'ard," shouted Joron, "they'll be sure to try and board us." The ship gave another titanic groan and shuddered, Joron staggering as he tried to stand. To seaward their fleet was passing, the black ships escorting the two unwieldy brownbones. Further out he saw Coult's *Sharp Sither* turning to come back. The Hundred Isles ship *Mother's Frown* a wreck, and behind it Chiver's ship, *Last Light*, was ablaze. Joron could see flukeboats leaving *Last Light*, rowing for *Sharp Sither*.

His gaze pulled for'ard as seaguard and crew ran past him toward *Tide Child's* beak. Then he was running toward the front of the ship, coughing on the settling bone dust. As he ran his eye was drawn by a tangled web of rigging and wing-cloth – the tops of *Tide Child's* for'ard and mainspine had come down.

"Someone get aloft and cut loose those spines!" he shouted. Women and men started to come over the beak of *Tide Child*, some bloodied, some not, all furious, all knowing their own ship was fatally wounded and eager to avenge it; all knowing that taking the black four-ribber was the only way to escape their own sinking vessel.

"Seaguard!" shouted Meas as she ran down the deck, sword aloft. "To your bows!" The seaguard knelt on the deck and sent a volley of crossbow bolts into the boarders, but as quickly as they fell more came. Another volley of bolts and then the short space between the two crews was crossed and the fighting was joined. Women and men, screaming, swearing, shouting. Joron running down the deck to join them, something in him singing, glad to be in in the fray and the fury. The sweat, the anger, the panic. Blade from seaward, block and dodge. Thrust at a body, feel the hit. Keep moving, trust to the crew to protect you. Trust to Cwell, behind him with her quick knives, to protect him. All around screaming, crying, begging, blood on the deck. Blood on his face. Hot bodies. Arm tiring. Can't stop. Mustn't stop. He saw Meas, face contorted as she beat at a man with her sword, all fury, no skill. Saw Barlay, swinging a boarding axe, protecting the shipwife. Saw Cwell forcing a knife into a woman's throat. Even Aelerin fought, face distorted with fury as they crashed a gaff down on a woman's head. Each of these people he knew, frozen for a moment in their anger and hatred and desperation.

And it was desperate.

Kill or be killed.

It was also freeing, to not think about the future. Not worry about where to go, when to go, how to command.

Kill or be killed.

Be killed or kill.

Only existing in the now.

And then it was over. Breathing hard, leaning over. Exhausted. Bodies all around. The ship creaking alarmingly, leaning at a strange angle.

"Get these corpses off my deck!" Meas, still full of energy. "Bring up wyrmpikes, get *Tide Child* free of their ship!" Joron, breathing hard, looked at *Tunir's Claw*. The smaller ship was listing heavily, the spars holding the wings had been broken by the impact and the for'ard of its two spines had collapsed completely, the ropes between it and the rumpspine stretched so taut they sang in the wind. With a groan *Tunir's Claw* leaned over further. "We need to get loose or we'll tangle their spines with ours!" shouted Meas. Joron looked over the rail. *Tide Child*'s beak had ruptured the hull of *Tunir's Claw* at the rear, punching into it and creating the hole that was causing it to list.

"He's sinking!" shouted Joron. "Barlay, take a crew and get on his pumps!" All was action, deckchilder pouring over the side and onto the smaller ship.

"Cut us loose!" shouted Meas. "Cut us loose or he'll take us down with him!"

While all was action and desperation on *Tide Child* the rest of their fleet passed serenely by, wings filled with wind. Deckchilder lined the rail of *Tide Child*, using heavy wyrmpikes to push against the hull of *Tunir's Claw* in an effort to free their ship.

"Hurry," shouted Meas, "put your backs into it or we'll have two whole fleets on us!" Joron glanced over his shoulder and saw the sea thick with enemy boneships, wings full of wind. It looked like they were pushing their gullaime hard.

He grabbed a wyrmpike, added his weight to all of those straining at the rail. With another groan *Tunir's Claw*'s rump sank further into the sea, dragging the beak of *Tide Child* under the water, making the deck slope dangerously. "Hag curse you all," shouted Meas, "push! Push you slatelayers or we'll be dragged down to the Hag!" Her words were what was needed, or maybe it was that the movement of *Tunir's Claw* had loosened something within the ship, or maybe the Hag smiled on them as at that moment *Tide Child* came loose, the long, metal-tipped beak pulling out of the stricken ship, ripping away bone and deck as it came. "Barlay! shouted Meas. "Get back on board!" *Tide Child* started to move, creaking and groaning as his hull scratched along the rump of *Tunir's Claw*, the spines and spikes of his side ripping away, sending shards of bone shooting across the deck, one cutting Meas's cheek. She ignored the blood, was too intent on Barlay and her small crew as they ran along the deck of *Tunir's Claw*, jumping from the ship's rump onto the hull of *Tide Child*, and then they were away. Flying toward Barcles Bight. Gullaime being called to add wind to their wings and help them catch up with their own fleet while the enemy bore down on them.

"What next?" said Joron as they entered the channel between two islands.

"Next?" said Meas, and she turned to look at the pursuing fleet. Her cheeks red with exertion, a huge smile on her bloodied face. "Well, that will be up to you and the keyshans."

56

The Broken

They flew on, through Barcles Bight, and it became clear to Joron that *Tide Child* was a broken ship. The tops of his spines gone, cut away after the collision with *Tunir's Claw*, and Joron could tell from the way he rode the waves, the way he creaked and groaned as he moved through the water, that something deep within the ship had cracked, something Joron felt sure was terminal. Something there was no coming back from.

But there was no coming back for any of them. Islands rose around them, two fleets pursued them and his shipwife had no plan of escape, no way out. Yet those around him remained confident — Barlay and Bearna and Gavith and Fogle had no doubt that Meas would see them right, that she had some clever scheme, and all those that flew with her would see themselves safe.

But he knew the truth. He would sing up the keyshans and they would hope that caused chaos for their enemies. They would skirt the Northstorm, and hope that *Tide Child*, battered and broken and limping *Tide Child*, would survive it better than those gleaming, fresh-to-the-fight boneships that pursued them.

He let out a deep breath, catching it before it turned into a sob.

"When do you sing, D'keeper?" said Barlay from her place at the oar. "When do them keyshans come to help?"

"When the shipwife commands it."

"Why wait?" said Barlay, a smile across her weathered face, "sooner them Hag-cursed ships there are eaten the better for us."

"I think Meas wants as much of their fleets drawn into the islands as possible." The cloud of his breath hung before him for a moment before it was whipped away by the cold wind.

"Joron Twiner." His name, said so softly he barely heard it. Then it came again, "Joron Twiner." He turned, found the Gullaime crouching on the deck in her fine robe which puddled around her like a shadow. Within the dark feathers of her shoulders Joron could see a second pair of eyes looking out at him.

"Yes, Gullaime?"

"Need talk," she said, but she did not orientate her face to him, and he wondered why, when all knew her secret, she was wearing her mask once more. "Need talk," she said again.

"I am always happy to talk to you," he said. Then stepped closer. "We should find some way to get you off this ship, you and Shorn," he said, pointing at the bright eyes nestling in her feathers. "It is not safe here for a child."

"Is my place," said the Gullaime, sadly. "Be here. Talk you. Talk ship woman." Then she looked up. "Keep Shorn safe? You worry?"

"Of course."

"Must stay," said the Gullaime, he had to concentrate to hear her. "My place."

"You need not," said Joron gently. "Meas sent Farys away with her child, I have told you, she would do the same for you."

"No no. Must stay," said the Gullaime again. "My place." It reached up with its wingclaw and pulled on Joron's arm.

"Come, come. Talk ship woman. Talk you. Come." It pulled him on, softly but insistently.

"Barlay," he shouted, "you have the deck!" Then he made his way down through the creaking, crying, moaning ship, out of the cold crisp air of the day, and into the cold dark damp of the underdeck. He knocked on Meas's door, the Gullaime behind him, shifting from side to side in the shadows.

"Come," she said. When he entered he found her standing with her back to him, staring out the window at the looming white ships. Aelerin sat at Meas's desk looking over charts. The shipwife held a nearglass to her eye with one hand, the other rested on the hilt of her straightsword, and the fishskin that wrapped her body glittered in the light. The great glass windows of *Tide Child* were cracked, a million pathways that showed the stress the great ship had put himself through at her command. "They split their fleet," she said. "Into thirds, one follows us the *Dread* led one going north-west, the other heads north-west and is mostly Gaunt Islands ships. They go around the islands we fly through and will try and catch us as we come out the other side to journey along the edges of the storm. Clear seas will give them a speed advantage while we must manoeuvre round islands and be careful of shoals." She let out sigh. "It will be a close run thing but the *Dread* may head off our fleet when we turn west along the storm's edge." As he watched something splashed into the ocean behind *Tide Child*, five, maybe six shiplengths behind them. "Their smallest ships, the newest, have gallowbows mounted on the front and are loosing at us."

"When will they be in range?" said Joron.

"Before Skearith's Eye closes," she said.

"We will have caught up with our fleet by then." She turned, a frown on her face.

"We should not," she said, "even the brownbones should be outpacing us, the condition we are in." She reached out and touched the cracked glass of the window. "Our fleet is under orders not to slow for anything."

"You should know your shipwives better," said Aelerin, not looking up from the table.

"And I imagine," added Joron, "that if you try and reprimand them they will have sundry tales of all the problems that have slowed them, lost spars, ripped wings, thrown rudders . . ." She smiled at him.

"Ey," she said, "like deckchilder caught shirking, there is always a reason."

"They love you," he said. "And they trust you." She shrunk then, he saw it, she collapsed in on herself, as if all the pain of her torture was visited on her once more.

"And I have nowhere to lead them to but their deaths." Stark words, real, hard, with no pity. Only a truth spoken out into the air. She crossed to her desk and Aelerin stood. "I will have you raise the keyshans, Joron, in the hope of buying more time. Hundreds more, on both sides, will die but it will all be for naught and we know it." She sat in her chair before her desk. Aelerin stood by her. Meas took a deep breath. "We are bound for the Hag, Joron, and nothing the Mother can do can stop it, no Maiden trick can help us. I have sent poor Aelerin spare with checking over these charts," she pointed at the maps on her desk. "But there is nowhere on either side of the Spine for us to run to, our enemies are too numerous and well equipped." She looked up, her one eye sparkling. "Maybe Adrantchi and Turrimore had it right, Joron. Maybe we should turn our fleet and attack."

"You said that is a fight we cannot win."

"Ey, and nothing has changed, but the more I think on it, the more I believe the best we can hope for is a good death."

"No."

A single word spoken into the cabin. Not by Joron, but by the Gullaime behind him, sunk into the shadows.

"No, Gullaime?" said Meas. "You have a better plan?

"Windseer," she said, head bowed.

"Fire and death," said Meas, "well, maybe that is what is deserved. Maybe you are right."

"No," said the Gullaime, and she shuffled forward. "Not want."

"What then, Gullaime? Can you spirit us away to another realm? Fly us over the Northstorm to another land?"

"Not over."

"Well, what use are you then?" she said, her exasperation rising.

"Listen to the bird, Shipwife." Garriya's voice. She stood in the door, hunched over, then came forward into the room.

"The Gullaime and now you, old woman, talk at me in riddles when what I need is good advice and clear heads."

"Listen, to the bird," said Garriya. "Me and her, we have been on this journey a long time." Meas took a deep breath, let it out slowly.

"At this moment, Garriya, I will listen to anyone who can offer me hope." Joron watched, unable to talk, because as the Gullaime had spoken, and as Garriya had spoken, the song within him had started to change, not in volume or pitch, but in rhythm and stress. As if some piece of music that had been slowly moving through a reprise was now reaching a crescendo, rising toward a final resolution. The music filled him. He knew, but not how, that his voice, his broken, tortured, damaged voice, was part of this song, a final key, the thing that threw open a cage of thousands of years. Any worry he had about raising the keyshans fled. For he knew he could, and more, he felt like he should, that he must.

"Garriya is right," said Joron. "Listen to the Gullaime." Meas focused on him, and he expected an outburst, something to put him in his place but instead she simply sighed, shook her head and took off her two-tailed hat.

"Speak then, Gullaime."

"Not fly over storm," she said. Shuffling forward, the Gullaime pulled off her mask, showing the bright eyes beneath. "Not over," she said again, "go through."

"Through?" said Meas. "Have you lost what wits you have? The storms are impenetrable, the Northstorm fiercest of all. It eats ships that stray too close. I have seen ships much bigger than *Tide Child* smashed into shards by those winds, and only barely escaped alive myself."

"Yes," said the Gullaime.

"And yet you think we can go through?"

"Through door," said the Gullaime. Behind her, Garriya nodded.

"Aye," she said, "You listen now, Shipwife. 'Tis the golden door."

"What do you mean, door?" said Meas, leaning forward. "I thought it was fire and death?"

"Yes yes, fire and death open door."

"Through the storm? A door through the storm?" The Gullaime nodded, and though Meas looked amazed, shocked, a smile started on her face, just at the possibility of an escape. Joron did not smile. He felt something was wrong. Very wrong. Because he knew the Gullaime, he knew how she acted, how she displayed, how her moods and emotions were drawn large through her body, and every display of cleverness brought with it yarking and dancing and noise and joy.

But here and now, in what must be her greatest moment, in the place where she had stepped in and told them she could save them all, where she had done her most clever thing she showed no sign of joy. None at all. Her beak pointed at the floor, her shining eyes were cast down and rather than dance she simply shifted and shuffled across the scuffed white floor of the great cabin until her delicate body was pushed against Joron and he could smell and feel the desert heat of her.

"What do you need to open this door, Gullaime?" said Meas.

"Gullaime," she said, "more. Five six seven. More come maybe." Meas nodded.

"And time? How long will it take to open? How long will it take us to cross?"

"Not long, not long," said the Gullaime. "Open quick." She looked up at Joron, keeping her head down, subservient, beaten, wrong. "Sea sithers, need sea sithers."

"Joron can help you do that, can't you, Deckkeeper?" He nodded. Then looked down at the Gullaime.

"Friend," he said, "what is the price of this?" The Gullaime looked up at him, blinked slowly.

"Fire and death," it said.

"Whose death?" he asked gently. The Gullaime blinked once.

"Mine," she said.

He could not speak. Could not answer. Could not think of it. After all they had been through this could not be how it ended. He felt a hand on his back and he turned, found Garriya looking up at him, and when she spoke, it was as if she used Meas's voice. Harsh with command.

"The sentence is passed," she said, "only the day is undecided."

"There is no other way?" said Meas. Joron turned back, found her standing. Though she had resigned herself to the loss of the *Tide Child* and all his crew moments before, now she stood straight and defiant as if her command could prevent this one death. As if she could bring all souls through the storm with her word alone. "I do not wish to leave any of my crew behind." The Gullaime shuffled forward so she stood before the shipwife's desk and raised herself up so she looked straight into her face.

"No," it said. "Gullaime open door. Cannot shut."

"You can stop it, surely," she said. "You can always stop something."

"Too much," it said. "Gullaime keep going, door not shut. All dead. Fire and death for all."

"There must be another way, Gullaime," said Joron. "Your death cannot be the only way to close this door."

"Only way," said the Gullaime. "Only."

"You would give your life," said Meas, "for us?"

"Friends," said the Gullaime and she reached out with a wingclaw to touch Meas's face. "Save friends."

Meas nodded and Joron saw, to his surprise, a tear track down her face.

57

Her Final Command

Skearith's Eye was two thirds across the sky, and provided little heat this far north. Cold winds whipped the deck of *Tide Child* as he caught up with the fleet and the Northstorm drew closer, huge towers of cloud swallowing up the islands before them, the storm advancing as if drawn to the ship. Joron watched their flukeboat as it scudded over the rough sea, taking Meas's messages to the other ships of the black fleet. Behind them loomed a different kind of storm, one of the three fleets of Hundred Isles and Gaunt Islands ships. It was steadily catching them. The tight passages through the northern islets had forced their pursuers to slow and break formation, falling behind at first. But now the islands were larger and more spread out and the enemy catching up, their lead ships loosing bolts to splash just behind *Tide Child*. Somewhere out there he knew the other two enemy fleets would be coming round the islands in a pincer movement, hoping to catch them.

Meas appeared on deck, he watched her make her way up the slate and wondered at her. She showed all her scars and pain, it was clear movement was difficult for her but she did not stop. She did not let anything slow her and when she joined him she stood as straight as him, the two-tail perched on her grey hair, tails twisting in the wind. She stayed there only a moment, gave him a nod and then turned to look behind her, lifting her nearglass and watching as another bolt was loosed and splashed into the sea behind them, and though she no doubt had watched this same thing happening from the cracked windows of her cabin, when she spoke it was as if she had only just realised, of so little concern to her was this enemy fleet.

"It appears that our pursuers are almost in range, Deckkeeper," she said casually.

"It appears so, Shipwife," he said, and another wingbolt splashed into the sea behind them.

"Well," she said, and closed up her nearglass, "I think it is time for you to sing."

It was as if the world changed.

It was as if the world slowed.

It was as if the world had been waiting for Joron and he for it.

This moment had been coming for ever, and now it was here and now he was here he realised that it had always been happening, felt it within. He stood in the centre of the deck and the ship flew on, and the wind whistled and their fleet approached and the enemy pursued. He stood in the middle of the deck as the Gullaime came forward to stand by him with its companions, who made a circle around Joron and the Gullaime. The crew of *Tide Child* paused in their work, and the ship quietened its groaning, and his shipwife stood behind him, her presence as warm and sure and as comfortable as that of the Gullaime.

"Now?" he said.

"Now," said Meas.

"Now," said the Gullaime.

He thought he heard Garriya chuckle. He thought he felt himself tense against an age-old prison. He thought he heard a call, as if filtered through all the oceans of the archipelago.

"Yes," he said. "It is now."

And Joron Twiner sang a song unlike any other. It powered through him, and he felt less like a singer than a conduit, his damaged vocal cords no longer mattered for his entire body was the medium of the song, it rang through him like a bell. The Gullaime joined him, a strange and painful counterpoint, not musically painful, not off-key, not wrong, only sad, so very sad and full of such longing. The song held them, it cradled them, their ship and the people in it, and across the water more voices joined, every gullaime in the fleet, both windtalker and windshorn, joined the song. And every deck-child and d'older and deckkeeper and shipwife joined, none were able to resist. The melody, rose and rose and rose.

And stopped.

Joron fell to his knees on the deck, breathing heavily. Beside him the Gullaime similarly slumped. She turned her head to look at him.

"Sea sither, come," said the Gullaime.

It was as if someone struck a massive drum, a single booming thud that rang out over the water, loud enough to make the sea and every ship on it shift. The wave of sound hit and the crew of *Tide Child* staggered, but remained standing, though it left every deckchild stood idle as if dazed and hypnotised, like something had been pulled from them.

"Look!" said a voice.

Another reverberating crash.

"The islands!" said another.

A groan, like every pain that existed in the entire archipelago was given a voice.

Then the call, the old and storied call coming down from the tops.

"Keyshan rising!"

And again, and again, coming from the ships of their fleet and echoed by their pursuers.

"Keyshan rising!"

Meas was there, at his shoulder, lifting him up by his elbow, pointing.

To seaward, down a wide channel between islands, came the Gaunt Islands fleet. To landward he saw the rest of the Hundred Isles fleet coming out from behind an island, the giant *Arakeesian Dread* at their head, and far nearer than any of them could have wished. But those things felt, at that moment, small and unimportant.

Because the keyshans were coming.

The air was alive with the sound of rock cracking and groaning, the thunderous noise of stone shearing away from landmasses and falling into the sea. Roaring fountains of white water followed Meas's fleet as all around the ships islands were disintegrating, shattering as they gave birth to giants. This was not the same violent, difficult birth that Joron had seen when he awoke the keyshan that had lived within McLean's Rock, this was more akin to the Gullaime's child, Shorn, emerging from her egg. The islands being sloughed off by the colossal forms within as they emerged, sounding and keening and singing out their freedom as they splashed into the water.

And more came, and more and more. And not only from the islands, keyshans began breaking the surface as if called from the depths, as if they had been waiting for this moment, this music.

So many different forms and sizes and colours of creature, churning up the water. Vast, blocky heads, as long as a ship, teeth as tall as woman or man. Fiery eyes, so bright they were hard to look at, some with bodies so huge they could crush an entire fleet. Some with frills that reflected their colouring, pinks and reds and greens and purples and blacks, all shimmering and shivering, so the keyshans appearing clothed in shining stars. Some had vast horns, curling back and around from their heads, some branching antlers, some had manes of slowly waving tentacles and others were as simple and smooth as a pebble worn down by years and years of tides. In among these huge empresses of the sea were smaller keyshans, just as brightly coloured, just as strange and terrifying to look at, toothed and clawed and bright; and even the smallest of them could have smashed *Tide Child* with a careless flipper. In among them, longer thinner keyshans darted, like serpents, twisting around their siblings, spinning through the water and not one person on *Tide Child* could tear their eyes away from this host of sea dragons as they broke from where they had slept or waited for eons, filled the water with their vast bodies. Long thin beaks poking from the water.

And then they sounded, each and every one in glorious unison, and every woman and man on the deck covered their ears. The sound like a wall, a shuddering violent call that sent the crews of all the ships staggering. It came again, echoing back and forth, and as more of the keyshans emerged the sound became softer, more pleasant. Until they were singing to one another in a huge and wondrous cacophony that filled the air where Joron's song had been, just as their bodies filled the water around Meas's fleet.

The Gullaime stood, shook her head and scuttled to the beak of the ship.

"Come, come," she said and they followed. When she reached the beak of the ship she jumped from the ship's deck and stood on *Tide Child's* battered ram and began to call. All around, on the other ships of the fleet as they were tossed up and down by the waves of the keyshans' passage, gullaime were doing the same, singing out in a loud and joyous song. The keyshans answered. The great beasts around them opened their huge mouths and sounded once more. And a wind came. Wings were raised by the sea dragons to catch it and the ships of Meas's fleet were caught up in it, dragged along with them toward the towering clouds of the Northstorm at a speed like no other, behind them the ships of the pursuing fleet were also caught up. He saw one go over, the crew not quick enough to react and the wind dragged the ship into the water, only to be smashed apart by a huge red and orange head, breaking the ship in two. To seaward and landward the incoming fleets were caught in the zephyr, pulled onwards whether they wished it or not. At the same time the looming Northstorm, almost as if it noticed them, rushed toward them, a tower of lightning-thick cloud. The Gullaime finished her song and turned, climbing up the side of *Tide Child*, and as she scaled the side a keyshan's head broke the water by them, bright yellow and green. From the centre of its head lifted a huge, pale spike.

"The windspires," shouted Meas above the roaring wind, clawing hair from her face, "they are part of them." As she said it the end of the spire on the keyshan started to glow, and a similar glow appeared on the head of every keyshan that filled the sea around them, a flotilla of massive bodies with glowing lights above them.

"Must leave ship before end," said the Gullaime. "All must go. All but one. All who stay die."

"What do you mean?" shouted Joron.

"Leave," screeched the Gullaime and she danced in a circle, frustrated. "One must stay, shut door."

"You mean kill you?" said Meas, fighting to be heard over the gale. The Gullaime danced forward, then stood before her, low to the deck, before raising herself to her full height.

"Already dead," said the Gullaime, "Windseer start, already dead. Power build. This ship, us, centre. Fire and water." She blinked her glowing eyes. "Ship woman. Deckchild. Joron Twiner. All must leave but one."

"Gullaime, we—" began Joron but it interrupted.

"Not have time!" she screeched. "Look, look!" He turned, ships were closing on them from three sides, powered by the unnatural wind of the keyshans. Behind them the fleet that had followed them through the islands, to seaward a Gaunt Islands fleet and to landward, much nearer, the Hundred Isles fleet headed by the *Arakeesian Dread*. And before them, the Northstorm rushing toward them as fast as they rushed toward it. All unnatural. All strange, the light of Skearith's Eye no longer bright, but bathing them in a violet unlike any colour Joron had ever seen. A finger of dark cloud reached out from the storm toward them. "Quick quick," shouted the Gullaime and for a moment even Meas seemed frozen by the onrushing cloud, the strangeness of the light, the feeling of power that crackled through the air. Then she was moving.

"Signals! Topboy, make signal, have the nearest ship come to us." As she shouted the weather became even rougher, the Northstorm nearer. Rain started, a cold and freezing downpour. Lightning cut the air and thunder crashed.

"Brownbone coming in!"

"Farys!" shouted Joron, and it was, she had taken command of the brownbone she rode in, bringing it near to Tide Child, already flukeboats were launching from it.

"Get our boat in the water, Tide Child will need a skeleton crew! Only volunteers, mind!"

Joron felt a scratching on his arm and he turned, the Gullaime stood by him.

"Must make sure, Joron Twiner. Must close door."

"You are my friend, I cannot kill you," the words tore at him, cut deep as any wound.

"Already dead."

"What?"

"Fire and death."

"I don't understand, Gullaime."

"Only stop pain, Joron Twiner." She blinked. Touched her chest. "Power grows. Fire inside."

"What you do will hurt?" The Gullaime looked at him, and nodded, then she reached inside her robe and took out her chick, passed her to him.

"Keep safe," she said.

"But Gullaime," he began as he tucked the tiny, squawking and complaining windtalker inside his stinker coat. The Gullaime no longer listened. She was standing on the tips of her claws, and with a shake she shed her colourful robe and stood before them, naked to Joron's way of thinking. She took his breath away, took all their breath away. Along her head a raised red and black crest, and the feathers of her body were a midnight blue, shining and glinting in the strange light, festooned with diamonds of moisture. That same midnight blue ran along the edges of her wings, huge wings that she stretched out, tested with a few soft flaps. The primary flight feathers were gold and bronze and breathtaking. Behind her strong legs stretched out a great tail of feathers that seemed to wink and look at him from a million blue and green feathered eyes. The windtalker turned her head to him, those burning eyes focusing on him.

"Goodbye, Joron Twiner. Good friend," she said. Then she began to beat her wings, huge, powerful motions. It had no effect at first. She called out, and Joron felt the familiar heat and pressure in his ears of the wind coming at the Gullaime's call and she began to rise into the air, getting faster and higher and higher and faster. From the deck behind him the acolytes also shed their robes to show feathers as pure and white as ice. They too flapped their wings and rose into the air. And from ships around them came more gullaime, as if there was a call that some of them could simply not refuse. All rising, flying out to meet the finger of dark cloud from the Northstorm. *Tide Child*'s glorious, colourful gullaime led her flock and when they met the finger of cloud he heard the Gullaime, their Gullaime, call out. Heard her familiar voice and all the gullaime of the fleet answered, as did the keyshans. Such a noise as he had never heard. The glowing points of the windspires on the heads of the sea dragons became brighter. Another squall of noise and every keyshan was joined to the one behind it by a line of light. A web around the ships that focused on one keyshan, at the head of their school. The greatest of them all. A vast mountain of a creature that rose out of the water far ahead of the fleet, water cascading down its sides. Every colour Joron had ever seen flashing down its body in a constant, hypnotic rhythm. The light above its head became so bright it hurt to look at. Then that same light leapt into the sky, a direct line from the keyshans around them to this sovereign creature and from there up to where the Gullaime hung in the sky like a jewel, on the point of being swallowed by the reaching black clouds of the Northstorm.

And the clouds blew apart.

A crack of air like the thunder of a million lightning strikes at once.

Fire in the sky.

First only a point of light from where their Gullaime was, then it grew, linking all the gullaime who had taken flight and creating the outline of a huge and fiery bird in the sky. Outside of the firebird the storm raged but within was open, flat and calm sea, a sea that dragged Meas's fleet forward into it, and as *Tide Child* entered he was held, along with Farys's brownbone, as if by a great hand.

"Off!" shouted Meas. "Abandon ship!"

All was action, crew piling into boats and rowing or flying hard for Farys's brownbone as the enemy ships bore down in them, until only boat one was left, waiting for the officers. They heard a crash, and the ropes holding the boat snapped. A moment later they saw it and the small crew Farys had sent sucked away, dashed to pieces on a wave. At the same time, the brownbone took aboard the last flukeboat; Joron saw Aelerin struggle onto the deck and saw Farys, pointing at *Tide Child*. Then the brownbone swung round, the gullaime on its deck driving it toward *Tide Child*.

"No," shouted Meas, "it is too risky!" but her words were whipped away by the wind and the boat came on. Grapples were loosed, catching on to *Tide Child* and the crew of the brownbone began to pull the two ships together beneath the silhouette of the burning bird above them.

"Joron!" shouted Meas through the howling wind. "You must leave, go to the brownbone, whoever stays to finish this will be consumed by the storm or taken by the *Dread*!" She pointed behind them, the massive five-ribber closing in, undeterred by the storm or the beasts in the sea around it.

"No!" he shouted back. "I will stay, you must go!"

"I am old, Joron, you are young, go!"

"No," he said, and ripped the scarf from his face, showing her the sores and marks of the rot. "I am dying, Meas. We both know it."

"I have given you an order," she screamed it at him, "an order!" He smiled, his ruined face hurting as seawater and rain hit the sores, as his skin cracked where it had scabbed over.

"And," he shouted back, water slicking his face, "it is the deckkeeper's place to tell his shipwife when she is wrong!"

She stared at him then, it seemed for far too long, though it may only have been a second, a moment within the maelstrom.

"You are no deckkeeper," she shouted, and dashed the one tailed hat from his head. He felt shocked, hurt, insulted, but for a moment only, then huge pride welled within him as she pulled the two-tail from her head. The symbol of command she had once taken from him, by force, and she pushed it onto his head, hard, so it jammed on the soaking braids of his hair. "You are a shipwife, Joron Twiner, and you are the finest I have ever known." Words failed him, had her face not been soaked with spray and rain he would have thought her crying, had his face not been soaked with spray and rain she would have seen his tears.

"I had the best teacher," he shouted back. Then before she could speak he carried on. "Now, get off my deck, off! And take this bird with you!" He pulled Shorn from her hiding place within his jacket and the tiny gullaime squawked and yarked in fury at the insult of the cold and rain as he passed her over to Meas, who nestled the chick into her coat.

"I once said, Twiner," she shouted, "that people like me do not have friends. I was wrong."

"Go!" he shouted, and he had to fight for his voice not to break. "Go now!" She looked at him, one last shared glance. "That is an order!" She nodded, then ran to the side of the boat, grabbed a rope and swung across to the brownbone.

He turned, found Cwell stood behind him.

"Go," he shouted.

"My place is by—"

"No!" He ripped his sword from its scabbard, grabbed Cwell's hand and pressed the hilt into it. "Take this, we both know I will only lose it without you." Cwell looked at him, seemed surprised. "Use it, keep Meas safe for me."

"You made my life worthwhile."

"Then," he shouted over the roaring wind, "do not waste it! Go!" She stared a moment more, then gave the smallest of nods.

"Ey, Shipwife," she said and then she was gone. Over the side and onto the brownbone.

A second later it released the grapples, raised its wings, caught the wind and moved away from *Tide Child*. The black ship stayed in place, held by the same powerful wind that had opened the door in the storm. Joron looked behind, the ships of the Hundred and Gaunt Isles were in the tunnel of cloud, bearing down on him, funnelled together by the howling wind. At the front of the combined fleet was the massive *Arakeesian Dread*. Joron looked for'ard, at his fleet. All around them the vast and shining bodies of the keyshans, powering through the storm, the raised spines on their heads glowing with eerie blue light as they surrounded the ships. He saw his crew on the rump of the brownbone, staring back. Meas looked old now. Old and hurt and haggard as she held up Shorn, the baby gullaime, so she could see her. By her was Farys, young and full of hope and fight, she held her infant daughter tight to her chest with one hand. He saluted them, not knowing if they could see him or not through the storm that whirled around them. But he felt sure he saw some movement, a return of his salute, in the moment before they were pulled on and out and through the tunnel of cloud. Then they were gone into the winds with an escort of sea dragons, to lands he would never know. To places he hoped would be so much better.

He ran up the deck, toward the gallowbow, Solemn Muffaz, and as he worked in the howling wind, untrussing and spinning, he felt a presence behind him. Turned to find Garriya, dragging a heavy bolt over.

"You should be with them," he shouted over the gale. He took the bolt from her.

"This is my world," she shouted back. With a grunt he slotted the bolt home in the gallowbow and started to pull it into its highest elevation. Centring it on the burning figure of the Gullaime and, even though she had said she was dead the moment this started, he did not know if he could do it. To have already lost so much, and then to be the one who murdered his friend. He felt weak. Broken. Like this was more than he could bear.

"Strength, Shipwife," said Garriya, "it is time."

"I cannot, they have not had long enough to be out, and—"

He felt Garriya's hand on his arm.

"The keyshans guard them now, they will be fine. They will build a new world and, we must hope, a better one. We must close the door on this one or we will be too late, and they," she pointed behind them, at the encroaching fleet, the massive *Arakeesian Dread*, "will take their poison through." He looked up, at the fire in the sky, the great burning wings and the constant crackling roar of the vast firebird filling the air. The Gullaime at the head of it. In the sights of his bow.

"My friend," he said. "I never even knew your real name." The words paralysed him. "I cannot do this alone."

"You are not alone, Caller," said Garriya. "We are all here." He turned, found *Tide Child* transformed. Across the deck, the rails, the ropes and every spar and wing ran flame, and yet it did not burn. This was not the same furious, hot flame that burned a hole in the storm or the vicious heat of hagspit that ate away the bone of a ship. This was a warm, blue comforting flame, and out of it, formed from it, came figures, gauzy, hazy, but with enough about them for him to recognise them. There was Shipwife Arrin who had died protecting Safeharbour, and there was Turrimore and Adrantchi. There was Anzir, killed in Cwell's mutiny, and by her Narza, and so many more, so many friends and faces that he had lost. With great joy he recognised the hazy form of Solemn Muffaz, massive in the back. And right at the centre, gathered closest to Garriya, Mevans, smiling at him, and with him was Dinyl, who saluted, his restored hand held over his heart and Joron could barely speak. Amid them all, closest to Garriya, was the Gullaime, twirling and dancing about the old woman and, watching her dance, a smile on his bearded face and his arm about a woman Joron did not know but felt sure he recognised, was Joron's father. Garriya reached out her hand.

"It is time, Shipwife," she said. "Take my hand and come warm yourself at my fire," and her voice was as gentle and welcoming as any Joron had ever heard.

"Ey," he said, and he pulled the trigger cord, felt the jerk of the gallowbow as the bolt escaped it. He watched it arc into the sky, saw it hit a tiny figure and the fire that had burned so brightly went out. The shape of the great bird dissipating as the frail bodies that had made it up fell into the sea until only the Gullaime's body was left, pierced by the bolt, somehow held in the sky. It became a point of brightness, impossible to look at. Then it became fire, raging, out of control, billowing out toward him. He looked back. Saw the tunnel closing, clouds rushing in, wind smashing ships. The *Arakeesian Dread* being overwhelmed by a huge wave, and he turned away from it all, from the death and the war. He took the old woman's hand. Smiled at those gathered around her.

"I am coming," he said as the fire reached out and surrounded him. "I am coming."

And for the first time in so long, the pain ceased.

The Song of Lucky Meas

She flew across the world
Bird passed her through a storm so
The Tide Child came 'n binded
Cwell there right beside her
Wise but melancholy rule
"Those left behind I miss so."

Our people they call out
"Children to the ships!"
And the sea it all cries out.
Shipwife Meas, you are missed.

Epilogue

The water was kissed with light, a thousand little bright points and she sang. Further out a keshun basked, its huge bulk almost as big as Home Island and Meyans thought that, when it was cooler, she may take the children over to it, the inshore sea dragons were safe and kept free of tunir. Or they may just swim instead, the waters were always warm and clear of danger around the seamothers. But not now, Gullam's Eye was at its zenith and it was becoming too hot for the baby, Fras, to be out in the sun, so Meyans brought the baby and the twins, Jeron and Mees, into the cabin.

"Why is the eye so hot, Mother?" said Jeron.

"Because it is the eye of a god, Jeron." The small girl squinted up at the cloudless blue sky.

"It does not look like an eye," said her twin, Mees.

"Well, it is."

"How did it get up there?" said Jeron.

"Well," said Mayans, "the story of how the world came to be, of the Maiden, Mother and Hag, and the man who died to save them, is a very long story."

"Will you tell us the story, Mother?" said Mees.

Meyans sighed, there was always work to be done on the deck. But it was hot, and the dekeper and her mate were sunning themselves on the roof of the cabin. Meyans could hear them gently cooing and chirping to one another. She sat back against the cushion in the small cabin and fanned herself with a gift of their discarded feathers, smiling as cold air moved over the sweat around her neck. Far toward the horizon the massive form of another keshun moved across the sea and Meyans thought that all was good and all was well in her world. Her husband had been right, this was the perfect sort of day to take the children out to fish. Then she wondered if he was fretting back in Safabbar, or if he was enjoying the peace and quiet. Most likely enjoying the quiet of an empty bothy, she thought.

"Please Mother," said Jeron. "The story." Meyans smiled, and as she knew it would be hours before the nets were ready to be pulled up.

"Very well," she said, "get yourself comfortable and I will begin." She sat and let the children squirm and fidget on the cushions until they were happy and would stay still for at least long enough for her to make a start. "Right," she said, "are you ready?"

The twins nodded.

"Good, now, these are not the sort of words you expect to start a legend. But these are the first words he heard her say. 'Give me your hat . . .'"

Afterword

Just before *The Bone Ships* came out, one of my writer friends said, "I think it's really brave what you've done, writing something completely different from your first trilogy." And I thought, very much, "Wot?" Then another friend in the industry said, "Yeah, I'm surprised your publisher went with it: naval-based fantasy tends to die a death." And I thought, very much, "It does?" Now, I'm sure you can imagine that these may not be quite the things you want to hear just before a set of new books is released. But I already knew that I'd chosen an idiosyncratic voice to tell the story in, made a deliberate decision to take my time getting into the world and to make my characters a little less than easy to like at first than in my previous books. And I have always been the sort of person that, when given a choice between what I want to do and what might be sensible, it's always the former and very rarely the latter.

So even if I'd known these things beforehand we'd probably be here anyway.

Nevertheless, it was still a nervy thing, waiting for the release of the first book, and you really cannot imagine how gloriously happy it has made me that so many people have taken Joron, Meas, the Gullaime (especially the Gullaime) and the crew of *Tide Child* to their hearts. So thank you for that, and if your heart is maybe a little bit broken now, then I am sorry but, as you have probably worked out from the last line of the book, it was always going to happen this way (and if you've read my previous books, the Wounded Kingdom trilogy, you shouldn't really be that surprised).

There's always a moment in a book where, as a writer, you

get a feeling about if something is working or not. It came in this book on page 361 when Meas sees *Tide Child* and says, "I never thought to see you again," and I got this sudden rush of feeling, because she has come home, and we all know that comfort, of coming home. I think the idea of home and finding the people you need to be with to be *you* is at the heart of my writing. Inventing worlds and big action set-pieces is all well and good and fun to do, but it's people that matter in the end, and people that fascinate me. War and violence are never glamourous or to be celebrated; they destroy lives and I try not to shy away from that in my writing. No one comes out of the events of these books unscathed; no one simply shrugs off their wounds, both physical and mental. The crew of *Tide Child* are not always the best people – indeed they do some terrible things over the course of the books. But, as I've said before, given the chance to do the right thing, they take it, as most people will. Even Indyl Karrad, our "bad" guy, is, in the end, motivated by a sense of fairness that has become twisted. In fact, it is the society of the Hundred and Gaunt Islands that is the enemy in these books (as is often the case in our world). Given leaders who shied away from war and chose a fairer society, or people who were less likely to accept others misfortune just because "that's the way it has always been", then the death and destruction wreaked over these books would never have happened (as is often the case in our world).

I have mentioned before the music that I listened to while writing, and during the writing of *The Bone Ship's Wake* I was mostly listening to the dark folk of 16 Horsepower and Wovenhand, who seemed to fit the mood of the book. I thought I'd also recommend some further reading if you've enjoyed the naval part of these books: C. S. Forester's Hornblower books are wonderful fun, and there would be no *Tide Child* trilogy without the brilliant Aubrey/Maturin books by Patrick O'Brian. In fact, if you're already familiar with O'Brian's work, I have no doubt you recognised my own homage to him in the relentless chasing down of *Tide Child* by *Beakwyrm's Rage*.

I didn't do a tremendous amount of research for these books as the age of sail is period of history I've always been fascinated by. There are loads of great biographies of Nelson of course, but I would recommend you having a look into Sir Edward Pellew who is equally fascinating, if not more so. If you're one of the (thankfully few) people who felt the need to tell me "women could never command ships", then I suggest reading up on the Chinese pirate Ching Shih, who had a huge pirate fleet. Her ships terrorised the seas of the early nineteenth century.

In the UK, there's also lots of history to visit, from HMS *Victory* in Portsmouth to the Ropewalk Museum in Hull (the supply chain involved in getting sailing ships running is something I find fascinating but, as with many things, came under the purview of stuff you leave out cos it's not needed for the story). In fact, if you are in the UK, it's almost impossible to visit a seaside resort without coming into contact with our naval history. It's also almost impossible to talk without coming across the navy too; not using the phrase "sailing" has been one of the most difficult parts of writing books in a world where that word does not exist. English is thick with metaphor and reference to ships.

There would be no Tide Child books without my agent, Ed Wilson of Johnson and Alcock, who always believed in it, and my editor, Jenni Hill, who has championed me as a writer from the moment she read *Age of Assassins*, and gently guides me toward better versions of the stories I write. There's also a whole host of people behind the scenes that you never see who get these books out to you and I am thankful to every single one of them. I'm not going to do a massive thank you list as I always leave people out (but will say a quick hello to Magnus and Steve Savile of the Swedish crew and Jan at The English Book Shop, oh, and Dave at the Espresso Coco book blog, I think I forgot you again). But you all know who you are and the army of book bloggers and writers and many other people who I count as friends that I have made through writing is a constant joy to me.

Anyway, I digress. Thank you for reading, and for sticking with me and with these books. I hope you have enjoyed reading them as much as I enjoyed writing them. Remember, everyone you meet out there is living a life and they may well be fighting a battle you know nothing about. So, just like Meas gave Joron space to change, grow and become a better person, it's a better world if we can all find the space to let others be who they need to be to get on. And, like the Gullaime shedding her robe to reveal the shining creature beneath, if we let them then people may surprise us in wonderful and magical ways.

Though, hopefully, without all the dying.

RJ Barker
Leeds, January 2021

extras

orbitbooks.net

about the author

RJ Barker lives in Leeds with his wife, son and a collection of questionable taxidermy, odd art, scary music and more books than they have room for. He grew up reading whatever he could get his hands on, and has always been "that one with the book in his pocket". Having played in a rock band before deciding he was a rubbish musician, RJ returned to his first love, fiction, to find he is rather better at that. As well as his debut epic fantasy novel, *Age of Assassins*, RJ has written short stories and historical scripts which have been performed across the country. He has the sort of flowing locks any cavalier would be proud of.

Find out more about RJ Barker and other Orbit authors by registering for the free monthly newsletter at orbitbooks.net.

If you enjoyed

THE BONE SHIP'S WAKE

look out for

THE BLACK COAST
Book One of the God-King
Chronicles

by

Mike Brooks

PROLOGUE: TILA

The Sun Palace, atop its mighty sandstone plateau, was the jewel of the city of Idramar. It blended beauty with fearsome defensive architecture, and had stood as the symbol of Narida's unquestioned power since the God-King Nari rose from obscurity to conquer the lands between the Catseye Mountains and the ocean. From the mighty Eight Winds Tower of the central stronghouse the current God-King could look east across the waves that lapped at his city's shore, follow the great River Idra west towards the Catseyes, hundreds of miles distant, or gaze north or south across the wide floodplain and its fertile fields.

Unfortunately the current God-King was doing no such thing, and Tila could feel one of her headaches coming on.

"Where is he?" she demanded. The servant, a scar-faced pox survivor, bowed and began to stammer a reply. Tila slapped him, and grabbed his tunic to haul him in front of her black veil.

"Let this princess make something clear," she growled. "She knows His Divine Majesty likes to disappear and keep his *advisors*" – the word got mangled as it passed her teeth – "unaware of his whereabouts, but she will find him eventually. You can either tell her where he went, or she can put you through that window and do this the hard way. *Where is he?*"

"The Oak Avenue, Your Highness!"

"A thinker." Tila snorted. "How remarkable. Congratulations on choosing to see another meal." She released the servant, wiping her hand on her dress and ignoring his miserable bow. She never exactly set out to mistreat the staff, but she always had so much to do – or at least, there was always much *that needed doing* – and they inevitably slowed things down.

She did indeed find Natan, God-King of Narida, on a bench catching the winter sun slipping through the bare branches of the oaks lining one of the private avenues within the Sun Palace. He was enjoying a goblet of wine from his northern vineyards, and he was not alone.

Tila didn't know his companion's name, but the youth was a dragon groom; a strapping fellow, whose clothes did little to disguise his well-formed limbs. Such vigour was hardly surprising, since a groom had to be both strong and quick on his feet. Even the most amiable beast could accidentally crush a man too slow to dodge a swinging tail.

Any other member of the Inner Council might have awkwardly cleared their throat, or made some other discreet announcement of their presence. Tila didn't bother with such niceties: she marched up to the groom and tapped him on the shoulder, causing him to hurriedly disengage his mouth from that of the God-King.

"You," Tila snapped, clicking her fingers. "Leave. Now." She eyed his half-unfastened tunic. Idramar had mild winters, but even so . . . "And cover yourself."

The poor youth glanced desperately at the God-King, back at her, and fled away through the trees, presumably towards his duties. Tila folded her arms and shook her head at her monarch.

"Are you happy?"

"His Divine Majesty *was* happy," her older brother replied sourly. "We need to talk about your propensity to interrupt his intimate moments."

"Do not take that form of address with your sister," Tila snapped. "And kissing a groom *here* is not 'intimate'."

Natan looked around ostentatiously. The royal guard stood in pairs some distance away, to intercept anyone intruding on their ruler . . . so long as that intruder wasn't Princess Tila Narida, since they weren't fools. Otherwise, there was no one to be seen.

"Besides, that is not the point," Tila continued. "It is unseemly for you to consort with such a lowborn man."

"And what do you know of his parentage?" Natan demanded, sipping his wine.

"It is clearly low enough for the stables!" Tila snapped.

"Your brother fails to see how it matters," Natan said, running a hand through his hair, which was starting to thin very slightly on top. Not from stress, Tila doubted. Natan Narida would reach forty summers this year, and she could count the number of difficult decisions he'd made on both hands with digits to spare. "We are Nari's blood. *Everyone* is lowborn, compared to us. It is just a matter of scale." He looked at her, eyes suddenly sharp. "This is presumably some prelude to trying to make your brother court a woman, is it not?"

"No," Tila said tiredly. She sat down next to him, in defiance of all convention that one should wait for the Light of Heaven's permission. "Or at least, not a specific woman. Quite frankly, anyone would do."

"You would be happy for the God-King to court a lowborn *woman*, then?" Natan asked in mock surprise.

"You need an heir," Tila said bluntly.

"Oh Nari's teeth, not *this* again."

"You *need* an *heir*," Tila repeated, even more firmly. "Preferably more than one, as well you know."

"Your brother does keep fucking the men, but so far they have stubbornly refused to get with child," Natan said, swirling his wine. "He supposes he will just have to try harder."

"Would it kill you to pick a highborn woman, marry her, fuck her until her belly swells, then go back to your men?" Tila asked bitterly.

"Tila, your brother would not have the faintest idea what to do with a woman. He understands the theory, but could never bring himself to enact it."

Tila closed her eyes and scrubbed her forehead with her hand. "Your sister cannot believe she is having this conversation with you, but Nari knows no one else will. What about if you were blindfolded? If you were only aware of the other person through touch, then—"

"Your brother is not some stud dragon for you to breed a prize calf from!" Natan snapped, hurling his goblet away. "He refuses to be held hostage to your notions of what he should be doing with his cock!"

"It's not about your cock," Tila said with a shudder, "it's about the future of the nation! An unbroken line of *male* succession, may Nari help us all. Woe betide Narida if it suffers another Splintering!"

Natan rubbed at his right eye. "Tila, you know your brother would give up the throne to you in an instant."

"Your sister knows," she replied, trying to keep frustration out of her voice now he was at least attempting to be reasonable. "Although she thinks you underestimate how different your life would be, once you were no longer God-King. But that aside, it cannot happen, so there is no point speculating. The thanes would rebel against a woman's rule in a moment."

"You cannot *know* it would lead to another Splintering," her brother said, and Tila sighed. No matter how many times they had this conversation, he never seemed to fully accept the truth.

"Yes, your sister can," she told him bluntly. "And that, incidentally, is why she came to find you. You missed another Council meeting."

"Resentful, power-hungry people your brother cannot stand, discussing things about which he has no interest," her brother muttered. "And you, of course."

Tila gritted her teeth. "So dismiss them, and choose others whom you like better, so long as they are competent. Your sister would not miss any of the current council on a personal level."

Natan waved one hand gloomily. "It would cause too much trouble."

Very briefly, Tila contemplated whether she would rather be remembered chiefly for regicide or for fratricide.

"More trouble than letting them run the country without you?" she said instead. "No, do not answer that. Your sister will just keep trying to control them in your name, and hope their respect for our bloodline wins out." She took a deep breath. "But she needs your approval for something."

"We both know you are a better ruler than your brother anyway," Natan said. "Write the decree, and he will sign it."

"No," Tila said patiently. "This will not be written down. But your sister will not do this without your approval."

Her brother's thick brows narrowed suspiciously. "Go on."

"The Council wants to move against the Splinter King again."

Natan's face hardened. "Remind your brother how many times assassins have been sent after that family, within our lifetimes?"

"Three times," Tila replied neutrally. She didn't need to. Her brother might be self-absorbed and uninterested in affairs of state, but he remembered these particular details.

"And how much success have we had?"

"The family is still there," Tila admitted. "When we were children, our agents were intercepted before they could even make the attempt. Father tried sending agents again a few years later, during a festival, but the guards stopped them."

"Alaban fighters are particularly deadly, your brother hears," Natan commented. Tila raised her eyebrows in surprise: she honestly hadn't expected him to know that.

"They can be," she acknowledged. "In single combat, at any rate."

"So you are suggesting we send sars on dragons?" Natan asked. "That is not in keeping with your usual preference for subtlety, Tila."

She snorted. "As entertaining as the notion is, no. The third time an attempt was made, shortly after Father's death, we had slightly more success. Archers killed the eldest male child, but both parents and the two younger children survived. The ruling Hierarchs take the safety of their poor foreign pets seriously, and limit opportunities for them to be seen in public."

"It all sounds impossible," Natan muttered. "Impossible, cruel and pointless."

"All the attempts so far have been made on the family when they appeared in public," Tila told him. "Yet most of the time, they are unseen. They live another life, unmasked, away from public view."

Natan frowned. "And guarded, your brother would have thought."

"Of course," Tila agreed. "But less so, to avoid attention. Day to day, their safety relies on being seen as nothing more than a wealthy family of a minor Naridan bloodline."

Natan's eyes narrowed. "You are not speaking speculatively, are you?"

Tila smiled tightly behind her veil. "Your sister is not."

"You know the family?"

"Yes." She still carried a faint shadow of the excitement she'd felt when she'd read the final pieces of the puzzle from her agents, and drawn her conclusions.

Natan rubbed his chin. "How? It is a foreign city that knows we have tried to kill them . . . however many times, over the last two centuries. Your brother knows you are clever, Tila, but how have you managed this when no one else has?"

"No one else asked the right questions," Tila told him simply. "They only thought of the Splinter King as a silver-masked imposter appearing in public, when he was an obvious target. They never asked where he was the rest of the time."

"It appears His Divine Majesty's low opinion of his Council is not inaccurate," Natan muttered.

"This took your sister ten years!" Tila snapped, angry at having the success of her hard work dismissed as simply due to the incompetence of others. And Nari knew, there had been incompetence, but that didn't diminish her achievements! "*Ten years*, Natan! Your sister infiltrated the City of Islands' society with her own agents and, more importantly, with locals who have no idea the people they take money from for tasks or information take *their* pay from her! She knows that city very nearly as well as she knows our own!"

"Forgive your brother," Natan said, scrubbing at his face to hide what might have been embarrassment. "He did not mean to demean your work. He had no idea . . . Ten years?"

Tila sighed. "Ten years. Your sister did not tell you, as she knew you would not be interested." She snorted a laugh. "And after all of it, one man was the breakthrough. A former servant with a fondness for drink, and not enough money to buy his own. His drunken speculation might have gone unremarked in a city where gossip is rife, but one of your sister's agents heard him, and provided further lubrication to his tongue. Not enough to be certain on its own merit, but when combined with what we already knew . . ."

Her brother actually had the decency to look impressed. "And would you make their deaths look accidental?"

"An extravagance we cannot afford," Tila said firmly. "We will get one opportunity at this. Once the Hierarchs realise we have discovered the family's identity, they will have no option but to guard their pets closely at all times, whatever the cost."

"So it is perhaps not impossible," Natan acknowledged reluctantly. "Your brother still feels it is cruel and pointless."

"The older child, the male heir," Tila said, deliberately avoiding looking at him, "has reached the age of majority. Hence the need to try again."

Natan tapped his chin with a finger. "What if your brother were to adopt?"

Tila gave him the sort of look she usually reserved for impertinent servants. "What?"

"Your shadows can place a knife in any city in the known world, given enough time," Natan pointed out. "Surely they could find a suitable candidate to become your brother's heir?"

"We are the divine blood of the God-King!" Tila hissed at him. "Our family, alone in all of Narida, *must* continue by blood inheritance! The people will accept nothing less!"

"Your brother is the divine blood of the God-King, and we both know he is not a good ruler," Natan argued. "The people would not know if any heir of your brother's was *truly* his blood, in any case. They'd know what they were told. Find a young, sensible, intelligent man. Say, sixteen years or so; of an age where we could claim he was your brother's bastard, fathered by laying with a woman in the depths of his low mood following Father's death. An orphan would be ideal. Your brother can adopt and legitimise him, and you can teach him to run this country well. Once he is ready, your brother can abdicate, and you can worry less."

"We cannot risk it," Tila told him. "There are rumours that Nari Himself has been reborn. The foolish mutterings of country folk, undoubtedly, but even so—"

"If Nari Himself *has* been reborn, as prophesied, your brother's rule is invalid anyway, doubly so the Splinter King," Natan said lazily. "Not to mention that we'll have bigger problems: the sun going out, dragons ravaging the land, and the ocean rising to swallow us all."

"This is no laughing matter!" Tila hissed.

"Who's laughing?" Natan responded, more sharply than she'd expected. "Tila, you have raged since we were children against the rules that bind us. *Let us break them.* Who is to say your brother's blood-son would be any better at ruling than he is? You won't live to guide Narida forever. Choose a competent heir, and we need not worry about the scions of our great-great-great-great-uncle, thousands of miles away in Kiburu ce Alaba."

Her brother was actually making sense, which was enough to make Tila consider his words carefully. She also couldn't deny the transgressive appeal of subverting the system that had held her back all her life. Even so, she'd always been cautious.

Well, apart from that one time. But she'd been wallowing in self-destructive grief, and it hadn't turned out too badly. In the end.

"It could be done," she said slowly. "But some nobles may

suspect the ruse, and view the Splinter King as a viable alternative. Narida's future is still at risk while that family lives."

"They must be almost pure Alaban by now," Natan objected.

"Even so."

Natan slumped back on the bench. "This, then, is the choice you are giving your brother? Your king? Marry a woman and father children, or send assassins after distant relatives, despite all previous attempts having failed?"

"Your sister would prefer you did both," Tila admitted. "But, yes."

"Fine." The God-King buried his head in his hands. "Go find your knife-men."